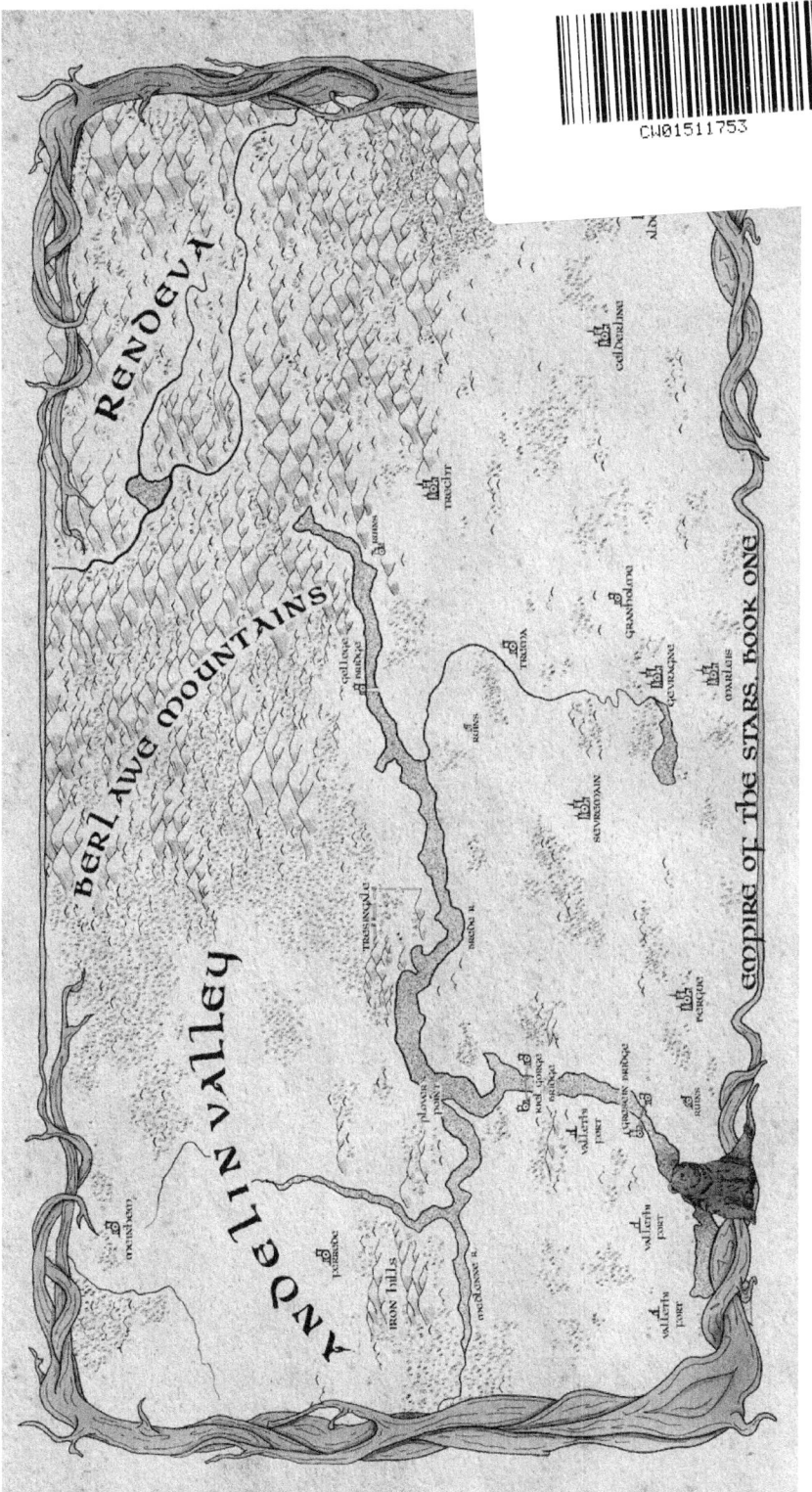

RENDEVA

BERLAWE MOUNTAINS

ANDELIN VALLEY

EMPIRE OF THE STARS, BOOK ONE

...for when those ancient kings had fallen, and all their lands were forfeit, they were brought to the seat of Starfall to make their oaths to Ospret Agnephus, the Far-Eyes. And with them he forged a sacred compact, the Covenant of Stars, that so long as his line endured, his people would be spared the ravages of magic.

- The Conquest and The Covenant, Vol II

TRAITOR SON

BOOK ONE OF THE
EMPIRE OF THE STARS

BY

MELISSA J. CAVE

CONTENTS

For my brother Daniel, who was listening to my stories
before I was old enough to write them down.

PROLOGUE

YEAR 817 OF THE DIVINE HOUSE OF AGNEPHUS

In the Greater Court of the Imperial Palace in Starfall, Remin knelt at the Divine Emperor's throne and prepared to be knighted.

Or killed.

He knew very well which the Emperor would have preferred. In the eyes of the Divinity, Remin was less than a commoner, less than a bastard. He was the son of traitors, born to a noble House whose name was now treason to speak, and he had refused to take any other.

"Squire Remin." The Emperor looked down from his high throne, a vision in silk and silver with the many-rayed crown upon his head. The name twisted on his lips. "You come before us after a great victory. We have heard it was you that broke the charge of the Eagle Knights of Valleth, who otherwise might have destroyed Lomonde, as they destroyed so many of our other cities. Perhaps you even saved the Empire itself."

"Yes, Divinity."

"We did not believe it, at first." The Emperor's starry blue eyes had a nearly tangible weight, the watching eyes of heaven. "But your actions were witnessed and attested by the Count of Lomonde himself, and a dozen other lords have sworn their names to the valor of your deeds. We must uphold the honors bestowed upon you. We name you Remin, Knight of the Empire of Argence. Rise, Sir Remin."

At nine, Remin had become a page. At twelve, a Squire. Now he was become Sir Remin, knighted with such acclaim that even the Emperor could only confirm the honor. His men called him Remin Grimjaw, impervious to pain. At seventeen, he had already survived five years of war, starvation, arrows, blades, poisoning, multiple attempted assassinations and two severe battlefield injuries only to grow almost insolently enormous, as if he thrived on mortal peril.

If the Emperor had not been raised on the sacred steps, Remin would have been unforgivably looking *down* on his Emperor. And he hadn't even reached his full growth yet; his hands and feet were still outsized on his lanky frame. But most offensive were those eyes, black and opaque as the eyes of a beast, the unforgettable eyes of a noble House that was no more.

"Thank you, Divinity." Remin was not grateful. He was only braced for whatever would come next. It was an expression duplicated on the features of his guardian, Duke Laud Ereguil, who watched from the periphery of the Court. Duke Ereguil was the only reason the child Remin had lived to become *Sir.*

"We shall reward such courage," the Emperor said, beckoning his servants forward. Six men in blue livery appeared, each bearing a jeweled casket clinking with gold, and set the heavy cases at Remin's feet. "One gold coin for every life you have saved. Another for every drop of barbarous blood you have shed in our defense."

It was a symbolic quantity, almost a mythic tribute, like a king being ransomed for his actual weight in gold. But the Emperor was wealthy enough to afford such trifles. Remin studied the caskets, his thick black brows lowering, then looked back up at the Emperor.

"Thank you, Divinity," he repeated. He wasn't old enough to manage his expression quite as adeptly as Duke Ereguil. The thought was clear in his face: *what's the catch?*

"It pains us to ask more from one who has given so much," the Emperor said silkily. "But for those to whom much is given, more is often asked. Your courage emboldens us to charge you with a greater task. You thwarted the invasion of our Empire. Now go and seize the lands that were lost to us in our great-grandfather's time. Bring back the Andelin Valley, the jewel of the Empire."

The periphery of the court had been alive with whispers, speculating about what a young man might do with so vast a fortune, but the Emperor's command silenced them as decisively as an execution.

"Divinity," Duke Ereguil objected. He was a burly man on the far side of his forties, with the sharp features of a hawk. "What you ask is impossible. The army of Valleth was defeated, not broken. If you—"

"You said the boy shattered them, Ereguil," the Emperor said, lifting one imperious eyebrow. "Your report claimed he scattered them to the winds."

"And those winds will assemble once more in the valley and become a whirlwind," the Duke replied steadily. "The Brede River remains an impassible barrier. Valleth holds all the bridges. The river is deep and swift even before the spring floods. It is a death sentence, and you know it. And you promised—"

"What will you give me if I do it?" Remin interrupted.

The Emperor smiled.

"What do you desire? Name it, and if it lies in our Empire and under the sight of the stars, we will grant it to you."

Remin could wish for the moon, and the Emperor knew he would never have to grant it. Duke Ereguil was right. The Brede was a devourer of armies. Let the boy drown in it.

"The Andelin for my duchy," Remin said. The words came to him like prophecy. "The Brede for my own. And your daughter for my wife."

CHAPTER 1 – THE EXILE PRINCESS

YEAR 825 OF THE DIVINE HOUSE OF AGNEPHUS

Beneath the gates of Ellingen, the last Warlord of Valleth was waiting.

Remin could see him from nearly half a mile away, swollen and glutted on suffering, twice the size of the men surrounding him. It was the sorcery of Valleth to reap magic from death and pain, and this man had feasted longer than any other. When they finally met, Remin had no doubt there would be a fresh necklace tattooed around his neck, a chain of screaming tongues.

The source of that power was still shining atop the gatehouse above him. Black mirrors, slick and gleaming as oil, and the husk of the man who had fed them so well. Sir Ludovin of Saccey had endured three days on the mirrors before he hanged himself, and Remin could do nothing but listen to his screams as he waited for reinforcements to arrive.

The reinforcements had come.

"Load!" Remin shouted, the command echoed and carried westward along the hilltops overlooking Ellingen. A dozen massive trebuchets rode the ridges, their heavy counterweights dragged backward, upward, in preparation for the next volley. They had already broken the main gates of the city and reduced much of the south wall to rubble, in preparation for the attack. And still the trebuchets pounded onward, hammering the city apart.

The same way he had broken so many other cities, over the last seven years.

He could hear them shouting his name in the distance. *Remin. Lore-Master.* Knight-General of the Empire of Argence. He kept always a little apart from his men, armored and massive on his warhorse, making sure the enemy could see him. He had waged a perfect war upon them. In seven years, he had not lost a single battle. They could not defeat him, only delay him.

Standing on the hill above Ellingen, he looked upon crumbling walls and the vulnerable lands beyond, a country that was ready to fall at his feet.

"Archers!" he called. There was a stirring among the knights massed behind him. That order meant their turn was coming.

Many soldiers of Valleth still wore scaled armor, better protection than mail against the bardiches and spears that were their preferred weapons. It was vastly insufficient against Imperial longbows. Remin lifted a hand, and at his signal, hundreds of arrows flew, humming toward the Vallethi ranks massing before the city.

"Trebuchets! On the towers!" he shouted, and there was grinding and creaking as those massive machines adjusted aim, targeting the remaining forward towers of the city. Valleth would have no covering fire. Remin had spent all the previous day maneuvering, breaking their defensive machines. Now the trebuchet to his left launched another load of heavy stones, and the black mirrors atop the gatehouse shattered.

Before the gates, the Vallethi warlord bellowed his defiance. As if Remin's men hadn't spared him deliberately.

Valleth had learned to use war machines from the Empire, but they still had no respect for them. Those killed by a trebuchet or even a crossbow were not counted by the Lord of Tales, and Remin would not allow his enemy to tell themselves that he had cheated, using mechanical means to kill their warlord. He must kill that man with his own hands.

That would be his task, when they charged at last for the city.

"Cavalry, forward!" he called, to a rumbling of drums and then the excited shuffling of horses, dancing with eagerness. He could feel the tension in his men, drawn taut as bowstrings, breathing the hot summer air. *"Charge!"*

A hundred mounted knights swept down the hill, pounding the earth flat with the terrible thunder of their approach. The knights of the

Empire carried heavy steel lances in the charge, metal monsters more terrible than any magic. But that magic still held sway outside the borders of the Empire, and so Remin set heels to his own horse and raced to the front, making himself the target of the surviving sorcerers.

The Vallethi thought him proof against magic, but that wasn't true. He could feel the stinging slices of their sorcery, Ludovin's pain that had been harvested from him over days, sharpened and husbanded. Remin let the magic wash over him, twanging like lightning up his nerves, singing to the roots of his teeth. It hurt. Stars, it hurt. But he had been learning all his life how to hurt, and every time he endured it, it increased the fear of his enemies.

They fled from his path as he arrowed toward the gates, where the First Warlord of Valleth was waiting.

He was a monster. Ten feet tall, dwarfing even Remin's vast height. His ice-blond hair had been shaved and black static crackled up his long, bristling beard, sizzling on the scales of his armor. That was the magic of Valleth, the summoning of the Inside to the Outside. Every life this man had taken, every drop of blood he spilled, every scream he had extracted became part of the story he told himself: the truth of his innermost self. He was the killer. The First Warlord of Valleth. He had cultivated a monster in his own flesh.

"Lore-Master," he said in Vallethi as Remin swung down from his horse and sent the animal away. "I will feed you to the Lord of Tales."

"I will send you to make your apologies to them," Remin retorted in the same tongue, more or less. The warlord bared his teeth, showing bloody gums.

It was rare that Remin fought an opponent larger than himself. His stomach clutched at the prospect of facing that hated magic, but he shook out his shoulders and drew a breath all the way to his toes. He had his sword. He had his shield. His plate armor would withstand a few knocks from the warlord's massive, spiked mace, and that should be enough time to get his rhythm.

All around them, the battle continued, and Remin heard the voices of his knights, shouting orders as they moved into the massed ranks of the Vallethi defenders, hunting for the magicians. They knew their business. They trusted Remin to handle this.

He charged.

He had always been faster than his enemies expected. He went straight in, shield first, twisting aside as the warlord threw up his own shield and slammed the mace down like a hammer. Fast. At close quarters the magic stung, the lightning fire of nettle spines, and Remin gritted his teeth, stabbing at his enemy's arm with the tip of his sword. The blade grated, as if he had struck the side of a mountain.

"You come with only steel?" The warlord sneered, and it seemed the ground should shake underfoot as he pursued, his heavy boots thudding.

So many warlords cultivated themselves this way. They reaped for size and power, chanting those words as they lapped at the blood of their victims. *Hamsa. Eska. Hamsa. Eska.* Stronger. Bigger. Stronger. Bigger.

So few of them said *faster.*

Remin lunged aside as that huge mace swung out again, a sweep that would've cleared a small patch of forest, trailing that loathsome magic like a cloud. Remin couldn't see it or hear it, but he could taste it on his tongue like acid, a stinging like wasps in the sinuses of his cheeks. He felt that pain and bulled right into it.

There was an opening. When the warlord's arm drew back for another swing, he left a gap between his arm and his shield and Remin was already in it, slamming his sword into his exposed side. The other man twisted aside with a snarl and black blood spurted from his ribs, smoking on the ground.

"Steel seems sufficient," Remin observed, sliding clear of the mace.

"You dance like a painted whore," the Vallethi grunted, swinging his mace and shield like two hammers.

"The better to teach you how," Remin countered, and made the warlord howl as he slammed his sword through one massive boot.

The duel brought the entire battlefield to a standstill. The sorcerers dead, the Eagle Knights staring, weapons falling from their nerveless fingers. Watching as Remin's sword sliced upward, a perfect arc that took off the warlord's fingers and sent that dread mace flying. Watching as he spun and slammed the edge of his shield behind the giant's knees, severing tendons. And a low moan rolled over the battlefield as the warlord fell with a bellowing cry, and Remin moved to finish him.

7

Even with the sorcerers dead, that magic was still in the air, crackling and snapping like the echoes of distant screams. Forever after, he would bear jagged white scars on his fingertips where his gloves burned away, and even Remin Grimjaw screamed in agony as he wrenched his enemy's head from his neck and flung it away, feeling as if he had grasped lightning in his hands. It hurt. It hurt, it *hurt,* nothing else in the world could hurt so much, but there would be Vallethi survivors to recount what they had seen this day, so Remin only kicked the huge body flat, resisting the urge to tuck his spasming hands under his arms.

"I'm fine," he said, reeling upright as his knights hastened over to him. Black blood sluiced down the runnels of his armor and he was still half-blinded with magic, like hornets crawling over his eyes. But a short distance away, they had finally cut Ludovin down, and so Remin went at last to see his friend and covered him with his own cloak.

"Finish the city," he said, looking at his brother knights. "Kill anyone that resists. Do not leave one stone standing atop another."

He meant it literally. Ellingen would be wiped from the face of the earth.

"My lord," they said, and went to execute his will.

Soon enough, he would follow. There were still a few more nightmares to acquire before the war was over, and Remin meant to make sure the lessons of Ellingen would travel all the way to Mindelind, where the King of Valleth would soon learn he had lost his last warlord.

But for a moment, Remin's black eyes turned away to the south, back to the Empire, where his sacred bride awaited. She was the last thing he needed to forge a dynasty that would last for all time, the foundation for a noble House that could never be destroyed again. And when he was done, Kings and Emperors would kneel before him.

A thousand miles away, on the isolated estate of Aldeburke, a certain young woman felt an inexplicable shiver down her spine.

* * *

Spring was a green dream trembling at the tips of the leaves when a column of black-clad knights rode through the gates of Aldeburke.

From the window of her secret perch in the library, Princess Ophele Agnephus glanced up from her book and caught her breath. She knew the heraldry of every major and minor House in the Empire, but she didn't recognize these banners: black and silver, bearing the device of crossed swords over a bridge. An ominous combination of symbols.

Were Lord and Lady Hurrell expecting guests? They wouldn't tell *her* if they were, but despite their exile and disgrace, Ophele's guardians had begun hosting infrequent gatherings over the last few years. Rich merchants and lesser nobles, poor and ambitious, hoping to capitalize on Lady Hurrell's greater ambitions. But never *knights*. Two score of them, some bearing lances and all bearing swords, with shields at their backs.

No one who wanted to see the Hurrells would spare any goodwill for the daughter of Lady Rache Pavot.

Slipping one of her smaller books into her pocket, Ophele shimmied over the side of the ceiling rafter and dropped soundlessly to the floor, scurrying off to fetch her cloak.

This late in the season, it rarely dropped below freezing at night, but this was not the first time Ophele had judged it prudent to disappear. Darting through the narrow halls at the back of the house, she could already hear the clamor of the servants, hastening to receive the guests. Ophele took advantage of the chaos to duck down the stairs at the back of the kitchen and slip into the pantry.

"Azelma!" Footsteps thudded past the door, and Ophele stopped short, making a rapid rearrangement of the apples and potatoes in her pockets. Voluminous as her cloak was, it would not do to appear too lumpy.

"Yes, I heard, I heard," came the old woman's voice, unruffled. "Does Her Ladyship want anything in particular?"

"A full luncheon, she says, and something sweet with tea afterward." That was the butler clattering silver together, sounding harassed. Maybe that meant *no one* was expecting these guests.

There was a squeaking on the stairs as he departed, and Ophele gave it another second before pushing the door open a cautious crack, peeking out. The only other person in the kitchen was Azelma, a round little figure in a spectacular lace cap.

"*Ssst,*" she hissed, without turning around, and set two loaves of bread at the end of her worktable, still steaming from the oven. "Out the back door, Your Highness. Should be clear for a few minutes yet."

Ophele snatched up the bread and scuttled away.

Maybe all this fuss had something to do with *her.*

That thought put wings on her feet. Ophele knew she was the Emperor's daughter, but it was in the same distant way she knew there was an Emperor and he lived in a palace; it was probably true, but she had no firsthand evidence and it didn't make much difference to her life either way. It wasn't like she was his *real* daughter. Lady Hurrell had always been very careful to explain the difference, and while Ophele's veins might contain the divine blood of the Emperor, they were stained by her mother's treason and irrevocably dirtied by her illegitimacy.

Somehow, the lady had always implied it was Ophele's fault. As if she had chosen to be born, and so choosing, had willfully defiled the Emperor's sacred lineage.

But it had been a long time since anyone had given a fig for her parentage, and no one noticed or called her back as Ophele set off into the forest. She had never ventured beyond the walls of the estate, but her mother had often taken her into the trees to forage, teaching her all the secret delights of mushroom, root, and berry. Though most of the trees were still winter-naked, there were several large stands of pine to the north that offered a good view of the road, and Ophele set up camp under the boughs of an obliging pine, plucking the book from her pocket.

It was hard to focus. Her eyes kept straying back to the road, recalling that grim column of men and imagining the many things it might portend. Try as she might, she couldn't think of anything *nice.* Armed men appearing at the prison of the sovereign's secret bastard weren't likely to bring good news.

Maybe they would be content with delivering it to Lady Hurrell, and would take themselves off thereafter.

It wasn't the first time she had slept outside. Ophele set a slow blaze to burn through the night and burrowed into her cloak, to wake up early the next morning, stiff with cold. Plucking up some dry pine needles, she poked them into the coals of her fire until she built up a small blaze. The hollow under her pine tree was nicely sheltered from wind and rain, and the boughs overhead dispersed the smoke. Raking the hottest coals to one side, she wrapped an apple and a potato in a stout strip of leather and buried them to roast.

The sun had barely cleared the horizon when she saw the first sign that something odd was happening at the manor.

Through the trees she could hear distant shouts, clanking armor, the neighing of horses and the barking of dogs. Was it a hunt? Sometimes Lord Hurrell hosted hunts for stag or even boar, but usually those events were held at a hunting lodge some miles away. The estate groundskeepers were careful that no animal as dangerous as a boar was allowed near the manor. And it was far too noisy to be one of Julot Hurrell's less official hunts. When Lord Hurrell's son went riding with his friends this early, it was usually because they were still drunk from the night before.

Ophele kicked dirt over her fire and retreated further into the forest, skirting around the west side of the manor. Julot had always thought it great sport to chase her about the estate, and she had no intention of letting two-score knights join in the fun. There was a patch of fir trees that offered better cover not far away, and she made for them like a light-footed little shadow, all but invisible in the morning gloom.

But it wasn't just Julot hunting her. Perched in one of the taller trees, Ophele was just in time to see people flooding out of the manor, bundled up against the cold and carrying lanterns. They had even turned out Azelma from the kitchen, her ruffled white cap bristling about her face. Azelma would not be happy to be forced out into the cold.

"Princess!"

"Princess Ophele, please come out!"

"Your Highness! Where are you?!"

It looked as if every single person in the manor was abroad. She even saw Julot and Lord Hurrell on the hilltop, and the young Lady Lisabe Hurrell in a blue gown and white fur cloak, walking the garden and calling, syrupy sweet. And those were knights, armored and fearsome, wearing that black badge.

Ophele's breath caught in her throat. Once before, Lord Hurrell had roused the whole manor to find her, and she pressed back against the trunk of the fir tree, covering her mouth with her hand to hide the white puffs of her breath in the frosty air.

Should she run? But where could she go? She wasn't ready yet to run away from the manor, though she had often dreamed of doing just that: fleeing to a place where no one knew her, maybe to one of the countries on the other side of the sea. Ophele knew that normally she would have had guards, to prevent such a thing, just in case she planned some evil against the Emperor; everyone knew bastard children were the seeds of treachery. But she had had no guards since she was a child.

Maybe that was the trouble. Maybe that was why the knights had come. Maybe they thought she was plotting against the Emperor, because there were no guards watching to make sure that she wasn't. There were books where just such a thing had happened, and most of them were histories. Ophele had read them all.

"Princess Ophele!"

She wasn't foolish enough to run, but no matter how much she scolded herself, she couldn't force herself to go down to them, either. Tam from the stables was close by. He wasn't bad. He had never actually been *mean* to her, and had even shown her a litter of kittens in the barn when she was nine. If she had to get caught, he probably wouldn't hurt her. Biting her lip, she watched as he drew nearer and nearer, within ten feet of her tree, and if she was ever going to speak it should be now, but her lips were glued firmly shut and then he had passed, and it was too late.

Now she was definitely guilty of treachery. Huddling with her hands over her mouth, she watched in an agony of guilt and fear as the sun rose and the hours passed and the search went on, wondering what they would do when they found her.

"No sign on the ground," said a man's voice nearby, and she was so startled she nearly toppled off her branch. "Unless she left the estate, there aren't many places she could be hiding."

"Miche said he found signs of a fire under one of the pines to the north. The ashes were still warm," said another voice. She didn't recognize either of them, and she knew everyone in Aldeburke. "Guess it's time to start shaking trees."

Oh, no.

Her heart pounded. She strained her ears, listening for the quiet steps. They weren't like Tam, blundering through the trees like an ox; there were two men, one to her left and one to her right, moving as patiently as if they were picking over every pine needle. There was nowhere to run. There was nothing to do but curl up as small as she could and wait, hoping they would pass her by.

The branches moved under her. A man's face, broad and grey-eyed, peered through them, then whistled and turned his head to call.

"Your Grace!"

* * *

"Your Grace?" Ophele echoed faintly, as a new face appeared below her.

"Remin of Andelin," he snarled, shouldering the branches out of the way. Ophele's first glimpse of the infamous Remin Grimjaw was of furious black eyes and shaggy black hair, his white teeth snapping the end off every word. "Get down here or I'll come and get you, if I have to rip up this tree by the roots."

He looked fully capable of doing just that. His voice sounded like a bear's would sound if they could talk, deep and rumbly as a landslide.

Petrified, she let herself bump down through the branches. Even in Aldeburke, they had heard of Remin Grimjaw. Over the years of his war with Valleth, the Emperor's command had been broadcast to the furthest corners of the Empire and taken on an almost mythic significance, as if the Age of Heroes had come again. And no one had forgotten the promised reward.

The Andelin for my duchy. The Brede for my own. And your daughter for my wife.

Hard hands gripped her arms and yanked her out of the tree, and Ophele shrank back automatically as he loomed over her like a rockfall.

"Was this some scheme of the Emperor's?" he growled, low enough that he would not be overheard. His clothes were surprisingly plain for a nobleman, rough wool and leather, with a heavy fur cloak over massive shoulders. His eyes were like two angry ink spots under thick black brows. "Did you think I'd give up and go away? Your father owes me a wife, girl. I am here to collect."

Her eyes flew open, and she turned her face away, hiding in the depths of her cloak in confusion. She felt as shocked as if he had ripped the tree up by its roots and clouted her with it. *Wife?* A scheme of her father's?

It all came together at once, an impossible series of events that led to the man glaring down at her, waiting for an answer as to why she had so deeply disgraced him as to actually *hide.* It was a grave insult. It was certainly an offense against the Emperor: direct disobedience of his orders.

But it didn't make sense. Everyone knew the Duke of Andelin was going to marry Princess Selenne. It was a story that had every maiden in the kingdom sighing, and even the maids of Aldeburke repeated it with relish, how the handsome knight had fought a war to win the hand of the fair princess. Lisabe had been complaining for months about how it wasn't fair; House Hurrell had given everything for the Duke's House, surely *she* should receive some consideration…

But Ophele knew that romantic tale was nonsense. People were strangely quick to forget that the Emperor's challenge was not a reward. It was not a magical task, like finding three grains of wheat in a wagonload of corn or sending him off to slay a troop of Skulkingmen. The Emperor *hated* Remin Grimjaw, and had been trying to have him killed since he was a child. Even saying the name of his parents' House was treason. Until Remin had crossed the Brede River, no one expected him to do anything but die on its southern bank.

And as payment, the Emperor had promised him *a* daughter. Not the Crown Princess.

Ophele's heart fluttered in panic. Stars, he must *hate* her.

She should greet him. She should apologize. But his hand tightened on her arm and that black glare was a weight on her head and her tongue stuck to the roof of her mouth as if it had been rooted there.

"Nothing to say?" he said after a long moment, and turned in disgust, escorting her firmly back to the manor house. "Best get your sulks out of the way now. There will be no time for such childishness where we're going."

Ophele's face flushed. She knew she looked like a child in her short gray skirts, showing a length of shin and bare feet as if she were still ten years old and wearing her hair in two plaits. His strides were so long, she nearly had to run to keep up with him, tripping along with his huge hand clamped around her arm. He didn't even look down at her. His black eyes were fixed on the manor house.

"Here," he said coldly in the grand foyer, thrusting her toward Lady Hurrell. "Have her cleaned and dressed. I don't think much of your guardianship if you let your princess sleep in the woods and dress like a beggar's brat."

"I must beg Your Grace's forgiveness," replied Lady Hurrell. She was a tall and elegant woman with blonde hair and china-blue eyes, exquisitely coiffed even for a search party. Her red smile made Ophele shiver. "We told you to stay in the house yesterday, silly child. Your feet are filthy. And you will cling to those gray rags, didn't I tell your nurses to burn them? Dear me…"

They had told her *nothing*. Ophele blinked as she realized what the lady was doing and dug in her heels, opening her mouth to protest. But Lord Hurrell was already blustering.

"Her Highness means no offense, Your Grace, she will wander no matter what we say. We try to allow her these small pleasures…"

He was making her sound like a simpleton. Lady Hurrell's fingernails sank warningly into Ophele's shoulders.

"Leise. Nenot," she said, and the maids took a firm grip on Ophele's arms, propelling her down the hallway to the back of the house.

This was terrible. Ophele had known that one day she would be married off and even suspected that Lady Hurrell intended her for Julot, and if that happened, she would climb straight to the highest rafter in the library and throw herself off it. But Remin Grimjaw was equal parts hero and bogeyman, like the Skulkingmen or one of the Stone Teeth, who chewed human flesh between mossy jaws. Remin Grimjaw was a brute stained with blood. They said after his victory, Remin Grimjaw had scoured the Andelin and slaughtered every man, woman, and child to be certain no one loyal to Valleth remained.

And her father had tricked *Remin Grimjaw* into marrying her.

Ophele sat like a block of wood as she was scrubbed and groomed, the pine sap combed from her hair, her maids going about the task as if they were doing laundry. It hurt. It always hurt. But the marks of harsh scrubbing and rough handling were easily concealed by her clothing, and Ophele knew better than to complain. All the while, Lady Hurrell stood and watched, twittering her brisk, cheerful poison.

"Such a skinny child," she said, shaking her head. "It is fortunate the Duke is not marrying you for your beauty. Stars, that hair is as common as a sparrow."

Ophele knew she was plain. Her hair was an unremarkable brown, her eyes a tawny hazel, and she was a skinny, unpromising creature, as if her base conception had stunted her growth. When they were done, she was swimming in one of Lisabe's old gowns, a faded pink that hung off her shoulders and bared four inches of her ankles.

"My poor Ophele." Lady Hurrell swayed toward her with the stalking grace of a hunting cat, her hands resting on Ophele's shoulders as she sat her down at a dressing table. The contrast between the fine lady and the ragamuffin in the mirror was stark. "His Grace is quite a fearsome specimen, is he not? He has been furious since yesterday, wondering where you were. What they say about his temper is true, I'm afraid."

There was no sensible reply to this. Ophele's face was as blank as a doll's, the only defense she had, but the pulse in her throat was fluttering frantically.

"I was fortunate in my marriage," the lady continued. Her fingers smoothed through Ophele's hair, tugging small locks loose and twisting them in her fingers. "Even after your mother disgraced us and brought down our House, my husband never lifted a hand to me. Lord Hurrell is a kind man. There are many who would have vented their frustrations on their spouse in such dire circumstances."

Lady Hurrell was a liar. She knew the lady was a liar. She wanted something, this was a trick, she shouldn't listen. Ophele's shoulders hunched as the lady tugged her hair, a gesture that looked like a caress but was actually painful little yanks, like a chicken pecking a weaker hen. Lady Hurrell's caresses were as painful as Leise and Nenot's punishments.

"No one would have helped me, if he had," the lady murmured. "For we were exiled, and I had not the refuge of my natal family. Can you imagine how desperate it would have been? My husband might have beaten me terribly, or starved me, or even killed me, and there was no one who would stop him. It is why I am so afraid for you. For you are only a bastard, and neither the stars in heaven nor your father on earth would even bother to protest."

As terrible as Lady Hurrell's lies were, it was this truth that made Ophele's heart contract with terror. She was right. Neither the stars nor the Emperor had ever shown the slightest interest in what became of her, not once in her whole life. If she married the Duke of Andelin, she would be at his mercy.

"And you have already made such a poor start," Lady Hurrell fretted. "The Duke is not a temperate man, and the very first thing you did was to insult him. What will he do, if the story spreads? Oh, no, don't look so frightened," she added quickly, her fingers curving around Ophele's right ear, caressing. "Everything will be fine, little mouse. You can just give him to Lisabe. It's the least you can do, isn't it?"

There were so many threats and debts tangled up in her words that Ophele was mute, frozen. The story of how the princess had been so horrified by her marriage that she had tried to run away *would* spread if Ophele disobeyed. Lady Hurrell would make sure of it.

"Now, now, I know perfectly well you can talk when you want to." The lady's thumbnail sank into Ophele's ear, sharp enough that tears sprang to her eyes. "Speak up, little mouse. Don't you want to make up for what your mother did?"

"Yes, yes!" Ophele gasped, pulling away and rubbing her ear, furious and ashamed of her own fear.

"Good. We have been kind to you all these years, in spite of the shame you brought us." The lady wrapped her arms around her tenderly, her smooth cheek pressed against Ophele's thin one. "Just leave it to me. I can't bear to imagine what would happen if His Grace learned what your mother did to his family."

* * *

House Hurrell must have once been mighty members of the Imperial bureaucracy.

They were masters of delay.

For two days, they had been dragging their feet with impeccable courtesy, from frittering away the afternoon with promises to produce the princess to airy assurances that she was just *hiding* by suppertime. It was only after a six course meal—when it was too dark to mount a search of the grounds—that they confessed she was nowhere to be found, and that apparently it was her *habit* to go wandering off into the chilly March night.

Having located her himself, Remin was once more cooling his heels in the parlor, listening to Lord Hurrell burble about his children and feeling distinctly out of place. Everything here was too clean, too delicate, and far too small. Including the sofa, which was so low he felt in danger of hitting himself in the chin with his knees.

"You have records of the princess's birth?" he asked Lord Hurrell abruptly. "Her Sacred Highness Ophele, daughter of the House of Agnephus. The Emperor claimed her birth was witnessed and attested by a Prior of the Temple."

Unfortunately, there was no way to prove that Rache Pavot, a lesser noblewoman whose House had been extinguished with Remin's, had actually conceived a child by the Emperor. He wouldn't put it past the Emperor Bastin Agnephus to lie, but so long as there was iron proof that he had acknowledged the girl as his daughter, that was sufficient. Remin would take whatever he could get.

Every last bit of it.

"Yes, Your Grace. I have kept them safe since her mother died," Lord Hurrell replied. He was a vaguely froggy gentleman with sagging jowls and a number of rings on his fingers, including one massive ruby that flashed as he pressed his hand to his heart. "We were charged with her care, you know, and we have looked after her as our sacred duty these many years. Those are the words of House Hurrell: *faithful unto death.* Your Grace may know the history between our Houses?"

"Yes."

Undaunted by the monosyllable, Lord Hurrell happily recounted it, pushing forward both his son and daughter as he spoke. Nineteen year-old Julot was a promising young man, he claimed, trained in the management of a noble household but also eager to stand beside the Duke of Andelin as one of his men-at-arms. Chewing on another tiny sandwich, Remin didn't dignify this with an answer. Julot Hurrell was a dandy in a velvet and silk jerkin, doublet, and garish red hosen. It looked as if the nearest thing he'd ever held to a sword was table cutlery.

The lord was equally enthusiastic in advancing the young Lady Lisabe. Over the next hour he had the girl sing, play a lap harp, and present samples of her embroidery, lovely and useless. Unaccustomed as he was to noblewomen, or any women at all outside the camp prostitutes that marched with his army, Remin had the odd feeling he was being offered something, and it was not what he had come for.

How long did it take to heat a lady's bath and clean her up? Lady Lisabe fluttered nearby as Remin waited with increasing impatience. Was this another insult? What was the purpose of these endless delays? The Emperor had set up a number of traps and ambushes for him over the years, and anything might happen in this isolated place.

But perhaps the Emperor's vengeance had taken another form. Since the day of his parents' execution, Remin had sworn that he would take back everything he had lost. His House. His name. His birthright. Remin did not care if the maidens of the Empire sighed for him; in practical terms, no one would give their daughter to a man so despised by the Emperor, no matter how she sighed. Anyone who extended a hand to Remin Grimjaw risked sharing his fate.

And yet Remin had set his sights on the highest woman in the Empire and gambled everything to win her. He was fully prepared to check her for weapons every night and employ tasters for his food, so long as the children he got on her inherited the untouchable sacred lineage of the House of Agnephus. The House he founded on the far side of the Brede could never be destroyed as his parents' house had been. And his descendants would be numerous as the stars.

But a simpleminded wife…well, that sounded just like Emperor Bastin Agnephus, who salted every gift with poison.

"More wine, Your Grace?" asked Lady Lisabe, with another dimpled smile. Even he could sense the invitation. Silently, he extended his goblet.

"How much longer?" he asked bluntly. "I mean to collect the princess and leave immediately. Get her things packed while we're waiting. I have a Prior ready to marry us in Celderline."

"So soon?" Lord Hurrell asked, glancing at his daughter, who rose and departed in a flutter of silk. "If I may say, Your Grace, the Emperor's daughter is as sweet a girl as one might wish, but she may be surprised at her good fortune. To be blessed with such an excellent marriage so abruptly, when she is young and possessed of a most maidenly shyness, I would ask for your forbearance so we might introduce her gently…"

"You told her I was coming, didn't you?" Remin's black eyes narrowed. "I sent a message a month ago. She's had time to get used to the idea. We are needed back in Andelin."

"Of course, of course we told her," the lord assured him hurriedly. "We fully impressed upon her what an honor it is. Why, every maiden in the kingdom is in despair to know that so mighty a knight was already promised to the Emperor's daughter…"

He kept saying things like that. The many despairing maidens of the Empire, and the implication that something was amiss with the princess. The sunlight made its slow journey across the floor, and Remin only halfway listened to the conversation, which carried on perfectly well without him. He was thinking.

"Once again I must apologize for the delay, Your Grace," Lord Hurrell said, when Lady Lisabe returned to whisper in his ear. "Can we offer you the hospitality of the house for another night? It takes some time to prepare a lady for the company of a duke, especially after such a …rigorous morning."

"Do that." Remin stood. "I will go inform my men. Thank you."

His knights were milling around the courtyard with the grumbling patience of seasoned soldiers, who knew that waiting was a vital part of life. Remin ducked through the doorway of the manor and strode toward them, his heavy boots crunching on the gravel.

"Edemir. Miche. Go wander, and keep your ears open," he ordered, jerking his chin toward the house. "Make friends with the maids. I don't mind if you get lost a few times. Huber, go talk horses with the stablemaster."

Huber said nothing; Edemir offered a courtly bow and headed for the front of the house. Blond, beautiful Miche had already taken to vanishing, no doubt into the beds of various maids, and he sloped immediately off toward the kitchen. It was thanks to Miche that they had found Princess Ophele at all. The old lady in the kitchen had given him the enigmatic instruction to *look in the trees* when he had been filching sausage rolls that morning.

"We'll be staying another night, then?" asked Bram of Lisle, a pockmarked former mercenary who had volunteered for the legendary charge at Gresein Bridge. As far as Remin was concerned, that excused him from noble courtesies for life.

"Yes. Probably a few days more," he replied, glaring at the manor house. Nothing in this world was ever simple.

"Nice beds and good food," Bram observed with a shrug, and whistled up a few lads to get the baggage wagons out of the way.

Did he dare refuse to marry the Emperor's daughter?

Remin was considering it. It wasn't any more foolhardy than most other things he had done, and it was one thing to risk his own safety on the Emperor's spawn, and quite another to risk the quality of his progeny. The Andelin Valley was rich in resources, but it was also wild and dangerous, a blank spot on most Imperial maps. Valleth had sacrificed thousands to their Lord of Tales over a century of occupation, then rounded out their depravity by summoning the devils in the latter days of the war. Those creatures had proven sadly indiscriminate in their appetites.

It was no place for a wandering simpleton.

A few towns had survived. Remin had undertaken a hasty survey after his victory that turned up a half dozen hamlets and a little less than two thousand people, clinging stubbornly to their land in spite of armies galloping about and ghouls creeping hungrily in the dark.

"It's no place for a wife," Duke Ereguil had told him when Remin explained what he meant to do. Laud Ereguil had always seemed as solid as a boulder to Remin, but he was a tired man after the long war in the Andelin and wanted nothing more than the peace and quiet of his own comfortable estate. But still, he found time to concern himself with Remin, honoring the oath he had made to Remin's mother. "You would be kinder to leave her where she is until you can put a roof over her head, boy."

Age twenty-four, more than six and a half feet tall, and Remin was still *boy*.

"I'm not giving that old snake time to wiggle out of his oath," Remin had replied flatly. "I will have a noble wife. The daughter of an Emperor."

"Be patient," Duke Ereguil cautioned for the thousandth time. "All men grow old. And die."

It was a warning, and a promise. No one was immortal. The Emperor would not be Emperor forever. And Duke Ereguil, Remin's only defender, was growing old.

This was a different sort of problem than the ones he had faced in Andelin, but Remin knew he had to learn to unravel the twisted social puzzles of nobility, and this was his first test. He would not fail it.

"I am afraid the lady has been taken ill," Lady Hurrell said apologetically at dinner, sliding into her seat. "She has always had a delicate constitution; it makes it all the more frustrating when she slips away before nightfall."

For some reason, this news did not surprise him. It was certainly plausible. Remin nodded slowly.

"Should I send one of my men to fetch a doctor?"

"No, we are accustomed to nursing our own, being so far away from town," the lady said, putting on a brave face. "My Lisabe will look in on her after supper. She is used to tending her, poor lamb."

Of course, he would be a brute if he removed a sick girl from her home. It would be an unpardonable insult if he demanded to see her and verify that she was really ill. Remin shoved roast pork into his mouth and masticated thoughtfully. Maybe he was too suspicious. House Hurrell was no friend of the Emperor. But meeting Auber's eyes, he saw a reflection of his own skepticism.

In war, there were times that called for a reckless charge, brute force, shattering strength. But other times called for patience and finesse, a slow and probing attack to find the enemy's weak points.

"That is good of her," Remin remarked, mentally settling in for a siege. "Loyalty is a rare thing."

His black eyes focused on Lisabe, and the girl smiled until the dimples deepened in her cheeks.

* * *

For the next few days, Ophele was a mouse.

It wasn't so different from how she usually moved through the vast manor, unseen and unwanted. The servants knew very well who the master was, and Ophele had never tried to contest it. To be sure, on paper, Aldeburke and everything in it belonged to her, but it was only right that she give it to the Hurrells to make up for what her mother had done.

"You are a fool if you let them do this," said Azelma in the kitchen, slapping Ophele's hands away from the sausage rolls she had just pulled out of the oven. The day's baking was done early in the morning, hours before dawn, and it was also the time Ophele felt safest to emerge from her hiding places and scavenge something to eat.

"I want a fig roll, too." Ophele dragged a wooden stool over to wait while the rolls cooled. They smelled so good.

"You aren't likely to get a better offer than His Grace, missy," the old lady said bluntly. Azelma had no awe of Ophele, and she was very willing to offer advice whether Ophele wanted it or not. "Why are you doing this? No, answer me and then you can have a fig roll."

In the absence of the Hurrells, the fig rolls were really hers already. The figs were hers. The flour was hers. Ophele met Azelma's steely blue eyes and wondered what would happen if she snatched a fig roll and ran out of the kitchen. Azelma was an old lady. Her reflexes were slow.

"It's for Lisabe," she said, looking down at her toes. "Or Lady Hurrell said she would tell him what my mother did."

Ophele had no idea what this was. She had been too young to receive an explanation when her mother died, but she knew Lady Pavot had struck the decisive blow against Remin's old House. And it wasn't just because Lady Hurrell said so, either. From earliest memory, Ophele's mother had warned her to be careful what she said, because there were some words that could never be called back. And she had always sighed and said, *that poor boy*, afterward. Treasonous words, filled with regret.

"Lady Hurrell wouldn't tell the truth if she was strapped to a Catherine wheel and set alight," Azelma said tartly. But she still turned away, because these were matters well beyond both of them. Ophele hadn't been born at the time of the Conspiracy, and Azelma was just an old lady who knew how to cook.

"Will you make cheese pastries tomorrow?"

"Your Highness's wish is my command." Flour puffed under Azelma's hands, stout and strong as a sawyer's from decades of kneading dough. She was rolling out more sausage rolls and set the pan to rise by the oven.

"It is not," Ophele objected. "You put prunes in the sweetbread again yesterday. You know I hate prunes."

"Good for my lady's bowels."

"The etiquette books say you should never talk to a lady about her bowels," Ophele said primly.

"I will put prunes in your food every day if you let Her Ladyship have her way. Princess." Azelma wiped the flour off her hands and deftly wrapped up a package of food, knotting the small bundle in a handkerchief. "You're a clever stitch. If Lady Hurrell says yay, you know to say nay, loud and clear. Here, now. Best you get along with yourself, His Grace's men wake up early and hungry."

Subdued, Ophele took the food and slipped out the back door of the kitchen. She had been haunting the library for the past few days, where she had a comfortable nest above one of the enormous bay windows, a space in the rafters wide enough that she could even sleep without worrying about rolling off. Hurrying through the servants' hallways, she pushed the heavy library door open and scampered up onto the shelves. From the edge of the long row of bookshelves, it was a short leap to catch the rafter above the bay window, and she scrambled up with a kick of bare legs and a flurry of too-short skirts.

It was true, what Azelma had said. Sitting cross-legged in her small, shadowy refuge, she kindled an oil lamp and unwrapped her breakfast, breaking the loaf of bread in half to save some for later. Of course, she knew that Lady Hurrell was not helping her. Lady Hurrell was helping herself and her family. She wasn't stupid. And anyway, the lady's motive wasn't the issue.

The issue was: what would she do if Ophele defied her?

On paper, the Emperor had acknowledged Ophele as his daughter. But as a practical matter, she doubted he had remembered she existed until there was an inconvenient marriage in the offing. No matter what happened, whether she was sick or unhappy or if the Hurrells locked her up or beat her, there was no evidence that her father had the slightest interest. She wasn't just a bastard; she was the daughter of an accused traitor who had threatened the rightful succession. Only the fact that Rache Pavot was pregnant with the Emperor's sacred child had saved her from joining Remin's parents on the block.

Ophele wanted to leave. She would have contracted with a demon if it promised to help her escape. She hated Aldeburke, and she was tired of being afraid all the time. Lady Hurrell and her twisting, slippery words, her pinches and slaps and fingernails. Lisabe with her mean, trilling laughter. Julot, who kept trying to corner her in quiet places. And Lord Hurrell…well, most of the time, he ignored her. But Ophele had never forgotten the time he had not.

But Remin Grimjaw was worse than all of them put together.

Ophele rubbed her wrists, remembering the feel of his hard hands. It was easy for Azelma to tell her to defy Lady Hurrell. Azelma was safe in the kitchen, tucking prunes into sweetbread. But who said Duke Andelin would believe her, or protect her? He wasn't a knight from a tale. He was a brutal conqueror who hated her father and had every reason to despise her, and Ophele had already made him angry. Azelma was proposing that Ophele place herself in his hands and hope that he believed her instead of Lady Hurrell.

When House Hurrell had served his father, and fallen with him.

Ophele buried her face in her hands and drew a long, slow breath.

No, it was safest just to obey Lady Hurrell. Ophele knew perfectly well what the lady's plan was; they had probably made some excuse for her absence and were trying to convince him that she was too stupid to be his wife. All she had to do was be quiet, be a mouse, and Lady Hurrell wouldn't hurt her and Duke Andelin might go away, and then…

Ophele paged through her small, permanent collection of books. Atlases, natural histories, a few favorite books of poetry and fiction. *The Habits of a Lady*, a book she had nearly memorized, if only to understand her lost mother. And there at the bottom of the stack, a book that described all the countries surrounding the Sea of Eskai. Some of them had very liberal attitudes about women acting as scribes and merchants.

She could run away.

There were only a few guards left on the estate; most had left after her mother died. If she set aside some food, and waited until all this fuss was over, she could likely make a good start before anyone noticed she was missing. The Emperor would probably never even search for her. Perhaps the Hurrells would; Ophele had long suspected that Lady Hurrell meant her for Julot, once she reached her majority. Bastard or not, the speck of stardust in her blood was priceless, especially to a disgraced House.

For the same reason, the Duke of Andelin would never stop hunting her if she fled now. But the Hurrells were fighting tooth and nail to get her out of it, so if he married Lisabe instead, then Ophele at least would have a sporting chance of evading whoever Lady Hurrell sent after her.

Should she play along, then? Act like a simpleton? Drool? Foam at the mouth? What was likely to impress him least?

Rummaging through her atlases, she found one with maps of Aldeburke and the surrounding areas. The nearest country was Rendeva, a mountainous land about a hundred miles away. She would need money. Might there be things in Aldeburke she could sell? She didn't have any real notion of what might be valuable, aside from jewelry; people in books were always selling jewelry. But Ophele had never bought or sold anything in her life.

She would need food. She would have to stay at inns, and be careful of rough men in taverns. Transportation: she couldn't possibly walk all that way unarmed, vulnerable to thieves and wild animals. She had never gone past the gates of Aldeburke in her life, but she thought she had *some* idea of the danger, and Ophele's precarious existence had made her both cautious and methodical.

It was possible. The dream of escape, and a safe place. But even as she imagined it, the words blurred on the page before her, because she knew that this was not what her mother would have wanted.

It wasn't fair to the duke, was it?

Ophele knew a truth that was treason to the rest of the Empire: his family had been innocent. They had been implicated in her mother's treason, the Conspiracy that had shaken the Empire to its foundation and almost broke the Covenant of Stars. By the time she was five, Ophele knew that she and her mother lived in this place because her mother had done something dreadful, and a boy named Remin had lost his whole family and his home and *everything* because of it. It was the saddest story her mother had told her, arming six year-old Ophele with the truth.

Lady Hurrell had made sure to reinforce the lesson.

The boy Remin had gone on to become a knight, wage a war, defeat Valleth, and win an Imperial Princess for his wife, fair and square. Ophele was sure that her mother would have wanted to help him, if she could.

Only…

She was afraid.

Duke Andelin probably wouldn't kill her, even if he did learn what her mother had done. Ophele was still a Daughter of the Stars, and no one would risk losing their blessing. But Ophele knew she could be hurt very badly, and no one would care. All he wanted from her was heirs, children with the sacred celestial blood of the House of Agnephus in their veins. Even if he didn't hurt her, what if he locked her up, or didn't like to give her food?

And in the Andelin Valley, she would be alone.

Shifting deeper into her shadowy refuge, Ophele opened another travelogue. She needed to learn how much she might expect to spend on inns on the way to Rendeva.

* * *

Azelma Bessin had, over the course of her long life, cooked for the highest tables in the Empire.

Of course, when she had begun her apprenticeship fifty years ago, she had never imagined she would end her days in exile. But when disaster had befallen Lady Rache Pavot, she had chosen to follow her even to Aldeburke. Rache Pavot had been the truest kind of lady, gracious to everyone down to the lowest scullery maid, keeping a harmonious home even with the contentious Hurrells. That was the mark of a noblewoman, and there were plenty that had the title of Lady who were no such thing.

And there had been the princess to think of, too.

Azelma didn't believe in wishing stories or magic. But she did believe there was a natural order of things, that the world gave with one hand and took with the other. Some people thought that things should always go their way even if they didn't put in the work to *deserve* it, as if bread would rise without a good slap and a hard, muscular kneading. And that just wasn't so.

"Keep your fingers out of my black pudding," she snapped when the handsome knight appeared again, just before sunrise. The duke's men took it in turns to supervise the preparation of his food. "The beasts in the field know to wait for breakfast."

"I'll still be hungry then," he said with a winning smile that revealed a dimple in his cheeks. Azelma studied him, marking the blond hair and hazel eyes, which looked a little red-rimmed. What had he said his name was? Miche? "Do you live in this kitchen, grandmother? I swear you're here every time I come in."

"How else would I save any food for the table, I'd like to know," she grumbled. "Locusts."

"I heard the princess is still ill," he said sympathetically. "I have a remedy from my mother, a sovereign cure."

"Do you, now?"

"Barley porridge with honey, and a few other things," he explained. His eyes went over the pots and pans on the stove avidly, no doubt searching for the soft, bland food usually offered to the unwell. "Have the maids already taken up Her Highness's breakfast?"

"You're a nosy fellow, aren't you? Here. Take these and be off with you." Azelma shoved an assortment of breads both sweet and savory into his hands. "If His Grace grants permission, I'll make that porridge."

"His Grace?" Sir Miche hesitated, his eyebrows pulling together.

"Are your ears full of wax? Go on, get out," she ordered, brandishing her spoon. "But only if Duke Andelin tells me directly! I know young men. You're all frightful liars."

* * *

The library was not the first place Remin would have searched for a simpleton.

Easing the door shut behind him, he paused to scan for danger. The old lady in the kitchen had all but shoved him down the hallway, and he doubted that a crew of assassins were hiding among the encyclopedias. It was a surprisingly large library for a modest estate; tall bookshelves lined every wall, and the room was broken up into sitting areas with deep couches and heavy worktables, generously supplied with oil lamps. The whole place smelled agreeably of leather and old paper.

It had been almost a week since he had arrived at Aldeburke, and other than their short encounter in the forest, he hadn't seen a hair of the princess. Moving silently through long aisles of bookshelves, Remin searched, wondering why the cook couldn't have just come out with it and told him where the girl was. At the back of the library, he came to a wide bay window that looked out on the rose garden. The last row of shelves was missing two bookcases, so as not to block the light, and his eyes drifted upward.

In the small space above the window, a light was glowing.

Remin eased back, peering into the nook. In the depths, a light gleamed on long hair, and he heard the distinctive rustle of a page turning.

"Princess," he growled. "Come out of there at once."

The head jerked. The light went out. And a moment later a pair of eyes peeped out of the shadows, round with terror.

"Do you think you're an owl?" he asked impatiently. "Get down here."

How had she gotten up there in the first place? There was no sign of a ladder; the girl must be nimble as a squirrel. But she accepted her fate. Her eyes vanished and a pair of small bare feet emerged, and Remin hastened over as she lowered herself off the side of the rafter, dangling. Her refuge was at least twelve feet off the ground.

"Drop," he ordered. "I'll catch you."

Silently, she obeyed, turning her body in midair so that he caught her neatly as a cat. She felt shockingly light, but then, Remin had never held a woman in his arms before; were all of them like this? More to the point, though her face was pale as paper and her tawny eyes absolutely enormous, she didn't feel the least bit fevered.

"You don't look sick," he observed, frowning down at her. "You've been hiding in the library all this time? Can you read?"

Uneasily, she shifted in his arms as if she wanted to wiggle away, and he tightened them like iron bands. He had no patience for any further games.

"Can you or not?" he barked, and she nodded frantically, shrinking back. "Can you *talk?*"

She nodded again. That was ambiguous at best.

"Tell me what you were reading. Don't think, answer."

"I—"

"The title of the book," he snarled, shoving his face into hers so they were nearly nose to nose.

"*A Survey of the Nations of the Sea of Eskai!*" the princess squealed, giving up all pretense and struggling to escape. "Please put me down, Your Grace!"

"Are you going to run if I do?"

"No!"

"You swear it?"

"I promise!" The cry burst from her lips, and Remin set her down and snagged her wrist before she could take to her heels. It was the first good look at her he'd gotten, without her face hidden in a hood. Small. On level ground, the top of her head barely reached the bottom of his breastbone, and the bones of the wrist in his hand felt as fragile as a bird's. Would she even be able to work? She didn't look like much in a dress that even he could tell was old, simultaneously too large and too short, with masses of untidy brown hair. She looked more hair than girl.

"This is the daughter of an Emperor?" he asked scornfully. "I guess I should be used to such gifts by now."

It had occurred to him that her shameful appearance might be intentional. She had already disgraced him once; was this some protest, a further humiliation? Her father loved such subtle insults. Gripping her chin with iron fingers, he forced it upward, catching a glimpse of those eyes hidden behind her hair. They were large and clear, flashing almost golden in the sunlight. There was nothing dull in those eyes.

Maybe this whole charade had been an attempt to get him to relinquish his claim. Remin was furious, because it had very nearly worked.

"Nine times nine."

"Eighty-one." She was quivering like a rabbit. Another trick.

"Sixteen times sixteen."

She paused. Blinked. He could see the calculation running behind her eyes.

"Don't *dare* to lie to me," he rumbled ominously, and she flinched, her head ducking.

"Two hundred fifty-six," she whispered.

"How many copper sens to a sovereign?"

"Twelve hundred."

"Spell *ballistae.*"

She spelled it down to the tricky *e.*

"Good enough," said Remin Grimjaw, shifting his grip to her upper arm and thrusting her toward the library doors. He had a wedding to plan.

CHAPTER 2 – A WEDDING

When he finally decided to move, the duke was like a tidal wave.

Ophele barely had time to jam her feet into a pair of shoes before she found herself swept into the manor courtyard with a thousand questions on her lips and a dozen things she was trying to do at once. He was barking orders so fast, she couldn't tell which were for her, and suddenly the area was boiling with men and servants and assembled baggage, two lines of blanket rolls and saddle bags forming as if by magic. There was another growing pile of foodstuffs requisitioned from the kitchen, and even as she watched, one of the squires trundled by covered in so many waterskins, he looked like a lumpy bipedal mole.

"But Your Grace," Lord Hurrell kept saying, hurrying after them, distinctly rumpled after the servants had had to haul him out of bed. The lord of the house preferred to sleep late. "The girl needs clothing! A lady-in-waiting! She has barely risen from her sickbed—"

The duke flashed him a glance like steel.

"She managed to rise into the rafters of the library. She's fine," he said curtly. But he did yield to protests about the weather and took a cloak from a nearby maid, jamming the hood onto Ophele's head with a jerk that hid her face to the tip of her nose. He had assumed command of the house as if it were a poorly trained army and a dozen maids were falling all over themselves to assemble some form of trousseau.

"Ophele? Ophele!" Lisabe appeared at the manor doors, panting, her blonde hair tumbling loose over her shoulders. Her hands clasped together. "Oh, please, Your Grace, we have barely had a chance to say good-bye!"

"They're still saddling the horses," the duke pointed out, striding toward the baggage line. "Say it."

Bewildered though she was, Ophele was not about to suffer a tearful farewell from Lisabe, who had once stolen her favorite doll and burned its hair off, who had always taken the last cookie rather than let Ophele have one, and who had never failed to offer Ophele up as a scapegoat for her own misdeeds. The list of grievances was long, a lifetime of petty torments and injustices, but it was the sight of those crocodile tears that made Ophele retreat in revulsion.

"Don't," she said, her hands held out as if warding the other girl off. "Good-bye, Lisabe."

Lisabe wasn't quite shameless enough to force her to accept an embrace, but Lady Hurrell had no such restraint. She swept into the courtyard with a keening cry, as if her heart were shattering to pieces.

"*Ophele!*" The wide sleeves of her gown flapped like wings and before Ophele could escape, her head was trapped in the lady's bosom, smothering in the scent of rose sachet. "Your Grace, please, it is too soon! She is like my own child, have mercy!"

Ophele couldn't hear the duke's reply; she was too busy trying to thrash free, and she was struck with a lunatic urge to laugh. This was ludicrous. It was a farce. Lady Hurrell's arms tightened and her voice hissed in her ear.

"Faint," she ordered. "Right now, or you know what will happen."

With a wrench, Ophele yanked free, panting. Her cloak was turned around the wrong way and her hair tumbled wildly around her face, half-blinding her, but outrage and hurt for once loosed her tongue.

"Do you think he'll take Lisabe if you make him kill me?" she whispered, disbelieving. Even after everything, she hadn't really believed that Lady Hurrell would do it. Her voice trembled. "He wants the Emperor's daughter," she said bitterly. "That's *all* he wants. He will never let me go."

Stars, it was *true*. She stumbled away, weaving between neighing horses. They were leaving Aldeburke forever, right now, and he was taking her with him.

She had to find Azelma.

Ophele darted up the long drive to the kitchen, dodging a few of the duke's knights, who hesitated as if they were unsure whether the princess needed recapturing. The kitchen had a separate delivery entrance around the east side of the house, and she could already see the old lady in the herb garden, hurrying forward with her apron still on.

"Azelma!"

"Oh, Princess!" Those soft, strong arms went around her and *then* it was real, and a sob burst from her throat as Azelma held her and rocked, a floury hand sinking into her hair.

"You shouldn't," Ophele wept, already regretting the intimacy in full view of a furious Lady Hurrell. "Let go, or push me away, quickly."

"Never. None of that, wipe your face," said Azelma, pushing her back to dab at her cheeks with her apron and applying a light dusting of what smelled like cinnamon. "Here. This is for you and His Grace. Make sure he eats, a hungry man is a terrible beast. Promise that you'll share it."

"I will." Ophele rubbed her nose and took the heavy parcel, wrapped in a knotted cheesecloth. The tears were falling faster than she could blot them away, and Azelma tutted, tugging her cloak back into place around her shoulders.

"Now, now," she said, more gently. "You can't go to him with a face like a wet Sunday. You're well away from here. They get letters even in the Andelin, make sure you write to tell me how you're getting on."

"I will," Ophele repeated, sniffing. "I need a handkerchief. Azelma, I can't go to Andelin without a handkerchief."

"Here, you silly girl," Azelma laughed, but for all her admonishments, the old lady's eyes were suspiciously bright as she tugged a square of linen out of her pocket. Her hand gripped Ophele's shoulder and gave her a shake. "Be brave, and don't tell lies. All will be well, I promise."

Ophele trudged back up the drive, tucking Azelma's handkerchief into her sleeve and wondering if she was going to her death. If she was, there was nothing she could do about it. Lady Hurrell would say what she wanted to say, and the duke would do what he wanted to do, and Ophele had no control over any of it. It was just as her mother had told her, with serene acceptance of life's vicissitudes: the only thing Ophele could control was herself.

But when she stepped into the courtyard Lord Hurrell was still trying to argue with the duke and Lady Hurrell was standing beside Lisabe and Julot, weeping theatrically and determined to go down with all flags flying.

"—a carriage at least, she is the daughter of the Emperor!" Lord Hurrell exclaimed. "If you give us but a little time, we can ready a carriage, as is appropriate to her station—"

"There aren't any roads where we're going." The duke swung up into his saddle, his eyes landing on Ophele as if he had assumed all this time that she would be exactly where he had left her when the time came. And here she was. "Princess, give me your hand."

At this point, it wasn't worth trying to protest. Obediently, she offered her hand and the duke hoisted her into his lap with one arm, tucking her cloak over her knees. The Knights of the Brede were already mounted and waiting in perfect order, shining down to their shin greaves.

"Good-bye, Your Highness," called Tam behind them as the horses started forward, and there were a few half-hearted farewells from the other servants. The Hurrells said nothing.

"Good-bye," Ophele whispered as the manor house receded behind her and was finally lost among the trees. She had never been on a horse before. She had never left the estate. It almost felt as if the air should be different as they passed through the gates.

"What's this?" The duke asked, poking at the parcel in her lap. "Give it to me, we can put it on the supply wagon."

"No," she said, clutching the cheesecloth as if it were Azelma herself. "It's mine."

"Don't complain when your arms get tired."

They rode in prickling silence. Ophele lowered her eyes, wishing she had a horse of her own. She was acutely aware of his chest at her back and his heavy thighs under her legs, thick with saddle muscle. She hadn't been this close to another person since her mother died. And he hated her. He probably didn't like touching her at all, any more than she liked touching him. But she had made a promise, and her mother had told her to always keep her promises.

She bit her tongue and screwed her courage to say, scarcely audible: "It's lunch."

"What?" he barked.

"This," she said, almost stuttering in fright. Why was he angry? Her voice died under that black glare, but she nudged the parcel and forced the words out. "Azelma gave it to me. To share with you. Your Grace. If you want."

His eyebrows lifted.

"I see." He sounded skeptical. "We'll be stopping to eat in a few hours."

He probably thought she was going to poison him. Ophele lowered her eyes, bumping along in his lap with his arms on either side of her like two walls closing in. The shoes dangling off her feet were tidy slippers of the sort worn inside the house, forest green with dangling gold tassels and vastly oversized.

They were Julot's.

* * *

If Remin had wanted to be married the same day they left Aldeburke, it wouldn't have been impossible. There were three small villages within a few hours of the estate, and at least one of them would've had a cleric available. But the Duke of Andelin would be married with the same thoroughness he did everything else: inarguably, irrevocably, smashing through all resistance to stamp the act on the pages of history, so even scholars in generations to come could not contest his will.

To that end, they were going to Celderline. It was a large town with a temple and a Prior, three days from Aldeburke. As much as he hated to waste the time, he would have smoke sent up from the Temple, call forth the town criers, and cram as many witnesses as possible into the temple. Songs would be sung. Oaths taken. The marriage certificate would be notarized in triplicate and then locked in the same casket where he kept proof of the princess's identity and parentage.

Even in the chaos of his departure from Aldeburke, Remin had collected every page of the records belonging to Lady Rache Pavot. His abrupt departure had served him well; the lord was too surprised to have time to conceal anything, and too rattled to lie convincingly.

From Celderline they would go straight to the Andelin Valley, a much longer journey and large portions of it through rough country. He had already decided that he and his new bride wouldn't have children right away, not until he had a respectable home in which to install them. But he meant to have a brood, as a hedge against the calamity that had plagued him all his life. The Emperor had wiped out his House down to the last infant. Remin was all that remained. And he would protect his children from suffering that fate even before they were born.

His eyes went to the princess, sitting alone by a fire and entirely ignorant of these plans. She looked tiny, huddling in her cloak, but according to the records of her birth, she had been born in 808 and would be eighteen this year. Old enough.

Surprisingly, she hadn't been much trouble so far. Remin had watched her carefully at lunch and only ate the things she ate, after she took the first bite. Sitting with her wasn't like sitting with his men and he frankly wasn't sure what to do with her. They ate silently and didn't make eye contact, an eternity of chewing.

"The bread is good," he had finally offered. The words fell into the silence like a stone dropping down a well.

"Azelma made it," she said, her eyes flicking up to him and quickly away. Her voice was so soft, he had to lean forward to hear her.

Their only other interaction that day had been when he caught her sidling away from the group during a short break in the afternoon, as if she thought she might slip off unnoticed. He had collared her before she got five paces.

"I'm just…to the bushes," she had explained, without meeting his eyes. The tips of her ears were scarlet. Accustomed though he was to his men doing any number of unspeakable things on the march, Remin released her at once.

"Very well," he said stiffly. "If I have to come find you, you'll never go without an escort again."

She nodded and sped out of his sight, and in the five minutes she was gone he hovered, for the first time uncertain. Suddenly it dawned on him that even if she wasn't actively trying to escape, the world was a dangerous place. There might be snakes in the underbrush; a red-mouthed adder could kill with a single bite. Badgers. Foxes with foaming sickness. Even a rabbit would bite, if startled; bites could turn septic even with treatment. It wasn't quite spring, and the nights were still cold, what if she did actually get sick?

He had commanded whole armies and ordered thousands of men to march to their deaths, but he had never been responsible for anything as fragile as a girl.

As if to punctuate his thoughts, the princess rubbed her hands together and held them out to the fire, scooting closer.

Remin went to take a look at the supply wagon.

He hadn't been lying when he told Lord Hurrell that there were no roads where they were going. The supply wagon rode high off the ground on two iron-shod wheels, so it could bounce along over the roughest terrain. Remin had no fondness for the Emperor's daughter, but he wasn't cruel enough to make her ride in that. She'd bite off her own tongue before noon. But as a bed, it might be better than sleeping on the ground.

After he ordered the load shifted off the front of the wagon and commandeered several large fur-lined cloaks from his grumbling men, Remin returned to collect the girl. She was sitting in exactly the same place by the fire, hunched in a little ball.

"Princess," he said gruffly, crouching beside her. Her eyes were closed, thick dark lashes curling over her cheeks, with her small chin propped on her knees and a half-empty mug of wine staining the hem of her cloak. If it had been one of his men, he would've administered a gentle kick, but he sensed that would not be appropriate. He shook her shoulder instead. "Princess. Wake up."

"Wha—huh?" She blinked up at him and instantly retreated, clutching the remains of her supper. Remin huffed with irritation.

"Come. If you want to sleep, do it somewhere safe," he said, pulling her up by her elbow and reaching for the bread. "Are you done with this?"

She muttered something.

"Speak up."

"F-for the morning," she said, clutching it closer.

"Give it to me, it'll attract vermin. We'll have breakfast before we leave, I don't starve my men," he added, irritated. It wouldn't surprise him to learn that there were such rumors about him. "Come, you're sleeping here."

Drawing her to the supply wagon, Remin stuffed the cloaks into the narrow space at the front, just enough room for a small girl, and folded the hoods over to make a rough pillow. "The furs should keep you warm enough. No, don't climb," he added, plucking her off the wagon wheel and depositing her in the wagon before either of them could think about it too much. "If you get cold, tell me. We don't have time for you to get sick."

She nodded without looking at him, and he frowned. What was wrong with her?

"I won't be angry if you get cold," he said sternly. "I will be angry if you don't tell me. Understood?"

"Yes, yes." Her knees drew up defensively and he thrust his own cloak at her, annoyed without understanding why.

"Go to sleep," he ordered, and beckoned to nearby Darri to guard her. Sir Darrigault of Ghis had eyes like a cat in the dark, and the good sense to be blind to anything his duke didn't want him to see.

He was much more at ease among his men. Taking his usual seat by the fire, Remin held out his cup for wine, nicely warmed to counter the night chill. Seven of his friends had survived the war, and they were now his closest counsellors: Miche, Auber, Bram, Tounot, Edemir, Huber, and Justenin. All of them were now properly titled, and some of them had been nobly born, but among themselves there was no need for courtesies.

They all remembered the same faces, missing from the circle around the fire.

"We have a wager," said Bram of Lisle, the firelight flickering over his narrow face. "Do you think that was the Emperor's orders at Aldeburke, or His Lordship's own idea?"

"It could be both." Remin grunted. "I sent two messages to Aldeburke. The guards at the gates of the estate saw three messengers."

"The Emperor has been in a generous mood," Edemir remarked, gesturing with a sheaf of papers, their seals dangling. The son of a count, he was the most educated of Remin's men and handled the duke's correspondence, official and otherwise. "To celebrate the victory over Valleth and in earnest prayer for lasting peace," he read from one paper, "the Emperor extends his mercy to his most unfortunate subjects... anyone who has committed minor offenses, excepting capital crimes...it seems he has decided to empty the prisons in advance of your announcement, Rem."

"The Brede will be well fed," Remin replied grimly. "No one with the brand of a criminal will be allowed across the bridges. I thought he would do something like this."

On the first day of spring, messengers from the Duke of Andelin would spread the word that for at least the first year, the Andelin Valley was open *by invitation only*. He would need that long to build the infrastructure to support them, roads and granaries and storehouses, to begin an orderly process so he would not become the Duke of Shanty Town.

Then he would open the floodgates. His lands were vast and almost empty of people, and he needed farmers. Miners. Chandlers and weavers, hunters, fishermen, people to sow and reap and spin. He wanted quarries in the mountains and fields of wheat as far as the eye could see on the Talfel Plateau. Remin could picture it as clearly as if the towns had already been built, and the long miles of road rolling to the horizon. It would be the work of many lifetimes.

But in spite of his orders, new people had already been arriving even in the depths of winter, and it would only accelerate once the weather was warmer. The Emperor's edict would salt criminals among the flood of people, yet another poisonous gift to endanger the innocent and plague Remin's lands for years to come.

It also made the Emperor look benevolent and rid him of prisoners that were expensive to feed and house. As far as Bastin Agnephus was concerned, it was a win all the way around.

"We'll have to leave a few more men on the bridges unless we want a repeat of the charge of Gresein," observed Juste.

"I've already sent warning," said Edemir, before Remin could order him to do so. The stars blessed a competent man. "And advised Their Lordships of Norgrede, Firkane, and Leinbruke that we will not be admitting criminals. I asked them in your name to keep a patrol on the south side of the Brede River, but…"

"People will attempt the crossing," Bram of Lisle said grimly. It was ironic that only a few years ago, he would have been one of the criminals they were trying to keep out. When one of the Emperor's freed prisoners mounted a suicidal charge onto an enemy-held bridge, then Remin would reconsider his position.

He couldn't blame them for trying. Many of the people coming to Andelin were fleeing all manner of hardship, but he could hardly fling open the bridges and let them throw his lands into chaos, never mind the dangers of the Andelin devils. So they would try the Brede, and he would send regular patrols to clear away the corpses to keep them from fouling the water.

"I'll draft additional orders tonight," he said. "You can forward them on, Miche, I'm sending you ahead to Celderline tomorrow. You too, Huber. Make sure the Prior's still in residence and pay some men to spread the word that the Duke of Andelin is getting married."

It still felt strange to say it, as if he were talking about someone else who was a duke, and someone else's wedding.

"Give me money," drawled Miche, sprawled out by the fire with his long limbs in everyone's way. He was never shy about asking.

"No more than ten sovereigns."

"Should I spread word that the duke is getting married in a barn?"

"How much do you think you need to bribe a few drunkards?" Remin retorted. "Pay the Prior and buy two rings. Plain silver."

"My older brother got married twelve years ago," said Auber. "I know it was twelve years ago because my sister-in-law complains about her silver ring every year on the same date. Not one diamond to grace it, not one star for her hand."

"Weren't we camped on the Talfel most of last year?" Tounot asked.

"I got letters. She mentioned it in the letters," Auber said, a little grimly.

Remin looked from one man to the other. There seemed to be an important message here.

"You're suggesting I buy diamond rings," he said slowly.

"And maybe some flowers," Miche put in, to a general murmur of agreement. "Even if she is the Emperor's get, Rem, she's going to be your wife for life. Women don't forget this kind of thing. Don't do anything you don't want to hear about for the next fifty years."

"Twenty sovereigns," he said, in a tone that closed the discussion. Wisely, his men moved on to another topic.

The subject had made him acutely uncomfortable. After he drafted his orders, Remin relieved Darri at the supply wagon and propped himself against the wheel, wrapped in a blanket. He could see the girl's sleeping face in the starlight, turned in three-quarter profile and undeniably pretty, when it wasn't hidden under a mass of hair. Had the third messenger at Aldeburke come for her? Would the Lord and Lady even know about it, if the girl had a habit of roaming around the estate unguarded? And if the message had been for her, what might it have been? Even if she was the Emperor's spawn, she hardly looked capable of assassinating him herself. And once they reached his lands, she would be utterly alone. She had no allies. She wouldn't be able to send so much as a smoke signal without his knowledge.

He watched her sleeping for some time, burrowed into the fur cloaks at the front of the wagon. Her hair was impractically long, cascading off the side of the cart and already tangled. Had any of those benighted maids thought to pack anything as useful as a comb?

"Here's fifty," he told Miche before dawn. The company's gold was distributed among a number of saddlebags and other unlikely places, including the soles of Remin's boots. "Buy diamond rings. And find her a dress."

"A dress?"

"One that fits. And one for the wedding." Remin scowled, daring the man to be amused. "If the duke is getting married, his bride shouldn't look like a beggar."

"They'll think she's a queen," Miche said, with his most elegant bow. Sir Miche of Harnost was a cynic and a womanizer, but he could charm birds out of the trees and for reasons known only to himself, had sworn his service when Remin was still a boy. "Size-wise, you think she's more like Lady Flavie or that seamstress back in Merelde? Chinot, that was her name."

"How should I know? You saw a great deal more of them than I did." Remin's eyes flashed a warning, because he knew exactly what was going through Miche's filthy mind. "Use your discretion about what else a woman might need, but make sure she's fit for travel. And don't waste my money."

"I will hire minstrels to sing the story of your love throughout the Empire," Miche promised, and ducked Remin's fist.

"Huber."

"Yes, Your Grace. No minstrels." Huber was already mounted, the humorless balance to irreverent Miche. "Quit fucking around, Miche, get in the saddle. We'll have to ride hard to make Celderline before nightfall."

Knowing Miche, Remin found himself wondering if maybe he should have given them a little less time. Idle hands were ripe for mischief.

* * *

The maids had not, in fact, packed a comb.

Hidden under the supply wagon, Ophele rummaged through her small bag of supplies, a pretty flower-patterned valise that might have been sufficient for a day trip in a carriage but was getting battered to bits in the wagon. Already something had been broken—she suspected a mirror—and she was carefully picking the larger pieces out of the bag and taking stock of the surviving supplies. It looked as if there were several changes of undergarments rolled into discreet little bundles of silk and lace, along with another of Lisabe's old dresses, two pairs of stockings, a small packet of various medical herbs (considerably crushed), several bolsters of sanitary cotton, along with cosmetics, perfume, and three jeweled hair pins.

Someone had thought of hair pins, but not a brush or comb. Muttering to herself, Ophele fished carefully through the case, hoping not to slice any fingers. After riding all day yesterday and sleeping in the wagon, she felt unspeakably grungy and would have traded all three pins for a toothbrush. One of the duke's men had appeared with a basin of water while she was still rubbing the sleep from her eyes, but she felt too self-conscious to wash in front of so many strangers. All she wanted to do was stay out of their way until it was time to leave.

"Princess?" rumbled a deep voice, and a pair of long legs clad in thick breeches and leather riding boots stopped beside the wagon. The duke's face appeared, sun-bronzed and stubble-jawed, his shaggy black hair damp from his own ablutions.

"A mirror broke," she said nervously before he could ask. The duke always made her feel like she was doing something she shouldn't. Plucking a curving shard of glass from the bag, she held it up as evidence.

"Let me see." He moved with animal grace as he crouched over her, reaching for the valise which contained multiple varieties of unmentionables. She snatched it away.

"Oh, no, it's all right," she said quickly. "I'll be careful, I—"

His black eyes narrowed in suspicion. "Give it here."

Did he think she was going to try to stab him? Or grind up glass to put in his food? Ophele's face reddened.

"There are…private things in it," she said, willing him to understand. "It's only—"

"Now," he snapped, his eyebrows lowering like thunderheads. Clutching the bag, she wondered wildly whether she would actually fight him over this, maybe even run for it, though she couldn't possibly win. His huge hand grasped the bag and twisted it out of her arms.

This was mortifying. Ophele looked at her feet as he rummaged, picking out more shards of the broken mirror, meticulously setting every object in the grass as if he were one of the Emperor's tariff men performing an audit. She couldn't bear to look at his face, but she could tell the precise moment he realized what the little bundles of lace and silk were, and realized that he was openly displaying her breast bindings and underclothes to two score milling knights.

"I told you," she whispered, humiliated beyond all description. "It was a mirror. I didn't even pack the bag."

"That is true," he said stiffly. And then, unbelievably, he went on removing the rest of the articles, all the way down to the bolsters of sanitary cotton, at which point she buried her face in her hands and wished she was dead. His one concession to decency was that he covered her underthings with the spare dress.

She heard rather than saw him slip out from under the wagon, and he shook out the smaller pieces of glass into the coals of a nearby fire. His boots returned, and he paused for a moment, then knelt back under the wagon and handed her the empty valise.

"We'll be leaving soon," he said, without expression. "Pack your things. Don't hide under the wagon again. If it rolls, you might get hurt."

She refused to acknowledge him. She had never been so embarrassed in her life, and growing up with the Hurrells had given her an extensive reservoir of experience. Biting her tongue, she looked down at her lap, furiously blinking back tears. She would not let him see her cry. That would be the final humiliation.

After a moment, he moved away without another word.

That man was going to be her *husband*. In a few days, he was going to be doing worse than touching her underclothes. Ophele had no concrete idea what went on between a man and a woman—the library at Aldeburke had little information on the subject—but she had overheard the maids gossiping often enough to have a vague notion.

She would die. She would be the first person in recorded history to actually expire of mortification. He was a brute, he was a cruel, callous, heartless bully and a *mean* man. Snatching up her violated undergarments, she stuffed them into her bag, every jerk of her hands punctuating a growing list of adjectives.

Unfortunately, once she was packed, the only place she could go was back to that mean man. At the front of the line of horses and men, the duke mounted his black warhorse and wordlessly held out a hand, a silent order to come, and lifted her in front of him. She tried to shift toward the front of the saddle, sitting stiffly upright to touch him as little as possible.

They moved out.

He spoke to his men, but never to her. She didn't want him to talk to her, anyway. She wanted nothing to do with him. There was nothing to look at but the rutted road and naked forest, and boredom slumped side by side with her resentment, a sore trial for a girl who had always had books for companions. The knowledge that marriage to a man who hated her waited at the end of this dreary road oppressed her.

"I had to be sure, Princess," he said abruptly, after they had been riding in silence for at least a year.

She said nothing. Even the word *princess* was loaded with his scorn. In one breath he was both condemning her for being the Emperor's daughter and ridiculing her for doing it badly. It wasn't her fault she had no dresses of her own, or that he hadn't given her time to gather the things she needed to look less like a beggar's brat. All she could do was try to bear it with dignity, and he wasn't even allowing her that.

"Don't sulk."

"I am not sulking," she said, her voice giving a traitorous quiver. She was too miserable even to be afraid of him. "I am humiliated."

He was silent for a moment.

"That was not my intention."

That was not an apology. Lady Hurrell had been punctilious about the proper parts of an apology. That had not included either an admission of error or an expression of remorse.

They rode in frigid silence until the noon meal, where he gave her a chunk of bread and cheese and told her to stay near his horse but absolutely not to touch it. When she took his hand to be lifted back in the saddle later, the worst of her anger and embarrassment had faded; Ophele had never been able to sustain a grudge. But she was desperately unhappy, and looking at a future that seemed so bleak as to hardly be worth living.

Was it always going to be like this?

It seemed impossible that it would be any other way. He was treating her like his horse, feeding her and bedding her down for the night, watching constantly to make sure she didn't wander off. She supposed she was lucky he hadn't tied her to a picket. But there was no chance of escape. The woods were still bare and her shoes were so big, she would have fallen flat on her face before she made it off the road. No, there was no way she could run away, and miserable though she was, she knew more than anything that she did not want to die.

How had her mother endured it? Lady Rache Pavot had never married. She had become the Empress's lady-in-waiting when she was seventeen, and then become pregnant with the Emperor's child, an event that precipitated the Conspiracy.

Had her mother *chosen* to lie with the Emperor? It was impossible to square the loving, gentle woman she remembered with something so ugly and tawdry, not to mention the bitter betrayal of the Empress she had served. But perhaps that was why her mother had told her time and again: *the only person you can control is you.*

They would arrive in Celderline tomorrow. And she hadn't bathed or brushed her teeth in two days and while her second dress lacked the slept-in wrinkles of the first, it was even more tatty and ill-fitting. She could see it in the duke's eyes when he dragged her into the saddle the next morning, a slap of disapproval that made her face burn. She spent the morning anxiously dragging her fingers through her tangled hair, craning her neck toward the horizon.

She had never been to a city. She had never *seen* a city. Her mother had been exiled to Aldeburke before she was born, and Ophele had only seen a few pictures of cities in books. She didn't realize the strange black clouds on the horizon belonged to the city until they connected to chimneys, and at last she saw the vague shadows of distant rooftops, unmistakably manmade in their angular lines.

"Is that it?" she asked, her fingers clutching the edge of the saddle.

"Yes."

Her heart gave a tremendous thud.

"Are we getting married today?"

"Tomorrow."

It felt like a nest of serpents had taken up residence in her belly. She could have cried. Could have pleaded with him to reconsider the virtues of Lisabe. She could have tried to flee when they stopped for lunch, forced him to drag her down the aisle to the altar and wailed her protest at the top of her lungs. She could make all of this as unpleasant and humiliating for him as it had been for her. It would please her father tremendously, if he heard about it.

But in her heart, she was not the Emperor's daughter. She was the daughter of Rache Pavot, who had accepted her fate with grace.

The city drew steadily nearer. There wasn't much to see but the high city wall and the rooftops beyond, taller than any building she had ever seen before. Around them, the duke's knights shouted and shook out their cloaks, black lined with silver fur, and produced that ominous black standard with the bridge and crossed swords.

Distantly, she could hear shouting.

"Why are there so many people?" she asked, squinting at the crowds lining the road ahead, and the duke cursed under his breath.

"Miche," he said, like an oath, and quickly rearranged her in his lap. "Turn this way," he ordered, before she could protest. "Both legs over my right thigh. Good."

With a flick of his hands, his heavy cloak fell over her, concealing everything but her face. One massive arm slid around her waist to press her firmly against his chest as he spurred his horse to the front of the column, managing the reins with one hand. It was just like the final bookplate in a romance she had once read, except his only reason for doing it was to conceal his bride's house slippers and ragged dress. Her long hair, unbound and unwashed, flapped loose to whip around them romantically and made the duke's horse very uncomfortable.

For all the evil tales about Remin Grimjaw, the Duke of Andelin was of higher nobility than most people would see in a lifetime, and a war hero to boot. His knights were a glorious sight with their shining armor and fluttering banners, and there were actual showers of petals as they approached the gates of the city. Flocks of children scampered ahead of them and formed a shouting mob behind, and Ophele was stunned by the sea of faces, more people than she had imagined there could be in the whole world, clustered ten deep by the side of the road.

A blond knight was waiting for them at the gates of the city, mounted and armored and bearing the duke's black banner.

"Your Grace!" He shouted, flinging out his arms in welcome. His voice boomed even over the noise of the crowd. "All of Celderline is waiting to greet you!"

The gates yawned ahead of them, the spikes of the portcullis bared like fangs, and Ophele prepared herself to be brave.

* * *

Miche had outdone himself, arranging all this with barely a day's head start.

It wasn't the first time Remin had received such a welcome. The triumphal progress through the capital of Segoile had lasted three hours, and for the first few months after Valleth surrendered, it seemed like all the roads before him were strewn with flowers. It had been strange and humbling, and almost made him feel like an imposter, even though he knew he had really done all the things they said he had done.

He accepted the shouts of the people of Celderline with the same stern, expressionless face with which he had received the war cries of the army of Valleth, holding his warhorse back to a dignified walk. Before and behind him, his knights paused to accept flowers from ladies, nudged their horses into a dancing trot, or lifted their banners and sang along with the crowd, each according to his own inclinations. They, too, had faced far more hostile crowds than this.

Belatedly, he remembered that the girl in his lap had not. The Exile Princess had never seen a crowd of any description, and she was pressed so tightly against him, he could feel her heart knocking against his ribs like it was trying to climb in and hide.

"Don't be afraid," he said, bending his head so his mouth was beside her ear. "They don't mean any harm."

She looked up at him, her eyes enormous. She had a small scar at the outer edge of one delicate eyebrow. Under his cloak, her hand was clutching the hem of his jerkin, and his arm tightened around her automatically, even as his back prickled at the remembered stab of a knife.

Fortunately, it wasn't far to the inn. Fifteen minutes was a satisfactory progress for everyone; it gave the townspeople a bit of excitement on an otherwise ordinary day, without disrupting the business of the city too badly. Following Miche, they wound through a large market square and then up a narrower avenue to a hilltop in the middle of town, passing through wide gates into the stable yard of a palatial inn. The innkeeper was already waiting, bowing low and declaring himself ecstatic to have the opportunity to serve so renowned a hero.

"Tell your lads to be careful of the horses," Remin replied, acknowledging the courtesy with a jerk of his chin. Swinging out of his saddle, he landed with a thud, doing his best to keep the princess concealed under his cloak. "They're trained for war. Feed and water them but leave the grooming to my men. You have a room for the princess?"

"The Prin—Your Highness!" the innkeeper exclaimed, prostrating himself on the cobblestones when he spotted the girl in Remin's arms. "Sacred Daughter of the Stars! Yes, of course, we are deeply...*deeply* honored!"

"Rise," Remin said, gesturing. "She needs maids. And a bath. And whatever else ladies require."

"I will ask my wife to personally attend her," the man replied, presenting a sturdy woman with an astonishing white bonnet. She too prostrated herself.

"Delaide Goel, if it please Your Grace. Blessed Highness, I will consider myself honored the rest of my days."

"Thank you." Setting the princess down, Remin transferred his cloak to her shoulders, tugging the hood over her tangled curls. "Stay with Mistress Goel, Princess. You'll be fine. Auber."

Auber nodded and trailed after the women into the inn. He was an unobtrusive sort with light brown hair and unremarkable features, and he had made an art of being overlooked.

With the girl off his hands, Remin went about the rest of his work with good will. His company occupied the entire third floor of the inn, luxurious accommodation in a part of the city renowned for their mineral baths. His own room was as opulent as anything he had seen in Segoile, with stained glass windows and a deep balcony that overlooked the river and the market on the other side. It would have been an outrageous expense under any other circumstances, but sometimes spending money was as good as flexing muscle.

Before supper, he and Edemir were ensconced at a worktable to deal with piles of correspondence, everything from invitations to balls that had already happened to reports of troop movements on the border with Valleth.

Remin did not fear another war. Yet. The wounds of the last were too recent, and he had harrowed every last Eagle Knight out of his valley, inflicting staggering losses that would take Valleth a generation to recover. With Hara Vos pressing from their east and certain other measures from Remin to compel their obedience, it would be decades before they needed another lesson. But Remin was hardly going to leave his borders undefended, and he planned to break the remaining units of his army into small local militias, lightly armed and mounted to respond quickly to reports of banditry and the like.

There were many other reports, less dire but all urgent in their own way. Some of it was good news; while he was in the capital, Remin had made the acquaintance of an earl from Leinbruke and persuaded him to part with a few head of his prized breeding rams, renowned for the quality of their wool. A dozen of them had arrived and were being duly coddled on some good grazing east of Tresingale.

All reports of Tresingale were of absorbing interest. It might be a few dozen huts on a muddy lane right now, but one day it would be a beautiful city, the seat of his duchy. It had everything: access to the Brede on two sides, rolling hillsides to the east for grazing, and acres of flat, rich farmland to the north, left fallow for nearly a century. In spring, work would begin on the network of roads that would connect Tresingale to the rest of the Empire.

He could have happily spent whole days planning his new city, if Miche hadn't insisted on interrupting every half hour with some question about the wedding. The ceremony had taken on undreamed levels of complexity, and Remin seriously doubted fifty sovereigns had stretched so far as a choir, but long experience with Miche had taught him sometimes it was better not to look too close.

"Your Grace, the tailor is here," said the irrepressible man, sticking his head through the door.

"What for?"

"To measure Your Grace for Your Grace's wedding clothes."

49

"I don't remember putting that on my list of requirements."

Miche stepped into the room. "With respect, Your Grace, you smell like a horse's ass. And you look like you've been sleeping on the side of the road for a month."

Edemir glanced at him with pity. "He's not wrong, Rem."

With the exception of their sojourn at Aldeburke, he *had* been sleeping by the side of the road for the last month. Sighing, Remin allowed himself to be measured for a new doublet and jerkin, stubbornly refused breeches in any color but black, and then submitted to the ministrations of a barber while Edemir read off more reports and noted down Remin's orders. But the jeweler was the last straw.

"I told you to take care of it, Miche," he flared. "I don't give a fuck whether you stick a sapphire or a lump of coal on my brooch. Don't bother me about it again."

He was silent at dinner, an excellent meal with hearty joints of beef and pork, thick crusty bread, and platters of turnips, beans, potatoes, and a variety of green things. It was pleasant to be clean, and clean-shaven, after so many weeks in the saddle, and his men were loud and boisterous. Seated at a long table beside a massive stone fireplace, the innkeeper rolled in cask after cask of excellent wine and ale, and their laughter rang to the ceiling.

Ordinarily, he would have been roaring and singing and exchanging insults right along with them. But tonight, for some reason he felt as if he were standing on the edge of a precipice, the same feeling he had had the night before the charge on the Gresein, and the day before he went to accept the surrender of Valleth. His men glanced at him, glanced at each other, and poured more wine into his cup.

"Your health, my lord," said Justenin, knocking his cup into Remin's. "We'll return to the Andelin in time for the spring planting."

"Sir Juste is eager to meet his sheep," said Bram knowingly. Justenin had taken charge of His Grace's livestock. "Think you'll find a bride of your own?"

"Better than the woolly sort of prostitutes you favor, Bram," Justenin replied placidly, to a round of laughter.

It was late when Remin finally stumbled out onto the balcony, breathing in huge draughts of the freezing air. The sting of it felt good on his hot cheeks.

"I wouldn't advise any more wine," said a voice from the darkness, and he turned to find Miche lounging on the stone railing against the side of the inn, holding a wineskin in one hand and a cup in the other. Miche always counseled against the vices in which he was indulging.

"I wasn't planning to." He wasn't drunk, but Remin was unpleasantly hot, and flapped the neck of his loose white shirt. "I just wanted some air. Why aren't you inside?"

"The same reason, more or less. I was quite busy today, on behalf of my liege."

"How did you get the whole city to turn out?" Remin wanted to know. "I figured out the rest, but you could hardly have bribed half of Celderline to show up."

"I bought minstrels." Miche smirked. "When Huber wasn't looking. A few rounds of *The Battle of the Brede* and *The Lady's Courting-Song* and they were lining the streets. It puts a nice finish on the war, doesn't it? And then His Grace married a princess and lived happily ever after."

"It's not like that." For some reason, hearing that made him angry. As if all of it, all those years of blood and dirt and misery had just been the lead-up to an hour in the temple of Celderline. "It was our land. The Andelin was part of the Empire for almost a thousand years. When Valleth invaded, the people—"

"Didn't give a shit." Miche poured himself more wine. "Neither do you, Your Grace. It's a rich land, but if the Emperor hadn't destroyed your House—"

"Miche."

"If you had grown up a proper nobleman's son, the Andelin Valley would still belong to Valleth and you wouldn't care," Miche said stubbornly. "I'm not judging, Rem. It's also true that they attacked us, and you likely would have been sent with all the other blue-blooded sons to lead an army and drive them out, one day. But that's not what we were fighting for. We were fighting because the Emperor took everything from you, and we had to go through the Andelin Valley to take it back."

Remin didn't want to hear that. It was easier to bear if he thought the dead men of the Andelin had given their lives in service of the Empire, not himself.

"Give me a cup."

"No. You're getting married tomorrow; you can't be nursing a hangover." The other man noisily drained his cup, because that was the sort of bastard he was. "You've gone to a lot of trouble to marry the daughter of a man you hate."

"You know my reasons."

"Yes." Miche's breath curled up white as he sighed. "But I was thinking. That's not good enough, Rem."

"What do you mean?"

"It's not what they'd want."

There was only one *they* among the Knights of the Brede. Even with the wine warming his veins and mazing his mind, Remin could see their faces as clearly as if he had spoken to them at supper. Rasiphe, Bon, Ludovin, Clement and Victorin. Rasiphe had died at the Gresein Bridge. Bon died of poison meant for Remin; Ludovin had been captured as a spy and fed to the Lord of Tales. Clement and Victorin had died together holding a narrow place in the Berlawe Mountains, slowing the arrival of enemy reinforcements. Victorin had taken twenty-six stab wounds before he succumbed.

"I was thinking," Miche repeated doggedly, "that they'd want the Duke of Andelin in new clothes for his wedding. They'd want to see you in a temple with a crowd of people smiling for you, and a pretty girl in silk next to you, with flowers in her hair. And they'd want you to be happy together, Rem. I know who she is. But she seems like a nice girl. Give her a chance. Give both of you a chance."

Remin was silent for so long that Miche finally relented and poured him half a cup of wine, setting it beside his hand with a click of metal on stone.

"Why me," Remin said finally, looking over the dark river. "Why should I have all that?"

"Well *one* of us should," Miche drawled. Remin gave a bark of laughter, shaking his head as he looked up at the sky. The stars in the vault of heaven looked down upon them, each one offering its own gate to paradise, reached only through great struggle and suffering. Victorin would surely be there. "And another thing," Miche added. "Tomorrow night."

"What about it?"

"Get her wet and take it slow," Miche advised, and made Remin choke on his wine. "No one's going to be witnessing the consummation. Make sure she's relaxed and enjoying it, don't just jam it in."

"Miche."

"The Knights of the Brede have a reputation to uphold," the knight said sternly, jabbing a finger at his lord. "It will be a tricky business for an unproven knight, but you've always been good at improvising. Let me tell you about that seamstress in Merelde…"

* * *

Lying in her room on the other side of the inn, Ophele could not fall asleep.

Any number of wild ideas were circling through her mind. The sight of her balcony had given her hope at first, but it was hanging over a river and she didn't know how to swim. After midnight, she slipped out of bed and padded quietly to the door in her chemise to peek into the hallway. Just to check. But there was a lean, dark man with a pockmarked face sitting on the floor outside her door, embracing his sword like a lover. He looked up at her mildly.

"Do you need something, Your Highness?"

"No. Thank you."

Shutting the door, she trudged back to bed.

There was no escape. Would Lady Hurrell really write to the duke and tell him what Rache Pavot had done to his parents? If she hadn't shouted it out before the duke left, did that mean she had given up? Forever?

That did not sound like the Lady Hurrell Ophele knew.

Sitting in the middle of a wide feather bed, she wrapped her arms around her knees. She never thought she would wish for her tiny, drafty room back at Aldeburke, but being in this strange place with its unfamiliar shadows only added to her fear. For the first time in days, she was warm and clean, dressed in a new linen chemise with the sweet scent of lavender wafting from her skin, a kindly attempt by Mistress Goel to help her sleep. But sleep had never seemed more impossible.

She couldn't stop picturing the duke's face and the narrow spectrum of emotions she had seen from him so far: irritation, annoyance, suspicion, scorn, and fury. Love matches were a wishing tale for little girls. She knew better than to hope for one herself. But the man she was to marry was infamous for his ruthlessness. People said he might have accepted Valleth's surrender years ago, but instead he had hunted them all over the valley, until the grass dripped red with blood. He hadn't shown the least consideration for her so far, other than doing what was required to keep her alive.

He was enormous. He didn't like her. And he didn't care what she was feeling.

Would he hurt her?

She was pale and red-eyed when the innkeeper's wife appeared some time past sunrise, tapping lightly on her door.

"Good morning, Your Highness," she said, throwing open the drapes over the casement windows. "There's plenty of time for a nice, leisurely breakfast, and then perhaps another bath?"

Accustomed to the scornful service of the maids at Aldeburke, frequently accompanied by Lady Hurrell's abuse, Ophele meekly put herself into Mistress Goel's hands and was surprised to enjoy it. Weddings in the Empire were conducted at dusk, and so it was a very leisurely breakfast indeed: endless courses of eggs, pastries, fruits, more food than she had ever seen, and nervous though she was, she actually ate until she was *full,* and then rose for her bath.

Ophele had never had a bath that didn't hurt. The maids tenderly scrubbed and lotioned and scented her skin until she felt as if she were effervescing, a new being made of flower petals. Her fingernails were filed and polished until they shone like little jewels, and then they wrapped her in fluffy towels and took her to a dressing table, where a hairdresser spent nearly two hours brushing miniscule amounts of scented oil into her hair. When she was done, Ophele's hair fell in loose curls past her hips and gleamed with a rich, silken luster she had never seen before.

Having made her into a clean palette for their artistic endeavors, they broke for afternoon tea. Sitting at a small table by the window, Ophele and Mistress Goel munched on sliced winter apples and oranges plucked from the inn's small hothouse.

"I was married twenty-one years ago," the mistress said reminiscently. "In the same temple, though ours was a much less grand affair. We married in summer, and I remember I wanted nothing more than to wear a silk dress, but that day it was so sweltering, I nearly fainted on the dais."

All day Ophele had been silently braced for some insult, some cruelty, out of sheer force of habit. But Mistress Goel had a pleasant way of rambling without requiring any response while still making her feel as if they were sharing a conversation. It gave her the courage to speak.

"Did you know him before?" she asked timidly. "Your husband?"

"Oh, my, yes. Our families were great friends when I was growing up. My father is a merchant in town, and he happened to supply most of the furnishings to this inn." Mistress Goel sipped her tea. As if in recognition of the importance of the day, her headgear was even more remarkable than yesterday, a conical hennin that required caution when going through doorways. "When did you meet His Grace?"

"Last week."

"That's the way of the nobility, isn't it," the mistress said kindly. "The Count of Dennel just married off his daughter last year, to a man of fifty-two, if you can believe it. You're fortunate to be matched to such a handsome young man. The girls will be breaking their hearts over him for months after you leave. But—and please forgive the impertinence—haven't you a nurse or a maid on the way to attend you? All the women who love you should be with you today."

"No," Ophele said awkwardly. It felt churlish to say that her mother was dead, or that she had never had a nurse of her own, or that His Grace had dragged her out of Aldeburke with someone else's shoes on her feet. "His Grace was in a great hurry to get back to Tresingale…"

"Ah. Then it will be our honor to be their hands today." The Mistress bowed her head and pushed the plate of sweets closer to Ophele. "Have another cookie, Your Highness."

After tea, they got down to serious business. The maids dressed her from the skin out in another new chemise, low-necked and richly embroidered with gold silk flocking. Her kirtle was a dusty pink silk, and the overdress a brocade in the pale green of new apples, slashed at the upper arms to show both kirtle and chemise.

"Are you sure it's all right for me to wear this?" she fretted as the maids sewed the tippets just below her elbows, long decorative foresleeves that cascaded in lacy ruffles nearly to the floor. "I don't have any money to pay…"

"These are gifts from His Grace." Mistress Goel looked surprised that Ophele didn't know this. "One of his men began bringing these things to the inn yesterday. He didn't tell you?"

Ophele shook her head, surveying the room dubiously. She had thought all these things—oils, lotions, cosmetics, clothing, even the apple-green silk slippers—must be some sort of wedding service the inn provided.

"And this, too," said a voice from the door, as a tall man was shown into the room and bowed courteously. "Sir Miche of Harnost, Your Highness, I regret we have not yet been properly introduced. I bring a gift from His Grace."

The songs were right. Sir Miche of Harnost was the most beautiful man Ophele had ever seen. For a moment, every woman in the room was too stunned to do anything but stare until he extended the gift: a shallow wooden box containing a necklace and earrings, delicate confections of pink and white diamonds on fine golden chains. Ophele tore her eyes from his extraordinary face.

"His Grace really sent this?" she asked, her brow wrinkling. He hadn't seemed to like her at all.

"Indeed. The carriage will be arriving in half an hour. I will have your flowers brought up."

Half an hour. Ophele bobbed her head in acknowledgement and stood rigid as a doll as the maids hastened their efforts. Their cheerful chatter swirled around her without making any impression on her consciousness, and she moved stiffly to let them clasp the necklace around her neck, clip the earrings to her ears, and then dab scent on her neck and wrists.

"Too much cosmetic is vulgar on a maiden," Mistress Goel said judiciously, giving only the lightest touch of rouge to Ophele's lips.

With her gown on, she couldn't sit down, so she bent her head as the hairdresser wove a coronet of roses into her hair and pinned a lacy veil over her head. When they held up a mirror to show her the finished result, she didn't know herself.

"You look beautiful, Your Highness," said the mistress, smiling with satisfaction. "The duke won't be able to take his eyes off you."

"He won't?" she echoed faintly. Her mouth was dry.

"No indeed." Mistress Goel pressed a bouquet of pink roses, alyssum, and small white lilies into her hands and led her into the hallway. "If my son were about to stand beside so lovely a lady, I would tell him to thank the stars for his good fortune. Please mind your train on the steps. Rosset, catch it before it snags."

She hadn't even noticed that her dress had a train; everything was so unreal, the added weight on her shoulders might just as easily have been the iron chains that bound misers and embezzlers in the Daitian underworld. At the foot of the grand staircase in the inn's entry hall, Sir Miche was just pinning a black half-cloak into place at his shoulder.

"His Grace is already at the temple," he said, before Ophele could ask, and offered another extravagant bow. "It will be my honor to escort you. Don't worry, from now on you're in the charge of the Knights of the Brede. You fear nothing in the world, eh?"

"Thank you." Kind words were always welcome, but he actually seemed to mean them.

With the warm glow of sunset lighting the town, she was transferred into the carriage, and Sir Miche swung up onto the rail by the door as if he intended to guard it with his body all the way to the temple. Through the windows she could see a sea of faces and another storm of petals, the crowd cheering and singing. They must have denuded every garden and hothouse in the city.

With all her heart, she wanted her mother. Somehow she was sure Lady Pavot would have known just what to say. But the only words she could recall were dim now, and too well-worn to be much comfort. Traditionally, both her mother and father should have driven with her to the temple, and her father should have escorted her down the aisle, to hand her to the man who would be her lord and master the rest of her life.

If she were going to be given away, it only seemed fair that *someone* cared enough to show up and do the giving. This way made her feel like the duke was taking in a stray no one else wanted.

The carriage halted before the steps of the temple and Sir Miche stepped down to open the door. As he handed her down from the carriage, someone cried that the Princess of Argence had arrived, and the crowd burst into *The Maiden's Meditation,* a traditional song about a maiden's thoughts on the morning of her wedding that bore no resemblance to Ophele's lonely vigil. Sir Miche arranged her train behind her.

"You look beautiful, Your Highness," he said, offering his arm. "Don't worry. I will be with you to the end."

She nodded, her eyes enormous. Inside the temple, people were squeezed together on rows of wooden benches, and incensors exhaled at the end of every aisle, giving off silver-blue smoke. Every head turned at once to stare as she entered, clutching her bouquet.

Ophele had never seen a temple before. She knew only the most elementary facts about the Temple of the Stars, the religion based on her own divine ancestors. Silvery starlight streamed through the crystal dome, the light of stars captured and magnified, glowing on the circular dais where the duke and the Prior were waiting.

The stars would witness this union. Before their all-seeing eyes, she would be joined to him inseparably, unto death and beyond.

Chimes rang. The choir sang a response. The duke watched her approach, tall and stern, his black eyes inscrutable. His immaculate doublet and jerkin were silver shot with green, undoubtedly styled to match her own ensemble, as if he were a sturdy tree and she its leaves and flowers. A black fur-lined cloak hung over his immense shoulders and made her think of a particularly elegant bear, and his black hair had been neatly trimmed and brushed back from his high forehead.

Sir Miche offered him her hand and moved to stand with the other knights, leaving her alone. There was nowhere to run, no protest she could make, no hope of an appeal. Ophele squeezed her eyes shut and drew a shaking breath, then squared her slim shoulders, to try and face this with grace.

"Greetings to His Grace Remin, Duke of Andelin," she said. Her voice was soft, but came out unwavering and clear.

"Greetings to Her Sacred Highness Ophele, Princess of the Empire of Argence," he replied with a low bow, and then straightened to lift the veil from her face.

CHAPTER 3 – A BED OF ROSES

She had flowers in her hair.

The vision of the princess danced before Remin's eyes even after he turned away, like an afterimage from staring directly at the sun. He had very rarely gotten a good look at her, these past few days; she was always looking at the ground, and hiding behind her masses of untidy hair. Even as the Prior began his opening blessing, Remin couldn't help watching her from the corner of his eye, as if it might be some trick. She looked like the maiden spring in pink and green, and her hair was beautiful, the rich umber streaming in loose curls down her back, with a crown of pink roses on her head.

The ceremony needed a few adjustments, as they went along. Neither of them had parents to approve the marriage, or at least, in the princess's case, no parent that was willing to stand behind her on her wedding day. And for the first time, the thought of the Emperor aggravated Remin for reasons beyond his own grievances. Surely the Emperor should have sent *someone* to witness his daughter's wedding. What Miche had said was right, and Remin found an unwilling pocket of sympathy. She had been a very nice girl so far, and she was all alone.

"Let us call the stars as witness," the Prior said, and Remin snapped back to attention.

The invocation was long and rather ironic, considering the number of verses calling for the blessing of the stars, and the Emperor who was their Beloved. It was very unlikely that the Emperor would spare any grace for this union. But the Prior made the best of it, and smoke from the silver braziers rolled in thick cloud around the base of the dais, cold and sharp to Remin's nose.

"Before these witnesses and under the light of heaven, we propose to bind this man and this woman as one, unto death and beyond, and even to their dwelling in the stars," said the Prior, lifting his hands. "Are there any here that will protest this joining?"

There was a terrible moment when Remin glanced at her, wondering if *she* might protest. But she said nothing, and at that moment the crystal chimes hummed along the periphery of the dais as the stars sang a wordless, ethereal accord.

The princess began to glow.

Remin had never been a particularly religious man, but even he was awed as the light shone from her fair skin, glowing in her eyes. Behind him, there were gasps from the crowd, and a rustling as everyone fell to their knees before a Daughter of the Stars. She was shining so bright, the lines of her body wavered in the radiance of their light.

The princess looked down at herself in amazement, and when she lifted her eyes to Remin, he saw that she was afraid.

"Sacred Highness." Remin had to force himself forward, to take the hands of this divine creature, his thumbs rubbing gently into her palms, warm and reassuring. "I am Remin Nicanot, the son of Benetot and Sidonie, and by the grace of the stars, Duke of Andelin. To you I swear the protection of my body and my house, from this day to my last day, and even unto our dwelling in the stars."

He meant it. Even if she was the Daughter of the Stars, the daughter of the Emperor, he would protect her to his last breath. The Prior was nearly as awed as the rest of the crowd, but he moved forward at Remin's sharp glance and began to bind their wrists together, the silk cords symbolizing the oaths that would bind them unto death and beyond.

"I—I am Ophele, daughter of Bastin and Rache, and by the grace of the stars, Princess of Argence." The princess's voice squeaked once before it settled. "To you I swear the submission of my body and my obedience to your House, from this day until my last day, and even unto our dwelling in the stars…"

Back and forth, they alternated vows, each vow another cord, another knot, another bond. A pattern emerged in silver and white and blue, gleaming with tiny crystal beads. If either of them had had a family, it would have been their responsibility to supply the cords of this binding.

As it was, they had been supplied by Miche. Possibly stolen.

"As your husband, I will build and guard the walls of our House, and forsake all others in fidelity to my wife," said Remin, taking the rings from the ends of the cords. They were nearly done.

"As your wife, I will govern well within the walls of our house, and forsake all others in fidelity to my husband," Ophele replied, taking his ring. There was a plain silver band for Remin, but her ring was small and exquisitely formed, with a diamond set in each scalloping scroll of silver. Miche had somewhat exceeded his mandate.

For a moment, they looked at the rings together, and then her eyes lifted to his as they spoke as one.

"With you, I will share my hearth and my home. The products of my labors." Together, they slipped the rings onto each other's fingers. "With you, I will share all my joys and sorrows, for all the days of my life."

The pattern was done. The Prior slipped it loose from their wrists, a perfect weaving, reflective, recursive, infinite. He lifted it over his head, that all the witnesses might see.

It was done. Remin was married. And no power on earth could undo it.

The light of the stars faded. Ophele tried to withdraw her hands, but Remin held them tightly, his heart thumping with emotions even he couldn't identify. Triumph. Happiness. Grief that his parents had not lived to see him wed. Satisfaction that he was moving, step by step, toward restoring so many things that had been lost. And looking into the eyes of his new wife, uncertainty about what lay ahead, because she was the daughter of his enemy.

"On this, the fourth day of March in the 826th year of the Divine House of Agnephus, I witness this marriage on behalf of the Temple of the Stars, and attest the shining of the stars upon it," the Prior concluded, and bowed his gray head, smiling. "Your Grace, you may seal this covenant, and kiss your bride."

When Remin bent to kiss her, it was only the second time in his life that he had kissed any woman. The back of his neck heated, aware that the Knights of the Brede had a reputation to uphold and that he had a certain dignity to maintain before the eyes of half of Celderline. But her lips were red and yielding and she smelled as if she had come from a bed of roses. Remin's hand sank into her soft hair to hold her in place, feeling the hesitant response of her mouth under his. It was as if someone was gently rubbing silk against his lips, and the surprising pleasure of the sensation made him lean into her for a moment before he collected himself.

Lifting his head, he had to force his usual impassive mask back into place, nodding to the Prior to continue. The man was dignified in his advanced age, raising his hands in benediction to the new couple.

"To the people of Celderline and all people under the dominion of the stars, I present the Duke and Duchess of Andelin!"

The cheers spread from inside the temple to the streets of the city as the temple bells tolled the news of the duke's marriage, and still Remin's knights were the loudest of all.

* * *

The rest of the evening galloped by like a panicking horse.

After the ceremony, the wedding party retired to the inn for a feast attended by anyone who impressed the innkeeper and the duke's knights. The food was tested for poison before it was brought to His Grace's table, and the only attendees permitted to carry weapons were the Knights of the Brede.

Ophele was ignorant of all these precautions. Seated at the high table beside her new husband, she picked at her food and tried to ignore the stares, unaccustomed to the attention of so many people. The duke was being unusually considerate, and she wondered why. It was impossible to tell from his expression; when he wasn't actively irritated, his face was at best neutral, if not grim. But he prepared a platter for her, cut up her meat, and offered her savories as they passed by, though his suggestions sounded more like orders.

"Do you have much experience of wine?" he asked as he poured her some, pausing with the glass half-filled.

She shook her head. The first time she had ever tasted wine was in his camp the night before last, and it had been sour and made her feel sleepy.

"You have to cultivate a taste for it," he explained, setting the jug aside. "Here, try it."

Obediently, she sipped, wondering if this variety might be any better. The taste filled her nose and tickled her tongue with a stinging heat, sour and acid. Her mouth puckered.

"No, eh?" The duke signaled a serving girl to bring her something else. Tasting his own cup, he frowned. "We will do better in the valley."

He meant to grow grapes? And he wasn't ignoring her, or barking orders. Ophele cast about for something to say, attempting to meet him on his own ground. "Are you going to—"

"Edemir." He was already speaking, leaning over to the knight on his left. "Before we leave, send out some inquiries..."

He probably hadn't heard her in the din. Ophele accepted a cup of fruit juice from the serving girl and sipped, trying not to notice that the sky outside the casement windows was completely dark, and the servants were lighting the oil lamps along the sides of the banquet hall. A space in the center had already been cleared for dancing, and musicians were tuning their instruments, the sounds of flute, drum, and mandolin rippling through the noise of conversation.

She caught the duke watching her from the corner of his eye and lowered her head, hoping he wouldn't ask. She could already hear his question in her head, punctuated by the derisive *princess.* She didn't know how to dance. Her mother had danced with her when she was a little girl, but after she died, there had never been a tutor or a dancing-master. Not even a nurse like Mistress Ursule, who taught Lisabe the proper arts of a noble lady.

Ophele looked up at her tall, imposing husband, wondering with renewed fear what he would say when he realized exactly how poor a princess she was.

"What?"

"Nothing," she whispered, looking hastily away. She watched the moon rise like a criminal counting down the minutes to their execution, and saw the key players in the final drama moving into their places: one of his knights came to murmur in the duke's ear, and a moment later Mistress Goel appeared at the far end of the table, flanked by two maids. It felt as if her heart stopped.

His Grace looked at her with opaque black eyes, and bent his head to her ear.

"Go on up, Princess," he said quietly. "I will follow shortly."

It occurred to her that dancing might have been a better alternative.

Traditionally, her mother and sisters should have escorted her from the hall, along with any other married female relations and close friends. Ophele rose and exited the hall alone, trying to walk with dignity, her head held high and her pace unhurried.

But they did not take her to her room. They went instead to a different room at the end of the hall, where Sir Auber was just coming out of the door.

"Your Grace," he said, moving aside with a polite bow.

The new bedchamber looked much like her old one, a large and luxurious room with a large and luxurious bed, littered with a small assortment of belongings that plainly belonged to a man: a large pair of boots on the floor, a familiar cloak over a chair, a rough leather bag. Patiently, the maids undid all their work, removing the layers of her gown and replacing her chemise with a lighter one of thin white silk edged in lace. Then Mistress Goel shooed them from the room and sat her by the washstand to remove the roses from her hair.

"Your Highness, please forgive me for asking," she began, looking troubled. "I assumed someone from your family was on the way, and had perhaps been delayed on the road. But…has no one given you your bridal lessons?"

"Bridal lessons?" Ophele repeated blankly.

"Oh, dear." The mistress glanced anxiously at the windows, marking the progress of the moonrise. "And His Grace will be here any minute, I wonder if I dare…you must be very honest with him, Your Highness. I believe he is a sympathetic man, he seemed quite taken with you. It was just as I said…"

A knock sounded at the door, and both women started.

"He hasn't been able to take his eyes off you," the mistress finished in a whisper, and gave Ophele's hair a final stroke with the brush before she rose and departed. There was a brief, whispered conversation in the hallway, and then the duke ducked through the door, and made the room small with the sheer force of his presence.

She had skittered halfway across the room like a frightened deer before she realized it.

"Wife."

The single word stopped her in her tracks. Her fingers tangled in an anxious knot before her as she lifted her eyes to his, ignorant that the fire behind her revealed the curves of her body through her thin chemise.

"Mistress Goel said no one told you what's to happen." As he spoke, the duke undid the silver buttons of his jerkin, sliding it off his shoulders and letting it fall on the floor. His tanned skin was dark against the open neck of his white shirt.

Mutely, she shook her head.

"We have to be together tonight. I will take your virginity." He was moving closer, too close, too tall, reaching out one huge hand toward her face. Her eyes fixed on it as if it were a snake and it took everything she had not to cringe backward. By the time his thumb brushed her cheek, she was trembling.

"Will it hurt?" she whispered.

"It might, a little." Gently, his hand stroked her face, curving around the back of her neck to slip beneath the warm weight of her hair. That didn't hurt. "But if I do it right, it is supposed to feel very good. I promise I will be careful. You must tell me if it hurts. Promise?"

She nodded. Her pulse was beating so fast, she could feel the tiny, frantic knot of it in her throat. His hand shifted to cradle her head and there was a sense of vertigo as his black eyes descended, his lips covering hers in the same slow, considering kiss he had given her in the temple. It was a kiss that felt strangely…patient, his lips gliding slowly, plucking at the soft curves of her mouth.

His hand touched her back and she flinched instinctively, her eyes squeezing shut. But he was only caressing her, his hand sliding up and down her back, his fingers in her hair, as methodical as if he was surveying the contours of her body.

It didn't hurt. He had said he wouldn't hurt her. Ophele thought of the romances she had read and tried to do what he was doing, her lips moving in timid, tingling brushes. Those books had never gone further than kisses, and the strange, fluttering feelings they provoked. But those girls *did* often fling their arms about their lover, and her hands crept tentatively upward to wrap around his neck.

His shoulders went rigid.

"What are you doing?" he murmured against her lips.

"I'm sorry," she whispered, removing her hands at once. "You don't like it?"

"No, it's fine." But he was frowning as he kissed her again, his thick black brows lowered ferociously. Ophele shut her eyes tight only for them to fly open again at the warm and shocking roil of his tongue into her mouth. He tasted of wine, and the honey-cakes they had had for their wedding supper. This was *not* the sort of kiss she had read about, and it made her feel very peculiar. It was hard to think when he was doing that, hard to breathe, and she bent back, and back, and back, and hardly knew she was falling until he caught her.

"See?" he murmured. Another kiss. "It will feel good. Don't be afraid. We have all night."

It was obvious to Remin that she had no idea what he meant, but that was his own fault; he had snatched her from Aldeburke without giving anyone a chance to explain things to her. Though he could not trust her, and she was the daughter of his enemy, he could not bring himself to be cruel to her. Not when she was looking at him like that, with her eyes eating up her face.

"Come here," he said, drawing her over to one of the chairs by the fire and sitting her on his knee. Miche had offered a painfully explicit explanation of how he should proceed, but it was something else to actually *do* it. Remin had never done this before, either, and it was all too easy to imagine accidentally hurting her.

Now that it came to it, he found himself unexpectedly nervous. They must do this tonight, to ensure there were no possible grounds to contest the marriage later, but he felt foolish as he brushed his lips over her cheeks. Her eyes slid shut and her breath shivered out and then it was easier, and he moved more confidently down her jaw, nuzzling into her throat. The sweet scent of her made his head spin and he lingered against that soft, warm skin. There was a fluttering against his lips that he realized was her pulse, speeding away.

"Does it feel good?" he asked thickly, and sensed her reluctant nod.

The more he kissed her, the more he wanted to kiss her. His hands at her waist tightened, sliding up and down, feeling her ribs move as she breathed, tiny and delicate as a bird. The slender frame of her collarbones called to him, and before he could think about it, he was licking her, sliding his mouth over those little bones and feeling her jerk as he bit her.

But she liked it. Remin was warming to his task, advancing steadily downward, and every time she squirmed, every time she stiffened, he retreated back to her lips until she softened for him. The back of his neck heated as he finally reached her breasts and sought one rosy nipple with his mouth, tugging her through her chemise. It was the first explicitly sexual thing he had done to her, and she rewarded him with a high, breathless gasp: the single most erotic sound he had ever heard.

The princess clapped her hand over her mouth and turned scarlet, and he couldn't bite back a chuckle. Drawing her nipple between his lips, he tugged again, wetting her chemise with his mouth. His other hand slid resolutely over her knee to the inside of her thigh, and she pushed it away, unthinking.

"But…what—why?" she stammered. He opened one eye.

"I am making you ready," he told her, and deliberately licked her nipple again, a lewd motion that made it darken and harden through the fabric. "We are going to be naked together, and I must touch you everywhere until you are wet. Then I will put myself inside you."

Ophele digested this.

"Like a goat?" she asked timidly. "I saw goats once…"

The corner of his mouth twitched.

"Like a ram, I should hope," he said. "Do not be embarrassed. This is what we must do together, as husband and wife."

She did not look entirely persuaded, but he could feel her response as he captured her other nipple, her body jerking with every stroke of his tongue. His fingers trailed lightly up and down her inner thigh, tickling that sensitive skin, making her jerk and shiver like a horse needing gentling. Both of them were breathing hard, and she could not be still.

"Let me look at you," he whispered, meeting her eyes for a moment before he slipped the wide neck of her chemise over her shoulders, and then her breasts were bare and he was cupping one in his warm hand. The sensation of his tongue rasping directly against her naked nipple was vivid and shocking.

"Ahh…" Her voice cracked. Her thighs tried to close, but Remin patiently eased them apart again. "Your Grace…"

"Does it hurt?" he asked hoarsely.

"No…!" She gave another cry as he stroked, circling with his fingers as he pressed his face into her breasts, licking and kissing and biting with his heart pounding wildly in his ears. Her nipples were so pink and tempting, quivering taut on his tongue as if they might melt. He tugged on one and then the other, and every time she jerked, every time she moaned, the pitch of his own desire burned hotter.

And then, nerving himself, he slid one long finger inside her.

"Oh—oh, y-your…what…" She stuttered in shock, her eyes flying open as she tried to squirm away from the invading digit.

He didn't stop. Ophele thought she would burst into flames as a second finger joined the first, and that handsome, forbidding face nuzzled again at her breast. This was Remin Grimjaw, the Scourge of Valleth, who had done nothing but glare at her from the moment they met. His lips moving, plucking at her. His tongue laving. His teeth nipping her skin. She could never have guessed what would happen, she certainly could never have imagined this, but the last thing in the world she would have expected from him was pleasure.

His fingers slid in and out, easier every time. It tickled. He made her body shake. In. Out. In. Out. Her breath burned in her lungs as a cry burst from her lips, sensation scorching along her nerves as she jerked and quivered through her first climax.

"I think you're ready," he said, as if from very far away, and his arm slid under her knees to lift her, striding toward the bed.

* * *

Deprived of her chemise, Ophele lay beneath her new husband and for the first time felt the naked skin of a man's body against her own.

She had never seen such a man. Well, she had never seen a man of any description without his clothes on, but the duke was a uniquely imposing specimen. The nuptial bed had been prepared for the wedding night with the blankets folded back and a fresh linen sheet spread out, scattered with rose petals and scented with amber, but Ophele noticed none of this. Her eyes were riveted on her husband as he undressed, revealing a body that was so unlike her own, it was hard to believe they were the same species. His chest and shoulders were massive, heavy muscle working in his arms as he stripped off his doublet and breeches. A rigid belly, with a trail of coarse dark hair leading to something she *definitely* did not have, springing upright from his clothing to pulse against his belly.

Her mouth fell open.

"Stop staring," he said flatly, moving over her on the bed so she couldn't see it anymore. "You'll make me embarrassed."

"But I've never—why doesn't it show through your clothes?" she wanted to know, trying to sneak another peek. Curiosity had not only conquered timidity, it was busily drowning it in a nearby river. "How do you hide it?"

"It's not always like that." The corner of his mouth twitched again, and he turned his eyes to her, his fingers moving between her legs. "Just as you're not always like this. Are you?"

"Noooo…" The word ended in a quavering gasp as he stroked her, slow caresses that proved she was very wet indeed, touching places even she had never dreamed existed, as if he knew secrets of her body unknown to her.

Maybe he did. The firelight burnished his back and shoulders as he moved over her, fluid as a beast. His body was covered in old scars, jagged and snarling lines in pink and silver-white, gouges where chunks of flesh had been torn away. He was so warm, like a stone that had been baking in the sun all day, and everywhere he touched her, her skin shivered against his.

"Your Grace—" she mewed, hardly knowing what she meant to say. His fingers moved inside her, pushing and wiggling as if he were looking for something.

"Your Grace, Your Grace." His fingers curled up, stroking inside, and she cried out. "I think we can dispense with titles when we're naked, wife. What's my name?"

"R-Remin," she whispered. Her tawny eyes shone as she looked up at him, so guileless that he doubted himself all over again. She was either a consummate liar or no liar at all, and it was hard to believe that any maid so young could pretend so well, or that a creature of the Emperor could place herself so trustingly in his hands.

"Again," he whispered back. His fingers circled and dived into her. Now he understood what it meant, that she must be wet, and her hips undulated with him, filled with innocent sensuality. He nipped the tip of her ear and wondered if he was falling into a trap. "Ophele…"

She moved under him, whimpering.

"Remin…"

"Again." His breath felt hot and thick in his throat, and he bit her neck. Her skin was littered with the marks of his desire.

"Re—Remin!" His name cracked in two as he found it at last, the rough spot inside her that Miche had told him to look for. There was a sudden flood of wetness as he rubbed her and she *writhed* in response, her heels digging into the mattress.

"Does it feel good?" he asked, panting with excitement.

"I—it…I feel, strange—*ohhhhh!*"

The cry burst from her as she jerked beneath him, her face twisted in beautiful agony. White flashed in waves behind her eyes. Ophele saw his face above her as if through a haze, his black eyes heated and intent as a hunter, his firm lips eagerly parted.

The sight of her climaxing sent such a rush of lust through him, it was all he could do to keep from shoving himself into her immediately. Stars, the way she sounded, crying his name! Remin sucked in a breath, his hips bucking involuntarily. What black magic was she working, the daughter of his enemy?

He hadn't had any idea how intimate this would be. How impossible it would be to keep her at arm's length when she was naked beneath him, her voice crying out with pleasure. He had checked her for weapons when he undressed her, but what defense had he against that look on her face? Those soft, trembling lips? Was it possible that she might be his, in truth? House Hurrell had been bannermen to his father; could it be that she was not the Emperor's creature at all? Could she be as innocent as she seemed?

What would it mean, if she was?

"Hold onto me," he said, his voice deepening with desire. Her eyes were blurred and soft, weaving up to his face as he pushed her legs apart and moved himself between them, angling into the small cleft between her thighs. The first *inch* of penetration felt so good, he had to swallow a gasp.

"Oh…" A crease appeared between her eyebrows. Her hands gripped the boulders of his biceps, very white against his brown hide.

"Don't…move," he warned, struggling to restrain himself. She was so tight inside, he couldn't see how he would fit, and the sight of his shaft sinking into her was making it very hard to think.

"Oh…oh, oh, *ow,*" she whimpered, reminding him that this might not feel good to *her.* Miche had said it depended. Slow, slow, he had to go slow, but Remin had never done this before either and she was *throbbing* on him, delightful spasms that ricocheted all the way from his balls to the back of his skull. Something gave way inside her and she yelped as he slid suddenly deeper, a white wave of pleasure that hit him like a hammer to the face. "Oh! Oh, Your Grace, it hurts!"

"I know, I know," he gasped, kissing her lips, her eyes, half out of his mind. "Shhh, shhh…"

He was trying to go slow. Trying to be gentle. Trying to give her time to get used to him, crooning to her, soothing her, but he could barely think past the exquisite, blinding pleasure of being inside her, feeling her tightness clinging to him. It felt *incredible.*

"Deep…deep breath, *ahhh…*" A moan escaped him and he bowed his head, his shoulders bunching with the effort not to thrust directly into her, all at once. "Breathe…with me…"

Wet eyes met his as she obeyed, breathing with him as he pushed steadily into her. She was so hot inside. Remin's shoulders jerked and shivers raced the length of his body. Even when he wasn't doing anything, even when he was perfectly still, he could feel her body quivering on him, waves of sensation rolling over and over him and there was a big one cresting, crushing, irresistible.

"Ahhh…" The noise burst from his chest, a deep groan as he went over the edge. "Ah…ah, ah, *stars…*"

Miche had warned him that this might happen. *It's your first time too,* he had said. *But don't you move a fucking inch if it does, even if it kills you. Hold still, let it happen, then continue.*

Remin thought he might be dying.

He understood now why it was imperative that he *not* do what his body wanted to do, which was pound into her as hard and fast as he could. His huge body rattled and his hips flexed, quivering with eagerness. But no. Even as his voice rose and he gasped and panted and spent himself inside her, even as he gripped and crushed the sheets in his hands, he *must*

71

not crush her. Stars. Stars. He was seeing stars. Static filled his brain, fizzing against the inside of his skull.

When he finally came back to himself, she was looking at him with big, sad eyes.

"It feels good?" she asked tearfully.

"Stars. Yes," he said, and kissed her. "You feel *so* good, wife. That's the hard part, I promise…"

Technically, they were finished. Marriage consummated; virginity taken. But though he could have rolled over and gone to sleep right there, Miche had said that on no account should she be crying when he was done.

Propping himself on his elbows, Remin kissed her again, careful not to withdraw from her. It would only be harder to get back inside her again, and with patience and persistence, her pained whimpers turned into soft cries as he stroked slowly into her, her body rocking beneath his. Her climax was not *quite* as loud as the first one, but her arms still went about his neck as she shuddered again, and he filled her a few moments later.

"Good?" he asked, winning a breathless nod, her head lolling on her neck. She didn't look *un*happy, and he drew back carefully, feeling a curious tenderness as he saw the droplets of red spattered between her thighs. They had been each other's first.

Now he understood why men made fools of themselves over women.

Lying beside her, he had all the time he wanted to look at her, her delicate profile limned with gold from the fire. A smooth, rounded forehead, little snub nose, and curving pink lips, like some exotic species of flower. Thick lashes curved over her cheeks, and his huge fist lay beside her upturned hand, the silver of her wedding band shining. She was small, and soft, and dangerous in ways he couldn't begin to articulate.

Remin sat up.

"Stay here," he murmured as her eyes blinked open. Padding over to the washstand, he rinsed their shared fluids from his body, enduring the cold without flinching. "It's cold," he told her as he set a shallow basin of water on the table beside the bed. "You must bear it."

It was another new intimacy between them, but he was very gentle as he washed her body. Ophele had to turn her face away as he washed her between her legs, wondering if this was really happening. Remin Grimjaw, the greatest hero in the Empire, was washing her. She had read extensively on the habits of ladies, hoping to educate herself, but no book she had ever read prescribed etiquette for this scenario. She had a lunatic urge to giggle and covered her mouth with her hand.

"Did I hurt you?" The duke paused in his washing.

"Oh, no," she said, guilty and embarrassed.

"Good." He set the basin aside and surveyed her through narrowed eyes, as if she were a puzzle he had not yet solved to his satisfaction. "I can do better," he said abruptly, and his long fingers trailed suggestively up her side. "Do you want to try?"

A shiver ran through her. Ophele was quite sure that whatever her virginity was, he had taken it very thoroughly, but there didn't seem any harm in letting him make sure.

"All right," she whispered, little dreaming of the night that would follow.

* * *

When Ophele slid out of bed the next morning, she kept going straight down to the floor.

"Ow," she rasped, squinting up at the unfamiliar ceiling and wondering where she was and why her legs wouldn't work. With the irregularity of life in Aldeburke, she hadn't kept a normal sleep schedule since she was a little girl, and she was never at her most intelligent first thing in the morning.

Gripping the side of the mattress, she pulled herself upright. The sight of rose petals scattered on the floor tickled her memory, and she sat down on the edge of a bed that felt strangely large and empty.

Ah. That was it.

Her husband had elected not to stay until morning.

Memories of the night before made her blush so hard she was nearly dizzy, and she looked down at her body, feeling so strange in her own skin, she hardly knew herself. The giggling of the Aldeburke maids made a great deal more sense now. She felt stained with the memory of his hands, his voice, his mouth, confused by the man she thought she had neatly categorized into *mean,* comma, *very large.* Burying her face in her hands, she flipped through a mental catalogue of books, searching for some applicable wisdom. The best she could come up with was the observation that life was suffering.

And she had been fortunate that Rem…the duke…had been kind.

The thought stuttered through her mental machinery, a set of new parts that had no place in the current design. She didn't know what it meant or what she felt about it and all of it made her feel tired and overwhelmed. A knock came at the door and she jumped, lunging for her blankets.

"Your Highness?" came the voice of Mistress Goel. "His Grace sent me to check on you. May I enter?"

Casting hastily about, Ophele found her crumpled chemise on the floor and grunted with pain as she reached for it and slid it over her head. The low neck did nothing to hide the red marks all over her chest. But *The Habits of a Lady* said a lady should be poised no matter how uncomfortable she was, to avoid making others feel uncomfortable, so she made herself answer and tried not to blush.

"Come in."

"Rosset will draw you a bath." The mistress didn't bat an eye, briskly going to open the curtains. The sun was already well up, streaming through the counterpanes in watery light. Turning to face Ophele, she clasped her hands and bobbed a curtsy, a tidy woman in a navy silk gown and a vast white cap on her head. "If you like, we will serve you breakfast afterward. Is there anything else you require, Your Highness?"

It was delicately put; the woman was tiptoeing around intimate knowledge that by rights belonged only to the princess's personal maids and closest family. And she was taking a risk with her offer, which could be regarded as impertinent.

"A bath will be good." Ophele took an incautious step toward the tub in the corner of the room and had to bite her lip to stifle a yelp. The pain between her legs was a dull, twisting ache when she held still, but that single step had felt like pulling open a wound.

"Perhaps some willow bark tea as well." Mistress Goel hurried over to offer an arm. "Please sit until the bath is filled, Your Highness. The hot water will help, and His Grace sent you a lovely new gown."

The bath was excruciatingly embarrassing. A lady might be poised in all circumstances, but Ophele was not yet made of stern enough stuff to endure the eyes of strangers with the red marks of the duke's mouth all over her body. It took her a moment to realize that the stripes on her thighs were marks from his hands: those could be nothing else but fingers, punctuated by a gripping thumb. It was as if she had been branded for a crime.

Sinking down into the steaming water, she tried to pretend that she was being washed by invisible spirits, and a friendly visitor from the aether was bringing her tea.

As might be expected from the finest inn in Celderline, they were sensitive to her mood and did their job quietly, washing her with the same care as before, lotioning, careful of all the sore places. The tea and the bath took the sharpest edge off the pain, and she hardly yelped at all as they wrapped her in towels and helped her to her dressing table. But when she rose to dress, Ophele was horrified to realize she was bleeding. She looked up at Mistress Goel, her face stricken.

"Could you send someone to find my valise, please?" she asked, crimson with shame. "Maybe one of the knights will know where it is. I'm so sorry, I didn't know, I will pay—"

"Sebire, go and see if you can find Sir Miche and inquire after Her Highness's things," Mistress Goel said promptly. "Please don't concern yourself, Your Highness, a spot or two never harmed anything."

"Is it normal?" Ophele made herself ask.

"Yes, dear, perfectly natural. I assume you have some bundles of cotton among your things?" She crouched beside Ophele, patting her knees in a motherly sort of way. "I remember when all my friends were getting married, some of them said it happened to them."

"My sister said she bled for two days afterward, Your Highness," offered Rosset, the lanky hairdresser.

"But you'll recover quickly," the mistress assured her. "I'm afraid marriage isn't always a bed of roses," she added, glancing humorously at the petals littering the floor on the other side of the room.

Ophele nodded, dumbly grateful. Everything to do with…everything was so embarrassing. She could hardly stand to look them in the eyes, but once she was wearing a fresh chemise and had another cup of willow tea, she could at least pretend some normalcy. She breakfasted lightly as they dressed her, and her new gown was both pretty and practical, fine violet wool over a black kirtle that would endure travel well and was deliciously soft and warm. Rosset was just plaiting her hair into a single thick braid down her back when there was a knock at the door.

"Princess." The duke ducked inside before she could reply, and Ophele rose immediately to her feet, flushing hot and then cold at the sight of him. He was back in plain wool and leather again, as if yesterday had never been, and spoke with his customary briskness. "Hurry up and pack your things. We're leaving now."

"Now?" she echoed.

"Yes, now. Mistress Goel, please let my man know how much all these things—" he gave a vague wave in the direction of the dressing table "—cost. We'll buy all of them. Hurry."

The memory of a man who had promised he wouldn't hurt her gave Ophele the courage to protest, her voice emerging timorously. "Your Grace, could we not—"

"What? Speak up," he said, glowering down at her. He looked impatient, as if she were keeping him from important business, and her fingers knotted together anxiously.

"Nothing," she whispered, looking at the floor. She couldn't possibly tell him something so embarrassing.

The door closed. She avoided the eyes of Mistress Goel and Rosset as she swept everything into her much-battered valise. She didn't know what had become of her wedding dress or diamond jewelry; the maids had taken them away after they undressed her the night before. All that remained were the cosmetics, brush, comb, and assorted sanitary items, creature comforts that were nothing compared to the parcel of willow tea Mistress Goel pressed into her hands.

"It was an honor to serve you, Your Highness," she said, her eyes flashing displeasure in the duke's direction. It had taken both her and Rosset's efforts to get Ophele down the stairs, and they bid farewell in the same place that they had met, with Ophele clutching her valise and feeling more than ever like a stray no one wanted. But she was glad she had held her tongue. All the knights were hurrying about the stable yard, swinging their saddles onto their horses and securing the supply wagon. The idea of asking the Knights of the Brede to wait until she felt better was unthinkable.

"Princess," the duke said, riding up to her on his big black horse and extending a hand. "Come, up you get."

He lifted her into her usual position, resting in the crook of his chest and arm, so large and solid it was like sitting in a chair. But the first bouncing step of the horse stabbed into her belly like a spear. Stifling a gasp, she clutched the arm wrapped around her waist, the steel of his vambrace cold under her fingers.

"All right, Princess?"

She nodded, pale. Her backside fit neatly between his thighs and rested on the saddle, and the jolting of the horse spanked painfully into all the places he had explored so thoroughly the night before. A few townspeople turned out to see off His Grace and the knights, waving and shouting so loudly, there was no chance for conversation until they passed through the city gates.

"We received word this morning that there are bandits near Tresingale," he explained as the horse settled into a brisk, ground-devouring walk that rolled like a small boat over an endless series of waves. "There are still a lot of deserters from both armies in the valley and we've just begun bringing in supplies and livestock, we can't afford to lose them."

That sounded important. She bit her lip and tried to find a less painful position, her head resting on his chest.

"Where is Tresingale?" she asked. It was the first time that he had spoken so many words to her at once.

"It's on a bend of the Brede near Drieze Watch, in Firkane," he answered willingly. "The nearest bridge is thirty miles upriver, but I've ridden the length of the Andelin and there's no better place. The grazing is good and there's a natural ridgeline for defense…"

It seemed she had found a subject the normally taciturn duke was willing to discuss at length. Ophele tried to focus on his voice. Adventurers in stories had to endure far worse than this on their quests; Beacon the Voyager had cut his own foot off to escape prison and make his way back to his ship before it sailed. Surely, the duke must have endured worse; wasn't that why they called him Remin Grimjaw? She had seen all the scars on his body with her own eyes.

And so, reminding herself of the misfortunes of every adventurer she had ever heard of, Ophele settled herself to endure.

* * *

It wasn't until they paused for the noon meal that Remin realized something was amiss.

The sound the princess made when he lifted her down from the saddle was similar to some of the less pleasant noises the night before, and he glanced back sharply. The princess was frozen in position behind him, biting her lower lip. Her face was very pale.

"All right?" he asked, his eyes narrowing.

"Yes."

But when she tried to follow him, the hitching steps were nothing at all like her usual quick, bouncing gait, and he frowned.

"What's wrong?" he demanded. "Don't lie. Are you injured?"

Her shoulders hunched and she glanced around quickly, as if frightened someone would overhear.

"It hurts," she confessed in a whisper, with tears of pain welling in her eyes and red to the tips of her ears. It took him a moment to realize what specifically might be hurting.

"Still?"

"Yes," she said wretchedly. "I have tea, Mistress Goel gave it to me—"

"I told you to tell me if it hurt," he said, lowering his voice. "All the way from the city? Why didn't you say something?"

"I thought—Mistress Goel said it was normal." She wilted under his black glare. "And you said there were bandits…"

It took an effort to keep from cursing aloud, but Remin swallowed the words and lifted her up, trying not to be angry with her. There was a small possibility that this was an intentional ploy to delay them on the road—she had become very friendly with Mistress Goel, and it was impossible to know what agents the Emperor might have in Celderline—but it was more likely that this was exactly what it appeared to be. The noise she made when he set her on a handy rock made him scowl ferociously.

"I'm sorry," she said, as a further heaping of coals on his head. "The tea helped before, I can keep going if—"

"Stop apologizing," he said shortly. "I'll go get it. Do you need to relieve yourself?"

Her face turned crimson. The blush spread all the way down her neck and chest, so dark it even disguised the livid marks of his mouth on her skin.

"Your Grace—"

"Yes or no?"

He was not easily embarrassed, but she was humiliated enough for both of them as he helped her into the bushes. He learned a great deal about women's clothing, anatomy, and the purpose of the bundles of cotton in her valise over the course of the next few minutes, as well as his deficiencies as a caretaker. He knew less about women than he knew about his horse.

He should have gotten her a maid.

Settling her by the fire to wait for water to boil for the tea, he sought out Miche to demand to know if all women endured this after their first night.

"I guess some of them must," the blond knight said, looking startled, as if the idea had never occurred to him. "I imagine being on horseback all day doesn't help. Sorry, Rem. My expertise is in deflowering, not the bit that comes after."

"Shut up." Miche's face had never looked more punchable. "Will she be all right?"

"I've never heard of a woman dying of it. Just what did you do last ni—"

"Shut up," Remin said again, and stalked off to find Tounot, who often served as medic when their camp surgeon wasn't available. If the princess had been one of his soldiers, Remin would have had no qualms about pushing on, unless it looked likely to kill her, and she didn't seem like she was going to die. But for some reason the sight of her sniffing back tears was intolerable.

"Willow bark tea is probably best," Tounot replied, when Remin pulled him aside to discuss the trouble. "Anything alchemical would be overkill. Or there's wine, if you just want to make her sleep. Does she have a head for it?"

"No." Remin brightened. Letting her sleep through the pain seemed ideal. Retrieving a skin of wine from the supply wagon, he went to dose her.

"Wine?" she said dubiously, when he presented the remedy.

"I know you don't like it, but just drink it." Guilt made him sharper than he meant to be. He probably could have foregone the fourth or fifth round with her last night, but at the time she had seemed to be enjoying it.

She nursed the wineskin with a sour face as they finished their meal of bread and cheese, and by the time he lifted her back onto his horse, she was already a little giddy, nestling into him like a kitten in a basket.

"S'warm," she said, slurring the tiniest bit. It had been less than an hour and she had consumed about one and a half cups of wine.

"Drink a little more," he told her, lifting the skin to her lips. He didn't want to make her wine-sick, but as the horse swayed into motion, a crease appeared between her eyebrows, and she shifted uncomfortably against him. "Does it still hurt?"

"Yes," she said. Her head was resting on his chest, her hair tickling his chin. "Sorry…"

"Don't apologize. You have to tell me right away next time," he said, more gently. "It's never my intention to hurt you."

"Really?" There was a plaintive note in her voice that made him look down at her, surprised and a little insulted.

"Yes, really. I took an oath to protect you, remember?"

"Those aren't real," she said with unexpected cynicism, and sipped from the skin again without being told. "The lord and lady took n'oath, too."

"Lord and Lady Hurrell?"

"Mmm." She sighed, rubbing her cheek against the fur trim of his cloak. Her eyelashes were very long and thick, curling over her flushed cheeks, and Remin shifted in the saddle, trying not to picture certain memorable interludes from the previous night.

"Why did they lie and say you were sick?" he asked, partly to satisfy his curiosity and partly to take his mind off the feel of her body against him.

"Lisabe," she said, as if it were obvious. "House Hurrell fell with House…Your Grace's house. They always said you owed. Because they were loyal."

"Why did you go along with it?" His mouth tightened. He had suspected something of the sort, but it was something else to hear it stated so baldly.

She was silent for so long, he thought she was going to refuse to answer. Or maybe she had already fallen asleep. Lifting her chin with his fingers, he found himself looking into troubled eyes, a warm and tawny shade like sunlight on the velvety hide of a doe.

"Tell me the truth. I won't be angry."

"Remin Grimjaw." Her eyes closed as his finger stroked the dainty length of her jaw. "You…you were so mad, 'member? And Lady Hurrell said she would tell…tell…she said, if you were my husband, and I made you mad, then you could do…*anything…*"

Her voice fell to a whisper and she burrowed against him as if she were trying to hide from that terrible *anything*. And he had lied. He *was* angry that anyone would insinuate he would abuse his wife, especially in front of that wife, for the despicable purpose of making her afraid of him.

"I have never harmed a woman in my life," he told her, stiff with offense. Assassins did not count. But this was the wrong thing to say, or at least the wrong tone in which to say it, because she lowered her eyes and nodded, clearly placating. "I haven't," he repeated with less heat. "I won't. I promise, Princess."

With his men nearby, he couldn't bring himself to reassure her more thoroughly. He had to satisfy himself with squeezing her briefly against him, her face pressed into his chest.

She hiccupped.

"That's nice," she whispered, her chin tilting up to look at him. Her eyes were hazy and her lips parted, pink and tender. "Remin Grimjaw said he promised. You smell nice."

He took the wineskin away.

"You," he said, trying to ignore a certain anatomical stiffening, "are drunk, Princess."

"Am not."

"I assure you, you are," he said, amused. She was bolder with a little wine in her veins.

"Not a *princess,*" she enunciated, sounding aggrieved. "But don' tell. S'a secret. Shh."

Remin frowned. He had all the paperwork to prove she most definitely was a princess.

"Your father is the Emperor," he said, looking down at her through narrowed eyes. He hadn't anticipated this when he gave her the wine, but he wasn't going to waste the opportunity. "Aren't you a good and filial daughter to him?"

"How? Never…never seen'n Emp'rer." Her eyes were closing.

"What about a messenger from the Emperor?" he asked, giving her a little nudge to keep her awake. "Right before I came to Aldeburke."

"Messjer?"

"Yes. Where did you meet him?"

"Never metta messjer," she said sleepily. "Not even'on my birthday…"

Her head sank against his chest, and she was asleep. Remin looked down at her thoughtfully. A sweet face could conceal sinister intentions. He had already learned that the hard way. It wasn't impossible that she was faking her intoxication, or at least pretending to be drunker than she actually was. He had known masters of deceit, spies and killers sent by the Emperor who must have been raised from birth to their calling. Child assassins.

Could she be one of them? Her lips moved, soft lips, innocent-looking lips, her head rocking gently from side to side with the sway of the horse, her delicate body as boneless as a doll's. Seventeen. He had never been so innocent; he had killed his first assassin when he was fourteen, and took command of an army three years later. Years of war and intrigue sometimes made him feel old and tired, as if he had already lived a lifetime. But if she was innocent…

"She out?" Miche drew his horse over, surveying the sleeping girl.

"Dead drunk," Remin replied, looking down at her ruefully.

"You still haven't introduced her to us formally," Miche noted. "We owe her our oaths too, Rem. She's our lady now."

"She is." Again, he wondered if it really might be true. "We'll do it properly tomorrow."

CHAPTER 4 – THE KNIGHTS OF THE BREDE

"Sir Tounot of Belleme." The knight lowered himself to one knee and laid his sword at Ophele's feet, a burly man with curling brown hair and a cleft in his chin. "I swore my service to His Grace eight years ago, when he was mustering in Norgrede."

They had heaped fuel on the fires tonight to illuminate these proceedings properly, a ceremony held under the night sky with the stars as witnesses.

"Belleme," she said thoughtfully. She knew who he was. She had memorized all the major and minor Houses of Argence over one endless winter when she was ten, along with all their banners and words, but even without that, everyone in the Empire knew the Knights of the Brede. "The Earl of Irenvale?"

"Speak louder," the duke murmured behind her, and she blushingly repeated herself.

"Yes. I am his son." Sir Tounot smiled and inclined his head. "And now my sword is yours."

Ophele smiled back shyly. She still felt a little strange from the wine, weirdly disconnected, and was trying very hard not to feel the gazes of forty other knights and a dozen squires on her; she couldn't find a place to rest her eyes or her hands. And it was embarrassing to be sitting on a tree stump as if it were a throne, with a cushion even, and His Grace looming behind her. All at once he was convinced that she was made of glass and wouldn't hear of her sitting on the ground.

He had explained the purpose of these formalities at length, as well as what she should and should not do. It wasn't just an exchange of oaths;

she needed to know the men who were sworn to her service, and so ideally, she should offer a few personal words to each of them.

It was a challenge for a timid girl, but the duke was being surprisingly kind. Every time she floundered, she could feel his hand press lightly at her back.

"I will accept your oath, Sir Tounot of Belleme," she said, just as she had said to Sir Auber Conbour, Sir Huber Adaman, Lord Edemir of Trecht, and Sir Darrigault of Ghis. It didn't feel real. These were famous men, heroes, the bravest and strongest knights in the entire Empire. What were they doing kneeling to her?

"Under the stars and before all here assembled, I, Sir Tounot of Belleme, swear my fealty and homage to the House of Andelin and its new lady, Her Grace Ophele, Princess of Argence, and now the Duchess of Andelin." Only a born nobleman could have so effortlessly ordered and recited her titles, and in the Empire, a woman's principal title devolved from her husband's. "I will defend the safety and honor of my lady even at the cost of my own life, and further offer the fealty of all my heirs, so long as House Andelin endures. Should I violate this oath, or fail in this trust, let my life be forfeit."

Ophele knew the proper steps of this ceremony. She had read it dozens of times in various books, sometimes in excruciating detail. At this point, she should take his hands—as if he needed her help to get up—and offer him the sword he had laid at her feet. But the duke had firmly vetoed the idea of her standing to accept the oaths of forty-some men, handling swords, or even allowing her to rise just for the amount of time it would take for the formal clasping of hands.

Ever since she had failed to tell him she was hurt the morning they left Celderline, he had been so determined to make sure it wouldn't happen again. Like a bear, she thought as she looked up at his forbidding face, big and black and *grumbling* in a way that was almost...sweet. It made her feel both guilty and grateful.

"Speak up," the duke reminded her now, and she sat up straight, trying to forget all the men watching from the other side of the fires. At least she didn't have to think of what to say. She had read these words countless times.

"In return, I swear to guard my honor with sincerity, so that I never bring shame to my House, my Lord, or his retainers," she replied. "And to be careful of my own safety, to honor the sacrifices of my defenders. Please rise, Sir Tounot of Belleme. I accept your sword."

It was sobering to look into a man's face and listen to him tell her that he was willing to die to protect her. What had she ever done to deserve that? And more to the point, considering what her mother had done to the man looming at her back, Ophele knew exactly how unworthy she really was.

But there was nothing for it. She was the duke's wife now, joined inseparably to him unto death and beyond, and her honor was now the honor of his House. The only thing she could do was treat her own life and honor carefully, so as not to betray these men further. And hope that they never ever found out what Lady Rache Pavot had done.

"Sir Justenin," said the next knight, a lean man with sandy hair and a scar bisecting his left eyebrow. "I joined His Grace's army as soon as the Emperor gave him command of the forces of the Andelin."

He gave no place name or family name. Was it because his parents died along with the rest of the duke's extinct House? She supposed that the children of some of their servants and retainers had escaped, and then gone on to serve Remin, the last son of their vanished House, because of the same oath Sir Tounot had just sworn. *The loyalty of my heirs.* These men were promising not just their own service, but the loyalty and service of their progeny.

She would have to think about that later. The duke's big hand pressed lightly against her back and she straightened again, searching for something to say.

"I…I never thought about the service all of you have already given His Grace," she began hesitantly, looking from Sir Justenin to the rest of the assembled knights. "I will do my best to learn from your example. Thank you for serving him so well, all these years."

She thought that was a good thing to say. Sir Justenin bowed his head and repeated the same oath Sir Tounot had given, and so the night wore on. Conscious of the solemnity of the oaths they were taking—and the long wait as the men shuffled forward to take their turn kneeling before her—Ophele tried hard to pay attention, and say her own words each time with the same sincerity she had said them the first time.

"You did well," the duke said when it was over, escorting her to one of the fires, which had burned low over the course of the ceremony. "Do you want more tea?"

She nodded, too tired to pretend she didn't. The second day of riding hadn't been as painful as the first, but the duke had still dosed her with more wine in the morning and she felt dull and achy from her head to her toes. She only dimly remembered getting on the horse after the noon meal yesterday, and things had been blurry until she woke up for supper today.

"Here," he said, handing her more bread and cheese. At night they usually had a hot meal as well, a sort of stew made with dried beef and root vegetables that were hard as stones after passing the winter in the bottom of a sack, but it would be some time before that was ready. A tin kettle was already on the fire, steaming its way to a boil.

"Thank you." To her surprise, he sat down beside her and stretched out his long legs, ripping into a chunk of crusty brown bread with his fingers. Uneasily, she watched him through her eyelashes. Before, he had given her food like he was putting down hay for his horse and then left to talk to his men, but lately he had been staying to talk with her.

"We'll be stopping in Granholme tomorrow," he said. "It's a small town, nothing like Celderline, but there's a market and a few shops. If there's anything you need, we can buy it."

"I'm f—" she began automatically.

"We will be buying more dresses for you," he interrupted, looking down at her with narrowed eyes. "And whatever other things women need. You're my wife, you'll have clothes that fit. The Knights of the Brede want a lady they can be proud of."

Oh. She looked down at her lap. She knew she wasn't a princess anyone would admire, but she hadn't thought that implicit in all the oaths she had taken tonight was the promise that she would try to be, that she owed it to the people in her service to try to make them proud of her.

"All right," she agreed quietly.

He sighed.

"You mumble," he told her. "Speak up. And you mistake my meaning. I don't know anything about the things women need. But I want my wife to be as comfortable and well-dressed as any other noblewoman."

"The maids at Aldeburke had four new dresses twice a year," she offered hesitantly, watching him from the corner of her eye.

"I would hope I could do at least that much." His eyebrows lowered ominously. "How many dresses does the Lady Lisabe have?"

"Oh, I don't need that many," she said, her eyes wide at the very idea. "Gowns are so expens—"

"How many?"

"I don't know," she admitted. "A lady dresses for afternoon and for supper, and then there are kirtles and chemises and stockings and br— other things." The Duke of Andelin could not be the least bit interested in women's fashions. "I don't need that much."

"Well, it will be a long time before we go back to the capital, and there aren't likely to be any balls in Andelin for a while either," he said, chewing thoughtfully. "I don't see a point in buying finery you won't have reason to wear. But I won't have my wife dressing like a maid. If you need something, tell me."

She nodded solemnly, and he looked at her hard.

"Promise?" And he actually extended his big hand to seal the bargain, as if they had agreed on some trade. He would buy her clothes, and in exchange she would tell him truthfully if she needed something? And she wouldn't look like a beggar's brat?

She gave him her hand, her small fingers vanishing into his vast palm. "I promise."

* * *

Though Remin increasingly doubted that his new bride was going to murder him in his sleep, he found there were plenty of other reasons to worry about her.

He should have gotten her a maid.

Remin was reflecting on his actions and repenting.

He'd had no idea how much tending women needed. The princess needed help dressing, she needed help undressing, she had long hair that took hours of maintenance, and he could hardly hand her over to one of his knights. At night, they hauled the supply cart off the road and screened it off with cloaks so she wouldn't have to sleep in her extremely limited selection of dresses.

"You don't have to do all this," she said as he lifted her onto the supply cart one night, doing his best not to notice the gentle curves under her chemise or the fluttering silk of her hair.

"Yes, I do," he said gruffly. It was his fault she didn't have anything to wear. "Go to sleep."

That was another worry. Remin was convinced she didn't sleep like a normal person. He didn't know if it was a thing all women did, or a unique vulnerability of her own, but there seemed to be a significant risk that she would kill herself before they ever reached Tresingale. The first two mornings after they left Celderline, he put it down to the wine. But the third morning he knew for sure that she was stone cold sober when she woke in the chilly gray dawn and tumbled off the front of the supply wagon, only to rise like one of the shambling undead of the Undebige Valley.

"Princess?" He started up from his place by the wagon wheel and caught her wrist.

"Muh." She pawed her hair out of her face. Her eyes were open, but unfocused, and she squinted up at him with none of her usual timidity and said, "privy."

"Over there," he said, gesturing to a clump of bushes. She wasn't usually so plainspoken; normally she tried to sneak away like a thief. "Your shoe," he added sharply as she stumbled off, seemingly unaware that one foot was bare. "Princess, are you well?"

"Mmm." It took several tries for her to slide her foot into the fur-lined slipper, during which time she seemed to forget where the bushes were. His long arm shot out to point her in the opposite direction.

"That way."

When she returned, she sleepily washed her hands in the basin he offered, then crumpled over in front of the fire, asleep in seconds. Maybe she had never really been awake. Remin fetched his cloak from the wagon and covered her with it, eying her uneasily.

The third concern was the reason he was sleeping against the supply wagon, rather than stretched out in a bedroll with her.

Having experienced sex with her, his body reacted to her presence with infuriating eagerness. He would have been within his rights to have her whenever and wherever he chose, but she was still recovering from the rigors of their first night together and he was not about to engage in such activities with fifty men listening nearby. It would be disrespectful to his wife. Who would probably die of shock.

And who also deserved a bed, not a filthy blanket on the ground, or being pushed roughly against a tree, or rolled under a hedgerow. Not that he had been contemplating such things.

His mind knew this. His body remained stubbornly unconvinced.

And so, though ordinarily he would never have considered paying money for an inn when there were perfectly good hillsides outside town, it only made sense to get an inn for the night, if they happened to arrive in Granholme before sunset. It would be irrational to force his gently bred wife to sleep in a supply wagon when there were beds available and she was clearly longing for a bath. And if she stayed at the inn, then as her husband it was only right—no, it was his *duty*—to go with her and sleep with her. At the inn.

Maybe this was compensation for all those years of deprivation. Remin had spent most of his adolescence suppressing his sexual urges with constant physical training, knowing that any woman he bedded might very well try to stab him to death in the middle of the act. Now, with the prospect of an inn, a bed, and his wife in the bed on the horizon, he was finding it very difficult to think of anything else.

"Your Grace," she protested, looking up at him with blushing cheeks the second time his lips inadvertently grazed her neck.

"The breeze is cold," he observed, adjusting his cloak to cover them both. She eyed him as if she suspected he had some other mischief in mind, and he pretended he had nothing at all to do with the hand sliding around her waist to stealthily caress her under the cloak.

"There are people," she whispered, but all he could see was the slow curving of her pink lips when she spoke, and his hand slid upward all by itself over her belly to cup her breast. *"Your Grace."*

"Watch the road." His breath felt unsteady. She smelled so good, it was making it hard to think. Remin bent his head, breathing her intoxicating scent and sorely tempted to tell his men to leave them for a half hour or so. He was fully aware that this was not the time or the place, but he could see the pulse beating frantically in her throat and all he wanted to do was bite it.

Her ears were red. Anyone who saw her could guess what he was doing; indeed, his knights were suddenly being very careful not to look in his direction. But she wasn't one of the hellcats that had marched along with his army, and he was not an animal. He could endure for a few more hours. He had always been contemptuous of men who couldn't control their baser impulses. He lectured himself severely and sighed.

"Tonight," he murmured, pressing his lips chastely against her forehead and trying to ignore the glint of her tawny eyes through her thick lashes. If he looked at her once more, he really might pull his horse off to the side of the road.

They arrived in Granholme that afternoon, and he dispatched his men to see to supplies, messages, and accommodations. He intended to look after the princess's new wardrobe himself. Left to her own devices, he suspected she would only dare to purchase four new dresses twice a year. Was that normal? It didn't *seem* right.

"Bertin, Ortaire, with me," he said, ordering two of the older squires along as escorts and looking down at the princess severely. "Stay in my sight, understood?"

She nodded, her slim shoulders hunching, and hung back behind him all the way to the market. Remin frowned down at her. Sometimes it was almost like she was nervous around him, and he didn't know why. He was keeping her close for her own safety as much as his own. Granholme was in the duchy of Firkane, whose lord was not just loyal to but *devoted* to the Emperor. If she wasn't actively in league with her father, that made her a potential hostage.

It was unexpectedly awkward, walking with her. Her strides were so much shorter than his own and he didn't know what to say. And it didn't help that she kept stopping to gawk. After months in the capital, the marketplace of Granholme looked small and shabby to him, but the princess was drinking it in with wide, solemn eyes, like a watchful little owl.

"Is there something you want to see?" he asked the fourth time he had to stop for her. She started and said something inaudible, hurrying over to his side. "And don't mumble," he added, scowling at her in perplexity. She was making him feel like an ogre. "We have time. If you want to look at something, tell me."

"It's just, I've never been to a town before," she admitted, looking at an inebriated lutist picking indifferently at his instrument as if he were a traveling fair.

He kept forgetting that. She wasn't just unaccustomed to crowds; she had never seen a town in her life before Celderline. She had grown up a prisoner in Aldeburke, in the questionable care of House Hurrell.

"All right," he said, laying her hand on his arm as he had seen couples in the capital do. "You choose where we go. Look at whatever you want."

"Really?" Her look of delight made the back of his neck feel hot.

"Yes," he said stiffly, his face freezing into hard lines. "Go on."

She was fascinated by everything, from the barking negotiations of the ironmonger to a cooper forming staves into a barrel. At a pastry stand he bought her a hot berry tart and repressed a smile when she bit into it too soon and yelped.

"All right?" he asked.

"Yeth," she said, fanning her burned tongue and looking up at him with comical chagrin.

At the glassblower's stand he watched her watch a sturdy bald-headed man delicately whisper molten glass into a chrysanthemum, so utterly absorbed that Remin had a momentary impulse to ask the fellow if he wanted to move his trade to Tresingale. Surely they'd need glass eventually, and the lady seemed like she could watch him forever and never get tired of it.

"Is it very difficult?" she asked, once the glassblower lifted his head from the pipe.

"Takes practice," he said. He looked from her to Remin and his men, taking their measure at a glance. "Want me to make you something, lady?"

She glanced back at Remin, and it would have taken a heart of stone to refuse. He nodded.

"Could you make a bear?" she asked. It was not one of the animals laid on the counter. Remin would have guessed she'd pick a flower or a bird or some such. But the glassblower nodded.

"Aye, can do," he said. "Even smoke the glass for you."

"To make it black?" She leaned over to watch as he made it, a tiny figure with tawny eyes bright with interest, filled with questions and talking more than Remin had ever heard her speak at one time. Even the gruff craftsman softened under her sincere interest, and by the time he finished the bear, he actually smiled at her.

Unexpectedly, she instantly turned around and presented it to Remin.

"It's for you," she said, her eyes fleeting away from his, and hurried back to the glassblower's display. Remin looked down at the useless object, flummoxed. It was small, hardly bigger than his thumb, and looked as if there was smoke contained *inside* it, crystal on the outside and swirling black within. The bear sat on its haunches with one paw extended, detailed down to the claws. Why had she given it to him? Was it some kind of message?

It was time they left, anyway.

"The seamstresses will need time to sew," he said, steering her to the side street where they had been told there was a tailor. It was a small place, but tidy. The lady inside looked as if she were about to swoon when Remin ducked in the door.

"Yes, this is my shop, my lord," she said faintly, her eyes as wide and staring as a fish's. A wise merchant knew how to recognize a nobleman at a glance. "How...you need...clothing?"

"The Duke of Andelin," put in Bertin, who was touchy of His Grace's honor. "And his lady."

"Oh. Oh, my. Please excuse me." She curtsied. "I am honored, it is ...I am Violet Courcy, and I will do my humble best to serve."

"My wife needs clothes," Remin said, pushing the princess forward. "By tomorrow."

"Everyday dresses, and kirtles, and...so on." Ophele glanced back at Remin's knights, her ears turning pink. "Um...do you need to measure me?"

"Bertin, Ortaire, wait outside." Remin wasn't about to leave her alone with a stranger, and it was nothing that he hadn't already seen, anyway. But his eyes still sharpened as Ophele reluctantly stripped down to her chemise with Mistress Courcy's help, baring that fine, velvety white skin, the soft shape of her breasts visible under the linen. For a moment, he considered ordering Mistress Courcy out of the shop, too.

"We have a pomegranate-patterned silk that will look lovely on you, m'lady," the seamstress said, scribbling down her measurements on a bit of paper.

"I don't need silk," Ophele said, gentle but decided. "Dark colors that are easy to clean, simple and comfortable so I can work. And I need to be able to put them on by myself."

From the look on the seamstress's face, this was the realm of maid's clothing.

"Two formal gowns, Princess," Remin said, as if he had the least idea what those were. He wasn't trying to humiliate her by making her dress like a servant. "Silk."

"Princess?" Mistress Courcy echoed, glancing between them, and he saw the shock of recognition in her face. "Princess Ophele? And you need—I beg your pardon! How could I make such a mistake, the Duke of Andelin, of course…"

But the look she had given the princess was fleeting, expressive, and unmistakable: pity. By now everyone in the Empire had heard of the Emperor's secret daughter, Princess Ophele, confined to Aldeburke since infancy, married to Remin Grimjaw in her sister's place, robbed of the rank she had never been able to exercise, and now here she was getting dragged off into another exile and told to buy simple clothes she could work in. That was what had happened, for very good reasons, but it put his back up. The opinion of the people wasn't irrelevant. This gossip would spread. The Emperor would have loved this scene so much, he could have written it himself.

"I am trusting her to you, Mistress Courcy," Remin made himself say stiffly. "We are just married and I know little about the things women need. Please take care of her."

He could almost see the woman flutter, if only in the mercantile part of her heart. That meant an open purse. Let *that* story spread.

And it wouldn't be bad, to see the princess in a pretty gown over supper. Remin sat back in the chair Mistress Courcy had offered, stretching his long legs. He remembered his mother and father's table, the grand banquet hall, the music, the murmur of conversation. That place was gone forever, and the Andelin Valley had been a battleground for a hundred years. But he wanted to make it a place fit for women and children, as safe and prosperous as the rest of the Empire, with a graceful banquet hall and the noblest of ladies at his side.

No. If he was honest, he wanted to make the Andelin the flower of the Empire. He wanted to make a garden that would make the Emperor sick with envy, not only prosperous, but a center of culture and learning.

And no one would ever look at his wife with pity again.

"You can have the rest sent along to the valley?" he asked, when they had agreed on a quantity of overdresses, gowns, kirtles, and other accoutrements that made Ophele look convincingly horrified and the seamstress very happy.

"Yes, Your Grace," she said, hastily totaling the figures with practiced flicks at an abacus. "I can call on half of Granholme if need be, everyone will be so excited to help with the princess's trousseau! We will see it done, never fear."

"Isn't it a lot of money, though?" The princess asked, clutching the first page of the bill of sale anxiously. "Your Grace, are you quite sure? You don't have to—"

"Yes. Give me that." He plucked the paper from her hand and added it to the sheaf in his own. Duke Ereguil had always said that there were many uses for money, with the acquisition of goods being only the most obvious. But between a bill of sale he could barely read—what the hell was a tippet?—and the glass bear in his pocket, Remin wasn't entirely sure what he had bought today.

He could only hope that such things as tippets and bears could lead to the building of a garden.

* * *

Unexpectedly, the princess had one more bit of business before they went back to the inn, the place Remin was longing to be with all of his soul.

The marketplace was closing for the evening as they made their way up the side of the cobblestone street, and the princess looked on with interest as the shops shuttered and the merchants cleared away their stalls, entirely innocent of the plans he had in store for her. But coming around the corner onto the town's main road, she stopped so suddenly, he nearly tripped over her.

"Rou?" she said in surprise, and then darted away with a cry, picking up her skirts to run. "Rou! Rou, wait!"

There was a small tinker's wagon ahead, but it rolled to a stop and a small, bearded man appeared from around the front, weathered as a nut and wearing steel-rimmed spectacles and a disreputable hat.

"Princess?" he said, disbelieving, and caught her hands in his own. "Princess! What are you doing here? Did you decide to run away with me after all? Or did Julot—ah." Hastily, he let go of her hands and stepped back as Remin appeared, looming and thunderous as a storm.

"She got married," Remin said, glaring down at the little man. "Princess, don't run off. Who's this?"

"Oh, I'm sorry, this is Rou," she said, flustered. "He visits Aldeburke sometimes, you know we can't go into town."

"I meant no disrespect, Your Grace," said the tinker with a deep bow. He had already guessed who Remin must be. "Rou Kurder, at your service. I have known Her Highness since she was a child."

"I am pleased to meet any friend of my wife's," Remin replied, surveying the cart. It looked like any other tinker's wagon he had seen, compact and rugged, with wooden awnings that could be lifted to display his eclectic wares or locked down to secure them. "Have you been long in Firkane?"

"Thirty years," said the tinker. "I added Aldeburke to my route by accident, you know. It's not so far into Leinbruke."

"It was kind of you, to serve Lady Pavot in her exile."

Rou scratched his chin. He understood what Remin was asking. "Well, I don't know about that, Your Grace. No one ever named the lady to my ears, and didn't seem like something that wanted inquiry, did it? Especially not from a tinker on the back roads of the Empire."

The princess watched this byplay curiously.

"It was very good of Rou to come and see us," she agreed. "Can I see Anzel, Rou? Is he dyspeptic?"

"No, he's always peptic when you're about. With His Grace's permission," Rou added, gesturing toward the front of the wagon, where a small donkey pricked its ears at her and immediately began nosing her pockets.

"I wish I had a carrot for you, clever boy," she said, stroking his gray muzzle.

"There are carrots in the front of the wagon, Your Highness, feel free to give him one." The tinker spoke without moving to follow her. He knew perfectly well that the duke wasn't finished with him. With a flick of his fingers, Remin ordered Bertin and Ortaire around to the front of the wagon, to keep an eye on things.

"Will you be staying in town tonight?" he asked. "I'd welcome the chance to talk to someone who knows my wife so well. I'm sure we could find space at the inn for you."

"I'm afraid not," Rou replied, and unwittingly passed the first test. Remin would have thought less of anyone who would accept a bribe so easily. "The moon will be full tonight and the roads are good, I mean to put some miles behind us."

"That's a shame." Remin made a decision. "We have need of tinkers in the Andelin."

"I had heard that Your Grace was taking things in hand," the tinker said, nodding slowly. "It might be an opportunity for an enterprising man."

Ophele appeared around the side of the wagon, pausing to make certain she wasn't interrupting. "Pardon…do you have new books, Rou?"

"I do indeed. Take any of them that you like as my wedding gift, Your Highness." The man's smile looked genuine. He even tapped the brim of his hat in a small salute, and then glanced up at Remin. "With your permission, of course."

"It's a generous gift. Are you sure I can't compensate you?"

"It is a gift." There was a gentle emphasis on the last word. And Remin would look through the books himself, later. He knew he was paranoid and accepted it. Any number of unlikely-looking people had tried to kill him.

But as the tinker doffed his battered hat to say farewell, Remin found himself hoping that the man would make his way to the Andelin. Trade between the small villages was almost nonexistent and he would prefer to keep his eye on a man who was such a good friend to the princess.

"Did you take all his books?" he asked as Ophele appeared, bearing a tottering stack of books that ended at her nose. "Bertin, Ortaire, carry those."

"No," she said unconvincingly as the squires relieved her of her cargo. "But Rou said I could have the ones I liked, and I haven't read these yet…"

She had to be bullied into accepting a second formal gown, but was willing to rob a tinker if it was books. The corner of Remin's mouth twitched.

"I would be surprised if anyone has ever read *A Second Treatise on the Will Immanent and the Will Absolute,*" he observed dryly, reading off one of the better titles. "We'll need another wagon to carry all these."

"Will we? I didn't think of that," she said, crestfallen.

"I am teasing you," he informed her, drawing her beside him to walk together up the hill. The sky was brilliant with sunset and it had been surprisingly pleasant to watch her wander the market. Lights glimmered in the windows of the houses as they went by, added a pleasant golden glow to the evening, but then the sight of a lamp in a window had always made him think, *home.* "There's plenty of room in the wagon."

She nodded, her hand resting lightly on his arm. He could see her watching him from the corner of her eye and waited until she finally said, "Rou is my friend."

"So I gathered."

"I only mean, I hope you don't mind what he said," she said, looking up at him anxiously. "He always likes to tease, he doesn't mean any harm."

"I am glad you have such a friend." He hadn't decided whether he would ask more about the content of the teasing, or whether he would ask it of *her,* but it would be cruel to make her worry in the meantime. Covering her hand with his own, he squeezed. "Are you feeling well? You walked a lot this afternoon."

"Yes." Ophele turned a little pink and glanced back to make sure Bertin or Ortaire were a discreet distance away before she whispered, as if it were a deadly secret: "Riding hardly hurt at all today."

"Good. You'll ride a little bit more tonight."

"I will?"

Stars, she was going to kill him. Remin stretched his legs, hurrying her toward the inn.

He was a civilized man. He let her eat dinner. It wasn't the finest inn in Celderline, but they still managed to find two maids to serve the Exile Princess, and he steadfastly ignored the subtle and not-so-subtle jibes of his men as he tried to estimate how long it would take them to bathe her. It took about half an hour to wash his horse, but she had all that long hair to tend, and the maids in Celderline had rubbed all manner of sweet things into her skin…

The image of his pretty wife lingering in her bath did not make it easier to be patient. Remin glared into his cup of wine for nearly an hour before he said goodnight and went up, pausing to give himself a scrub in the common baths. For some reason, he was more unsettled tonight than he had been on his wedding night.

But something in his chest seemed to loosen when he opened the door to find her sitting alone by the fire, cross-legged on the floor with a book in her lap.

"No," he said quickly. "Don't get up."

She watched him with those solemn eyes as he approached, her cheeks still rosy from her bath. It was clear that she expected him to pounce on her, and perversely this made him want to draw things out. She was the Emperor's daughter, yes, but she was surprisingly sweet-tempered and he was finding her company far more pleasant than he had expected.

Silently, he sat down behind her, lifting the end of the thick plait that streamed down her back. The maids had put her hair back for the night, but he wanted to feel it in his fingers and see it fall in a curtain around her.

"May I?" he asked, plucking at the ribbon, and saw her tentative nod.

Untying the ribbon at the end, he pulled it loose, and the plait came apart like skeins of silk, so long and luxuriant that it coiled around her on the floor, shining in umber and maple.

"What are you reading?" he asked, maneuvering her slender body into the shelter of his own.

"The Will Immanent." She clutched the book as if she thought he might take it from her. Her dark lashes lowered, hiding her tawny eyes, and he couldn't resist tugging her hair aside to bare her beautiful shoulders, brushing his lips over her skin. Just a little taste.

"What's it about?"

"Theology," she said. "About how the divine manifests in the world and how the will of men conflicts with the will of the divine."

"Oh?" Her chemise was loose around her shoulders, a wide opening that bared the back of her neck and several inches of her spine, the contours of fragile bones and smooth, light muscle under skin like sugar.

"It's interesting," she was saying. "Like this: *If we assume the divine infinite as a perfect presence, then what purpose has the divine for creation? If the divine is a perfect presence manifest in all things, what is the purpose of imperfect beings? The divine is the divine, its supremacy is innate. Therefore, the contest of wills is the will of the divine.*"

It had been a very long time since Remin had a tutor.

"What does that mean?" he asked, more interested in what she would say than what the book said.

"Well, I haven't read the arguments yet," she began, "but I think it's saying that if there is a divine presence like the stars, then the fact that they created the world and put people in it that contradict their will is proof that they want the conflict to happen. If you were a god and you created me, and you didn't crush me like a bug when I argued with you, it must be because you want me to argue with you."

"And they tried to convince me you were simple," he said, after a moment.

"Well, that's just what I think," she said, embarrassed, and looked up into his eyes as he took the book from her and set it aside.

"I want you to stop thinking," he murmured, and covered her mouth with his.

* * *

In the Daitian cosmogony, there was a demon of desire that seduced women with such sweet words, his love-talk lingered in their ears forever afterward, until they starved their hearts out with longing.

His Grace wasn't much for talking, but he certainly *looked* like he could be a demon of desire.

Stretched out on the rug by the fire with his jerkin undone and his boots kicked partway under the bed, Ophele couldn't understand what someone like him could possibly want with someone like her. He was so big, so male, so serious and forbidding. *Husband.* In what mad world was Remin Grimjaw nibbling on her fingertips? And why did she *like* it?

"Come here," he said, pulling her to him to torment her some more. She sprawled over his chest as he kissed her, his hand framing her face so the rough pads of his fingers brushed her cheek, curling back into her hair as if he were learning the shape of her bones.

Ophele still felt shy when he kissed her, uncertain what she should do, how she should respond. It wasn't at all what she had imagined it would be, neither the chaste kisses from the romances she read or the fearful and repellant act she had imagined in a loveless marriage. He teased her with the slow motions of his mouth, drawing her in like a whirlpool, slow and dizzy and sucking her under before she knew where she was. He bit her lips. One hand moved stealthily over her body to cup her breast and when she gasped, he stroked his tongue into her mouth, a diversionary tactic to precipitate an invasion.

This was not chaste. It didn't feel loveless.

But he didn't love her.

"I wonder if you'll ever tell me what's going on behind those eyes," he said against her lips, making her blink in incomprehension, and then he crushed her mouth under his own, his big hand gripping the back of her neck to eliminate all hope of escape. He kissed her as if he were drinking her down, the muscles of his neck and jaw working as his tongue plundered her. There were sounds to the kiss, liquid and hungry as the sea, the sound of his heavy breathing like the roaring of waves.

He sat up. Somehow she was in his lap with her arms around his thick neck, feeling his hands sliding over her body from her shoulders to her thighs, eager caresses that made her feel as if she was melting. When he lifted his head, he looked so handsome he almost didn't seem real, and she thoughtlessly lifted a hand to touch his broad cheek, her thumb brushing the swooping scar over his cheekbone before she realized what she was doing.

She jerked her hand back.

"You can...you can touch me," he said, low. "Ophele..."

He closed his eyes at her tentative caress. The corners of his eyes tilted upward; she hadn't noticed that before, an almost exotic curve at their outer edge. After everything they had been through over the past few days, it wasn't quite so embarrassing to touch him, to feel the stubble on his jaw and the line of his straight nose, the bristle of his thick black brows. Like a huge dog, he pushed his face into her palm and made her giggle.

"I won't hurt you," he promised, stern-faced but with a twinkle in his eyes. She touched him with her fingertips, brushed the grim line of his jaw with her thumb, and even wondered what it would feel like to stroke his rough cheek with her smooth one.

That was a little too bold. Her face flushed.

"Do it," he whispered, angling his head to catch her thumb between his lips, his black eyes glinting like a proper demon of lust. "Whatever you were thinking."

She wasn't thinking anything. The feel of his teeth nipping her thumb had driven all capacity for thought from her head. She stared at him with wide eyes, feeling as if her heart and breath had frozen together as his mouth moved down, biting her wrist, licking at her pulse point like a flame. His breath burned the sensitive skin of her inner arm, scorched her shoulders, and her breath exploded out in a gasp as he tugged down the neck of her chemise and buried his face in her breasts.

"I have wanted to taste these for *days*," he said, muffled, as his hungry mouth found her nipple. Why did it feel so good when he did that? Every tug of his lips seemed to lift her up all the way from her toes, short jerks that made her head fall back and something clench tight in her belly. Her hands sank into his hair, thick and unruly, curling at the back of his neck.

"Your Grace…" She moaned breathlessly as he sucked both breasts, one and then the other, ravenous. His tongue circled each nipple, licking them into hardened peaks, and between her legs she felt his finger pierce her.

"You're already wet," he murmured, lifting his head to look at her. "You want me so much?"

"Well, it feels good," she admitted honestly, feeling her cheeks heat, and gasped as a second finger entered her, a taut stretch inside that made her voice quaver. "Hoooow do you…haaa…know what…know what feels good?"

"I asked Miche," he answered, with a glint of humor. "I didn't know myself. I never had a woman before you."

"Never?" That shocked her. Especially since he said it while his long fingers were sliding in and out, circling inside, seeking out places that made her mind haze white. She wanted to think about it, what it meant, whether it made her happy, but then his fingertips bore down on that tickling, troublesome spot inside her and a wail burst from her lips.

"Never," he said hoarsely, and bit her neck, licking up her throat with his tongue. "So you have to be careful, you can't claim a man's body and not be responsible for it."

The thought tickled her.

"Are you saying I should…o-ohhh…I should be gentle, Your Grace?" she asked breathlessly, daring a small joke, and then clutched his shoulder as his fingers slid deep. What was he doing that felt so good? His fingers stroked, circled, rubbed again at that place inside her and it was making her dissolve as if he were rubbing away at the edge of her sanity.

"Remin," he panted, low and excited. "Call my name."

She could feel that hardened part of him straining underneath her, pushing hot and urgent at her backside. And though she vividly remembered the pain, she was crimson with the thought that *that* felt even better than his fingers, she wanted him to do it to her again. Did that make her a lewd woman? Shouldn't she pretend like she didn't like it so much?

She bit her lips, her body straining toward release, fighting back her cries so hard that tears streaked from the corners of her eyes. Her breath came in gasps and she couldn't even hear what he was saying, she knew nothing but feeling, his fingers inside her and his hard arms around her, as if he were the only thing keeping her tethered to the world.

"Remin," she managed, trembling as if she were going to shake herself apart. "Hnnnnn, *ahhhhnn, ah, Remin!*"

She didn't even know the word for what was happening to her, vulgar or technical. It just *happened,* her breath seizing in her lungs and then exploding outward, and she felt his hot lips on her belly, his hand on her breast, his fingers stroking, stroking, heating her to boiling. She felt like she was bubbling, she was water, so wet she was dissolving as she climaxed in high, gasping cries.

"Wife, wife, Ophele…" Remin was rapidly disrobing, yanking at his jerkin and dragging his shirt over his head. She had the impression of his naked body, a glimpse of a hard and reddened member, but everything was hazy as a dream until he plunged it inside her.

* * *

Both of them cried out together. Remin was shaking with the effort of restraining himself. He didn't want to hurt her again. He didn't know how hard it was safe to go, though he knew how hard he *wanted* to go, it felt so good inside her that all he wanted to do was grab her and pound himself blind, to etch his body into hers like a hammer and chisel.

"Tell me if it hurts," he rasped as he began to move. He had always enjoyed the feeling of his own body working, the coiling flex of muscle and sinew, but he had never been so intensely aware of it as when he was with her. The twin cords of heavy muscle in his lower back, the long muscles of his thighs, even the negligible burden of her body on the muscles of his arms, so much strength leashed and quivering as he pressed into her with torturous care. Her body stretched around him, inner walls pulsating.

Ophele clutched his wrists, gasping. Was it good that he had made her climax first before he put it in her? Maybe it was too much. He could see tears trembling on her eyelashes, but her thighs were squeezing his waist, lifting her hips to meet him as if she wanted it.

"Do you like it?" he panted, dragging himself back out of her and feeling her body cling to him, a heated wet grip that made him feel hard as iron. It must feel good, it couldn't possibly feel this good only to him.

"Y-yes…" she breathed, her eyes screwed tight shut as he stroked back into her, a reedy whisper. "Yes…yes, ohhhhh, feels good…"

He wasn't going to last long if she was going to make noises like that. Not with her devouring and massaging him until he could feel the heat flood all the way up to his face. A vast buzzing filled his ears and the pulse of the blood in his veins was so hard and deep he could feel it to the root of his manhood.

Her breasts heaved. Her lips parted as she gasped, and he gasped with her. Again, a deep thrust that she met with intoxicating eagerness, her silky insides sucking him in. Again, their bodies meeting with such perfection that it felt as if they were breathing together, moaning together, their hearts racing together, throbbing and pulsing and beating together in flawless rhythm. His hips withdrew and plunged forward and she was there to meet him, straining her small, lovely body to take all of him in.

"Ophele," he groaned. He was so close he was seeing stars in his peripheral vision, golden sparks like he was on fire, or maybe both of them were, blazing. "Ophele, wife—"

"Yes, I am too, yes, yes," she breathed, her back arching in a sudden spasm of pleasure, understanding him in a way that went beyond words because she was with him and the time was now. Gripping her hips in his hands, his lips peeled back from his teeth as he *pounded,* a rumbling grunt huffing from his chest. More. More. More, more, more, she was gripping him so hard he didn't know how he was going to pull himself out of her, balanced right on the flash point of their conflagration.

He was going to have to pull out of her *soon*. He could feel the shuddering spasms wracking her body, like the tremors before an earthquake. Harder, harder, hammering into her, and he felt her erupt in a blaze of heat and a flood of wetness, working him violently to completion. Remin yanked himself out of her as he came, pinning her to the floor as he climaxed on top of her.

Stars. It was so intense, so searing, so vast, it was like the immensity of the sky, dark and trembling with the blaze of distant stars behind his eyelids. He held her to him as he finished, his sides heaving as he inhaled huge lungfuls of air. His heart was beating like a Vallethi war drum.

"It's cold on the floor," he said dazedly, turning his face to kiss her. Honestly, he never wanted to move again, but he wanted her to get sick even less. "Can you stand?"

In bed, he rested and then had her again, slower. He had wanted her too badly to prolong the first time, and their wedding night had been such a revelation, all he could do was drown himself in her body. Now he wanted to experiment.

He wanted to learn every inch of her. Her body fascinated him, her long, narrow waist, her slender legs, her sleek curving thighs. He wanted to taste every inch of her velvety skin, and lap at her round breasts. And he was wild to feel her mouth on him, though her shy kisses and caresses roused him so unbearably, he couldn't endure it long before he wanted back inside her, and streaked her thighs white with his seed.

It was dangerous, letting someone get close enough to touch him. When she looked at him with those large, solemn eyes, suddenly his heart was beating so fast. The merest brush of her hands made him shiver, as if he had been starving to be touched all these years and never known it.

But he made himself stop early, nevertheless. He wouldn't repeat the mistakes he had made on their wedding night, and it was strangely satisfying just to hold her, her head resting in the crook of his shoulder, her silky hair streaming off the side of the bed in the river. Long after he should have sought his own bed, Remin lay looking at her sleeping face, soft and curving as a flower. Inexperienced as he was with women, he'd never thought about why maidens were said to be *blooming*. Nothing bloomed, in the places he had been. But his wife did. She was so fresh and so lovely, he hardly knew what to do with her.

What if she wasn't his enemy? It was far more likely that she was exactly what she seemed to be: a timid girl who had grown up a prisoner, too frightened to speak up for herself but brave enough to raise her voice for a friend. He liked that about her, very much. As a matter of fact, he had enjoyed almost every moment he had spent with her for days now. She was so smart, and funny, when she forgot to be shy.

He wanted her to stop being shy with him.

Embracing the soft, warm bundle in his arms, Remin dozed, breathing her sweet scent.

Only a whisper of a sound alerted him. A little past midnight, a shadow eeled its way through the window, cloth rasping against the windowsill, and Remin's sharp eyes saw the darker shape in the shadows of the bedroom.

It was like a slap of icy air in his face. His sword was by the fire, but he was instantly so angry, he didn't need it. Rising grimly from the bed, he stalked forward and smashed his arm into the tall wooden poster at the end, snapping it off. Ophele woke with a cry.

"Stay under the covers, wife," he ordered without looking back. "Close your eyes and don't open them until I give you leave."

Reversing the broken poster in his hand, he advanced, angling to put a small worktable between himself and the assassin. There was the gleam of a blade in their hand, a shortsword, but there were many other, fouler means of murder. He watched the blade, but he also watched the assassin's other hand, and the hooded face. There was one assassin in the Masaron Basin that had actually *spat* poison at him, like a frilled lizard, and only missed his eyes by chance.

"Miche! Tounot!" he bellowed. One of them should be at his door. "Get someone outside!"

The assassin's free hand shoved inside their robes and Remin exploded into motion, kicking the edge of the worktable up and twisting his body behind it. Several sharp metal objects thudded into it as he bulled forward, intending to slam the bastard between the table and the wall, but even if the assassin hadn't expected to find an awake and furious Remin Grimjaw, they were still quick to fling themselves right back out the window. Swearing, Remin thrust the table aside and grabbed for their hood.

It tore away, revealing short blond hair, and he whipped the bedpost at it as a parting shot. He couldn't tell if it landed. The assassin slid down the slate tiled roof and over the side like there weren't two stories between them and the alley below.

Yanking the shutters closed and noting the broken lock on them, Remin went for his pants. He hated having to face assassins when he was naked.

"Y-Your Grace?" the princess asked from the bed, her voice quivering.

"You can look," he said shortly. "He's gone."

"Who—what…" She yanked the bedcovers up to her neck as Miche burst into the room, followed by Justenin.

"I guess someone decided to try their luck," Miche said, grim. "Tounot and Ortaire went out the window as soon as you yelled, we'll know in a minute."

"I almost got a hand on him," Remin replied, tossing him the assassin's hood. Miche lit a lamp and they inspected Remin's impromptu shield. Three short throwing knives were sunk into the worktable, sharp silver steel with black edges on the blades. All of them knew better than to touch it. The black edge was likely poison.

He glanced at the terrified girl in the bed, pressed against the headboard with her knees drawn up to her chin and one hand covering her mouth. Was she really frightened? Had she known? Could there have been some signal passed between her and one of the people she had spoken with that day, the glassblower, the lady at the pastry shop, the seamstress, the tinker? How had the assassin come unerringly to this room, when Remin ought to have been in another?

Had she pretended to enjoy his affections to keep him here, long enough for the assassin to attempt his task?

"I'm afraid you'll have to get used to this, Princess," he said coldly. The thought that he might have kissed her and let her touch him and moaned his pleasure in her arms after she had arranged for his murder made him burn with hurt and humiliation. He *knew* better, but he couldn't help dreaming that just once, it might be otherwise. "Your father wants me dead quite badly."

Her face went as pale as if he'd slapped her.

"Rem, maybe—" Miche began, just as another voice shouted from outside in the alley.

"Rem!" It was Tounot. "You'll want to see this!"

"Get up and get dressed, Princess," he ordered. "Juste, guard her. Miche, with me."

"Oh, b-but, Your Grace—" The princess was white with terror, but he was already shrugging into his shirt as he headed for the door. "The window, w-what if—"

He didn't hear her. He didn't have time for her mumbling right now.

Outside in the alley behind the inn, there was a very dead assassin.

The maddening thing about assassins was that they were like a bolt of lightning: impossible to anticipate, impossible to track back to their source. The dead man was not going to be carrying anything that identified his client. His knives were simple steel, without decoration or even a maker's mark.

Remin had been set upon by everything from paid local thugs to—once—a painted journeyman of the Dream Flower Guild. That was the one that tried to spit poison in his face. The blond man in the alley had stabbed himself in the heart with a stiletto rather than be captured, which demonstrated considerable dedication to his client. Bertin had already stripped him naked and was going over his clothing an inch at a time, searching for any concealed pockets.

"Here," said Tounot, kicking the dead man onto his belly. The moon was as high and full as the tinker had promised, clearly illuminating a tattoo between his shoulder blades, a clock with many spokes and an eye in the center, slit-pupiled and lividly red. "That one's new to me."

It was new to Remin, too. It might not mean anything, or it might be another one like the Dream Flower guild, who rubbed dye into their eyelids and lacquered their fingernails.

"Drag him inside," he said. "Make a copy of that tattoo."

"Innkeeper won't be happy."

"We'll pay him extra." Remin scowled. "Though he's the one with assassins creeping through the windows of his establishment trying to murder guests in their beds. Get Bram to have a quiet word with him. Maybe he knows something."

"No one's getting any sleep tonight," Tounot observed sourly, and gave the dead man a kick on the strength of that alone.

This was Granholme, in the duchy of Firkane, whose duke was fanatically devoted to the Emperor. It would have been surprising if someone *hadn't* taken a chance to curry favor by eliminating the perpetual thorn in the Imperial side.

And of course, no one knew anything. The innkeeper threw a small fit about having a dead man sprawled on one of his dining tables, but after Bram explained things, he elected to retire back to his own room, with the courteous request that they knock if they needed anything else. With no other evident threat, it didn't seem dangerous enough to warrant leaving town immediately, so Remin sent everyone back to their beds to try and get a few more hours of sleep before sunrise.

He himself sat downstairs, watching as Tounot painstakingly reproduced the tattoo and contemplating the grisly possibility that it might be better just to slice it off and take it with them.

No. It would just curl up and go black. And stink.

It was a silent company that left Granholme later that day, after receiving a very large order of women's clothing from a yawning Mistress Courcy. The clothes were packed along with the princess's books in the supply wagon, though the princess herself showed little interest in either. She was silent, with red, swollen eyes, and she sat so stiffly in the saddle that Remin wondered if he'd hurt her after all. The pleasures of the night before felt like a distant dream.

"Are you hurt?" he asked wearily.

She shook her head.

"Do you want wine?" He was going to make a drunkard of her at this rate, but he didn't know what else to do. She *looked* hurt.

When he gave her the wineskin, she gulped it down like water.

CHAPTER 5 – AN IMPERFECT CREATION

Ophele was never drinking wine again.

It might have surprised her husband to know it, but she was seldom ill. Spring colds and flus came and went in Aldeburke without ever touching her, and she had slept in the forest in all but the most bitter cold without so much as a sniffle. But she was unquestionably weak to wine, and by the time the duke realized how much she had swallowed, it was already on the way back up.

She had never been so sick in her life.

Throughout the many miserable hours that followed, she remembered being both mortified and terribly, terribly sorry for something. She remembered clinging to a tree as she vomited, and someone holding her hair back, and then blackness, and then more vomiting, even though there couldn't possibly be anything left in her body to eject. The periods of blackness and vomiting went on for a very long time before it was just black.

When she finally swam back to consciousness, it was afternoon, and she was buried in a pile of furs and cloaks. Why was she sleeping in the afternoon? For a dazed moment, she thought she was back in Aldeburke, napping in the long grass by the stream, but then the sun struck her naked, defenseless eyeballs like a hammer and she squeezed them shut, shutting her mouth against a swell of nausea. Her mouth tasted disgusting. Everything stank of wine. She felt like she was *sweating* wine.

"Princess?"

The voice sliced into her brain like a rusty saw, but she slitted her eyes open. The eclipse looming over her could only be one person.

"Do you still feel sick?" The duke's voice was softer than usual as he knelt beside her, pressing his cool fingers to her cheek. And she couldn't lie. If he'd asked her to stand up, her head might have exploded.

"Yes," she whispered.

"Drink some of this. It's water," he added, when one of her eyes cracked open in alarm. "Slowly."

He had to help her sit up. And when she saw the camp around her, and all the knights with their backs politely turned, and the horses grazing on their pickets, she realized with a horrible shock that all that vomiting had *not* been a dream. She had gotten drunk. She had gotten so drunk, she was too sick to travel. She had gotten drunk in front of *the Knights of the Brede,* and made them sit by the side of the road and wait for her to stop being drunk.

If she could have died right there, she would have.

"We stopped," she said faintly. "We stopped?"

"Don't worry about it."

"I'm sorry," she said, so humiliated that she couldn't look him in the face.

"Just drink," he said, propping her up with one arm and lifting a cup of water to her lips. "Your body needs water."

She drank, but the water seemed to be pouring down her cheeks as fast as she drank it. She choked and turned her face away, clapping her hands to her mouth to keep the disgraceful noise in, the wail of misery that was strangling her. This time, it was too much. Burying herself in the pile of cloaks, she sobbed herself sick.

He hated her.

That look on his *face,* she could never, never forget it. Even Lady Hurrell had never looked at her like that, as if she hated her enough to die. And when Ophele thought of how he had touched her, and how nice he had been in the market, the sobs welled up and sliced her throat like razors, because for a little while she had really thought things might be different. He had been gentle. He had talked to her, listened to her, even teased her. It had been almost…friendly between them.

More than friendly.

But she had been stupid. How could he ever care for her after everything her father had done? After what her mother had done? Her family had *destroyed his life*. Her father had been trying to have him killed since he was a boy. Oh, this *particular* assassin might not have been sent by her father, but whoever had ordered it had done so in accordance with the Emperor's will. Ophele would never forget the sight of the assassin creeping through the shadows, and His Grace had gone to face him with nothing but a broken bed post.

How could he ever forgive her for that? The things her family had done to him could never be made right. He was right not to trust her. She was the child of his enemies, and a bastard, too. Everyone knew that bastards were the seeds of treachery.

Ophele pretended to be asleep for the rest of the day, and the next morning, when the duke asked her if she was well enough to travel, she nodded without lifting her eyes from the ground. How could she dare to even meet his eyes? How could she face any of them? She had disgraced herself before the *Knights of the Brede*. There were actual songs sung about them. She had sworn an oath to make them proud to serve her and then done the most shameful thing she had ever done in her life.

She spent the whole day looking blankly at the road ahead, so painfully aware of the silent wall at her back that it was all she could do to keep from bursting into tears again. But she would not do that, she *would not*. As soon as they stopped for the night, she went to bed, wishing that she would never wake up.

The first thing she saw the next morning were her books, a boxy lump in the supply wagon wrapped in oilskins.

Thank the stars, she had run into Rou.

Books were a familiar refuge. She was a coward, hiding from her troubles in their pages, just as she had always done in Aldeburke. She should say she was sorry, but that word was so hopelessly inadequate it would be an insult to the duke, and the bare thought of standing before the Knights of the Brede to apologize made her tongue wither in her mouth. Day after day, she felt the duke's icy presence at her back and all she could do was read and read until the letters danced before her eyes, so ashamed that every time they passed a large body of water, she honestly contemplated throwing herself into it.

"My lady." Sir Miche had begun bringing her supper to her, since the duke no longer wanted anything to do with her. "Please eat. You can empty the pot, if you like."

"Thank you," she said, without lifting her eyes.

"It is the privilege of a knight to serve a lady," he said, angling his head to catch her eyes. His beautiful face was filled with sympathy. "Even if it is only rabbit stew and biscuit. Though if you don't like it, I'm sure I could find something in that stream. Catfish, maybe."

"No, this is fine." She took a bite.

"Are you sure? I bet I could catch a juicy toad or two. Or maybe some pollywogs for tea."

"No," she said again, though that almost won a smile. He was a very kind man.

Surprisingly, it was *The Will Immanent* that offered her some solace. It had many things to say about the concept of balance and order, and the struggle between divine order and the chaos of creation. No one *really* wanted to believe in fate or destiny; what was the point of anything, if everything was preordained? Who wanted to think they were a puppet in someone else's play? But there was no question that in the case of Remin Grimjaw, there was considerable imbalance, and a great debt owed.

This was a familiar thought. She had been told all her life that she must pay for the crimes of her parents. But maybe there was a way she could, beyond the simple function of providing His Grace with heirs. Perhaps she could help him, or at least not hinder him. It would be a beginning, anyway.

"Will you let me borrow that book when you've finished it, my lady?"

Seated by the fire one evening, she looked up in surprise. The knights rarely spoke to her, except for Sir Miche. But this time it was Sir Justenin looking down at her in a friendly sort of way, and lending him a book was the least she could do.

"Oh, yes," she said. "You can have it now, if you like."

Instead of accepting it and walking away, though, he waved a hand and crouched down beside her.

"I can wait. Do you enjoy theology?"

"I haven't read much," she said, a little nervously. They called Sir Justenin the Coldest Knight, and he was famous for his defense of the fort at Iverlach three years before, a critical stronghold that he had held through a winter siege, though he and his men had been reduced to eating their boot leather before the end. The maids at Aldeburke used to sing a song about it, *The Snow Kept Falling Down.*

"You picked a hard one," he said. "I know the writer, Vigga Aubriolot. Very dense writing."

"It is, that's why it might take me a while," she said apologetically. "I have to stop reading to think about it sometimes, to make sure I understand."

"That's how it should be. Important ideas should take some thinking." He leaned over to add a few branches to her fire, sending sparks into the sky. "What's one that you had to think about?"

"I liked the part about how the divine perfect made room in the universe for imperfect creation," she said, pointing to a passage in the chapter she was currently working through. "Here. Mr. Aubriolot explains that that was the purpose of the earth and the heavens, that the earth is an imperfect place for imperfect beings."

"He said something of the sort in his first thesis. It seemed a rather self-evident contention," Sir Justenin observed. "An excuse for bad behavior."

"I guess so, but...but I didn't take it that way," she offered. "I thought they were doing us a kindness, so that we could have a place that we *could* be imperfect while we try to learn better."

"I will have to pay attention to that chapter," he said, looking thoughtful. And while they were on the subject of imperfect beings, Ophele nerved herself to say what she had been wanting to say for more than a week.

"Sir Justenin," she began, feeling color burn from her cheeks to her ears, "I have been wanting to say...not just to you, to all of you...I'm very sorry. About what happened after Granholme. And...everything else."

Everything else, including the deaths of his parents, along with the rest of the duke's House. But he didn't know that she knew that, and she didn't know how she could even begin to apologize.

His eyebrows went up in surprise.

"No one blames you for that, my lady," he said firmly. "His Grace said you weren't used to wine, and wine is a dangerous remedy. If anything, we failed you. That man should never have gotten anywhere near you. It would shock anyone, waking up to find an assassin in the room."

Her father's assassin.

"That's very kind of you." She bobbed her head in a small bow. "I won't ever do such a thing again. I…"

Will do my part, when we get to the valley.

Will make you proud.

Will spend the rest of my life making up for what you have lost.

"I won't be a disgrace to you," she finished, looking away. It seemed like the most she could aspire to, at present.

* * *

He should have gotten her a maid.

Remin thought this at least half a dozen times per day.

It wasn't because the princess needed the help. On the contrary, now that she had books and simpler dresses that she could manage by herself, she was surprisingly self-sufficient. She knew where to get her own food and drink, she ate from the common stew pot, she competently tended her own fire, and from sunup to sundown her nose was buried in a book. She had even begun waking up on her own when the camp started moving, though she still stumbled around for the first half hour or so and, three times so far, walked into things.

A week out of Granholme, they were on the outer edge of the Empire and moving through rolling hills where wide swaths of forest were bursting into new leaves and flowers. Fast-running streams, icy and swollen with snowmelt, ran along the sides of the road, and every day was warmer than the last. They would pass through one more town before they came to the Brede, a little hamlet called Trema that was to Granholme what Granholme was to Celderline. There would be no inn there. The best they would find was a share of a cowshed.

He should have gotten her a maid, Remin thought again. Maybe that was the real purpose of servants: to serve as a buffer to avoid any unnecessary intimacy in this kind of political marriage. In the normal course of things, he and his wife would hardly have needed to communicate at all. They could have lived separate lives in the same vast house, coming together only to discuss household business and conceive children, in brief encounters as passionless as the mating between a prized stud and a mare.

He should have gotten her a maid, and a horse of her own, and taught her to ride it, because maddeningly, his body *burned* for her. He tried not to notice, but sometimes he thought she really might be a witch. All it took was the breeze wafting her scent to him and he flashed back to their nights together, every sound, every sigh, every touch. He touched her as little as possible and avoided her whenever they weren't sharing a saddle, but no matter where she was, his eyes found her as if she were a lodestone.

It was worse than when he was a teenager. At least he hadn't known what he was missing back then.

"Rem, you're being an idiot." Miche sat down at Remin's fire one night, which was on the opposite side of the camp from his wife. "Remember what I told you before you got married?"

"Shut up, Miche." Remin was eating his supper and not watching her. Every night she sat down to take her hair out of its plait and painstakingly brushed it from root to tip until it gleamed, an almost hypnotic ritual, like she was casting some feminine magic. She was just finishing, and turned to climb up onto the high wheel of the supply wagon to put away her brush. She really was as nimble as a squirrel.

"I told you not to do anything you don't want to hear about for the next fifty years." When Miche had something on his mind, nothing could shut him up. Remin could have threatened him at spearpoint and he would have cheerfully impaled himself and delivered his remarks with his dying breath. "When that girl finishes growing up, she's never going to forgive you."

"She'll reach her majority this year, and she's plenty old enough to marry. She's not a child." But watching the princess burrow into her usual nest of cloaks, she looked so vulnerable that Remin had to look away, his jaw clenching. *A trick.* "The sooner she understands her position, the better."

"If you're going to treat her like poison every day of your life, why did you marry her? If I'd known you were going to do that, *I* would have objected at your fucking wedding."

"I asked for an Emperor's daughter and I got one," Remin snapped. "Don't make it more than it is."

"You're making a big mistake." Miche met his eyes, flat and angry. "I told you I'd tell you if you were. She can't help who her father is. If you just gave her a chance—"

"Drop it, Miche," he said shortly, and walked away.

Remin was not prepared for this. He had expected a spoiled, haughty noblewoman, sly and conniving, the Emperor with breasts. It would have given him immense satisfaction to use the Emperor's blood for his own ends, to defeat whatever machinations she might attempt and get heirs on her that would establish his House for all time. There was no possible vengeance so complete or enduring.

But the princess refused to play her role. He kept giving her opportunities to reveal her true colors, so he could catch her in some lie, some deception, but every time it failed to manifest. Perversely, it only made him more determined to trap her. It could only mean that she was more cunning than he had expected, more subtle, more patient.

It meant, when she inevitably betrayed him, that it would devastate him.

It was his own fault. He had almost been taken in by her. He had let her get too close, close enough to hurt him. It would be a painful correction, but soon they would both get used to it and understand what lines should not be crossed, and then they would...

He didn't know how to end that sentence.

At any rate, soon they would be back in the valley and working too hard to care. The matter of the bandits was his biggest concern, but until they got back to Tresingale and saw how things stood, there wasn't much he could do about it. But as the Andelin drew near and they left Trema behind, he and his men often sat up late at night, planning everything that would have to be done.

"The surveyor sent a preliminary map," said Edemir, spreading a large piece of parchment in the space they had cleared between lamps. He had collected the messages waiting for them at Trema's small garrison. "This is the proposed town site, and he's even included the grade of the hills and their elevation. Here's the river, and here's that hill you suggested for the manor, Rem. It'll be a steep climb for horses unless you circle the road around the back."

"Daitians do a terracing thing to manage steep terrain," said Bram, who was the most well-traveled among them. "If you don't mind climbing a lot of stairs yourself."

"Not if it means we'll have a view of the town. The city," Remin corrected. Tresingale would be a city in his lifetime. On the far side of the fire, he didn't notice the princess turn slightly toward them, listening. "The hill to the east would be good for a training yard. And the barracks could go here."

"With a view of the sheep," observed Tounot. It was true that the hills Remin had designated as grazing land were immediately adjacent.

"What you do with your time off is your own business," he said, to a rumble of laughter. "But I won't force any of you to stay," he added, looking at the map. Specifically, the blank space that lay beyond the borders of the town: the mountains to the north and east, the Talfel Plateau northwest, the moors to the west. It was a lot of land. "I told you I'd give you all lands and titles of your own."

"What sort of bannerman leaves their lord sleeping in a croft?" Tounot asked lightly. "Which, if I recall correctly, was located about here. Next to Tounot Boulevard."

"Auber Avenue," Auber corrected. "His Grace said everything had to be alliterative."

This was true, though Remin had consumed a considerable amount of alcohol at the time.

"If that's the main road going to the new bridge, it can only be Harnost Highway," said Miche loftily.

"Miche Marke is going to be on the bad side of town. Where the brothels are," Tounot retorted.

"How dare you, sir."

"There will be no bad side of Tresingale," Remin decreed, putting an end to the argument. He was glad that they were all steadfast in their desire to stay. Eventually they would have to go and begin settling those wider lands, or someone else would beat them to it. But he wasn't quite ready to give up his knights yet.

Each of them had a task, according to their own inclinations and aptitudes. Juste, who had lived in an orphanage run by the Brothers of the Shepherd Star, had learned how to manage sheep, cows, and goats. Auber was a farmer's son, and several of his many siblings—including the older brother that had made the error of buying wedding rings without a single diamond to shine for the stars—would be arriving in autumn, to farm lands more vast than the niggling acres in Engleberg.

Huber knew horses, Tounot and Bram would manage the incoming settlers, and Edemir did the work of actually procuring the experts and materials they needed to accomplish everything else: the surveyor who was charting the lands around Tresingale, followed by the architects and planners who would decide what to do with it, and the builders to make it real.

Miche pronounced himself useless but willing to lend a hand wherever he was needed.

Already hundreds of people were converging on the valley at the duke's invitation, and they were going to have to ride hard to beat the first shipments of supplies. Remin had left behind a few trusted knights and a small force of soldiers, but the amount of work to be done was staggering. Thoughts of bandits weighed on his mind, and he took some solace in the knowledge that he had left Genon Hengest and Jinmin of Oskerre behind to look after things. Genon Hengest was a surgeon and veteran that had kept them alive through seven years of war, and Jinmin had once crushed a Vallethi soldier's head in the palm of his hand like he was cracking a walnut. The two men could be trusted to keep a grip on things.

"We'll be arriving in Andelin in two weeks, if all goes well," he told the princess the next day as he lifted her into the saddle. With practice, they had managed to find positions on the horse that allowed them to touch as little as possible.

She nodded. He couldn't remember the last time he had heard her speak.

"There won't be much there," he said, wondering how much she had heard, or guessed, about what he was taking her into. "There's no manor house, like Aldeburke. If we're lucky, we'll have the main house built by winter, but that's just the central structure. It won't include things like libraries or ballrooms."

The princess nodded again, solemn as ever.

"You won't have time to be reading all day," he added. It came out more harshly than he intended. "It won't be the life you knew before. You'll have to be useful."

"I will," she said, almost inaudibly. He kept telling her to speak up, but if anything, she was getting worse. "I'll work hard."

For some reason, her meekness infuriated him. Why wasn't she angry? She was a princess, the daughter of the Emperor, she should expect to be treated like one. She should demand better than a wattle-and-daub shepherd's hut. Even a serving girl would have balked. A noblewoman should have raised hell.

"You don't have much pride, for a princess." It just slipped out. But he wanted *something* from her, a flicker of temper, of outrage, of hurt. He had expected a spoiled, haughty princess and kept digging to find her, sure that she must be hidden under this shy, lovely façade. But she just looked away, her narrow shoulders drawing together.

Whatever her reply was, it was so soft, it was trodden under the heavy thud of his horse's hooves.

* * *

Ophele didn't think she would ever walk normally again.

Every day was a grueling marathon, her backside and thighs battered to bits by the spanking rhythm of the horse. They ate in the saddle and only stopped briefly at noon to allow everyone to carry out the necessary bodily functions, then were ahorse once more, pulverizing her bones to dust and making her wonder how the duke—who had to actually do the work of riding, rather than sitting like a sack of grain in the saddle—could endure it.

They had come so far, so fast, it was a little overwhelming to think how many miles she was from Aldeburke and everything she knew. So far to the north, even the forests looked different, thick with fir and pine and other trees she didn't recognize, hoary and massive. She spotted a few edibles like pecan, hazelnut, and walnut; she had always loved fall back home, when she could gorge herself on the season's produce and Azelma would bake pecan tartlets and mincemeat pies.

After three weeks on horseback, Ophele would have given anything to just *walk*. The duke's horse was immense and his back correspondingly wide, but no matter which way she turned, she just couldn't get comfortable anymore. In the evenings she walked endlessly back and forth at the perimeter of the camp to ease the cramps in her legs, and even when she was lying in the back of the supply wagon, it felt like the world was swaying underneath her like a ship.

Sometimes Sir Justenin joined her for her walks. She wasn't sure what to make of him. He was so much older, he could nearly have been her father, and she didn't know what such an important man could possibly want from her. But she was grateful to have someone to talk to, all the same. Just because she was used to solitude didn't mean she *liked* it.

"Did you ever think of going back?" she asked one night, walking carefully to avoid horse droppings. Sir Justenin had been describing the place he had grown up, a peaceful mountain monastery that took in inconvenient children. She thought she would have liked to be sent there. "To the Brothers?"

"No," he said thoughtfully. "Though there was a time I thought about joining them; there are worse ways to spend one's life than contemplating the stars. I liked learning. And I miss the quiet," he said, looking at the noisy camp with mingled fondness and chagrin.

"Was it an oath?" she asked hesitantly. "That made you decide to join His Grace."

"Yes. My father was one of his father's retainers."

"Oh." Well, she had thought as much, but she still had to bite her tongue to keep from apologizing. "That's very honorable of you, to keep his promise."

"Honor cuts both ways, my lady," he said with a small smile. "A pledge of service also means that your husband pledged to keep a position open for me, if I wanted it. And I thought I wanted to see the world, and serve the son of the man my father served."

He often said that. *Your husband,* as if it were a firm foundation upon which to rest their conversations. But though Ophele had come to understand a little of the relations between men and women, it never occurred to her that anyone might want her with that strange, thrilling madness that had briefly possessed His Grace.

"It must have been difficult," she said, though she was a little at a loss. Of course it had been difficult; he had survived seven years of war and eaten his own boots one winter. "For all of you. Is it the same for the others? Did their fathers swear, too?"

"A few, I think." At the end of the picket line, they turned together, reversing their course. "Tounot for certain; his father was the duke's bannerman, and Tounot fostered with His Grace's father every summer. Edemir's lands border the Andelin, and Huber was a fosterling of Duke Ereguil's and came up with His Grace as a knight. Bram was a mercenary your husband hired to do some tricky work, and then he decided to stay on. And Miche—well, as far as I know, Miche just got a whim in his silly head one day."

Ophele giggled. It sounded like something he would do.

"You're all very brave," she said. "I often heard the maids talking about you, back home."

"There are many kinds of bravery, my lady. The subtler variety is no less worthy."

"Oh, that's from…" She hummed, rummaging through her memory. Sir Justenin liked to pepper quotations into the conversation, as if he were testing her. "Deregas. *A Primer of Virtues.*"

"Aldeburke has an impressive library." The compliment was roundabout enough that she was not embarrassed. "Do you agree with his definition?"

She loved this kind of conversation. Sir Justenin was so patient and encouraging, she forgot to be nervous, and he was a very methodical thinker. He often trapped her with her own logical inconsistencies, and it taught her to think more thoroughly, to consider not just the words on a page, but all their implications, and everything that must follow, if they were true.

Like the travelers. They saw occasional travelers on the roads, but as they drew close to the river, there were more. Ragged families with hand carts, single men with heavy baskets on their backs, and twice, huge wagons bogged down in the middle of the narrow path, blocking the way and requiring the knights to hitch up their own horses to pull them free. A vast migration had begun, and though she had heard the duke and his men talking about it at night around the fire, until now she hadn't thought through what it meant.

All these travelers wanted to be the duke's people. They wanted to settle his lands, they would pay taxes to him, take oaths of loyalty to him, and he would be responsible for protecting them. Riding on mules, seated in wagons, or tramping barefoot through the mud, they were coming, to build new lives, to till the soil and raise their families.

And if they wished to belong to the duke, and she was his wife, then it logically followed that they were going to be her people, too.

Ophele closed her book and watched.

Few of them were actual beggars. Beggars would never make it so far. It must cost a lot of money to uproot a life and buy food and supplies to journey for months. But some of the travelers had clearly underestimated the cost, or run into misfortune, and when she saw a woman with a young child sitting in the shade by the side of the road, she couldn't be silent. The child did not look well at all.

"Your Grace," she made herself say. "Can we help them?"

"Who?" He glanced over, following her eyes. He and his knights were not indifferent to the people they passed on the road, but she knew they were pushing hard to reach Tresingale, worried about what they might find there. "We have somewhere to be, Princess."

"But that little boy looks sick." She would have gone to help them herself, if she could, but Ophele was well aware that she was of no practical use to anyone. "They're on their way to your valley, Your Grace. She wants to be one of your people."

His black eyes flickered. After more than a month on the road, he was looking very shaggy indeed, with a thick black beard darkening his jaw and making him almost a stranger. She wasn't sure whether it made him more or less easy to talk to.

"Tounot!" He called up the line, and the curly-haired knight swung around on his horse. "Go see if you can help the woman back there."

There were others that needed help, too. An elderly man with swollen ankles, a family that had broken a wheel on their cart, and too many other hungry-looking travelers to count, but after the third time she timidly asked him to help them, he flatly refused.

"We can't stop for everyone," he said curtly. "They're responsible for their own lives, Princess. They chose to leave their homes and come here uninvited, indeed, against my orders. They passed a dozen towns on the way here where they might have stopped for help."

"But maybe some of them didn't have any choice—" she began.

"I have people I am responsible for waiting in Tresingale," he interrupted, looking down at her sternly. "People who have already sworn their loyalty to me. Some of them have risked their lives for me. I will keep faith with them first."

Once again, she hadn't thought things completely through. The duke met her eyes as if he were waiting for her to produce another objection, but he had already offered enough counterarguments to silence her. She looked down at her lap, her eyebrows drawing together as she thought about the problem. Honestly, there were too many things she didn't know to offer a solution.

They pressed on. The horses devoured the miles to the Brede and then followed its winding course to the bridge at Gellege, a plain but impressive structure that was so large, a shout from one side of the bridge would have been inaudible from the other. And that was the narrowest place on the river she had seen. The Brede River was called the devourer of armies for a reason. For most of its dark and churning length, the further bank was only a smudge on the horizon.

"Your Grace!" shouted one of the men at the gatehouse on the far side of the bridge, and the duke rose up in his stirrups, lifting a hand. "What's the password!"

"Hawthorne!" The word boomed out like thunder. The duke knew how to make himself heard. But the drawbridge didn't budge.

"Beg pardon, m'lord, it's the other one!"

"Grimjaw!" Sir Miche shouted gleefully from behind them.

"I told you if you added that to the rotation, I'd reassign you to Kiel Gorge!" The duke bellowed. "Drop the bridge, you fu—" He glanced down at Ophele, who was looking fascinated, and declined to complete the sentence. "Now!"

The drawbridge lowered. Glowering, Remin Grimjaw spurred his horse forward, the saddle spanking Ophele's tortured backside like she had done something to deserve it. Inside the gatehouse, soldiers crowded around to welcome them, including the wit with the password, who the duke kicked lovingly in the back of the head.

At last, they had crossed the Brede.

* * *

Nothing appeared to be on fire.

In his dreams Remin had seen black smoke rising from miles away and descended to the valley to find burning huts, burning wagons, burning horses, and dead men, all the sights he was accustomed to seeing in the Andelin. But from the rolling foothills at the southern end of the Berlawe Mountains, he looked on distant Tresingale and saw a pastoral paradise, every bit as beautiful as he remembered.

From the heights, the valley stretched before them like the pleats of a fan, lush and verdant from frequent rainfall, so green it dazzled the eye. Dark stands of old-growth forest carpeted the sides of the mountains, and the mountains themselves were almost relentlessly scenic and reminded Remin of old white-headed soldiers, marching away to the northeast. Soon it would be warm enough that the dark things in those mountains would begin making their way to the valley, and the city walls would need to be up by then, with solid gates.

They had already begun the spring planting. He could see it on the north side of the city, dark acres of freshly turned soil in slightly uneven furrows. War horses did not turn into plow horses overnight. There were more crofter's cottages lining the town's only road, carefully spaced so that there was room for each cottage to turn into a proper city house one day. One drunken night in Segoile, he and Tounot had gone out and measured the lot sizes for three blocks of Aben Road, to give themselves a base measurement in planning Tresingale.

There were his sheep, white dots on the green hills. There was a wagon track veering down toward the river, the area where they had found clay. There was another trail winding west into the trees, a quarry site they had begun to build last winter. His men had been busy.

He had to fight the urge to kick his horse into a gallop and race down to the town. His town. His city.

"That's Tresingale," he told the princess, who had closed her book and was looking at the town with her solemn-owl face. "Probably smaller than you imagined."

"The valley is beautiful," she replied, which was a clever way to sidestep the subject.

"You should have seen it before. I left two hundred men here, midwinter, and most of them were sleeping on the floor of the cookhouse. We've a dozen more cottages than when I left and it looks like they've been busy on the wall. We're going to be doing nothing but hauling stone this summer."

He hoped the oxen had arrived. Remin had dozens of items on his mental lists that he wanted to check, and Edemir maintained even longer lists, endless catalogues of tasks and plans that extended years into the future. Even the horses seemed to know that home was nearby and picked up the pace as they descended, watching the trees break to provide tantalizing glimpses of the town.

There was a palisade under construction on the north side of town, and another around the storehouse, the only building of substance. Its stone walls were three feet thick and contained all their food, weapons, armor, and other crucial supplies. He was half-tempted to keep the princess in it.

The sun was westering toward evening as they rode into town amid distant cries from laborers at the city wall and a few people taking their turn watching the sheep. He felt his heart lift. Most people would still be out at work, but Wen should be in the kitchen and Genon would be along as soon as he got word the duke had returned.

"There's the storehouse," he said to the princess as they approached. "Over there is the cookhouse, it doubles as a barracks right now, until we get an actual barracks built. Kitchen's on the back. We have a camp cook that can make something edible out of almost anything. Plain food," he added, as a warning. "It won't be what you're used to. Wen's used to feeding an army, not gracing a nobleman's table."

He paused, giving her an opportunity to protest this, but as always, she let it pass in silence, looking at the tiny settlement. Tresingale was to Trema what Trema was to Granholme. There wasn't even a cowshed in Tresingale yet.

"What will happen to all the people we saw coming here?" she asked.

"We're still discussing that," he answered, reining in his horse, who had spotted the stable and wanted hay. "Technically, they're Firkane's problem. But we'll see what we can do for them."

It would take a lot of time and money either way, and he had to bite his tongue to keep from cursing the Emperor aloud. He had started this flood with his talk of open lands to the north. They were Remin's lands, and they weren't open yet.

"And...the bandits?"

"I'll deal with them," he said, grim lines deepening in his face, and lifted his hand to greet Genon, who was pelting toward them on his gray mare.

If he'd thought about it, Remin would have warned her about Genon beforehand. It would have been a kindness to them both.

"Genon!" Remin swung down from his horse, reaching for the princess to set her down beside him and then striding forward to clasp hands with the surgeon. Genon was a big man, vast in the way some men could be big without being fat, burly and heavy-boned with forearms like hocks of ham. "Still alive."

"Too cursed stubborn to die." Genon clapped his shoulder. "Thought you'd never get back, it's been tense, Your Grace. Been feeling like we're out here naked with our boll—that is, it would be nice to have more defenses in place," he hastily amended, glancing at the princess, who was hobbling toward them and trying to hide it.

"This is my wife," Remin drew her forward, noting the line of pain between her eyebrows. No matter what she said to the contrary, the ride had been grueling for her. "Princess Ophele of House Agnephus, Lady of Aldeburke, and now my duchess. Princess, this is Genon Hengest, our surgeon."

"Pleased to meet you." Her eyes were round as she looked up at him. Remin was used to Genon, so he hardly noticed the man's wounds anymore, but they were a graphic illustration of the reality of war. Thirty years ago, Genon had been doused in boiling oil while assaulting a Vallethi fortification. The upper right quarter of his head, including his right eye, was a melted mass of silvery-pink scars that extended down the right side of his body, pulling his shoulder into a permanently crabbed position.

"It's my honor, my lady." Genon bowed and gave her a glimpse of the scars seaming the top of his head. "I've known His Grace a long time, it will be a pleasure to serve his lady. You ever need anything, I'm your man."

"Thank you." She was staring, her fingers knotting together in an anxious gesture that Remin recognized. He was willing to let her timidity pass, to a point, but he was going to have to talk to her about that. He would not allow her to embarrass Genon. "I have heard of you, I think," she said hesitantly, so softly even Remin didn't catch all of it, and he was right next to her. "Some of…Genon minding the valley. And…good hands. On the way here."

"Is that so?" Genon gave a booming laugh, having made out enough of it to understand it was complimentary. "That's kind of you to say, my lady. There's a lot of work to be done. But we've kept His Grace's croft ready against your arrival, to make you as comfortable as we can."

The look Genon was giving Remin from his one yellow eye was as good as words: *see to your lady and then come talk to me.* There was news, and it could wait, but not for long. And as much as he wanted to plunge straight into the work of the valley, his first responsibility was to his wife.

"I'll find you in the cookhouse shortly," Remin said, catching the princess's elbow and steering her toward the cottage. "Tounot, have some of the lads bring the princess's things up. The rest of you, be about your business."

The princess nodded politely to Genon and moved with Remin, picking up her skirts and tiptoeing to keep out of the mud. His cot wasn't far, the second one down the narrow lane, a thatched cottage with a recent coat of whitewash on its thick daubed walls. Weeds and scrubby dandelions filled the front yard.

"I told you it wasn't much," Remin said shortly, plodding across the muddy yard. By rights, he should be taking his new bride to the ancient and beautiful manor where he had been born, one of seven separate estates that had belonged to his murdered House. That place was gone, burned to the ground on the Emperor's orders. The rest of his ancestral lands had been seized.

What he had now was a peasant's cottage. Dark, dusty, dingy, though he could see his men had tried to keep it up for him. The rushes on the floor looked fresh, and so did the bedding. The bed was the one concession to his rank, an actual bedstead that took up the rear third of the small cottage, vast enough to accommodate his size.

The princess said nothing. She stood in the simple doorway, dusty and disheveled from weeks in the saddle, her eyes moving from the small hearth to the rough table and chairs to the single heavy trunk under the window. It was most charitably described as *humble,* and the contrast between this hovel and the dignified estate at Aldeburke made Remin flush with humiliation.

"Not what you were hoping for, Princess?" he asked, tossing his own rough pack into the only empty corner. He wanted her to be angry. She *should* be angry to be brought to a place like this. It was her father's fault she was here, and her father's fault that Remin Grimjaw had nothing better to offer his wife.

"You told me it would be a cottage," she said, blinking. "Is there— could I have a bath before supper? I was hoping—"

"There will be no maids to draw baths for you here." Best she knew the worst of it now. "If you want to wash, you'll have to fetch water from the well."

"I will." Her hands pressed together, her fingers twining an anxious knot. "I—I was p-planning to dress for dinner, I wanted…a fresh…"

Her voice wavered, each word quieter than the last, and the last of it was completely inaudible.

"Speak. Up," he said impatiently. "We don't dress for dinner here. There won't be room for half your dresses in this cottage. You'll have to get used to living simply."

"I know," she whispered. "In Aldeburke—"

"Does this look like Aldeburke?" Suddenly, he was furious. "There's no great house here, Princess. No servants, no maids to wait on you, no groundskeepers to chase away foxes. In a few weeks, there are going to be hungry things coming out of the mountains, and no one's going to have time to coddle the Emperor's spawn. There's *nothing* here, do you understand? We have *nothing!* We are going to have to build all of it ourselves, because *your father—*"

"I *know!*" She burst out, her eyes round with fright. "I know, I will do it, I will get water myself, I won't trouble you, I just don't know where anything is and I wanted to look nice when I meet your men, I'll be careful, you just have to tell me and I'll do it, I only need a bucket, a b-basin, I'm sorry, I'm *sorry!*"

Tears spilled from her eyes and she covered her mouth with her hand, shocking him out of his temper. What was he *doing?* He had backed her up into the wall, and she was gripping the windowsill like she was about to go over it. Automatically, he reached for her, but she ducked back, cringing into the corner.

His hand dropped.

"No," he said into a heavy silence. "No, I'm sorry. Go sit down. You can draw your own bath next time."

"I can do it," she wept, scrubbing at her face with her sleeve.

"I know you can." Carefully, he nudged her toward the closer of the two chairs, keeping his hands low and unthreatening. "I'm sorry. I went too far. Don't cry, Princess. Stay here, I'll be back."

Ducking through the door, he closed it behind him, trying not to hear the soft sounds from inside the cottage. He felt like a brute, and a bully, and he deserved to. Even if she were feigning her tears, she had done nothing wrong. He had just been so *angry*.

"Leave her things here," he said to the approaching squires, laden with the oilskins containing the princess's books and clothing. There was no place to put them but on the ground, in the mud. "I'll deal with them. Go and see if we have a large tub in the storehouse. Or a cauldron, from the kitchen."

The boys exchanged glances.

"How big, Your Grace?" Ferme wanted to know.

"Big enough for a lady's bath."

* * *

The cauldron His Grace had acquired from the kitchen was just large enough that they could have cooked her in a stew.

Ordinarily, Ophele would have found this very funny.

Heating bathwater was a tedious process, especially given the size of the hearth. She knew how to manage fire and boil water, and she figured out the hearth mechanisms easily enough—there was a cast iron bracket that swiveled to hold the pot over the fire—but she was literally watching water boil, and by the time she got one potful steaming, the previous one was already beginning to cool. A series of buckets marched from the hearth to the door of the cottage, waiting their turn over the fire.

That was fine. All she wanted was to be *clean,* as if she could wash not just the road and aches of riding but the whole day from her body.

She didn't understand what she had done wrong. Her head throbbed dully as she gazed at the fire, trying to reason her way through the puzzle. She had tried so hard to fix things, on the way to the valley. She had kept quiet and stayed out of His Grace's way, sick at the thought that she had delayed them so much. The duke might have come home to find everything in ashes, of course he would be furious.

But then, why was he angry now? Hadn't he said he wanted her to look nice, like a princess instead of a beggar's brat? She hadn't meant to complain, she wasn't *going* to complain, it didn't matter to her whether she lived in a cottage or a palace. Either was better than Aldeburke.

But maybe it wouldn't be. Her stomach knotted as she glanced toward the window, wondering *what* hungry things would be coming out of the mountains.

Slipping out of her sweaty gown and chemise, Ophele climbed into her stew pot, ducking her head to soak her hair. She still had all the soaps and lotions and sundries from Celderline, and she reserved a few buckets of cold water to rinse herself off, shivering. There were no towels. Wrapping her arms around herself, she went to stand by the fire, hoping no one would come to the door and nothing hungry would come through the windows.

Spread on the bed was the gown she would wear tonight, as beautiful as anything Lisabe owned. It was an unlikely combination of bronze and dark blue, studded with pearls on the bodice and skirt. She could dress herself as far as her chemise and the bronze silk kirtle, but there was just no way to put on the overdress herself. The duke might say that there was no one here to wait on her, but ladies' gowns were complex constructions with many layers, fastenings, and laces, and often there were pieces that had to be sewed on after the lady was dressed.

Imagining the duke clutching a needle and thread in his huge hands made her mind boggle.

At least he had brought her books to the cottage. Ophele sat down at the table and hung her hair over the back of the chair to dry, then promptly fell asleep.

"Princess?"

She woke up to find the duke frowning down at her, as shaggy and black and bearlike as ever. He had taken time to wash and shave, and it was strange to see him without a beard, his bare cheekbones high and arrogant.

"Sorry," she said at once, skittering nervously away. "Sorry. I fell asleep."

"It's all right. You need help with your dress?" he asked, taking in the many pieces laid neatly on the bed. Ophele had already donned the kirtle, a simple underdress studded with topaz along the neck.

"Yes." Silently, she showed him how the overgown went over her head and how the slashed sleeves fit over her arms, puffing out to reveal her white chemise and held in place with bronze ribbons. She couldn't tie bows on her own arms.

Neither could the duke, apparently. He scowled at the ribbons as if they had mortally offended him, and the final bows were decidedly lopsided.

"I don't see why it's so complicated," he grumbled, kneeling behind her to thread the laces through their eyelets. "Princess," he added, more gently. "I am sorry for what I did, earlier today. You did nothing wrong."

"I didn't mean to complain," she said, not daring to look back at him.

"I know. And you need to know that I will not strike you. Ever."

She flushed. Lady Hurrell had said he could do whatever he liked as her husband, and it was Ophele's part to bear it. But she had gotten scared, again. Lady Hurrell used to scold her for cowering, like a little brown mouse.

"It's all right," she said, subdued.

"No, it isn't. Look at me, wife." He turned her around to face him and took both her hands in his big ones, looking at her seriously. Even kneeling, his head was almost level with hers. "If I ever lay my hands on you with violence, then may the stars in heaven strike me dead. I will speak that oath before every man in Tresingale, if you like."

"You don't have to do that," she said, alarmed at the prospect. What would his men think, if he did such a thing?

"I mean it, nonetheless." His mouth pressed into a flat line, and he turned her back around, returning to the lacing in a businesslike way. "We can at least be civil to each other, and I don't want you to be afraid of me. If you have questions, ask."

She had many questions. But she didn't know how he would react, and she wavered for a minute before she finally ventured, "...what did you mean, about things in the mountains?"

"Devils," he said seriously. "They didn't used to be there, when Argence held the valley. Maybe Vallethi magicians conjured them somehow, in the last days of the war. They were pretty desperate. But a few years ago they started showing up on battlefields, ghouls coming out to eat...to eat," he said evasively, as if Ophele wouldn't guess what. "There's something else that comes after nightfall that we call stranglers, and there's a thing that looks like a wolf and isn't. The men call them wolf demons, though I don't know if they're actually demons. I'm not sure I believe in demons."

"They say they are real in Bhumi," she said, trying to find some ground on which to meet him. Devils. Magic. She looked again at the shutters on the windows, the wattle and daub walls, which basically meant sticks and mud. That didn't sound like it could stand up to wolf demons.

"Bhumi think there are ten thousand different kinds of spirits. This ribbon is fraying at the end." His deep voice rumbled the complaint.

"If you singe the end, it will curl up."

"So long as I don't singe you." He stood and went to light a bit of kindling, searing the end of the ribbon and blowing it out before it caught fire. "I didn't tell you that to scare you, though," he said, returning to the previous subject. "They've been quiet all winter, and we're pretty sure they go up in the mountains to hibernate, then come back down in the valley once it warms up. You'll be safe. I'll be with you at night and you're not to go wandering by yourself otherwise. None of the nonsense you did at Aldeburke."

Ophele was glad her back was to him. Of course, he would be here at night. This was his house. Their house. His bed. And now that there was a bed again, did that mean he would want to…?

"Promise," the duke said sternly. "No wandering off."

"I won't, I promise," she said, trying not to look at the bed. The bodice of her gown drew tight and she carefully tugged at her kirtle, lining up the jeweled neckline to neatly follow the edge of the overdress. Behind her, the duke stood, and she tilted her head back. "Does my hair look all right? There was no mirror and it's still a little wet…"

"It looks fine. I don't think we'll do this every night," he said, looking down at her thoughtfully. "Much as my men would like to see a real lady at table. Up you get."

And he swept her off her feet, never minding any crumples in her dress. Ophele squawked.

"You don't have to, I'm wearing my slippers, see?"

"So you can lose them in the mud?" he replied, looking at the dainty blue slippers. The cottage door banged shut behind them and he stepped out into a cool violet dusk, with torches lining the lane from the cottages to the cookhouse. A few men were hurrying in that direction and paused to bow, eyes popping. Ophele nodded, feeling dreadfully conspicuous.

"When will there be roads?" she asked, remembering the firelight conversations she had overheard on the journey. She felt him stiffen and hastened to add, "I don't mean it like that. I mean—sometimes I heard you talking about it with Sir Edemir and Sir Tounot and everyone, and I was interested, so I wondered—"

"They'll start laying real road in a few months," he replied. "It's trickier than you think, you can't just throw stones in the mud." It was hard to tell whether he was offended or not; pressed against his chest, she could only see the square line of his jaw and the fringe of surprisingly long black eyelashes. "But we'll begin as we mean to go on. We don't want the roads flooding, so we'll plan for runoff and put in drains, grade it properly, and so on."

She would have liked to know what *and so on* entailed, but the duke was already striding up the graveled path to the cookhouse doors, and when they stepped inside it was like walking onto a stage, a place filled with staring eyes and a sudden and profound silence. The cookhouse was large and echoing, with rows of long tables extending far into torchlit gloom, and every table was filled with rough-looking men staring at her. The pungent miasma of unwashed male struck her even from the doorway, but she would never let such a thing show in her face.

The duke's hand pressed behind her, as if he sensed she wanted to retreat right back out the door.

"I'm glad to see all of you," he said, projecting his voice all the way to the back of the hall. "I've already spoken with Genon, and he told me not one of you buggers managed to get yourself killed while I was gone."

There was a low ripple of laughter.

"I won't keep you from your meat, but I will remind you to mind your manners before your new lady. Ophele, Daughter of the House of Agnephus, Princess of Argence, as was. Now my wife, the Duchess of Andelin. You'll give her your oaths tomorrow."

This was where she should speak. Ophele swallowed, but all those eyes were looking at her and suddenly her mind was blank as sticky heat blazed along her hairline. A lady's first care was the comfort of others. A lady should be gracious. A lady offered honors to those who deserved it, and these men surely did. But it felt as if her breath was stopped in her throat and her tongue was rooted to the roof of her mouth in abject terror.

"Eat," said the duke, as if nothing had happened, and Ophele's ears burned as he led her through the rows of tables. There was no high table, like there had been at the wedding feast, but toward the middle of the room, some men were budging over to make a space. It was hard to climb over a bench in long skirts.

"Welcome, my lady," said one of them, and she nodded, trying to smile. They all must be soldiers; most of them bore visible scars, and there was a much higher than average number of missing appendages, from ears to hands to whole arms.

"Thank you," she said, as one handed her a bowl of bread rolls. It was a little easier to speak in a small group, but heads were still turning up and down the rows on either side of her. The duke had not been exaggerating, there wasn't a single other woman in sight.

"This is Josue Orris," said His Grace, gesturing to the man who had handed her the bread. "He has charge of the hunters."

As he spoke, he was heaping meat, bread, and spoonfuls of green things onto her plate, and Ophele looked from the dripping red joints to Josue, who laughed.

"Aye, though I probably didn't kill that one personally, Your Grace," he said, bowing his head. He had the flat, burring accent of the Midland Empire.

"Thank you, all the same," she said, looking uncertainly away as the duke sliced her meat for her. It had never occurred to her that they would be lacking something as basic as utensils, but all the men nearby were tearing into their food using only fingers and belt knives. She was fairly sure both methods were forbidden to ladies.

"How is the hunting?" asked the duke.

"Better. Fatter game since the last frost, though we've been trying to go easy, let them graze before we run them to sinew," answered the hunter.

The duke grunted. "The first wagon of pigs should be arriving in a few months. That ought to help."

"With respect, Your Grace, I'd keep them penned up and domestic, you haven't seen the tuskers in these woods," said Josue. "Big as cows. We'd be eating one of those fu—things for days, if we could kill it."

Ophele nibbled on a bit of bread, wondering what word started with *fu-* that they were so reluctant to say in front of her.

"We were planning to coordinate a few hunts, if we could borrow some men," said the man next to Josue. "It's no fish story, there would be three hundred pounds of meat on just one of those boars. But it's not something one man ought to tackle by himself."

This was fascinating. Ophele had never considered how her food came to the table, much less how that small miracle fit into the creation of a town. For weeks she had been listening to the duke and his knights plan how they would build the town, from the walls to the herds to the drains, and it made her wonder who had built Aldeburke, who had planned it, how all that stone and glass and plaster had become a house.

These men had built everything here. The benches. The tables. The two stone hearths, blazing away at either end of the room. It was such a monumental undertaking, and she wanted to know all about it, every bit of it. She wanted to help, if she could. Even if it was only in a small way…

The sounds of their voices faded away as she drifted into the dream, and then into a doze, her head drooping over her plate.

"…wife home," said a deep voice close by, and she lifted her head, blinking owlishly.

"Oh, I beg your pardon." She looked around, trying to shake the fuzz out of her head. For some reason she thought she had fallen asleep on horseback again. "I'm sorry."

"It's time we left." The duke caught her elbow and lifted her over the bench entirely, minding her long skirts as he set her back down. "Good night, lads. Go easy on the ale, I'll make you work it off tomorrow."

"Good night," Ophele said over his shoulder. "We don't have to go," she added, looking up at the duke as he strode toward the doors of the cookhouse, opened to admit the cool night breeze.

"You were falling asleep in your seat, Princess." He didn't sound annoyed. Outside, he lifted her up into his arms again, his boots crunching down the gravel path to the lane. "Besides, the wine is flowing, and they'll soon be in their cups. It's no place for a lady."

Would he take her to the cottage and then go back to the cookhouse himself? Or would he stay? Heat washed through her, reddening her cheeks, and she was glad the darkness hid her face. It hadn't hurt at all, that night in Granholme. She had liked it. He had been so tender, so passionate, but then the assassin had come, and ever since, he looked at her as if she were his enemy.

What if that was what he wanted, though? Should she ask? Should she try to apologize for her father, as little as that would mean? The duke was silent, carrying her up to his cottage. Its front window glowed golden from the oil lamp she had forgotten to blow out, and it didn't look so bad like that. It looked like a home.

"Stand still, I'll unlace you." Once inside, he set her down gently. "We'll put this in storage tomorrow, and find another trunk for your things. If there's something you need that you don't have, tell me."

"I will." His hands moved over her back and she lowered her head, standing perfectly still. She remembered how he had pushed his face into her hand like a huge dog, and that look in his black eyes, and...why had he done that, if he hated her? How could she bear it if he touched her again tonight, and then pushed her away in the morning?

Silently, he removed her overdress, hanging it over the back of a chair. His hands settled on her shoulders, such big, warm hands, his rough thumbs gliding over her skin to undo the fastenings of her kirtle. It slid off her body in a whisper of silk, and he laid it with the overdress. For a moment, she was sure she would feel his lips on the back of her neck, and even imagined she felt his breath, a tickling warmth against her skin.

"I'll sleep on the floor." He said into the silence, low. "Go to bed, Princess."

"Oh. Oh, but...but no, it's your bed," she stammered, turning to look up at him. His expression was unreadable. "You'll get cold, and...you don't have to sleep on the floor."

"No," he said quietly. "It's too soon for children."

She had forgotten that. Of course. Of course, that was what she was for. That was why he had married her, to have children with the Emperor's blood. In time he would touch her again, but only to get a child in her. This was what he wanted from her. This was *all* he wanted from her.

"You don't have to do that," she said through the tightness of her throat. "It's your bed, too. I can sleep on the edge. I don't take up much room at all, I've slept in very small spaces. You'll get sick if you sleep on the floor."

There was a peculiar look on his face.

"No. Go to bed," he said, turning his back. "Don't argue with me."

And that was that. He couldn't stand her enough to sleep beside her, but soon enough he would put a child in her. Silently, she turned away to slip under the blankets. The mattress was filled with lumpy wool, but it was soft, even if the bed was so big she felt like a single potato bumping around in a very large barrel.

She didn't look at him as he laid down the same bedroll he'd been using for more than a month, but she heard the rushes rustling under him as he stretched out. There was barely enough room for him to lie down in the small room.

"If you wake up and hear something outside, don't be afraid." His voice rumbled from the dark. The coals in the hearth had burned down, and there was only the faintest glimmer of starlight through the cracks in the shutters. "It'll be one of the lads. There's always a guard on this house, watching every window and door."

"All right."

Despair would have been easy. And for a time, she indulged it, and let the tears streak her cheeks in silence, well-practiced after many years of soundless weeping. But Ophele's mind was a busy place, and her life had never been her own. No matter how limited her options, no matter how cramped her prison, she had never been able to stop seeking a way out. A pattern she might exploit. A solution to the problem.

The Will Immanent said there was a purpose to everything, especially in this imperfect creation. Purpose was the gift of imperfection. The divine world was perfect, flawlessly ordered, but in a perfect world there was no purpose, no reason to learn, to work, to grow. There might be debts owed in an imperfect world, but they could be paid. An imperfect world was a work in progress. An imperfect world could be changed.

She could change it, if she was brave.

CHAPTER 6 – A POISONED SWEET

His wife did look as if she could fit in very small spaces.

Remin woke up early his first morning back in the Andelin, when the outlines of his furnishings were just visible in the morning gloom. A cottage floor was an improvement over the side of the road, but he grimaced as he sat up, rubbing the back of his neck. For a moment, he wondered if he'd overindulged the night before, but then he spotted the small shape in the middle of his bed.

The princess was a nester. Even with the whole wide bed to stretch out in, she was curled up in the center, hugging a pillow and burrowed into the blankets so only the top of her head showed. The Emperor's daughter, sleeping in his bed at the far end of the empire. Alone.

This was what he had wanted.

There was a small washstand next to the hearth, and he took the opportunity to strip down and wash, then brushed his teeth. He had long waged an internal debate between fashion and practicality; he had been born the son of a duke, but he had grown up as something worse than a peasant; more like a particularly insidious species of vermin that the Emperor just couldn't kill. The affectations of nobility most often felt like a waste of time—for example, shaving—but people set store by appearances. One of the reasons he had brought his wife to Tresingale was to begin civilizing the place.

Beginning with himself.

Grumbling inside, Remin shaved. They needed a public bath. There were such places in the capital, everything from practical and minimalist facilities for peasants to luxurious places where nobles met to socialize and connive while they were scrubbed, massaged, and beautified. The princess was too polite to show it, but the stink from his men last night had singed his own nostrils, never mind what it must have done to her aristocratic little nose.

Maybe he'd bump the bathhouse up a few spaces on the list of priorities. Genon had been nagging about personal hygiene for months anyway.

Tugging a fresh shirt and pair of leather breeches on, Remin went to wake the princess, who generally needed some time before she was sensible. He had applauded himself for his restraint the night before, but as soon as she sat up, foggy-eyed and disheveled, with her chemise slipping off one slim bare shoulder, it all came roaring back.

"…time izzit?" she mumbled, squinting into the middle distance.

"Almost dawn." Remin's jaw tightened. Why did she have to look like that? He refused to confuse himself or her any further. They had a political marriage, and he knew he was already dangerously soft-hearted toward her, or her tears wouldn't make him feel like he deserved nothing more than a hanging. "Get up and get dressed."

"Mmm." She covered her mouth with the back of her hand, yawning, and he turned away to build a fire so he wouldn't forget himself.

The thing about traitors and spies was that one had to consider the work from their point of view. Assassins were lightning bolts, but traitors and spies were chameleons, blending in, biding their time, wearing the face of a trusted friend, servant, or sweetheart. He would rather face a hundred assassins than one spy. He had never once felt guilty for killing an assassin. Killing a spy who wore the face of a friend was something that haunted.

Remin was sure that traitors didn't think about their treachery every moment of the day. They couldn't; no one could live that way. Those moments of friendship, affection, and trust had to be real, part of a complex web of manipulation and—he was sure—cognitive dissonance from the traitor. They would do whatever it took to get close and stay close, and then await their orders. It might be days, weeks, or even years, but the order would come.

It had always come. He knew how these things worked. He was a fool if he let himself forget it.

"Usually we go to the cookhouse for something to eat in the morning," he said as he lit the kindling and slowly added larger branches to the blaze. "Food isn't allowed in the cottages to minimize vermin, though you'll still hear field mice in the thatching. Between Wen and Genon, we mostly keep them at bay, but I hope you're not afraid—"

He glanced back to see if the temptress was dressed yet and stopped talking.

She was asleep.

Sitting up. Her elbow on her knee and her chin propped on her hand, with her eyes closed and the curves of her breasts plainly showing at the neck of her chemise. Through her parted lips, she was very softly snoring.

This sort of thing was why he had to lecture himself about assassins and spies. Bending, he shook her shoulder, trying to keep the corner of his mouth from twitching. This was not funny. It was not cute.

"Wake up."

She sucked in a breath and her eyes opened up wide.

"I'm awake."

"Lies," he said, pulling her bodily out of bed. He had seen her do that trick before, her eyes would slam shut again just as quickly. "Get dressed."

A few minutes later, the realization that there was nothing like a privy in the cottage and the Duchess of Andelin could hardly go in the bushes thoroughly woke them both up, and Remin once again regretted the lack of a maid.

It was time to consider more fixed sanitation facilities anyway.

"Don't be sorry, it's not your fault," he said gruffly, closing the door of the cottage behind them. He genuinely didn't mean to keep embarrassing her this way.

His decision to bring her to the valley had not been entirely spiteful. Even a man like Miche didn't know all the things that were needful for a woman's comfort, and Remin had thought the Emperor's daughter should face a little deprivation. He had expected her to tell him—often, loudly, and at length—exactly what was lacking. Never in his wildest dreams had he imagined the daughter of Emperor Bastin Agnephus would look at a woolly bed in a crofter's cottage and tell him she could curl up smaller.

In every other way, though, she perfectly suited his purposes. She looked like a shepherdess from a pretty pastoral painting in her green wool gown, even if she was a little red in the face, and the men outside were falling all over themselves to doff their caps and bow.

"Good morning, Your Grace."

"Morning, m'lady."

"Good morning," she said, looking a little startled, but nodded graciously and left them staring, with very foolish expressions.

This was the other reason he had brought her here, over the objections of the Duke of Ereguil. After years of war and questionable female companionship, his men badly needed civilizing. He wanted to give them the first opportunity to settle his lands. He wanted the veterans of the Vallethi War to send for their wives, their children, their sweethearts and their extended families, and spread out across the valley for which they had bled. They had earned it. But right now, Tresingale was a rough and dangerous place, and someone had to be the first.

If the Duke of Andelin was willing to bring the Emperor's sacred daughter to the valley, then surely it was safe to bring their own families.

It was going to be a little rough for the princess, though.

"Get out of me kitchen and stop nibblin' at me cheese before I take a cleaver to ye!" Wen the cook shouted as Remin entered the kitchen. Where Genon was massive, Wen was just fat. Enormously fat. The fact that he could fit in tiny camp kitchens seemed to defy all natural laws of space and physics, and Remin's personal theory was that Wen's bulk was just more fungible than the average person's. He didn't squeeze into tight spaces so much as ooze. "Shiftless bastard, ye'll do without bread today and see whether ye go filching my fine aged cheddar, ye skiving arse—"

At the far end of the galley-style kitchen, a boy vanished out the door, accompanied by the cook's curses.

"Wen. Wen. Wen!" Remin raised his voice and fought the urge to cover the princess's ears. Taming Wen was going to be her version of crossing the Brede. "Watch your tongue."

The cook drew a breath as if he were about to treat His Grace to a similar diatribe, but then he spotted the princess. His eyes narrowed.

"So," he said, inflating like a frog. "It begins."

"My wife," Remin warned. "This is Princess Ophele, who is now your duchess."

"I don't care if she's now me bloomin' Empress. I told ye, I won't have women in me kitchen. I'll quit." Wen slapped a grubby wet towel onto the counter as if to punctuate the point. "I will quit. Next thing she'll be asking for pudding and saying where's the coriander and I won't have it, I tell ye, I won't have it. I do good plain cooking me *own* way."

"She's not here to cook," Remin growled. "I told you yesterday I would be bringing her by so you could pay your respects."

"Oh aye, an honor," said the cook, glaring. "Then what's Her Highness got to do with me, eh?"

"Princess, sometimes you'll come here to fetch lunch for the men." Though Remin was reconsidering the wisdom of this course. "Wen will have it packed up in a basket."

"Will I get lunch, too?" she asked anxiously, so soft he wasn't entirely sure he had heard her right.

"Of course you will," he said, insulted. Did she think he planned to starve her? "Wen will have something fit for a lady, as thanks for saving him a walk."

"In a pig's—" The cook began, but cut himself off at Remin's warning glare. The duke was willing to tolerate certain liberties from his men, as long as they did their work well, but his tolerance only went so far.

"The princess doesn't need to hear your filth, Wen."

"Then why'd ye bring her to me, then," the cook grumbled, but finally, grudgingly, bowed. "Pleased to make your acquaintance, m'lady. Name's Wen. Just Wen. Consider me hands your own, unless you ask for bleeding pudding."

"Pleased to meet you," the princess said a little faintly, looking at him as if he were a bomb that might go off. But she was trying; she had taken Remin's advice about offering a few personal words to each person she met to heart. "Thank you for supper. Last night, I mean. The bread was good."

"Aye, aye, glad to hear it. Ye're not to come in me kitchen." Wen jabbed an enormous finger at her. "Ye want something, ye stand in the doorway and wait 'til I stop chopping. Princess or no princess, never talk to me when I've a knife in me hand, understand?"

She nodded silently, round-eyed. Imagining this scene with the haughty princess he had expected to retrieve from Aldeburke had entertained Remin no end, but this was like watching someone shout at a kitten.

"Breakfast, Wen," he said flatly. The sun hadn't even cleared the horizon yet and everything was much more complicated than he expected.

* * *

"We'll be at the south side of the wall," said Sir Miche later that morning, walking south beside Ophele along the lane to the wall. The maids at Aldeburke had sighed over Sir Miche in the few days he was there, and loudly enough for even Ophele to hear about it; he was very, very beautiful, with long golden hair and light hazel eyes, seven or eight years older than the duke. "You might have seen it on the way in, they finished almost a mile of wall while we were gone. Eventually it'll be the base for a new bridge over the Brede, they've already finished one caisson and are working on the footings."

"What's a caisson?"

"A wall that holds back the river, basically." Sir Miche nudged her around a mud puddle. The road was almost all mud, but it was very picturesque otherwise, with the sun casting a golden light over green hills and the birds singing their morning songs. "Not the sort of thing that a lot of ignorant soldiers can tackle, I assure you. We're just laborers for the experts."

"What do you need me to do?" she asked.

"Fetch and carry, though I beg your pardon for saying it. Normally the sort of thing we'd have squires to do, or pages, but we're short of both and it's a waste to have a grown man doing such work. Just having someone to haul water will save them coming off the wall or up out of the ditch for a drink."

Ophele pondered this. "That will really be helpful?"

"Every foot we can add to the wall matters." Sir Miche glanced down at her. "Did Rem tell you about some of the…problems we have in the valley?"

"Wolf demons?"

"Oh, thank the stars." He heaved an exaggerated sigh of relief, hand over his heart, and made her giggle. "Rem's spreading the word about the beasties through the Empire now, to dissuade some of the settlers, but now all the scholars are curious and the only thing worse than a rabble of farmers is a passel of academics from the Tower. But it's no joke to us, I'm afraid."

"Keeping the hungry things out," she guessed, and he nodded.

"We have a palisade coming down from the north, but stranglers don't think much of a wooden fence. It has to be stone, and stone takes time. We're lucky we've got the river on two sides. That gives us nine miles of stone wall to build, about five and a half running north to south, and four miles east-west. In a few months, hopefully we'll join up with the north wall crew. But don't be scared," he added quickly. "We've been in this valley for seven years, and contending with the beasties for almost half of that. We know what we're about."

The only thing she could do was trust him when he said that. But Ophele still looked over the hills to the distant mountains and the tangled forest at their feet, where the hungry things were, and wondered if she was afraid.

The wall itself was amazing. She was used to the almost decorative walls of Aldeburke, fine white plaster and short enough that she could have climbed over them by herself, if she wanted to. The stone wall cutting through stands of black pine had to be at least twenty feet tall, with the dark water of the Brede flowing behind it at the foot of a steep bank.

It was early enough that the work crews were still gathering, brawny stonemasons and mortarmen, an engineer named Guisse who was very eager to explain absolutely everything, and an ever-increasing number of laborers whose task was to dig and haul stone. The wall was covered with wooden scaffolding, ladders, pulleys, and ropes, and several blacksmiths were on hand to repair and cast new metal parts as needed.

Before work began, Sir Miche gathered them all together.

"Most of you were introduced to Her Grace last night," he began, suddenly all business and looking from one man to the next as if he were memorizing faces. "To show you how seriously His Grace is taking the construction of this wall, he has asked his lady to lend her own fair hands to help. You will never in this life have such an honor again. I trust you will be appropriately humbled."

Deeply uncomfortable under the weight of so many eyes, Ophele wished she at least had a crown or something. She felt a very poor specimen of the princess variety.

But at least Sir Miche didn't expect her to make a speech. He clapped his hands and sent them off to work, then bent down to mutter, "Don't worry, they're as scared of you as you are of them."

That startled her into a laugh, and she quickly covered her mouth with her hand, giggling. He grinned, dimples flickering in his cheeks.

"Come, I'll show you where the well is. We didn't mean to dig one, actually, we just hit bedrock and up came the water. Did Rem already warn you to stay away from the wall and the ditch?"

"Yes." All through breakfast.

"Then I won't belabor the point. But you're to be careful, for the men's sake if not your own, and if you're not sure of anything, I'll always be in shouting distance. And don't be climbing things," he added with a flicker of humor, reminding her that he had been there that day in Aldeburke, when the duke plucked her out of a fir tree.

A proper princess should be horrified by this. It was squires' work, the lowest kind of labor, so far beneath her that she should be unaware of its existence. And it was also much harder than she expected. Ophele had to stand nearly on tiptoe to push the windlass on the well, and after five buckets she was puffing and reminding herself that thirteen year-old boys did this work. Boys that wanted to be knights, true, but still. She was stronger than a thirteen year-old boy, surely.

There were nearly a hundred men working on just this section of the wall, and she could see the construction process in all its stages. At the furthest end were the excavators, digging all the way down to the bedrock to give the wall an unshakable footing. From there came the men with mortar and stone, building a thick shell of carefully cut and fitted blocks that would rise up twenty-some feet, with a hollow space in the middle to be filled with a thick, chalky powder and crushed stones.

Wagons creaked back and forth from the wall to the quarry to the west, oxen groaning as they trundled away, and Ophele was careful to stay out of their path as she set down the buckets where Sir Miche had told her and then waited to be told what else to do.

And waited.

And waited.

The men didn't refuse to drink the water she had brought for them, but an hour passed before she realized that no one was going to ask the Duchess of Andelin to fetch a shovel for him. She didn't think they were being rude. They said thank you every time they came for a dipper of water, drank nervously, bowed, and then hurried back to their work. And she didn't want to bother Sir Miche; he was working as hard as any of them, stripped to the waist and pitching in with a shovel at the far end of the trench.

"Is there anything else I can do?" she asked the next man who came to drink, reminding herself to speak up, as the duke so often admonished her.

"Aye? That is, no, lady, I'm fine," he said, looking startled. "Very grateful for your help. Thankee."

And he was gone, as if a wolf demon were on his heels.

She sighed and moved to the shade of a nearby oak tree, sitting down on a high root to watch.

Remember your rank, the duke had admonished her as he left her with Sir Miche that morning. *Don't let them order you about.* It looked as if that would not be the problem. Sir Miche was right, what she was doing wasn't useless; so many men went through water buckets remarkably fast, and when there were only two full buckets left, she went to refill the rest, picking her way down the hillside to the well, which stood on a paved platform overlooking the river, sheltered by tall trees.

Drop the bucket. Crank the windlass. She tried carrying two buckets at once up the hill, but a wooden bucket filled with water was surprisingly heavy, so she went back and forth eight times, puffing. They would go through them faster as the day warmed, and her busy brain fastened on this problem, for lack of anything else to do.

There were three places where the men came down from the wall. There were only two ways they came out of the deep part of the trench. It was convenient for her to put all the buckets together in one place, but if it were about her convenience, she would have left the buckets by the well. The stated objective, as defined by Sir Miche, was to reduce the amount of time the men spent off the scaffolding or out of the trench.

"Your buckets are there," she told the next man who came down from the wall, pointing to the three buckets she had placed in the shadow of a nearby lilac bush.

"Ah, thank you, lady," he said, and inwardly she breathed a sigh of relief. It might have been a small thing, but she had worried he might scold her for changing something, or that there might have been a reason she had overlooked for the original placement of the buckets.

The diggers seemed to go through water faster, so she took away one of the masons' buckets and moved it down by the trench, then hurried to fill the buckets for the blacksmiths. She liked problems of this sort. Someone on the wall dropped his trowel as she was passing, so she dared to approach the scaffolding, stretching on tiptoe to hand it back to him.

"Sorry, m'lady, thank you very much," he said, tugging his forelock. He had an eyepatch over his right eye, a lanky man as brown as a bean and just as stringy.

"It's no trouble," she said, as awkwardly as he, but then he gave her a crooked smile and she smiled back, and hurried away to gather her empty buckets with a lighter heart. That was one man who hadn't had to get off the wall.

Putting the filled buckets back in their new configuration, Ophele went to stand under her oak tree again, her large, watchful eyes open, taking everything in.

* * *

"There's about a hundred of them, Your Grace," said Remin's scout. Eude was still winded from his fast ride back to Tresingale, a short and slightly built man who was born to lurk. In Remin's absence, Jinmin had dispatched scouts and trackers to locate the bandits, and reports had been coming in for the last week.

They were not all bad, but they weren't good, either. The number was less than originally supposed, but a hundred men was a formidable force. On the north side of town, Remin had resurrected his old commander's tent and set up a worktable, just as it had been through all the long years of the war. He even had his maps rolled up in their usual corner, stored in oilskin cases and neatly labeled.

"They made winter camp in the Veralde Forest." The scout pointed to the place on the map. "I saw a lot of old Vallethi army insignia."

"That's a lot of men to be living off the land," remarked Bram, who had come in from the Gellege Bridge early that morning. All of Remin's knights had some degree of tactical genius, or they would never have become knights at all, but Bram of Lisle was uniquely attentive to practicalities. A hundred men would clear a forest of game inside a month.

"They cleaned up the camp some, sir, but we found this." Eude held up the remains of a rough burlap bag, burned in the middle but whole enough to get an idea of size. "There were many more like it. Near their cooking pit."

"A grain sack," said Remin, his jaw tightening. Men living as fugitives in a forest should not have sacks of grain. Men living as fugitives in a forest should not have access to trade. Men living in a forest over a long, bitter winter should have been eating each other's frozen carcasses by the new year.

Which meant someone was supplying them.

"The nearest villages are Ferrede and Meinhem," said Bram, tapping each with a fingertip. "Ferrede is three or four days away, if I remember right. Meinhem, nearer a week."

The scandalmongers of the Empire claimed that Remin had put every man, woman, and child living in the valley to the sword, to make sure no one loyal to Valleth remained. He had not. But if he had, he would not currently be having this problem.

"I'll leave that to you, Bram," he said after a moment. "Go watch the villages, see who goes in and out. Stop any wagons you see on the road. Take eight men."

Bram nodded. He always reminded Remin of a rather moth-eaten ferret, with button-black eyes, a narrow, pockmarked face, and long black hair, peppered with gray.

"Where are they now, Eude?"

"About ten days out, Your Grace. Marching south-southeast on foot. Mostly spears and clubs, but I saw some swords and about two dozen bows."

The tent was silent as they let him think. Remin knew every ripple and fold of the valley; he had been riding it for seven years and had an excellent memory. He wasn't worried about dispatching a mob of deserters, though the fact that they were men of military experience shouldn't be taken lightly. The greater concern was that every man he sent away from Tresingale was leaving some necessary work unfinished. If the walls were delayed, then they would be increasing night watches for Andelin devils; if the spring planting was delayed, then they might be hungry, come winter. And more than anything, he resented having to take his war horses from their plows.

"I'll lead a force out tomorrow afternoon," he said finally. "We're not going to sit and wait for them to come to us. They're in rough, rocky hills, with a lot of choke points. We'll intercept them when they're moving in column and hit them with our archers, then send in some horsemen to mop up. How many can we spare, Auber?"

"Dozen horses at most, unless you don't mind stopping some major projects. Most of them are doing draft work."

"Tounot, pull some archers out of their work details today, and give them some practice time." Remin scowled ferociously. "Edemir, report to me later about how we can minimize the impact on planting and wall building, but I'm willing to give up a few acres of planting before we lose a foot of wall."

These were familiar problems, too much to do and not enough resources, and not even gold could buy a solution to everything. Between grudging rewards from the Emperor and tribute from Valleth, Remin had more money than he knew what to do with. The thing he was lacking was time. Finding and securing the experts and supplies he needed didn't happen overnight, much less transporting them to the valley. By late summer, Tresingale would be bursting with men and materiel, but they would have to survive that long, first.

He would take Juste, Huber, and Jinmin along. Sir Jinmin of Oskerre was a stolid man of nearly forty who went about his work on a battlefield the same way he went with his belt knife at dinner. A knight on horse was worth twenty bandits. A Jinmin of Oskerre was worth forty.

After he dispatched more scouts under Eude's command, Remin reviewed the rest of his plans with his knights, to make sure nothing was overlooked. The only remaining trouble was what he would do with the people supplying the bandits. It might not be the whole village; it could be only two or three people who had taken it upon themselves to commit treason. The loyalties of the Andelin commonfolk were complicated. After a century of war, they might regard themselves as citizens of either Valleth or the Empire.

But he had offered them amnesty. He had offered to escort anyone who considered themselves citizens of Valleth to the border, and even gave them a few silvers to help them on their way. Someone had refused that offer and then stabbed him in the back.

Remin Grimjaw had no mercy for traitors.

For now, he handed the problem over to the back of his mind and went to have a look at the spring planting.

It gladdened his heart to see the furrows of rich, dark earth stretching away on the north side of town, acres of fresh-turned soil that would soon sprout, green and living. There were small dots in the distance, men and horses plowing and seeding, singing out their commands to the beasts under Auber's experienced eye.

"Looks good, doesn't it?" Auber asked, trotted his bay over to stand by Remin's warhorse. They only had a few horses to spare for riding, but the quantity of acreage would have made it impossible for Auber to manage on his own feet. "We've got about sixty acres plowed and forty planted, so far. Based on Edemir's figures, that ought to see us through the winter comfortably. I agree with the men, though, we ought to plant the carrots and such inside the wall. Birds are already stealing seed and next it will be deer in the carrots."

The wooden palisade on the north side of town was a stopgap measure. Both men glanced at it automatically, a ten-foot wall of heavy logs planted upright, spiked on the top and currently three miles long. It would keep deer out, but stranglers would go up and over it as easy as a ladder.

Deer. Ghouls. Stranglers. Demon wolves, regular wolves, human wolves, traitorous villagers and the coming winter and no doubt a host of other hazards that Remin hadn't even conceived. It was overwhelming, if one started a list.

"You want a turn with the plow, Rem?" Auber glanced at him sidelong, and Remin decided he would.

"Let's see if you beat me this time," he said, kicking his horse into a gallop toward the nearest plowman and grinning as Auber swore and raced after him.

Of course, Auber was a farmer's son and had taken his first toddling steps behind a plow, so the contest wasn't exactly fair. But it was nearly time for the noon meal and the men welcomed any excuse to stop, much less the treat of another contest between the Duke of Andelin and Sir Auber Conbour.

"First to five?" Auber handed his horse to one of the men nearby. "And the row doesn't count if it looks like a drunkard plowed it."

"That only happened one time," Remin protested, but he didn't mind the good-natured mockery. Manual labor sounded like just what he needed. A few minutes later, Remin and Auber were standing at the end of their respective rows, plows and reins in hand, waiting as the spectators excitedly counted them down.

"Gee up, there!" Remin shouted, starting his horse off with a jolt. Until last year, he had never touched a plow in his life. It was hard work; the soil of the valley was rich, but wet and heavy, and the muscles in his shoulders and back burned pleasantly as he pushed the nose of the plow down, dragged forward by the horse in front of him. The soil rolled up and outward like the wake of a ship, and the primal smell of fresh earth filled his nose.

"One!" shouted Auber distantly, to cheers from the spectators, who had already placed their bets. The odds heavily favored Auber.

"One!" Remin shouted back, clicking his tongue to get the horse to turn at the end of the row. He reset himself, pushed the plow into position, and called again, "Gee up, there!"

Five rows were a solid bit of work, and he was sweating when he was done, scarcely twenty seconds after Auber. But his rows weren't bad at all, following the curve of the hillside, and there was quiet satisfaction in this work that had been lacking even when the warlords of Valleth had fallen at his feet.

"I keep telling you, you don't have to push the plow down so hard," Auber said, mopping his sweaty face with a handkerchief. Even years of campaigning hadn't browned his skin, and he turned red under the slightest exertion. "We're planting wheat, not digging a mine."

"When I plow a furrow, the earth will never forget it," Remin said gravely, to the sniggers of the listening men, who received all vulgarities with the delight of twelve year-old boys.

Remin rode the length of Tresingale twice that afternoon, checking on his prized breeding rams, the progress of the wooden palisade, two sites where wells were being dug, and then met his town planner on top of the east gatehouse to look at the town site. Nore Ffloce was a twitchy, excitable man with the angular limbs of a grasshopper, but he had an eclectic experience that was worth a little twitching.

"You can see we have the stakes up to mark the first two streets, Your Grace," he said, holding up an enormous parchment so Remin could see the beautifully visualized depiction of a future Tresingale, with artisans' quarters, shops, and houses, a temple, and a market square that Remin could already imagine decorated for the midsummer Turning of the Stars.

The grubby reality was a bunch of stout sticks and string in the mud, like a Bhumi wind graveyard.

"What about the flooding around the back of the temple site?" Remin asked, pointing to the large stagnant pool that the men called Mosquito Pond.

"Ah, we have been working on the drainage system, look here, Your Grace," Nore said, as if he had been dying for Remin to ask. Rapidly, he shuffled through his parchment. "It's fortunate that we've had a year to observe the troublesome areas, I've modeled your sewage system on the city of Indhigi, in Daitia…"

Even the drains were fascinating. Remin listened, asked questions, and then left to bolt down the noon meal and head to the forest with his hunters, to see if they might get a look at a boar. None deigned to make an appearance, but they did hear some distant grunting from deep in the trees that was either an enormous boar or a very localized earthquake.

By late afternoon, he had postponed going to look at the wall for long enough. It was visibly longer than it had been even the day before, but Remin only watched the work from a distance. He didn't want to distract his men, who were doing hazardous work in high places, and the less he saw of his wife, the better.

Leaning over his saddle, he watched as the earth was shifted and stones moved into their places, one backbreaking rock at a time. The figure in green scampering past the scaffolding might not even have been the princess. From this distance it was impossible to tell who was who.

It wasn't like he was looking for her, anyway.

* * *

There was a very slight incline on the lane into town. Ophele hadn't noticed it at all that morning, but she was sure she could have calculated the exact angle that evening, just from the pitch of the shrieking in her legs.

"All right, Your Highness?" asked Sir Miche beside her. He was unspeakably filthy from digging all day, with his muddy shirt slung over one shoulder and his sword slung over the other.

She nodded. She was tired, but complaining about it wouldn't change anything, except that maybe they wouldn't let her help anymore.

"If you ever need to rest, say so," he said, eying her critically. "You've already done more than anyone should expect."

Exactly how low were their expectations? She had filled buckets with water. Helpful, yes, but minstrels would never sing songs of it.

"I'm all right," she said. "But you don't…mind? Digging all day? You're a knight and everything."

"You're a princess and everything," he noted, with a wry twist of his mouth. "Still not sure I like watching you sweat. But I like work, myself, even if it's digging. It's clean work. That was Rem's idea."

"What was?"

"This," he said, jerking his chin toward the valley. "Andelin's a poisoned sweet, just like all the Emperor's gifts. He gives Rem a knighthood, then orders him over the Brede. Gives him the valley, but it's filled with Vallethi demonspawn and deserters and who knows what else, and then he pardons a pack of criminals and sends them to settle it. No one would've blamed Rem if he just sold off what he could and retired to Capricia. But he wants a grand city right on the Brede, and he wants to give all of us a chance to build something instead of destroying it."

The last part buzzed right by her, unnoticed. Ophele was appalled.

"The Emperor sent…criminals?" she echoed.

"It's nothing to worry about, my lady. They'll never get across the river. Oi, Rem!" Sir Miche lifted a hand as they approached the cottage. The duke was coming out of the stables further down the street, looking almost as grimy as Sir Miche; his boots were black with soil and his jerkin was covered with burrs. "Wall's coming on well, thanks to your lady," Sir Miche said, according Ophele a sweeping bow.

"I'm glad she was useful." The duke didn't look at her. "Go into the house, wife, I need to speak with Miche. I'll be in in a moment."

She went. After the news about the criminals, she couldn't look him in the eye anyway. How was she ever going to pay him back if her father kept adding to the debt?

Was there any point in trying to write the Emperor a letter? Ask him to please stop being mean to her husband? No, her father had never given her any consideration before. The fact that she was now the wife of his enemy would not help her cause.

A poisoned sweet, like all the Emperor's gifts. She wondered if Sir Miche knew that *she* was one of those poisoned sweets, too. A princess that was no sort of princess at all, an honor that was a backhanded insult.

She was tired. Thinking about all of it now just made her...more tired. After a day sweating at the wall, she felt unspeakably grimy, but if she wanted a bath, she was going to have to heat water herself, and the wood wasn't going to set itself on fire. Groaning internally, she reached for the kindling box. There was a nice blaze going by the time the duke knocked at the door.

"Already started a fire?" He slid his jerkin off and hung it on the back of a chair. His white shirt was sticking to him with perspiration.

"I want a bath, please."

He gestured to the buckets by the door. "You can bathe whenever you like."

Ophele looked at them grimly. More buckets.

"Can you tell me where the well is?" She pushed herself back to her feet with a screech of quadriceps. "I can get the water myself."

"I'll go with you. Wait, look at me." The duke caught her elbow as she went by and tilted her face up to look at her, his eyes narrowing. "Your face is burned. Wear a hat tomorrow, we'll get one from the storehouse. And try to keep in the shade, as much as you can."

The noblewomen of the Empire were famous for their aristocratic pallor. He wouldn't want his princess to embarrass him with a peasant's tan. Ophele looked away. This was enough to *almost* make her angry, which was very difficult to do. She didn't mind working hard, but being rebuked for not looking regal enough afterward was too much.

"I have something to tell you anyway," he added as they walked to the well, behind the row of cottages at the top of a small hill. "You remember we heard about bandits in the area when we were in Trema? I'm going to have to go and deal with them. I'll be gone a few weeks."

Ophele was silent, absorbing this.

"You're not going to tell me to be careful?" he asked dryly.

"I do want you to be—"

"The men will be giving you their oaths tonight," he said, as if he hadn't heard her. Ophele shut her mouth and looked at her feet as he filled the buckets for her, cranking the big windlass. "You'll need to dress nicely after your bath. In future we'll do something more formal for those that mean to live in the valley, but I want everyone to make their oaths before I leave. You'll be safe, Miche will keep an eye on you."

A bear. She followed him back to the cottage, hauling her heavy pair of buckets. An angry bear, roaring away in front of his cave, and in the end all of his roaring meant *stay away*. Don't talk to me, don't bother me, don't come near me.

Putting water on to heat, she trudged back to the well with more buckets, and returned to find the angry bear naked at the washstand. Ophele's face instantly flamed and she almost dropped her buckets in her haste to turn her back.

"What are you doing?" he asked testily. "Come in and close the door. You're not a maiden anymore, Princess, we don't have time for your blushes. You'll have to get used to it."

Would she? Could she ever get used to this? His comment about her maidenhood struck her like a slap and she set her buckets down without looking at him, crouching by the fire to wait for her water to boil. This was just like back home, when all she could do under Lady Hurrell's bullying was to be small and quiet, like a mouse, and hope to go unnoticed. The duke scrubbed himself from head to toe, dunked his head in a bucket, and then shook his black hair like a dog.

"I'll be back soon," he said, pulling on a fresh shirt and clean breeches. "Be quick about your bath."

It was lukewarm at best. As she scrubbed, Ophele wondered that a man eighteen inches taller and two hundred pounds heavier than she could clean up in five minutes, while she took at least half an hour, most of it painstakingly soaping and rinsing sweat and stone dust out of her long hair. She was nowhere near ready when he knocked at the door.

"Wife?"

"Wait!" Maiden or no maiden, she still bolted for the bed and pulled on a fresh chemise that instantly clung to her soaked skin. And then she hesitated, her fingers knotting together as she looked at the door, because she wasn't ready yet and if he scolded her one more time she didn't think she could take it.

"Princess?"

"Come in," she said, as if to an executioner.

The duke ducked through the doorway and then stopped as suddenly as if he had struck a wall. He didn't speak. He just looked at her with those opaque, unreadable black eyes, and the room filled with a deep and dreadful silence, as if to make room to allow her to contemplate the totality of her failure. He looked at her for so long that Ophele wrapped her arms around herself nervously, her eyes on the floor. Lady Hurrell used to do this, too. When Ophele was in trouble, the lady would just sit there in silence, staring, letting the pressure build and build until Ophele didn't care *what* cruel thing the lady did as long as it happened and was over.

"We don't have any towels," she said at last, when she couldn't bear it any longer. "I had to wash my hair, it got all dusty, but it takes too long to dry. It's too long, I'm sorry, most noblewomen don't have their hair so long, I could cut—"

"No," he said instantly, and then blinked and seemed to shake himself. "No. I told you to tell me if you need something. I'll find some towels before I leave. Come, I'll help you with your hair."

"You'll…" The vision of the duke clutching her hairbrush was nearly as mind-boggling as the idea of him sewing tippets to her sleeves. "…help?"

"Yes. We're not cutting it. Come, show me what to do." Crossing the room, he pulled a blanket from the bed and wrapped it around her shoulders. "Here, you—cover up. Now, explain."

It was probably like brushing his horse to him, she told herself. A prized horse that he needed to tend so he could trot it out to be admired. But it was still surreal to have him stand by the hearth and brush one side of her hair while she combed the other, separating and untangling the long locks so the heat of the fire would dry them faster.

"That looks well enough," the duke said when they were done, shifting back from her so carefully that it was as if he thought he might catch fire if he so much as touched her. "Tell me if you need help with such things."

"All right," Ophele said to the floor, thoroughly bewildered and wishing he would just be hateful, if he hated her. At least then she would know what to expect and have no hope for anything different.

"Be quick," he said, striding to the doorway without looking back at her. "It's dangerous to keep a hungry man from his meal."

* * *

Any large gathering in Tresingale was a cause for concern.

With the exception of those on guard duty, every single person in town was assembled in the field behind the cookhouse, a ragged and somewhat mangy mob, worn from the day's labors. Even Wen the cook was standing in the doorway of the kitchen, his arms crossed over his chest and a ladle in one hand. Soldiers turned farmers, soldiers turned hunters, soldiers who had apprenticed themselves to the masters and craftsmen Remin had brought to the valley. There was even a literate few who were acting as Nore Ffloce's hands, and learning the science behind the building of a town.

But with so many people gathered, security was an issue, so the Knights of the Brede were present and impressive in their armor, standing at the perimeter of the crowd. Tounot and Edemir flanked the duke and his lady, and the cat-eyed Darri stood outside the circle of torches, watching for danger in the dark.

"All of you that have come to this valley, as soldiers or as builders, have already sworn an oath," began Jinmin, whose gravelly command voice could cut through any crowd. "As soon as you set foot on this side of the Brede, you swore to do no harm to the Duke of Andelin or any who have sworn loyalty to him. Tonight, you will extend that oath to his Duchess."

There was no cleric among them yet. Remin had already sent a request to the Holy City of Jaen, the seat of the Temple of the Stars. But these men would be standing under the stars when they made their oath, with all of the eyes of the glorious dead to witness.

"Kneel," said Jinmin, and sank to one knee himself, turning to face Ophele. He would swear another oath as a knight later, just as all of his brother knights had, but it was good to set an example. "With all the stars as witness…"

The men's voices echoed him, and Remin searched the faces in the crowd, looking for any who had refused to kneel, any who did not say the words. As more people came to the valley, it was likely that sooner or later one of them would be in the service of the Emperor. His wife's case was a complicated one: she might be a target for assassins, or she might be an assassin herself.

The princess herself didn't seem to know *where* to look, and for once, he could sympathize. Remin was dimly aware that she was wearing a red gown. He liked her hair. But in his mind's eye there was a vision of her standing by the fireplace with her chemise clinging wet and transparent, showing the shape of her breasts and her narrow waist and rounded hips. The sight had actually, literally, embarrassingly paralyzed him. It was as if his brain had temporarily ceased all nonessential function.

It was the first time that had ever happened to him. Just remembering it made the back of his neck feel hot.

He was *not* going to stand here picturing his wife's nipples while everyone in the valley was swearing to protect her honor.

"Say what you said to the knights," he murmured to her in an undertone. "Thank them for their courage and say you will try to learn from them. Promise to bring them honor as their lady. And speak up."

Among the nobility, elocution and oratory were considered fundamental subjects, usually taught by a tutor. There was no evidence that his wife had ever had a single lesson.

"Th-thank you," she began, looking terrified. Remin laid a hand on her back, which usually seemed to steady her, and she straightened her shoulders. "Thank you all for serving the duke so well. Especially those of you who fought with him. Now you're working to build this new place, and I want to thank you for that. As well. I hope to learn from your good example. I will do my best to bring honor to you. As duchess. Thank you."

This speech was probably only heard by the front two rows of men, but the virtue of a speaker who was petrified of their audience was that at least the speech was short. The men filed past their new duchess to go to their meal, doffing their caps and tugging their forelocks, and a few even offered her a bow and a smile, making her smile in return.

Remin's knights and officers stayed behind to make their own oaths, the same oaths that Miche and Tounot and the rest had already sworn, that night on the road to Granholme.

"Your Grace." Genon Hengest was last, and remained on one knee even after he had said his oath. He wasn't a knight, but Remin counted him their equal nonetheless. "I've served His Grace as herbman and surgeon for a long time, and will be honored to do the same for you. I know a young lady might be afraid or embarrassed to talk about such things with an old gargoyle like me, but I'll give you my oath to listen to any worry you might have, and never repeat what you say to anyone else. That includes your lummox of a husband."

The princess's eyes widened.

"May the stars in heaven strike me dead if I break your trust," the surgeon concluded.

Genon had already chosen not to discuss this with Remin. And he had chosen to swear it publicly, before all his knights. Remin's jaw tightened.

"I—that is, thank you," said the princess, looking from Genon to Remin as if she suspected there might be a fight and was trying to figure out how to stay out of it.

"In matters pertaining to the princess's health," Remin corrected. He understood what the surgeon was doing, and why, but even for a man who had saved Remin's life a dozen times over, this was going too far. A pretty face could disarm even a wily old man, and he wouldn't have Genon bound to silence if the princess chose to confide things unrelated to the condition of her body.

Genon bowed his head.

"Aye, that's fair. If you tell me you're planning to fill His Grace's boots with manure, I'm afraid you're on your own, my lady. I so swear."

"Thank you," she said again, covering her mouth with one hand to hide a smile.

"On the other hand," drawled Miche, "If you ever want to give it a shot, I will swear to the stars to assist you, lady."

"No, I won't," she protested, but she was giggling and his knights were laughing and she looked up at Remin with a glance that asked, *is this all right?*

Honestly, he wasn't sure. He had chosen to have his men swear to protect her, and it was inevitable that they would come to know each other and be easier with one another, but he didn't like to see her laughing with them. That felt dangerous for reasons he couldn't even articulate.

"Let's finish our business," he said, unsmiling. "There's a great deal to be done tonight."

He could almost hear Miche saying *Grimjaw*, but no one could argue that he was wrong. After a quick meal, he left the princess back in the cottage under guard, then headed back to his tent to confer with his knights. All of the day's business, and plans for the days to come, had to be discussed in all their many variations, and he and his men worked late into the night. Plans were all well and good, but success often depended on anticipating not just that the plans would fail—they would—but *how*.

"You should have asked me first, Gen," he said as he walked with the surgeon back to the cottages. It was late enough that the torches lining the lane had burned out, and the sky overhead was enormous, dark and starry, clear enough that even the blue-violet clouds of the celestial tides were visible, sweeping between the stars like foam on the sea.

"I didn't know if I would," Genon replied frankly. "Hadn't had much chance to see you together."

"And you decided it was necessary tonight."

"Aye." Genon rolled a yellow eye in Remin's direction. "If I thought she'd confide in you, I wouldn't have bothered. But that girl wouldn't ask you for a bandage if she was bleeding to death."

Remin stopped walking.

"I told her to tell me if she needs something," he said, turning to look at the older man. "And you thought the solution was to volunteer to keep her secrets? No matter what they may be."

"No," the surgeon replied. "No, not necessarily. We're all watching, be sure of it."

"You were expecting me to object," Remin said slowly. "When you swore yourself to silence. You promised too much to get her to trust you, and counted on me to make you walk it back."

"Wouldn't get very far if she's on her toes, thinking everyone's her enemy," said Genon reasonably, and they continued on together in the dark. "But while you're bracing for a storm, Rem, someone's got to be ready in case the sky is just blue."

That was a very gentle warning, and he was right. Hadn't they spent all night making plans on just that principle? The princess could be exactly what she appeared and entirely innocent, and in that case, Remin had already wronged her in more ways than he could count. But...

He couldn't forget how terrible storms could be.

There was a phantom twinge in his back at the memory, as of a wound yet unhealed, and he bade Genon good night and ducked into his cottage, shutting the door. The lamps were out, but there was still a red glow of coals from the hearth.

"Your Grace?" came the princess's voice from the dark.

"You should be asleep. It's late." Pulling off his breeches, jerkin, and boots, Remin stretched out on the floor. Tomorrow night, he would be sleeping outside again. There was silence from the bed for a few minutes, and then…

"Your Grace?"

He sighed. "Hmm."

"You'll be safe? With the bandits?"

He did not want to hear this question from her. "Quite safe. I know it would grieve you, if I didn't come back."

"It would," she whispered.

"Don't worry. If your father wants me dead, he'll have to do it himself."

"But I don't—"

"Be quiet," he said, rolling over to turn his back to her. He would not give himself to her again. "Go to sleep."

CHAPTER 7 – CLEAR BLUE SKY

The duke and his men marched out of Tresingale the next day.

Ophele did not see them go. She didn't even realize she wouldn't see him again until he handed her over to Miche and said *I'll be back in a few days.* She thought there would be more…ceremony. Marching out the gates, cloaks fluttering, while she at least got the chance to tell them to be careful.

Maybe she had just read too many romances.

She had little to say as she walked to the wall with Sir Miche, so stiff from yesterday's work that she could barely move. She had never had to do work like this in her life, and while she assumed her soreness was normal—she could hypothesize cause and effect well enough—the intensity of the pain still seemed excessive. When the duke woke her up that morning, she felt like someone had cast her in clay, fired her in a kiln, and then pushed her off a tower.

Dressed in a long-sleeved gown, with a hat, veil, and gloves to protect her skin, the only thing before her was more of the same, and the depressing thought that maybe the duke would never realize what she was trying to do for him. It was one thing to resign herself to brutally hard work in the name of atoning for her parents. But it would be nice if the person she was doing it for appreciated it just a *little*.

"I know where he keeps his other pair of boots," Sir Miche offered, and it took her a moment to realize what he was suggesting.

"No, that would just mean I have to smell it until he gets back," she said without thinking, and then clapped a hand to her mouth as Sir Miche roared with laughter.

"I do like a practical girl," he said, wiping his eyes. "Feel better? And stretch yourself out before you begin, my lady. It takes a bit to get used to this sort of work."

"Did you have to get used to it?" she asked, a little plaintively. The thought of hauling buckets was making her wish her arms would just fall off right now.

"I'm not used to it *now,*" he said frankly. "I've been a knight thirteen years, my lady, it's been some time since I used my ditch digger muscles. Right this minute I'm so sore I'd sooner throw myself in the pit than dig it. But here, watch me. Stretch your arms out before and after you work, like this…"

It did make her feel better. And even if he was sore, and a knight, and hadn't had to dig ditches in thirteen years, he was still pitching in and doing it cheerfully. She might be fit only to fill buckets of water, but she would try to do her best with it. Ophele nodded to the men on their way to the wall as she gathered her buckets, smiling when she saw friendly faces from the oath-taking last night.

"Thank you, lady," said one of them, marching past with a shovel over one shoulder. "Good of you to help."

It was interesting to watch everyone at work, like a complex machine with many parts. Ophele tried unobtrusively to stretch, as Sir Miche had advised, looking with pleasure at the length of wall that had been completed only yesterday.

But that meant it would be a farther walk to the well today.

She hadn't thought of that. And it would continue to get further, as the wall got longer; it would take her longer to carry the buckets every day, and she would have shorter periods to rest between rounds. As she returned with her first bucket, Ophele tried to measure the distance with her eyes: there was the oak tree she had sheltered under yesterday, and there was the wild lilac bush that had shaded the water for the builders, but today would be used by the men filling the gap between the walls. And tomorrow, would not be used at all.

After she finished setting out buckets, Ophele went to go see Master Guisse, a middle-aged man with splendid gray muttonchops. He had a worktable set up under a canopy, with all his parchments weighted down by tools she didn't recognize.

"Master Guisse," she began hesitantly. "How much longer does the wall get each day?"

He looked delighted to be asked.

"An average of two hundred feet per day on the south wall, my lady," he said, puffing out his chest. "The north wall averages only a little less. There are certain techniques we are pioneering that have been most effective, you see the pulley system we have devised—"

Ophele nodded politely as he rattled off a quantity of information about pulleys and levers and slides, but for once she wasn't interested in the details; there seemed to be a more immediate problem. The blacksmiths needed water, too; they were rolling it back and forth by the barrel. Two hundred feet per day? But surely someone else must have spotted the issue, there were masons and builders from all over the Empire here, but maybe just in case…

"Sir Miche," she began as they walked back to town at the end of the day, "are there any horses that might be spared?"

"Not without a da—very good reason," he said, looking at her curiously. "And you can call me Miche, my lady. Why?"

"Nothing." It was presumptuous to think she knew anything.

"Well, now I'm curious," he said, offering an encouraging smile. "Go on, I won't tell another soul."

"Well, I just thought maybe there might be a problem with fetching water soon," she said hesitantly. "It's not that I don't want to, but I asked Master Guisse how much longer the wall gets every day, and I was doing some sums, and I think I refilled all the buckets nine times yesterday and ten times today. And I kept track, I averaged seven minutes per bucket, going to the well and back, at about thirty seconds per hundred feet of wall, so if we keep adding two hundred feet per day, then in a few days …"

He was looking at her very oddly.

"I don't think it will be mathematically possible," she finished, small.

"No," he said slowly. "No, you're right. On the north wall they've got a stream handy, so water's not an issue. I wonder if in all his pioneering Guisse has got a plan for hydrating his work crew."

"The blacksmiths were complaining, too," she said, encouraged. "That's why I wondered, I could do it if I had a horse to pull the wagon."

"You can't lead these horses, my lady," Sir Miche replied seriously. "War horses are dangerous. Trained to bite and kick if anyone but their handler gets close. That's why Rem wouldn't let you near that black monster of his. But I'll look into it tonight. Could be I could scrounge up a donkey."

"Oh, a donkey!" Ophele forgot all about being sore, filthy, sweaty, and so tired she could have laid down in the grass on the side of the road and gone to sleep. She whirled toward him, clapping her hands together with excitement. "Really? We have donkeys?"

"I think I saw a couple in the stable." Sir Miche looked amused. "Most people don't think much of the creatures."

"They look like a rabbit and a horse had a baby," she said, bouncing beside him. "And I'm really not trying to get out of working, you know, it's just that if you do the math…"

"No, no, I can't argue with your reckoning." He laughed, shaking his head, though Ophele didn't see what was funny. "Could you manage a donkey by yourself?"

"I think so." Though now that it looked like a real possibility, she wasn't entirely sure. "I had a friend back at Aldeburke who had the sweetest donkey…"

She told him about Rou and Anzel as they walked up the lane into town, and how Rou had always saved some new books or some small surprise for her whenever he visited. Usually, they walked together all the way from the manor to the gates, and once she was old enough, he let her lead Anzel a few times. Of course, that was a well-trained donkey over a paved road, but still…

"We didn't get to see much of you in Aldeburke, when we were there," Sir Miche remarked. "I suppose you must miss it."

Ophele looked away, searching for an answer that was both truthful and innocuous. The fact that it took some time to produce one spoke volumes.

"I—I miss the library," she said finally. "And Azelma."

"I…see," he replied, and was quiet until they reached her cottage. "I'll come collect you for supper at full dark," he said at the door. "Don't go anywhere else, and if anything frightens you, run to the cookhouse. Wen is always there. But you're safe here," he added, meeting her gaze with unusual seriousness. "If anyone looks at you crossways, you tell me, and I'll set them right."

"All right…" she said dubiously. She had no doubt Master Wen would be there, but it seemed to her that she could stagger through the doorway with a knife in her back and he'd yell at her for bleeding on his kitchen.

Supper came with the news that there was indeed an elderly donkey that might be fit to haul water, and inside Ophele hugged herself with delight. She had always loved animals; they were easier to talk to than people.

"We'll go see him in the morning," Sir Miche promised. "Tounot, will we be getting any more human assistance on the south? We're having to recruit donkeys now."

Sir Tounot sat down on the other side of the table and reached for a platter of roasted meat.

"Maybe next week," he said. Ophele hadn't had much opportunity to exchange words with him, but Sir Tounot looked friendly enough, ruddy and curly-haired, with a cleft in his chin. "Your Grace," he added, with a nod of his head for her. "I hope you're well. A lovely lady at table makes even the humblest meal a feast."

"Y-yes," she stammered, reddening. Such extravagant compliments were considered an art among knights, but having never received one, she hadn't the least idea how she was supposed to reply.

But Sir Miche was happy to help her.

"This is where you say something like, 'And your good company adds spice to every dish,'" he said, bending his head and speaking from the corner of his mouth. "Except it's Tounot. I'd only stretch him to salt."

"Oh? Then what would you call your nonsense, Miche?" Sir Tounot replied, without the least offense.

"Cardamom," Sir Miche said promptly. "The spice of kings."

Anise, Ophele thought. *An acquired taste.*

It would have been funny, if she had said that.

Both men made a kindly attempt to include her in the conversation, but as the rest of the knights joined them at the table it felt a little too much like making a speech, with so many eyes on her. And anyway, she was much happier just to listen as all of them talked about the planting, the wall, the horses, the construction, and the thousand and one other details of building a town. She wanted to know everything.

Things felt less strange when she was sitting among the Knights of the Brede; she was used to them, even if she was still too shy to talk to them. But once Sir Miche had left her at the cottage for the night, with the promise to pick her up early to go get the donkey, she realized just how far away she was from everything she had ever known. It was amazing to think that this was only her fourth night in Tresingale.

And alone, in a house of her own. Ophele kindled a fire and lit an oil lamp, then sat down with a book. All she needed was a cup of tea and one of Azelma's hazelnut cookies, and it would have been perfect. For the first time in her life, no one would come to bother her. No spiteful Lisabe, no sneering Lady Hurrell, no Julot saying strange things and standing far too close. And, though it felt disloyal to think it, no duke hurrying her or scolding her or icily ignoring her.

She didn't blame him for not trusting her. Ophele tried to be fair about such things. She just wished he would stop showing her glimpses of what he could be like, if he *didn't* hate her. When he talked to his knights, sometimes he even told jokes. He wasn't mean to anyone but her.

By now, she had been married for over a month. She didn't feel married. She felt like she had acquired a very strict guardian. Since leaving Aldeburke, His Grace had been with her almost every moment of every day. He loomed so large in her life, figuratively and literally, and now that he was gone, she felt curiously bereft.

Especially once she put out the lights.

Ophele was sure she would sleep as soon as her head touched the pillow. A day in the sun had left her feeling like a wrung sponge and her limbs were in such agony, movement seemed impossible. But suddenly the cottage felt very big and shadowy without the shape of the duke on the floor, lying between her and the door like a small mountain range.

It was fine. She wasn't a child. Ophele hugged a pillow to herself and shut her eyes, trying to empty her mind. And when that didn't work, she reminded herself how sorry she would be if she didn't sleep, and that she was going to get a donkey in the morning, and she needed to hurry up and go to sleep so there would be time to stop by the kitchen and ask Master Wen for a carrot or an apple.

Outside, there was a very soft scraping noise.

That was just one of the guards. The duke had said there were guards on every window and door. But Ophele found herself wondering what a strangler looked like. Sir Miche said they had long fingers—presumably for strangling—and that they could climb right over a wooden palisade. And there were ghouls, too, that ate the dead on battlefields. And maybe not just the dead; anyone that couldn't get away, probably. And though both men said they wouldn't come down from the mountains until it was warmer, it had been very warm today...

It wasn't *impossible* for them to come earlier, was it? It wasn't impossible that something could slip into Tresingale in the dark, creeping between braziers and torches unnoticed. And it certainly wasn't impossible that something like a strangler could creep up on her guards and strangle them, and they wouldn't even be able to call out because they were being strangled. And then it could sneak up to her window...

Another scraping noise.

"Is someone there?" she asked, her voice quavering. She was being silly, she knew it, but she was six hundred miles from home and all alone and people had been talking about stranglers ever since she got here.

No one answered. She sat up.

"If you are, please say something," she said, clutching her blankets. Turning, she addressed the daubed wall behind her headboard. "It's fine, I know I have guards, I just want to know what...who's there."

"One of your guards, m'lady," said a reluctant male voice. "Just sharpening my sword. Beg pardon, didn't think you'd hear it."

Ophele closed her eyes.

"No, please keep it sharp," she said. "What's your name?"

"Dol, m'lady."

She slid back under her blankets. "Are you here every night?"

"Aye, lady. Night watch doesn't change much."

"One of the watchmen back home said that. He said once you got used to being up all night, it was best to stay that way." It was easier to talk to a stranger if she couldn't see him. "His name was Alou."

"I don't mind it. But you probably ought to sleep now, m'lady."

Now that she knew she wasn't about to be strangled, she thought she could. It wasn't just that she was alone in a strange and frightening place. She had never been on her own before, ever. She had never had any control over her life. She had been born in fetters, pushed into marriage, with no choice in what she was and the inescapable destiny thrust upon her.

But maybe now, even if she couldn't choose her own path, she at least could go down it her own way.

* * *

To call what happened in the hills west of Tresingale a battle would have been a wild exaggeration.

It was a slaughter. Brisk and ruthless, a barrage of arrows followed by the thunder of heavy horse, with the dreadnaught Jinmin in the front. People called Remin a giant, but Jinmin was nearly as tall, and so massive it was hard to find a horse that could carry him. The hundred bandits had rough shields and threw them up after the first volley of arrows, but they might as well have been waving daisies at Jinmin.

Remin, seated on his black warhorse, watched from a nearby hilltop.

His participation wasn't necessary, and there was always a small chance there could be a secondary force nearby, or a weapon hidden among the rapidly decreasing number of surviving bandits. Years of warfare had taught him to always hold a force in reserve. But in this case, it wasn't necessary. In less than fifteen minutes, the remaining twenty or so bandits had thrown down their arms and knelt in the bloody grass.

Then he rode down.

"Who is your leader?" he asked curtly. Almost every man before him had the pale skin and ice-blond hair of Valleth.

The bandits exchanged glances. It was possible their leader was already dead, but curiously, there was one man that no one was looking at.

"Who supplied you?" he asked in his adequate Vallethi, watching them carefully. Again, they looked at each other, but the man fifth or sixth from the left looked at no one, and no one looked at him. "Does that mean your leader's dead?" Remin asked conversationally, leaning forward over his saddle. "Or ran away? I guess if you weren't cowards, you wouldn't have deserted in the first place."

Now the man on the left was looking. Glaring. Remin sat up, nodding at Juste.

"That one," he said, pointing. He wasn't always right about this kind of thing, but even if that fellow wasn't the leader, the others would wonder why he had been chosen. The rest of his knights waded in to split up the other survivors, binding their hands and leading them off in small groups, too far away to see or hear each other.

Remin had learned the principles of interrogation when he was a squire. It was filthy work that usually left him feeling drained and discouraged, no matter what the outcome. But Juste was the best of his men at the task, and very rarely had to resort to actual torture. It was he that had struck upon the idea of separating enemy units and pitting them against each other. It left them wondering what was happening in the other groups. Were they being tortured? Were they talking? Juste made the same offer to all of them, out loud, for everyone to hear: talk, and you'll live. Or rather, talk *first,* and you'll live.

Sometimes it was even true.

A disciplined unit could withstand the technique. Remin did not believe he was looking at a disciplined unit.

"Huber," he said, waving over the master of his scouts. "Send some men to Bram. He should be in Ferrede. Let him know we've wiped out the bandits and to expect us there in five days. Send the rest of your men to make sure we haven't missed anyone."

The Iron Hills were four days from Tresingale, and the question he most wanted to ask the bandits was what they thought they would accomplish by going there. It was true that if Remin had been away when they arrived, or if he had been incompetent enough not to send scouts out into the surrounding country, they might have succeeded in surprising and overpowering his forces. Temporarily. They had no hope of holding the town.

"We weren't going to hurt anyone," said the bandit named Drazhake, in a Vallethi accent so thick that Remin had to look to Juste to interpret. "We were just planning to take some things we need. We're in a bad way and we can't go back to Valleth."

That was a third option: they could have been planning to raid, then retreat. But it was a lie to say no one would have been hurt. Remin's men would have fought to the death to defend what they had worked so hard to build.

"The war ended a year ago," said Juste. "You could have accepted the amnesty."

"No, we couldn't."

Loyal enough to Valleth to refuse an amnesty, but not quite loyal enough to finish their service. Remin might have been sympathetic; most of Valleth's army was composed of conscripts by the end of the war, and it was hard to blame a man for not giving it his all when he was a slave in all but name. And all a deserter would find in Valleth now was an execution. But Remin had offered them a way out. They could have settled peacefully in the valley, or gone anywhere else in the world, and had chosen to stay and be his enemy.

"Who was supplying you?" Juste asked. "We know you didn't survive the winter on your own. It will go hard with you if you lie to us."

"Do we look well-supplied?" Drazhake spat. He had a point. The bandits were long-haired and unshaven, with ragged, patched clothing. But they weren't starving.

"Jinmin." Juste turned to the behemoth knight standing a few yards away, arms crossed and silently observing. "How many did we capture?"

"Twenty-two."

"Twenty-two." Juste crouched in front of Drazhake, somber as a confessor. He even looked sympathetic. "I'm going to go and ask the other twenty-one men this question, and promise to spare anyone that tells me the truth. Do you think all twenty-one are going to give me the same answer? The stars have blessed you with the opportunity to answer first."

He let that sit there. The sun beat down on the bare hills, brown rock and iron deposits. Interrogators were gamblers at heart, playing the odds, watching for tells.

"Very well." Juste stood up. "I'll go and speak to your friends. Truth is important."

"You're going to kill us anyway," Drazhake said angrily. "Why should I tell you anything?

"No. It may be that we will spare someone useful." This was a lie. Drazhake knew it was a lie. But he wanted to live.

"We went to Ferrede," he said, bitter, angry. "Twice, over the winter. They have a mill. We ordered them to give us grain and said if anyone complained, we'd come back and burn it all."

That was a good one. It might even be true. And Juste knew it, too; he gave Drazhake a long look and then turned away without another word. He had been asked and answered. Now they would see what the other bandits had to say.

Over the next hour, the source of the grain was variously given as theft from a grain cart they encountered on the road, theft from a mill, supplied voluntarily by an elderly man and a teenage girl—which made everyone else glare ferociously at the man who said it—and supplied directly from Valleth. That last was so transparently impossible that Juste only looked sadly at the man who had said it, as if he were ashamed for him.

They might have gotten more details if they had tortured a few of the men, but what they had was enough. This did not look like a complex conspiracy. Remin took his own turn killing the bound, wailing men. There was no glory in it, he didn't like it, but he wouldn't ask his men to do anything he wasn't willing to do himself. His knights and squires silently performed the same task further down the line, lifting their swords to plunge them into dirty, squirming backs, the heavy steel slamming through flesh and bone, aimed for the heart of a man who was doing his level best to wiggle away. Remin had to put his boot on the back of one dying man to wrench his sword free before he went on to the next.

He reminded himself that the bandits had chosen to march on Tresingale, where he and those loyal to him were breaking their backs to carve homes out of the wilderness. His soldiers had laid down their arms and deserved some peace. There were hundreds of other men who had come to the valley at his invitation, who might have been injured or killed.

And one seventeen year-old girl. What might these bandits have done to her, given the opportunity?

Remin's jaw tightened. That thought made it easier to do what was necessary.

In less than half a day, they had positioned themselves to intercept the bandits, killed them, questioned the survivors, and left over a hundred corpses on the bare crowns of the Iron Hills. Remin left a few men to search the dead and dispose of them, sent his archers home, and moved on with his remaining force for Ferrede, five days away, riding hard.

Remin had all but forgotten Drazhake's name by the time they were on their way. There were so many other names and faces in his memory already.

And when he arrived in Ferrede, he suspected there would be at least two more.

* * *

"My lady?"

"My lady."

A gentle poke.

"My lady, wake up."

"Lady, it's morning…"

"*Ophele.*"

Ophele's eyes snapped open, meeting a pair of bemused hazel eyes. Sir Miche straightened.

The donkey.

"Oh, no," she said, bolting upright in bed and clinging to her blankets. "I'm sorry, I'm so sorry!"

"Another slugabed," he said, but he was smiling as he headed for the door, which he had left carefully open. The duke's knights were scrupulous that there would be no opportunity for misunderstandings.

Ophele flew to get dressed. She hadn't even wondered how she would wake up on time in the morning; she had never had to, and the duke hadn't been the least bit shy about shaking her awake when he wanted her up. Stumbling out of bed, she tugged a dress out of her trunk and put it on the right way round on the second try, then buried her face in a basin of cold water until some of the fog cleared. In ten minutes, she was outside with her veil and hat in hand, and had only fallen over things twice.

"I thought Rem was exaggerating," Sir Miche said, amused. "No, don't trouble yourself to apologize, my lady, I knew someone else who had the same trouble. Stable's this way. Sure you're awake?'

"Yes." Her eyes were open very wide.

She had often visited the stables in Aldeburke, so she was familiar with the smells, the sounds, the stomping, blowing, curious horses. There was a lone donkey in a small corner at the back of the stable, an elderly little fellow whose head was roughly level with Ophele's.

"Hello," she said softly, holding her hand under his muzzle and wishing she had a treat for him. "Do you know his name, Sir Miche?"

"Just Miche. Drover said they called him Eugene."

He looked like a Eugene. He lipped at her fingers, searching for food, but didn't bite, and Ophele looked him over. She would feel horrible if he were hurt or too old and she made him work anyway.

"Some of the masons used him to carry their kit on the journey," said Sir Miche, who seemed to intuit something of her thoughts. "But he's too small for most work around here. They were talking about putting him down, but he makes do with scrub, so it's not like he's costing us in feed. I think he could handle a small cart."

"Of course he could," she crooned, stroking his ears. He needed a good brushing. "Can't you, Eugene?"

The donkey seemed a little shy of hands around his head, but she gave him a few minutes to get used to her, moving her hand from his shoulder to his neck so he would know where she was. Tam had told her it was like that with horses; they were big animals, and they couldn't see what was around their sides unless they turned their heads to look. Tonight, she would give him a good wash and scrub.

"Let's get him hitched up." Sir Miche straightened and untied the ropes that blocked the donkey's improvised stall. "Most days I'll have the stable boys get him ready for you, but you'll need to learn to manage his tack yourself, just in case."

Two helpful stableboys were nearby to explain the harness and cart, a tiny four-wheeled wagon that showed signs of hasty repair. The leather harness looked like a tangled mess until they got it on Eugene, but Ophele soon saw how it all fit together, with an additional bit of complex strapping in the wagon to keep the barrel from bouncing out.

She was delighted with all of it. Not just because of the donkey—though she already considered Eugene a gentleman and bosom friend—but also because this meant she really *was* doing something valuable, however humble.

"He can start by carrying my shovel," said Sir Miche, cheerfully pitching the tool into the back of the wagon as they set off. His sword was strapped in its usual place on his hip, never absent even when he was digging ditches. "I finally got one with a decent handle yesterday, they'll have to pry it from my cold, dead hands."

"Can we see if there are carrots or apples in the kitchen?" Ophele asked as they approached the cookhouse. They were already a little late; the sun was a finger-width above the horizon, but she could make up any lost time now that she had Eugene.

"I'm sure there are, but you'll have to talk Wen into parting with them," Sir Miche said dubiously. "If you can do it in five minutes, my lady, I'll make friends with Eugene in the meantime."

Ophele blanched. She had secretly been hoping that he would get them for her. And he likely suspected as much; there was a teasing look in his eyes as he reached for Eugene's lead rope, and before she left, he sketched the sign of the stars' blessing over her head and intoned, "When you find yourself in the void, may the light find you."

She could do it. Hadn't she just been telling herself last night that she could make her own way? Ophele hurried to the kitchen at the back of the cookhouse, braced herself, and opened the door.

The massive cook did not have a knife in his hand. That was a good omen.

"Master Wen?" she asked timidly, remembering not to cross the sacred threshold. "Excuse me?"

His vast back to her as he stirred something over the fire, and he showed no sign that he had heard.

"Master Wen?" Louder.

He didn't so much as twitch. Ophele bit her lip.

"Master Wen," she said loudly. "Excuse me!"

"What, what, what what *what?!*" He went off like a volcano. "Your Grace, I am *stirring.*"

"I—I just wondered if you had some apples or carrots to spare," she stammered. "If you point to where they are, I won't trouble you—"

"You are not setting *foot* in me kitchen," he said, pointing at her as if he were a Vallethi sorcerer about to level her with a curse. "What d'ye need them for?"

"A donkey." This answer did not impress him, and she hurriedly explained. "They gave me a donkey to help at the wall. He's old and he's just been living on scrub brush and he's going to be hauling water for everyone all day. So I want to give him something good to eat. Like carrots? Even old ones. Please." The words tumbled out in a cluster of fits and starts and Master Wen looked more incredulous with every syllable, but she had to try. "His name is Eugene."

"The donkey's name is Eugene."

She nodded, petrified.

"What a coincidence, me sainted mother's name was Eugene," Wen said, hands on his vast hips. "Well, I suppose if it's for Master fu—bloody Eugene, of course, of course." It was a soaring fit of sarcasm, but he still abandoned his stirring and reached into a cupboard to produce a small bundle of ancient carrots. "Not one foot in me kitchen," he warned, and tossed them.

Ophele clung to the doorframe with one hand and snatched them out of the air.

"Thank you!" She said breathlessly. "Thank you, Master Wen!"

"You're a blooming duchess, me name's just Wen!" He roared after her as she escaped, clutching her prize.

"You actually managed to wheedle it out of him?" Sir Miche looked impressed.

"Carrots for Master Eugene," she said, tickled by the title, and broke off a bit of one to present it victoriously to the donkey.

They spent the day getting used to each other. It was a different routine, only a little less arduous even with the barrel. It was a relief not to have to haul buckets up and down the hill, but her hands were blistered from the windlass after she filled the barrel for the third time, and Ophele tore up her handkerchief to bandage her palms, hoping no one would notice. The cart and barrel were also *just* short enough for her to reach on tiptoe, and she didn't dare to climb on the cart. In the first place, it might fall to pieces, and in the second, Eugene sometimes took it in his head to start walking while she was busy with the buckets.

"No, no, not yet," she admonished, hurrying to grab his lead rope. He might be elderly and small, but he was still surprisingly strong; when she tried tying the lead rope around her waist to keep him from wandering while she refilled buckets, she found herself being dragged along with the cart for a dozen paces, to the amusement of the watching masons.

"Need help, m'lady?" called one, as she snatched at a passing gorse bush.

"No, thank you!"

But she didn't hold it against him. Master Eugene was learning his new job, he was bound to make a few mistakes. And he was such a sweet and grandfatherly little fellow, a little absent-minded perhaps, but he never shied once from the racket on the wall.

The smiths also approved of this new arrangement. At the noon meal they sent a delegation to propose that Eugene haul their own water barrels to and from the well, and in exchange they would spell her on the windlass. As Ophele was working assiduously to hide her blistered hands from the eagle-eyed Sir Miche, she happily agreed to this arrangement.

"That was wise," he said approvingly from behind her, where he was lazing against a tree. "Never give away anything for free, my lady, or the next thing you know these swindlers will have you begging for an hour of the donkey's time."

"Never," Ophele vowed, feeding Master Eugene another carrot.

She bathed and brushed him before she bathed and brushed herself that night, and only left after the stableboys had promised to look after him as respectfully as the big war horses.

It had still been a hard day. She would almost have preferred to skip dinner rather than leave the steaming comfort of her cauldron, where the boiling water was the only thing that soothed her aching legs. She had done the math as she walked endlessly back and forth at the foot of the wall, and she reckoned she had walked nearly fifteen miles that day. Only the thought of Sir Miche having to fish her out of her cauldron kept her from falling asleep in the water.

She was almost asleep later that night when her remaining trouble popped into her mind, and she jerked instantly back to wakefulness. Turning over, she faced the wall behind her bed.

"Dol?"

There was a moment of silence, and then… "Yes, m'lady?"

"Can you do me a favor?"

"Might do," he said cautiously.

"Could you wake me up a little before dawn?" she asked. "I'm sorry to trouble you, but I don't wake up on my own, and I don't want to be late. Could you bang your sword and shield together or something?"

"Folk in the cots next door would hang me if I did that, lady," he said. He sounded like he was trying not to laugh, but at least he hadn't refused. And he was right; she didn't want to trouble the neighbors. But she could hardly let him come into the cottage, the duke could have his head for such an outrage.

"Just call, as loud as you dare," she said finally. "And maybe have one of the other guards knock on the door? Who else is out there?"

"Yvain," said a new voice from the wall at the foot of her bed, startling her. "Sorry, lady. Walls are thin."

"Oh. Nice to meet you," she said, glancing from one wall to the other. "Would you mind knocking, Yvain?"

"Don't mind. I'm a heavy sleeper myself."

"Thank you both." She burrowed back under her covers with a lighter heart. "Good night. I hope it's not too boring, just sitting out there."

"We like boring," Dol assured her.

"Good night, lady," said Yvain.

* * *

They met Bram a few miles outside Ferrede five days later, and Remin was impressed again by the sheer size of his own duchy.

"No wagons in or out of town," Bram reported as they sat together at dusk, forgoing campfires to avoid arousing suspicion in the nearby town. It was better if the townspeople didn't know they were being watched. "My Meinhem scouts reported back yesterday, no movement on their side, either. These towns are just too far apart to communicate regularly, Rem."

He agreed. These were small towns, backwaters. There was only one road in Ferrede. Forty-some cottages spread across the countryside surrounded by acres of planting, a windmill creaked on a lonely hilltop, and eight houses clustered together in a hollow and were likely considered "the town." It was an isolated place that had survived a century of armies tramping by mostly because it wasn't near anything of tactical value and the people were too stubborn to leave.

He wondered how they'd been coping with the ghouls.

"What do you think?" asked Huber. There was a glint of copper in his eyes in the sunlight, the legacy of a Noreveni ancestor. In the distance, they could see a single horse and wagon trundling from the town toward the mill.

"I don't think the whole town was behind it," Remin said slowly. "If they were, then we would've seen more contact between them and the bandits. I'm betting there's an old man and a girl somewhere in town. Might be someone's sister or sweetheart that just wanted to help the deserters. We're far enough from the border that they're more Vallethi than Empire up here."

"Rem," said Huber. "If it's a girl and an old man—"

"I offered them amnesty." And if the girl had been helping her sweetheart, or her brother, she would have done better to tell him to build a hut and start farming. The deserters could have settled anywhere in the valley, and Remin would have looked the other way, as long as they were peaceful.

But they hadn't done that.

"I need to talk to them first," he decided. "As their lord, I'm worried about the bandits that have been harassing other villages in the area. I also want to help them prepare for what'll be coming out of the mountains in a few months. We'll see how they respond, and keep our eyes open for an old man and a teenage girl. Juste, you go to the mill while we're making our greetings in town. See who's in charge of the grain."

He suspected that that was where they would find the pair in question. And the behavior of the townspeople would determine whether he took the betrayers away quietly or hanged them from the larger of the two trees in the town square.

There was no hint of trouble from the village elder, a very elderly man named Yewen Brodrim who was a little hard of hearing, but seemed in full possession of his wits otherwise.

"The Duke of Andelin?" he said loudly, looking automatically toward Remin, who had a nobleman's bearing even when he was in the middle of dismounting his horse. "Himself? Well, well, we must be honored, honored indeed! We will be pleased to offer whatever we have, Your Grace."

He bowed, hands together in the Vallethi style.

"We heard there were bandits operating in the area," Remin said, equally loudly. He wanted friendly relationships with even his smallest villages; Duke Ereguil was always saying that happy people were productive people. "We won't strain your hospitality, elder, but would you mind calling your folk together tonight? We also want to see how you're coping with the new Andelin wildlife."

"Bastard devils," Elder Brodrim declared loudly. "It's good of you to trouble yourself, Your Grace. Folk are busy with the planting, but I reckon I can gather a few together."

The size of the gathering that evening made Remin fairly sure that this was not a town with a guilty conscience. The people came to the square dressed in their finest, lit lanterns, and generously offered the little food they had to spare after the long winter. There was no sign of fear among them, and he and his men were careful not to give them reason. Huber and Juste were at their most charming, the squires behaved themselves, and Jinmin kept out of sight. The giant knight was alarming under the best circumstances.

As much as he preferred to be in Tresingale, it might be a good idea to visit his other villages, at that. Remin listened gravely to their troubles as Juste sat behind him at a table, scribbling notes. They had indeed been troubled by the devils, and lost seven people before the winter snows fell.

"Most of them from ghouls, while they were in the fields alone," said Elder Brodrim. "Two of them were stranglers who crept through windows in the night. And they are growing bolder, Your Grace. Ronze over there, he says he saw a big wolf running through the trees at the end of his north pasture. A very big wolf. Ronze's not one to exaggerate."

Remin did not curse aloud.

"Seems early for that," was all he said, but in his mind, he was picturing the miles of empty land in Tresingale, where there was no wall.

"Folk don't go anywhere unarmed, Your Grace," said the elder. "And the doors are barred after dark."

Except for tonight, when they had turned out to honor their lord.

"We're taking many of the same precautions in Tresingale," Remin said, looking out at the packed square. He supposed now was as good a time as any to address them. He hardly needed to signal for silence; as soon as he stood, the crowd quieted. "We're as worried about the Andelin devils as you are," he told them. "And we're doing many of the same things. I can't promise that we'll get rid of them in a night, or even a year. And we can't wall off your fields. But I will see that you at least have a place to sleep at night where the stranglers can't get you."

Last year, in Tresingale, they slept in the cookhouse and the storehouse, and posted guards. He could at least give them the option of doing the same. Next year, they would have something better.

"That's very generous, Your Grace," Elder Brodrim said amid murmurs of agreement. After the terror Valleth had inflicted on the valley, the devils were just one more damned thing. The people of the Andelin were realists. Life was short, hard, and often ended violently.

That left one other bit of business.

Juste had pointed out the girl and her grandfather as soon as they arrived in the square. The miller and his granddaughter were obviously of Vallethi stock, the girl almost wraithlike with her pale, thin hair and skinny frame. They claimed not to have any grain to spare for their duke, even at a high price. Remin had glanced at them from time to time, but avoided staring. The old man hadn't a word for anyone else in the square, and there was something off about that girl's smile.

As much as he hated to ruin the mood, it would be best to deal with it before the wine started flowing.

"There is one other thing that brought me to Ferrede," he said. He had already planned what he would say. He did not want this place to fear him when he left. "Five days ago, my men dispatched a large group of bandits, over a hundred strong. They were marching to Tresingale. They confessed that they meant to raid it."

He paused, watching. There was surprise on many faces, discomfort in a few, and anger on two.

"My men would have resisted," he continued. "They're soldiers. They don't know how to farm as well as you yet, but we have sixty acres planted so far. We've been building homes. I just brought my wife to the valley. It may be that I will bring her here one day, to see how one of the oldest villages in the Andelin has endured a century of hardship and still prospered."

He hoped he wasn't laying it on too thick, but everyone was nodding; they liked what he was saying. He was making them relate to his men, to his wife, to his fears for her safety. But he also saw puzzlement, because what did this have to do with the people of Ferrede?

"Someone from this village was supplying the bandits with grain."

The charge hit them like a rockslide. Remin watched, waited, and sure enough, the girl from the mill turned at once as if she meant to slip away. Jinmin was already there.

"You fools." Elder Brodrim's voice trembled as he spun, searching the crowd. "Jutte, Tymmon, you foolish old bastard, do you realize what you've done? After everything we said? Do you realize what you've done to *all* of—"

"I'm Vallethi, you craven dog!" The miller suddenly roared. He had a long white beard and was just going stringy with age, and he yanked ineffectually away as two of Remin's men grabbed him. "This bastard sweeps the valley clear and the lot of you can't wait to drop to your knees! Maybe if more of you had—"

Juste shut him up with a hard knock to the head. Remin was inclined to let the rest of the drama play out, and watch the reactions of the people. It was clear that there was little support for the miller and his granddaughter. Every face he could see was frozen in horror, and they drew back from the pair as if they had something catching, clearing a path for Remin's men. The girl spun around as Jinmin carried her off, livid, as if all the power and venom in her body were concentrated in her pale eyes.

"The Lord of Tales will be back!" She screeched. That false smile had vanished and now there was only rage. "And he'll punish you all, he won't forget who the traitors are! You're cowards, weaklings, *worms!*"

Shrieking, she was born away. How old was she? Fifteen? Remin's stomach twisted, but nothing showed in his hard face. That girl had been barely more than a child when Valleth surrendered. But there were holdouts after any war.

Before him, the townspeople were slowly sinking to their knees. Clutching their children.

"Your Grace." Elder Brodrim's voice trembled. "I am sorry. We knew their feelings, and we suspected—but we didn't think they would go through with it. I thought they had seen sense. It was my error in not reporting it. Please, punish me—"

"Stop." Remin lifted a hand. "I offered you amnesty once. I will repeat that offer now. If any of you do not wish to live under the Empire of Argence, then you may go, now. My men will escort you to the border, and you will be given coin enough to start you on your way. I swear to the stars in heaven that no harm will come to you if you wish to go. This is the last time I will make this offer."

He paused, giving them a chance to take him up on it. No one did.

"Then any support for Valleth or further lawlessness will be punished accordingly. You will give me your oath. Now."

Every single person said it. Even the little ones, kneeling beside their parents and looking around in confusion, but game to play along. Shrill, piping little voices swearing their loyalty. Their happiness was gone. They were relieved; they were all but fainting with relief. Other lords might have swept the square clear, and killed them to the last child.

But Remin knew what it was like to be the last child.

"In return, you have my oath to return loyalty with protection, and trust with trust," he said. "I regret that we had to endure such unpleasant business tonight. I will send men to build you a sleeping house safe from stranglers. Elder Brodrim, I will hope to return after the harvest. May our next meeting be under more pleasant circumstances."

"Y-yes, Your Grace." The old man stood, slipping his hands into his wide sleeves to hide their trembling. Great drops of sweat stood out on his bald head, but he gave a good bow all the same. "I hope…I hope you will bring the Duchess of Andelin so we can offer our hospitality, Your Grace. We will be honored."

Remin offered them a cordial farewell, but kept it short. He was about to execute two members of their village. Regardless of their guilt, it would be insensitive to linger.

But when he returned to his camp in the hills, he found Jinmin had already beaten him to it.

"That's them," said the knight, pointing to the two corpses a short distance outside the camp. The girl's pale hair was stained red with blood. "Didn't see any point in delaying."

"I did not order you to kill them." Remin's voice was frigid. The giant knight met his gaze squarely, small brown eyes in a flat brawler's face. "What if I had wanted to question them?"

"Then I'd say sorry," said Jinmin. He bowed, his face expressionless. "Meant no disrespect, Your Grace."

"If I can't trust you to withhold your sword, then I won't ask you to draw it." Remin said it quietly; this was only between the two of them, not a show for the consumption of the camp. "Go."

Jinmin lumbered away, a small mountain.

Sometimes he thought that Jinmin had only chosen to follow him on a whim all those years ago, and if he hadn't, then Remin likely would have been obliged to kill him. They had been together for the entirety of the war and Jinmin had been a loyal and formidable weapon; he had once taken a crossbow bolt intended for Remin, and killed the assassin without so much as a twitch. But for all that, Remin still felt sometimes that he hadn't the least idea what was going on in that giant skull.

They camped under the stars, though this time they lit fires. There was no need to hide their presence, and the warnings about wolf demons had them all on edge. When the moon was high and the middle of the night was passing, Juste came to sit with him. The rest of the camp was quiet. In the distance, Remin could see the massive shape of Jinmin in his bedroll, snoring like a congested ox.

"Sometimes I think he'd do anything I ordered," Remin murmured to Juste. *"Anything.* And then he goes and does something like this."

"Fortunately, the rest of us are here to argue with you," Juste replied. "In this case, he saved me the trouble, my lord. I was on my way to do it myself."

"What? Why?"

"You weren't going to question them. They know nothing," Juste said curtly. "But you were going to force yourself to kill that girl."

"Why would I do that?" But the question lacked his usual conviction, and Remin looked into the fire as if he might find the answer there.

"To prove that you can, if you must," Juste said, with quiet sympathy. "It is unnecessary, my lord. We will not ask this of you."

"You know." It wasn't a question.

"Yes. I saw you after you killed that girl in Ellingen. It did not seem like a *new* trouble, so I asked Huber about it."

Huber was the least likely of all Remin's knights to gossip, or indeed to talk at all, barring some pressing need. Remin understood and allowed it when he would never have tolerated it in anyone else. But trust Juste to sniff it out and know exactly where to go for an answer. Miche would laugh and laugh, and never tell the truth.

Thoughts of Ellingen always filled Remin with a complicated mix of guilt and horror and shame, and the belligerent sense that he should feel none of those things. He had offered them a chance to surrender. He had promised that if they returned Ludovin, and opened the gates, he would do them no harm. Instead, they had tortured Ludovin for three days before he killed himself, and so Remin had knocked down the walls, killed everyone who resisted him, and tore down the city until not one stone stood on top of another. Ellingen was destroyed for all time.

Valleth had done far worse, when they invaded the Empire. They had rained terror on the Andelin Valley for a century, offering its cities and its people to the Lord of Tales. But all that history and self-justification evaporated like smoke when Remin heard the word *Ellingen,* for that would only ever conjure a girl of fourteen, maybe fifteen years old, who had come at him with a broken sword.

And he had killed her with one blow of his fist.

It was only afterward that he realized what he had done. He could have disarmed her. He should have just taken the strike; the stars knew it wouldn't have been more than a scratch. But he had seen that shape, that motion from the corner of his eye—

Remin had wrenched off his helmet and stumbled away to be sick in an alley, revolted by what he had done. And that was where Huber had found him, alternately sobbing and heaving his guts up, and guarded him until he had recovered enough to go on.

"And you fear it will happen again," Juste said softly. He was not speaking from idle curiosity. Juste had always been simultaneously the gentlest and most vicious of Remin's knights. He never hesitated to take on tasks that would have kept Remin awake for weeks afterward, and he did them with an air of gentle regret that made even the ugliest work seem sadly understandable. "Do you really think it will be necessary?"

This was a dangerous gift. It would be far too easy to rely upon it.

"I don't know," Remin said, and drained his cup in a single gulp. "I can't tell anymore. I don't...*think* she would. I don't think she would want to."

But he knew all too well that the Emperor had ways of bending people to his will, and even if he hadn't found a way yet, there was no guarantee that he would not, in time. In his dreams, Remin had already seen the shape of a girl lying broken on the stones of Ellingen, with a face like a solemn owl.

Juste nodded. His pale blue eyes were as placid and peaceful as a pool of water.

"Then rely on me," he said, as he had for all that other unpleasant work. "If it comes to it, my lord. I will do it."

* * *

It was amazing to see how much Tresingale had changed in a few weeks.

Remin and his men galloped through the north gate under a clear blue sky, after nearly a week of riding in the rain. The fields were more vividly green than ever, sweeping off to the mountains in rolling hills. On the north side of town, the dark furrows of planting stretched farther away, and though he wasn't farmer enough yet to guess acreage at a glance, he thought they might just get all the wheat into the ground after all.

Home.

"They've been busy," said Juste beside him, rising in his stirrups to look. Even from the gatehouse, the two white lines of the north and south wall were visible in the distance, like arms stretching out to embrace the east road.

If his horse had been a little fresher, Remin would have gone straight to look. He wanted to see everything and know every detail of how the town had grown in his absence. But he owed it to man and beast to let them refresh themselves before he put them back to work, so he grudgingly trotted them all to the stables and tended to his warhorse, who the stableboys still regarded with popeyed awe. Another year or two of peace and he might finally be able to make himself name the beast.

Then he went home to give himself a scrub. After two weeks in the saddle and sleeping by the roadside, the layers of filth were about to crack and fall off, like flakes of shale.

But when he opened the door to his cottage, he stopped. Stepped back. Looked again.

This was *his* cottage, wasn't it?

Yes, that was his trunk under the window, and his bed. But there was a new awning on the north face of the cottage housing a collection of buckets, tubs, and the princess's bath cauldron, and a small room added to the opposite side that turned out to be a privy closet. He'd forgotten he'd asked Edemir to have that built. And there were several other minor construction projects he had *not* authorized: sturdy shelves were mounted above the bed bearing the princess's books, and the washstand was a tiered marvel of shelves and cubbies, with a mirror that could be put on a shelf at his own height.

It didn't look like a single surface had escaped unscathed. There were bunches of flowers in cups on the table and windowsills, new blankets neatly folded at the foot of his bed, and under the bed were two little pairs of slippers, neatly lined up. The princess's smaller trunk and battered valise were underneath the other window, and a tin kettle hung on a hook beside the hearth. Which now had a mantle. And more flowers on the mantle.

Remin stepped inside and let the door close behind him.

Most of the shelves on the washstand contained all the soaps and lotions and strange little jars the princess had acquired in Celderline, but one shelf had his own things, along with a bar of plain soap. He put water on to heat in the kettle and stripped down to wash the filth of the road from his body with *hot water and soap,* then shaved with more hot water in an absolute orgy of good grooming. It all felt so amazing, he was almost ashamed.

His horse needed rest after weeks of hard riding, but it felt good to stretch his legs and he didn't mind beginning with a look at those projects within walking distance. All weariness had fallen from him at the sight of Tresingale. He was clean, freshly shaved, and reenergized, and now his men were going to pay for it.

Like all other valuable things in town, Edemir and all his records and plans were housed in the storehouse.

"You're back," said the stocky knight, looking up from his worktable in his closet of an office. Edemir was a compact and efficient man, economical with word and motion. "I guess we're lucky you didn't come straight from the stables."

"Tell me everything," Remin ordered, dragging over a stool.

With Edemir, it was a long list of arrivals and departures. A dozen cows had arrived and departed immediately for a new field adjacent to the horses' paddocks, and Tresingale officially had its first cowshed. More masons had arrived. Bricklayers. Carpenters. A third architect, the renowned Master Sousten Didion, had arrived, seen the cottage prepared for him, and pitched a fit that required an additional bribe of gold. He had been obsessively surveying the proposed site of the manor house ever since.

Remin was willing to forgive a tantrum. Several of the craftsmen and masters he had hired were best described as charmingly eccentric, and Sousten Didion had a reputation not just for building beautiful houses, but unfolding them in stages, planning years of gradual growth as new parts of a noble house became necessary. It was exactly what Tresingale needed.

"...seed for the kitchen garden, shipments of medical supplies, and two new journeymen to work under Genon," Edemir continued. A single surgeon was not sufficient for the growing population. "And you saw the work in your cottage? The Duchess asked for a few things, and I didn't see why not."

"That's fine." Remin waved this away, though he was surprised his shy wife had actually gathered the courage to request something.

"And if you see her today, you can tell her we'll be sending a crew to dig the third well tomorrow," Edemir added. At Remin's blank look, he explained, "They need water on the wall. You'll see when you get there."

With the warnings about demon wolves fresh in his mind, Remin had been planning to go to the wall anyway, but what did new wells have to do with the princess?

"The folk in Ferrede said the devils might be coming out early," he said, shaking it off. He had been working to push the princess out of his mind since the day he left, but she insisted on peeping back in. "Someone there saw a wolf demon. It's early, but it's been a warm spring. Has anyone here seen anything?"

"Not that they've reported." Edemir's eyebrows lifted. "They're sure it wasn't just a big wolf?"

"The man who reported it doesn't have a reputation for exaggeration. And they've seen their share of Andelin's new wildlife by now."

This was not good news. They took some time to talk through various preparations, from increasing the night watch—which meant decreasing the number of men available to work by day—to the supplies needed to keep torches and braziers lit.

"The wall is proceeding on schedule, though," Edemir noted. "You ought to take a look, Rem. In a month or so they'll start work on the gatehouse, and we can send a third of the workforce immediately to start on the north wall. I took some men off the palisade since it seemed we'd finish the wall in time, but with your news…should we have them close the gap? It'll slow building the permanent wall if we have to rip up all the earthworks."

"Don't do anything yet. We'll discuss it first," Remin decided. The sighting of a single wolf demon might not justify going that far.

Leaving Edemir to his lists, he went to find some food, hungry enough to tolerate Wen's shouting about how unreasonable it was to expect meals outside of mealtimes. In the kitchen, the vast cook was taking a cleaver to what looked like the remains of a deer.

"A bit of bread and cheese will be fine," Remin said from the doorway. "And a sausage. And wipe the blood off your hands before you touch my food."

"Well, welcome back, Your Grace." Wen glared and didn't move from his spot. "Ye can get it yourself, and welcome. Right next to the door. Ye know how to work a cupboard?"

"When did you get those? And you're letting people over the threshold now?" There were three tall sets of cupboards on the wall by the door, and Remin opened the doors to find bread, cheese, sausages, apples, carrots, and other portable items neatly stored in bins.

"Only so far as that white line." Wen jabbed his finger at a stripe of whitewash on the floor. "No one crosses that line. But it's easier than having His Grace nagging when I'm up to me elbows in yesterday's buck, innit? Ye can thank Her Grace for the favor, if you like it, she's the one wheedled the cupboards out of that skinflint Edemir."

"Wheedled? Her Grace?" Remin echoed.

"Aye, like a tinker. Came in asking for bloody carrots every morning, I was hearing *Master Wen, Master Wen* in me dreams. And then one day she says, *Master Wen, would it be easier to keep the apples and carrots here by the door? I don't like to trouble you. For Master Eugene.*" Wen produced a credible impression of the princess's shy, start-and-stop speech pattern, though the batting eyelashes were a little over the top. "Next morning it was bread for Miche, and then the ruddy stable lads wanting their breakfast, and so off she was to Edemir with a ration scheme worked out and just needing a new set of cupboards. So put that box back where ye got it from, if ye please, now I've been fucking *organized.*"

"Her Grace did this. The princess. My wife." He was sure he had misunderstood something.

"The Duchess," Wen corrected. The foul-mouthed cook was a stickler for proper etiquette. "Became the Duchess when you married her, didn't she? And aye, t'was her notion. So Your Grace, I can now say, get your own bleeding rations and sod off. And close the cupboard doors, we're not fucking animals."

It wasn't until he was some way down the road that Remin realized he hadn't asked who Master Eugene was.

Gauging the progress of the wall from his glimpse at the north gate, he elected to head down the east road rather than the southern loop. It was incredible to think that in a few months, he would already be seeing a stone gatehouse in the distance. And he really needed to name the roads.

East Road was utilitarian, but an East Road could be located anywhere in the Empire. Remin wanted people to *know* when they were in Tresingale.

Even if there wasn't much to see there yet. On the east road was the stick-and-string outlines that marked off the lots in the main town, with wide streets that would one day accommodate not just carriage traffic but foot traffic along the storefronts. And, of course, the all-important drains. Until the wall was done, Nore Ffloce had no one to actually *build* roads or drains, but he occupied himself with the surveyor in the meantime, taking exhaustive measurements to determine where digging—or filling—would be required.

"Your Grace!" The gangly man hailed Remin happily, speeding over with his usual armload of parchments. Three assistants were hot on his heels, laden with sticks, strings, and tools. "How fortunate that you happened by! There are some revisions to our plans for the outer areas of town…"

Remin was just as happy to see the plans as Nore was to show them, and for an hour they bent their heads together as Nore explained where he had adjusted this road or that set of lots, and how he planned to terrace off the back of the temple gardens to get rid of Mosquito Pond.

"And I must say, Your Grace," he added as they were saying their farewells, "please thank Her Grace for me, when next you see her. Those wells might have caused quite a mess in the artisans' quarter, when we begin construction there."

"What does the princess have to do with the artisans' quarter?" Remin asked, his black eyebrows drawing together ominously. The princess seemed to have her dainty fingers in a lot of pies and he was beginning to think he was due an explanation.

"Just the wells, Your Grace." Nore was quick to see which way the winds were blowing. "Really, it was Guisse that approved it, perhaps it would be best if he explained it…"

He escaped soon after, leaving Remin frowning at the distant walls.

On foot, he had the pleasure of watching them slowly loom ahead on both left and right, though the gap between them was still dauntingly large. Both were wrapped in a lattice of scaffolding and so covered with people, they looked like vertical anthills, with the racket of hammering, chiseling, and yelling men audible a mile away. The land on the outside of the wall was being cleared of trees for a hundred paces to make sure nothing climbed over, and Remin had to walk through a mile of forest before he reached the construction area of the south wall.

He wasn't looking for the princess. He was doing the opposite of looking for her, trying to dismiss her from his mind altogether, but she was the first thing he saw all the same. A tiny figure in the distance with one hand on her hat and the other embracing a small gray donkey, her head tilted back to look up at a blacksmith. Behind the donkey was a long, low wagon bearing three large barrels.

This by itself was sufficient to raise a number of questions.

Even as he watched, the blacksmith said something that made her eyes widen and she covered her mouth with one gloved hand, giggling. Where was the silent, solemn little owl he knew? She was smiling. Her eyes were so bright, so quick to see everything. Even veiled, hatted, and covered in white dust, he couldn't help thinking her beautiful. She looked like nothing so much as the clearest and bluest of skies.

Until she turned and saw Remin.

CHAPTER 8 – THE GROWTH OF TREES

"No, it was her idea," Miche said at the stable that evening, as they stood at the far end of the long aisle and watched the princess brush Master Eugene, who kept affectionately butting her with his head. "At first, she was just worried about getting the water to the lads on the south wall. But then she wondered whether the stream on the north wall dries up in summer, which apparently happens to the stream in Aldeburke. Next thing I know, she's consulting with Guisse on the placement of wells, and then the day before the first one was due to be dug, she suddenly wondered whether or not someone else might have plans for that bit of dirt. She'd caught sight of Nore's sticks on the east side of town."

"And you gave her a donkey."

"She was right." Miche spread his hands helplessly. "I can't argue with her math, Rem. On day two she was counting her footsteps and taking averages of how much ground she could cover on her own. She's a smart girl."

Remin knew that. He had sometimes glanced at the books she was reading on the way to Tresingale, everything from her favorite *The Will Immanent* to histories, poetry, plays, and one book that was more diagram than prose. But he had never expected her to start *applying* her intellect the minute his back was turned.

"Sort out the bandits?" Miche's eyes twinkled, as if he were enjoying himself.

"We did. Supplied by a miller and his granddaughter, out of Ferrede. I'll tell all of you the rest over supper." At the end of the stable, the princess was crooning as she brushed the donkey, her voice rising and falling musically as she assured him that he was the handsomest and cleverest and most darling creature alive.

As if the donkey understood a word of it. Remin folded his arms, scowling.

"You could go help her," Miche suggested, following his eyes. "She'd be happy, Rem, if you just—"

"Any trouble while I was gone?"

Miche sighed. "Nothing major. Accident on the north wall, one fellow took a tumble and broke his arm. We're trying not to tell the men to hurry. Hurried men make mistakes."

It would be nice if they could accomplish as much in two weeks as a single princess apparently could. But for all Miche's assurances, it was still hard to believe. Her greeting for Remin had been as timid as ever, accompanied with something that might have been *I'm glad you're safe*. And even then, she had looked as if she had expected to be scolded for saying so.

"I need to get washing water from the well," she said when they reached their cottage, hanging up her hat and veil on a nail by the door. Her hair was almost gray with stone dust. But she paused, her fingers knotting together, and asked softly, "...do you like it?"

She clearly meant the cottage. And for some reason, he just couldn't make himself say it.

"It was good of Edemir to spare the men for the extra work," he said. "I hope you thanked him."

"I did." And she slipped back out the front door without meeting his eyes.

The thought of awkwardly not speaking to each other when she came back with the water did not appeal.

"I'll fetch you for supper when it's full dark," he said when she returned, lugging a pair of full buckets, and departed without looking at her.

That was more or less his plan for the foreseeable future. But it was difficult when his own men persisted in bringing her to his attention. At supper, Edemir wanted to talk about the blasted wells, Juste had heard about the donkey and wanted to know how much weight he was hauling, and Miche teased her endlessly, albeit with a gentler version of his usual biting wit. All of it made Remin feel like he had been away for much longer than a few weeks.

"It turned out as well as it could have," he said, when Miche inquired after the bandits. "I don't think we'll have any further problems with Ferrede, but we'll need to send them some builders, Edemir. They had a couple stranglers crawling in their windows last year and I promised them a safe place to sleep. They're cooperative, but we should send a few armored men along, just in case. And maybe one of the squires. Who do you reckon, Huber?"

"Rollon," the quiet knight said, after a moment's consideration. "Folk generally like him, and he's ready for a small command."

"We'll make it eight men. That's the other trouble." The cookhouse was emptying by now, but Remin still spared a glance at the men nearby, who quickly found somewhere else to be. "I already mentioned it to some of you, but a man in Ferrede said he spotted a wolf demon. It's early, but I don't want to take any chances. We'll have guards in the sleeping areas, braziers, and the new arrivals need to know what to watch for."

"We'll need to get the animals out of the field before nightfall, then," said Juste. "I'll go now. They've been leaving the sheep and goats out overnight in the near pens."

"Any livestock missing?" Bram asked suddenly from the end of the long table, and Juste stopped.

"Yes," he said slowly. "They told me today. A goat and one of the ewes."

"It could be regular wolves," said Remin into the silence, but none of them believed it. "Go on, Juste. And hurry back."

"I guess we're moving some men back to palisade building tomorrow, then," Edemir said, resigned. "Blast it. We were just starting to get ahead on the wall. If the wolves are out, the others won't be far behind. We'll need to put some nursemaids on our more delicate masters, Rem. Some of them don't have the sense to come in out of the rain. I wouldn't like Sousten Didion to take it in his head to get a midnight view of Tresingale. Which he might do."

"Tell him what happened to that mason last year," said Huber flatly. "The one that decided to get drunk and take a walk outside the north gate."

"That was a wolf demon, wasn't it?" Bram tossed a bone into the bowl in the center of the table. "All but gutted the poor bastard, I'd sooner a pack of ghouls got me, at least they can't take my leg off with the first bi—"

"Rem," Miche said sharply, and Remin glanced over to find the blond knight radiating extreme displeasure, his eyes flicking pointedly at the princess, who was listening to the talk with round, horrified eyes.

"Excuse me," Rem said abruptly, taking her elbow. She'd barely done more than pick at her supper anyway, and she didn't need to be sitting in on their councils. "Come with me, Princess. Edemir, send word to the night watch. They need to be warned. I'll be back."

The pools of torchlight lining the path outside hadn't seemed so insubstantial in quite some time. Last year, their defenses had been fewer, but they had also been a much smaller target. The Andelin devils only came out after nightfall, and Remin's men were wary and disciplined. It was almost worse this year. They were a sprawling settlement of hundreds of craftsmen, journeymen, and apprentices, many of them sleeping in tents, and folk wandering about in the dark like it was a summer festival.

"You'll be safe here," he said as he ducked into the cottage behind the princess, bending his head under the rafters. Sometimes he felt like he lived half his life in a crouch. "Don't go outside, for any reason."

"Do Yvain and Dol know?" she asked, looking at the window nervously. "If a wolf demon can bite off a leg, couldn't it come through the wall? And surely the folk in Ferrede have shutters on their windows, how did—"

Ah. This was why Miche had been glaring.

"My guards know what to look for," he interrupted, before she finished that thought. She needed to know the danger just as much as Sousten Didion, but there was nothing to be gained from terrifying her. "We've been dealing with them for three years. Go to sleep. I'll be late tonight."

"Oh, but…" She caught his sleeve. Her eyes were enormous, shining gold in the lamplight and so vulnerable that he had to look quickly away. "Couldn't you just…I—I know you must…"

Her fingers slipped from his sleeve.

"At least warn the stableboys," she said, her head bowing. "Eugene isn't as big as a horse, and he's old, and he doesn't even have a proper door on his stall…"

"You're worried about the donkey," Remin said incredulously.

She nodded and went to sit on the bed, her arms wrapping around herself, and at once he wanted to go to her and recoiled at the sight. Everything in him rose up and roared a warning. *A trick. A trap.*

"I'll have a word with the stableboys," he promised, and shut the door.

Normally guards pretended not to overhear anything, effectively blind and deaf to everything that passed in their presence. But tonight, both of the house guards were waiting for him as soon as he came outside. Guards with whom the princess was already on a first-name basis, Remin noted. Yvain was a short, sturdy man who would never win a race, but who could march to the ends of the earth, and Dol was taller and weedy-looking.

"They're back, Your Grace?" Yvain asked.

"It looks like it. I'll send someone with extra torches. Keep your eyes and ears open."

He did send someone to warn the stableboys to lock up, but only because it was good sense. It would be devastating if the devils got into the stables.

"And tell them to make sure that donkey is put somewhere safe," he added before the messenger departed.

It was a late night. Remin and his knights occupied Edemir's small office long past midnight, wrangling over which men could be spared for what tasks, and whether or not they needed to build some sort of hardened structure for the masons' camp. They had a duty to protect the folk of the valley, but there was also a concern about provoking panic, or even an exodus out of town. If such a thing happened, it would take years to recover.

"The worst part is, it will slow down the wall," Edemir said grimly, surveying his new lists. His secretaries had been writing their fingers off, keeping pace with the flow of orders. "It's going to be full summer before they even begin the northern stretch."

"At some point we're going to have to find out where the devils go during the winter, and why," said Juste. "Are they hibernating? Breeding? Or one spring night we may find they've bred up more than we expected over the winter."

"Maybe that's what they did this winter," said Huber, who was always good for a bad thought.

"Let's not make any assumptions," Remin said firmly. "We know what we're dealing with, if not how many. Let's call back a reserve force from the Vallethi border, and we can discuss tracking the devils to their burrows come fall."

With the next day's work divided between them, they broke for the night, far more warily than usual. The devils feared the sunlight and avoided torchlight, but it wouldn't stop them. Outside the cookhouse, Remin found Miche leaning against the wall, waiting.

"She was scared," Miche said, without preamble. "I told you to take her home because she was scared, Rem, not so you could get her out of the way. I know you're an idiot about women, but you're verging on being cruel. If she's scared, you stay with her until she's not."

"My wife is not your business."

"You made her my business. And you're my business too, you giant git."

Remin had been at odds with his men before. It was inevitable; all of them were accustomed to command, all of them had strong opinions, and though Remin bore the title of the Duke of Andelin, it wasn't a card he cared to play often. He wanted his knights to argue with him if they thought he was wrong.

But this was the first time *Miche* had ever cared enough to have an opinion.

"I know we've always had to be wary of the Emperor's gifts," he was saying. "But she's not a knighthood or a duchy. She's a seventeen year-old girl and no one asked her if she wanted to come to the edge of the Empire and listen to devils howling. And she's a good girl, she's been working like a dog, which you would know if you ever *talked*—"

"It does not please me to find her hands in the kitchen, in Nore Ffloce's planning, in Guisse's construction, and managing the water supply for both the north and south wall." When Remin was angry, it came out in the all-but-forgotten tones of his father, stiff and icy and snapping like a whip. "Have you considered for an instant how much damage she could do?"

"We're talking about the same person, right? Five feet tall, timid, calls Bastard Wen *Master?*"

"The one who has you eating out of her hand." Remin leveled a black stare at him. "You've never cared about a woman before, why does this one matter so much to you, Miche?"

"Don't even try to tell yourself that lie." Miche glared right back. "You're the one that handed her off to me. I'm telling you that if you're wrong, you're going to be sorrier than you've ever been in your life."

There wasn't much more to say, after that. Remin stalked into his cottage and stripped down in the dark, rolling out his bedroll with a snap. The last straw would have been a timid question from the darkness, but if the princess was awake, she had the sense to hold her tongue.

In the morning, he found out where the flowers infesting his cottage were coming from.

"What the hell are these?" He asked, turning back through the cottage door with several ragged bundles of wildflowers in his hands. A number of them had been lying on the front step. The princess was sitting up in bed and her eyes were open, but that was all the progress she had made so far.

"The flowers?" She rubbed her eyes. "Someone leaves them."

"Who?"

"I don't know." She wilted visibly under his stare, her voice shrinking. "They're just there in the morning…"

Under the codes of courtly love, there was nothing inappropriate about anonymously leaving flowers for an admired lady. Indeed, it wasn't even necessarily romantic; knights frequently left small tokens for a lady that struck them with her beauty, grace, or skill at some noble pursuit. Remin was effectively clutching notes that said, *you have a fine wife.*

Most men would have been proud that she was so—

Remin's arm snapped back to strike before he could think about it, and Ophele, who had materialized at his side on her light little feet, ducked backward with a gasp.

Name of all the stars. He had almost *struck* her.

"I—I was just—" She began, her voice high with fright.

"It was just a reflex," Remin said loudly. He set the flowers on the table and retreated, looking at her small white face. He hadn't hit her, thank the stars. But his mouth was dry, and his heart was hammering so hard, he was almost dizzy. "Please do not…surprise me, wife."

"I won't," she whispered.

"I'll send Miche to take you to the wall," he said, backing away, unable to take his eyes from her hands. Empty. Of course, they were empty. But for a second, from the corner of his eye…

"Get dressed," he said, his stomach churning. Whatever Miche said, he wasn't a complete idiot. He could see that she was frightened, and hurt, and it gave him no pleasure. This was why he was doing his best to keep away from her. To train his eyes to pass her by.

But no matter what he did, she persisted in being seen.

* * *

That was how all her days began.

"Get up."

Black eyes. Thick black brows. Chiseled lips pressed tight together, stern and forbidding. Every morning the same frowning face swimming above her, as if sleep were an affront.

"Uh?"

"Up," the duke repeated, pulling her into a sitting position. Left to her own devices, Ophele would have kept going straight over onto her face. It felt as if she had barely closed her eyes.

"…izzit?" she mumbled, rubbing her face with her hands.

"It's dawn, time to get up."

Blearily, she watched him put on a kettle to heat washing water and then strip off his shirt, dirty and sweaty and a little blood-spattered from guarding against the devils. It wasn't his blood. It was never his blood. And he had been very careful to wash the worst of it off before he woke her ever since that first time, when she had opened her eyes to see him glaring at her through a mask of devil's blood. Half the town had heard her shriek, to her lasting humiliation, and it had taken some time before she could be *sure* it wasn't all a nightmare.

To be fair, he had been sorry about that.

Ophele understood something of her father's frustration, watching him shave. Didn't he ever get tired? Was he even human? Night after night, he was standing watch, sometimes returning at dawn to wake her and wash before he went to work for the day. She knew this because often she was still awake when he came home. Yet somehow he looked as fresh as if he had come from a good night's sleep, while she was so exhausted she was starting to believe in the Bhumi night hags, ephemeral demons that rode on the shoulders of their victims, whispering nightmares in the dark and leeching away warmth and strength by day.

Hands gripped her shoulders and lifted her bodily out of bed, standing her on her feet, and she had to catch herself. She had almost fallen back to sleep.

"Awake now?" His finger pushed her chin up to look at her, and Ophele shrank away. She knew she was nothing to him, neither wanted nor useful, nothing more than a chore.

Once, she had wanted to say so many things to him. Apologies, explanations, and an endless number of questions. Now she just felt paralyzed in his presence, afraid to do or say anything. Sometimes it seemed as if just the sight of her infuriated him.

He had made it very clear that he wanted nothing from her. Not even her help.

That hurt her more than almost anything else, including the incident with the flowers. Ophele had unraveled *that* mystery inside twenty minutes; of course he would not want her near him, and would see her as a threat: her father had spent almost twenty years making sure of it. But she had thought he would be pleased, when he saw the other things she had done. Wasn't it better if Master Wen didn't have to stop cooking to fetch things? And both Master Ffloce and Master Guisse had said they were glad she thought of the wells, especially with the stream by the north wall already drying up.

But maybe they hadn't meant it. She was their duchess. Maybe they had been afraid to tell her she was wrong. What did she know of wells and walls?

"Get dressed," the duke said as he shrugged into a rough jerkin, belting it around his waist. "I'll see you at supper."

The cottage door thudded shut behind him.

Safflower. That was the Bhumi remedy for night hags. Ophele stood in the silent cottage, feeling the rushes with her bare feet, and then moved stiffly to dress.

There was always a bouquet or two of flowers on the front doorstep, and she put them in water and hung the old bouquets over the bed to dry, filling the cottage with the sweet scent. There was no sign of Sir Miche yet, so she stood by the new road, looking with pleasure at the cobblestones. They had just been laid yesterday; was it safe to walk on them? Did the mortar have to set, or something? Cautiously, she stepped onto them, feeling the rounded river rocks through her small, sturdy boots.

"Admiring the metropolis, my lady?" Sir Miche's voice said from behind her, and Ophele retreated guiltily.

"It will be, one day," she said, brightening as he approached with Eugene. The donkey's hooves clopped onto the road and the wagon wheels bumped upward with a sound that was like a touch of civilization. "Do you think that's the first time anyone's heard wagon wheels on cobblestone in the valley?"

His eyebrows lifted.

"First time in a long time," he said, glancing back at the wagon with appreciation. "Since the first invasion of Valleth, anyway. That's a milestone, isn't it? The official opening of Harnost Highway."

"I thought it was Tounot Turnpike." She fell into step beside him, petting Master Eugene. The Knights of the Brede squabbled like boys over the naming of things.

He gave her a wounded look.

"Of all people, I never thought you would abandon me."

"I would never," she protested. "I think it should be Eugene Street, in memory of the first wagon to touch it."

"We are not naming the first major road in Tresingale after a donkey, no matter how distinguished."

Bickering amiably, they stopped for breakfast and carrots and then headed for the wall. It was a fair distance, two and a half miles along the curve of the road that went south, then east. But it gave them a chance to see the progress of all the new projects along the route, from two buildings at the end of a long lane by the river to the wooden frame of what Sir Miche said would be the town's first store. A merchant named Guian was already on his way to the valley.

It promised to be a fine, hot day as the sun rose in a clear sky, and Ophele was already beginning to perspire in her hot woolen dress as they reached the cob barracks, a prominent structure on a hillside overlooking the sheep pens.

"They're putting in windows?" she asked in surprise. The building was made of white Brede River clay, and the large, regular gaps in deep sills could be nothing else. It seemed foolhardy, with stranglers creeping about every night.

"One in every room," Sir Miche said, with mingled satisfaction and defiance. "The east wall will be finished before the barracks are. We'll have all the windows we want, and laugh at the devils."

"I like the tower." It wasn't in her to laugh at the devils. She didn't even want to think about them. "What's it for?"

"That'll be the council room," he replied, nodding to the large round tower on the east end of the complex. "Have you heard of the Five Courts?"

She nodded. They were the five bodies that supported the Emperor in Segoile: the Courts of Nobles, Merchants, Artisans, Scholars, and the powerful Court of War. It would have been blasphemous to count the Temple of the Stars as merely a court, though the essential divinity of the Emperor made it very difficult for the Temple to oppose him.

"That will be the Andelin's Court of War," Sir Miche was explaining. "The Emperor considers us a buffer region against Valleth, expendable if necessary. We're not going to count on the House of Agnephus for support, if it comes to it. We'll have our own Court of War, our own standing army, and our own Academy. Just in case."

Ophele digested this. The ramifications might have escaped most seventeen year-old girls, but she had read a great deal of history. No one in Segoile could protest if the duke maintained his own army, not with Valleth sitting on his doorstep. But she couldn't help wondering if anyone in the Five Courts had considered that Remin Grimjaw, son of an extinct House, might not think that Valleth was his only enemy.

"The Brede belongs to the duke, doesn't it?" she asked. "Even the docks on the south side of it?"

"Every mile," Sir Miche agreed, looking at the dark water churning beyond the trees. "Nothing moves on the river without Rem's permission."

They were so clever, the Knights of the Brede. Had anyone thought, when the duke claimed the river as part of the Andelin, that it would mean his duchy was all but impregnable? Everyone said Remin was a genius, and he must be; the greatest military commanders in Argence had been trying and failing for a hundred years to take back the valley.

And now the genius held it to the south bank of the Brede.

Was that what the duke was planning? Or maybe *planning* was too strong a word, she thought, frowning. He was maneuvering. He was putting himself in the most advantageous, unassailable position. The House of Andelin would be very difficult to destroy the way his original House had been.

Had Remin really thought of all that when he was only seventeen?

"My lady?" Sir Miche asked, and Ophele looked up, startled to see they were nearly at the foot of the wall.

"I'm sorry, I was thinking of the Court of War," she said, which was the truth.

"It'll be some time before it's ready." Retrieving his shovel from the wagon, he saluted her with it. "I wish you luck with the windlass. Sit down if you get tired."

"Be careful," she replied, as she always did, and turned the wagon south to the well.

Ophele knew her routine now. She knew where water would be needed and had found the patterns in the men's work, slow and uneven in the morning, accelerating into a perfect, humming machine as everyone woke up.

"Wayyyy I wake up, up high on the hill," called one of the foremen from the top of the wall, raising his voice over the clatter and clang of all the tools, and all the men on the wall sang the answer.

> *Wayyyyy I wake up, before the sun*
> *Got a cup and a bite against the chill*
> *Got a mountain to climb before day is done.*

"Wayyyyy I wake up, down in the valley," came Sir Miche's voice from the trench, and there was a ripple of appreciative laughter from his fellow ditch diggers before they called back.

> *Wayyyy I wake up, under the stars*
> *Got to grab my shovel, no time to dally*
> *Got a mountain to shift, so far…*

"So far!" called Sir Miche in answer, as all the shovels bit into the wet earth at once, dirt flying up in a wave from the trench. Stone thwacked into place on the wall, and there was the scrape of mortar, trowels flicking, a rhythmic accompaniment to the music.

After a few days, Ophele had learned these songs well enough to sing along, softly because she had no more notion of music than a sheep. But that was the time she liked best, when they all sang together so that the wall almost seemed to assemble itself. She nodded and smiled and waved as the men went by, fetched their tools when they dropped them, and before noon, she topped off everyone's water and then turned back to town, where Wen and his kitchen boys were waiting to load the noon meal onto the wagon.

"No, they'll load it, you're a bleeding duchess," Master Wen barked when she tried to help. The irascible cook stood in the door of the kitchen with his hands on his hips as he watched the proceedings, red-faced in the afternoon heat. "Do ye think they need consultation on stacking their baskets? Go. Sit. *Eat!*"

The abrupt bellow made her jump, and Ophele scuttled over to a pair of tree stumps set in the shade of a nearby tree. There was a trencher of bread, cheese, and a sliced apple waiting for her there, covered with a cloth. Wen glowered at her until she was done, and when she rose to return the plate and cloth, he looked pointedly at the remaining bit of bread and cheese.

"Does it not suit your palate, Your Grace?" he asked, soft and dangerous, like the warning gust of a tempest. Ophele stuffed the remainder into her mouth and escaped.

It was hard to eat when she was so hot, and so very tired. Sir Miche had said that eventually her body would adjust to the work, like he had gotten used to his ditch digging, but it had been weeks and still she was just barely keeping up. Her hands were blistered, blisters on top of blisters, and she washed and bandaged and padded them under her gloves, wincing as she dragged the buckets out of the well. The burn of her aching muscles blended with the heat of the day until it was as if she moved through a waking dream, where everything hurt and nothing was real and it was impossible to tell one day from the next.

Unfortunately, the nights were all too vivid.

"I'll be back late," said the duke after her supper, just as he did every night, clanking and jingling in his armor. He kept it on a stand in the cottage, battered steel that was disappointingly utilitarian, though he carefully cleaned and inspected it every day. His sword was an object of fascination to Ophele, who had been nourished on fantastical tales of legendary weapons forged in magical fires and engraved with sorcerous writing. His Grace's two-handed broadsword was nearly as tall as she was, but it didn't look the least bit magical.

"Be careful," she said from the furthest corner of the bed, where she was already trying to hide behind her book. She couldn't let him go face the devils without saying *something,* even though she knew he would have preferred that she didn't exist.

"Go to sleep," he said, as if she hadn't spoken. "You're safe. Nothing will harm you."

And he was gone, slinging his sword into its place on his back. Outside, the light was fading.

For the first week after he returned from Ferrede, it hadn't been bad. There had only been the occasional noises of devils, faint and faraway, quickly dispatched before they could approach the town. But their numbers had grown with the heat of the days, and Ophele knew about every one of the gaps in the town's outer perimeter because she heard the duke and his knights discussing them over supper. The palisade wasn't completed on either the western or eastern ends. There was a gap of nearly two miles in the middle of the stone wall. Stranglers climbed over the palisade, exploiting the least shadows to slink into town.

Every night, there were more of them. Every night, they came closer. Louder.

Why did they make those noises? Ophele sought patterns as naturally as she breathed, but she did not have enough information to make sense of these nighttime horrors. Why did stranglers make that sound? It was a high and cackling *eh heh heh heh* that echoed through the night air for miles. Were they communicating with each other? Could the devils talk amongst themselves? It seemed to her that it would be more sensible to go after forest animals than to face armed and armored men, but the hunters reported no shortage of game. The devils wanted the flesh of men. And occasionally livestock, out of pure spite.

She could find no patterns in their behavior. The deafening howls of the wolf demons came nearer and nearer, and only two days ago she had heard a pack of ghouls down the lane, like a particularly hoarse and raspy dogfight. She had never seen these creatures, and no one would describe them to her, and it let her vivid, well-stocked imagination run wild.

Ophele tried to be brave. She tried to be logical. She lit lamps and blew them out, unsure whether lights might not attract the devils. As the night wore on, she moved from her bed to the table and back again, trying to reason out where the safest place in the cottage was. From her bed, she could see all the doors and windows at once, so if a strangler crept inside, at least she would have time to scream.

But she had also seen the damage a wolf demon could do. A creature that could rip the front box off a wagon would think nothing of a bit of wattle and daub. It could tear off the whole corner of the cottage if it wanted to, and take her with it. And she hadn't any idea how strong stranglers were, either. It was entirely possible that one night, as she tried to squeeze herself back into the corner of room, two hands might smash through the walls and wrap around her throat.

Could they hear her breathing? Could they smell fear, the way people said dogs could?

Hiding behind her book, she tried to be deaf.

"Strangler!"

The call was distant, but not that distant. She heard running feet heading up the road to the north, somewhere further along the line of cottages, and suddenly she hardly dared to breathe. Her ears strained.

"Don't see it," said another voice. It was hard to tell how far away. The walls of the cottage muffled sound a little, but not much.

"Well, he's dead, you nit, it's somewhere close by," said a third voice. "Weren't you watching? Search the crofts."

Ophele clutched her knees to her chest, curling up as small as she possibly could, as if she could eventually collapse on herself and disappear altogether. She wished she would. Oh, stars, someone was dead. A strangler had killed someone right outside. This second it could be outside the cottage, killing Yvain or Dol.

"Dol?" Terror turned one syllable into three. "Are you all right?"

"You're not asleep?" Dol sounded displeased. "We're both here, you're safe, my lady."

"They said someone is dead."

"Dunno who yet, lady. Oh, but it's not His Grace," Dol added quickly. "He's on the east watch tonight, at the gap between the walls."

But he could die there. He could already be dead. And Sir Miche might die, or Sir Justenin, or Sir Tounot, any of them could die, all those men she saw at the wall or sat with at supper. They tried not to let her see the devils they killed, and every time someone died on the wall, they moved heaven and earth to make sure she didn't lay eyes on the corpse, but she wasn't stupid. The devils were there. Men could die. A man *had* died. She could die.

They kept saying she was safe. The duke said it every night, that no devil would ever get so far as the cottage, but how could they *know* that? It was only May and all anyone could talk about was how there were more devils than they had ever seen before. In her mind's eye she could picture dozens of shadowy goblin-shapes crawling over the palisades, wolf demons smashing through the barricades that lined the main road, and frothing packs of ghouls charging behind them, snarling and slavering. One night, they might come in like the tide.

No one could say it wouldn't happen. No one could *know*.

"…lady? Your Grace?" Dol repeated, and Ophele started, turning in the direction of his voice. "Are you there?"

"Yes," she breathed. "Yes?"

"Don't be scared. You're safe."

"How do you know?" She wanted him to know. She wanted desperately for him to make her believe it.

"If we ever thought there was danger, our orders are to take you to the storehouse, my lady," said Yvain, who was standing at the opposite side of the cottage, outside the door. "Stone walls. No windows. If we thought it was necessary, even for an instant, that's where you would be right now."

"All right," she whispered. She shouldn't be talking to them anyway. They needed to watch and listen. There was a strangler outside, and while she was distracting them, maybe it would creep up and kill one of them. Would she even know? Did people make noise when they strangled to death? Ophele strained her ears, her heart lodged in her throat.

At that moment something howled so loud, it seemed it would shake the roof off the cottage, and she clapped her hands over her mouth to keep back a scream, tears of terror streaking down her cheeks. She wanted to go home. She wanted to go home. She didn't want to be here anymore, even Aldeburke was better than this. Would she even be able to run if she had to? Oh, she could imagine fleeing to the storehouse, with the snarling shadow of a wolf demon barreling after her to rip her apart. Sir Bram said they could rip off a man's leg with one bite.

"Try to go to sleep, my lady," said Dol, once the howl had faded into ringing silence. "I swear under the light of the stars, no harm will come to you."

Ophele wished she could go to sleep and never wake up again. Burying her head under her covers, she called herself a coward and a mouse and still couldn't argue herself out of her fear. Knuckles pressed to her mouth, she silently sobbed, and some hours later, her tears accomplished what logic, reassurance, and sacred oaths had failed to do. A little bit before dawn, Ophele sobbed herself to sleep.

It felt like *minutes* passed before a hand gripped her and sat her up.

Black eyebrows. Black eyes. A firm mouth, set in a disapproving line.

"Wake up," rumbled the duke's voice, and Ophele rubbed her face with trembling hands. The Bhumi night hags were very much clinging to her shoulders, even after he shook her. "Are you well?"

"I'm fine," she whispered, at the dawning of another day.

* * *

"Twenty-foot sections and six-foot gaps," said Remin, who was confronting a much less impressive wall on the north side of town. The palisade had already advanced eastward beyond the wheat fields to the edge of the old forest, and he had to raise his voice to be heard over the din of shouting and sawing and falling trees. "We'll fill in the gaps later."

"It'll be a fortnight before there's enough wall to be worth defending," rumbled Jinmin, stumping along beside him. Having taken command of the night watch, the big man was deeply concerned about the progress of the palisade. "It's still a long way to the east wall, m'lord."

"It'll be a fortnight before we're trying to stop them here," Remin replied, pausing by one six-foot stretch of wall, the raw timbers lashed together with wet rope. It would dry and shrink tight quickly in this heat. "Save the pines for pitch. We're going to need a lot of torches."

Ahead of them were hundreds of men busy at every stage of construction for these defenses, from clearing the land to deny the devils cover to dragging the trees in for processing. Sawyers, busily hewing them into planks. Rope-makers, pressed into service to soak long strips of bark and grasses in water and then weave them together. Pitch-makers, hauling away the pine branches as fast as they were trimmed, to be burned for their resin. Tounot was overseeing the construction of the palisade itself, the finished timbers thudding into the earth, braced with heavy stones to keep the devils from simply digging under it.

And other trees were reserved for barriers like the one lying at Remin's feet: six feet wide, eight to ten feet tall, lashed together with two cross-braces on the back to make them strong.

"Break walls," said Jinmin, eying them with foreboding.

"They'll fill in the gaps in the palisade, when we're ready," said Remin, and confirmed Jinmin's worst suspicions by bending to lift the nearest barrier, jerking his chin at the other man. "Get the other side."

Normally such work was reserved for draft horses, but Remin and Jinmin made a reasonable substitute. It was a long walk to the cluster of cottages by the north gate, wattle-and-daub structures already obscured behind three lines of break walls. Every section was braced with two sturdy logs behind it and banked with earth at the base, designed to withstand even the deadly charge of a wolf demon, so that a single man with a sword could pin them between sections of wall. Behind the last line of walls were stands for archers, with baskets sitting ready for their arrows and sturdy braziers to give them light for shooting. The land had been cleared for twenty yards from the last line of break walls.

There were many lines of defenses. More soldiers guarded the nearest gaps in the palisade, funneling the devils into a gauntlet of archers. Each of Tresingale's small camps had been built on a hilltop, with excellent visibility and no cover for the devils, so that even the sneaky stranglers could not approach unobserved. Devils did not fear torchlight, but they had sufficient animal intelligence that they would not attack an alert, wary target unless they outnumbered it.

Remin was still dissatisfied.

In this part of the valley, the devils usually didn't arrive until late April, then escalated to a peak in late July and August. So far, his men had been keeping pace with the beasts; they had only lost a single guardsman, and there was no doubt the early warning from Ferrede had saved lives. They kept the devils' corpses out of sight to avoid alarming the camp, but Remin knew exactly how many there were.

He felt with deepest instinct that this was only the beginning.

He managed a few hours of hauling sections of wall before Juste appeared to protest the activity, galloping up as urgently as if he had been informed that the Duke of Andelin was running around the north gate with no clothes on.

"My lord," he said pointedly, swinging off his evil-tempered roan, which immediately tried to bite him. "Please let me take your place. My horse could use some exercising."

"Thanks, Juste," Remin said agreeably, surrendering his section of wall. Jinmin was busy propping it up with two heavy braces. "I want this line finished by sunset. I'll go look in on the barracks, if you'll give Jinmin a hand."

"Please let the bricklayers haul the bricks, Your Grace!" Juste called after him, correctly guessing what he was off to do. Remin waved a hand.

A few of his men had strong opinions about what work was appropriate for the hands of a nobleman, and Juste and Edemir in particular objected to Remin including himself among the town's beasts of burden. But Remin thought it was good for his men to see him working. They could hardly complain about their own labors if they saw the Duke of Andelin trundling by with a load of bricks on his back, and it wasn't as if he had any other useful skills. Remin was not a mason or a bricklayer or any sort of craftsman. He was a knight and a general, and he had spent his life learning to break walls, not build them.

There was plenty of work for his unskilled hands. He was pulled in a dozen different directions every day, and he genuinely loved all of it. One day he was helping mix clay for bricks, then juggling them as they came scorching out of a kiln. He took his turn felling trees, digging wells, digging trenches. There was no part of Tresingale that he had not touched, and he was learning right alongside the rest of his men how to mix mortar, how to build a foundation, how to plow and sow and one day, if it pleased the stars, to reap a bountiful harvest.

After supper, he donned his armor and took his place in the lines of soldiers, secretly glad of the excuse to get out of the cottage and away from the princess. Soon, construction would begin on their house, and then they would hardly see each other at all.

And so, congratulating himself on how well he was managing everything, he walked in on her in the bath.

"Your Grace!" She squealed, ducking behind the lip of the cauldron, but it was already too late. The sight of her smooth white shoulders and bare breasts had already been seared onto his eyeballs.

"I'm sorry," he said, electing to brazen it out rather than retreat like a coward. "I came to tell you, we're looking at the manor site with Sousten tomorrow morning. He wants to show us his plans. Would you like to go?"

"The plans for the house?" she asked, peeping over the lip of the cauldron. He had never seen her in the bath before, and he was struck by how ridiculous it was; she looked as if she were about to be cooked into a soup.

His lips twitched until the back of his brain observed that she would make a very meager meal.

"Yes," he said slowly, his eyes narrowing. Had she always been that thin? Surely her cheeks had been more rounded before, hadn't they? Her eyes had always been splendid, thickly lashed and luminous, but now they looked almost *too* big in her small face.

"I would," she said, her shoulders hunching under his regard and red to the tips of her ears. Remin politely yanked his eyes away.

"I hadn't realized how cramped that is," he said abruptly. "I'll find a proper tub."

"I need something deep enough for laundry."

"You've been washing your own laundry?" he snapped, and then could have kicked himself; who else would do it? The squires were responsible for tending their masters' clothing and armor, but the Duchess of Andelin could hardly send her underclothes to a bunch of teenage boys for washing.

She nodded, looking as if she wished she would drown in her bathwater.

"I'll think of something," was all Remin could say, and left her to get on with her pitiful bath. All this time, he had never thought of such a basic chore. When had she found the time? Or the energy? He had done his share of laundry when he was a squire, and it was hard work that demanded a great deal of strength. There was a reason washerwomen had hands like blacksmiths.

Once, it would have given him pleasure to put the Emperor's daughter to such work. Now he couldn't imagine how the prospect had ever pleased him. Well, he would have to do it himself, whether she protested or not.

At least she seemed happy to be going to see where the manor would be built. The next morning, she woke up on only the third try and was already dressed when he returned to pick her up, soft and pretty in a modest violet gown, and doing her best to be invisible.

The planned site of the ducal estate was on the southwest hill overlooking the river. Two smaller hills hugged its side, flattish on the top and gently sloping toward the back, perfect locations for outbuildings. The front of the hill was a bit of a climb through tall grass and there wasn't much to see at the moment; the old forest was still thick here, and an immense oak stood at the summit, hoary and ancient.

Sousten Didion was already on the crest, equipped with a worktable and disdaining a tent, which he claimed would ruin the atmosphere of the entire hill.

"Ah, you must be His Grace's lady wife!" He exclaimed, hurrying over to kiss the princess's hand. "I am charmed and delighted, blessed lady, charmed and delighted! What an honor to build a home to shelter the daughter of the stars! I beg you to speak freely if our plans are not perfect in the slightest particular."

He had the habit of simultaneously over-pronouncing and swallowing his words, like an actor's parody of an aristocrat. But even if he was a little flamboyant for Remin's taste, he couldn't argue with Sousten's work. The man was a genius.

"Thank you," said the princess, bobbing her head.

"It may be difficult to imagine now, but the finished house will have a tremendous view," said the architect, flinging out his arms to embrace both the town and the river. "Imagine the great city that will lie at our feet, bustling by day and lit with lamps of an evening, nestled beside the river. Decorative trees will line the streets, and there will be the temple, with its gleaming crystal spires. And in the distance, far white walls and green hills. That is what you will see from the front doors of your home."

He snapped his fingers, and two assistants produced an enormous canvas depicting this vision, a watercolor that was like a dream of the town to come. The princess drew a breath, her large eyes absorbing every detail.

"And we promise a view every bit as spectacular from the opposite side," Sousten went on, smug with this success. "A natural view of the river, the forest, and eventually the new bridge. As such, there will be no back of the house…"

Another picture. Tounot, Juste, and Miche had accompanied Remin to the site; they had been with him longest and deserved to see the rewards of their hard work. Remin drew the princess in front of him as they crowded around the picture, to make sure she got a look. As Sousten said, this would be her home, too.

"There will be extensive terracing on the grounds," said the architect, beckoning them onward. Every time he stopped, his assistants unrolled another picture or diagram depicting the things he was describing. "Imagine, my lady, that here you see gardens and follies and manicured lawns descending, with a manmade pond over there…"

There were places that would be raised and others that would be flattened, connected with paths and bridges and stairs. High walkways would look down on lower gardens, with arches and cascading flowers and connecting tunnels that made the gardens spectacular and multi-dimensional, a fanciful construct like nothing Remin could have imagined.

"I have designed it for all weathers, you see," Sousten explained. "The whole estate is meant to be *experienced:* walked, ridden, circumnavigated by carriage and in the winter, by sleigh. One must consider all seasons, how it will look under snow, where the cool places will be in the summer."

It was a masterpiece. No, it was dozens of individual masterpieces flowing together in elegant harmony. It would be the wonder of the Empire.

"But you took out all the trees," the princess said timidly.

"Yes, Your Grace?" The architect said, pausing mid-sentence.

"All these trees," she said, gesturing at the forest surrounding them. She looked nervous with so many eyes suddenly upon her, and her hands pressed together, her fingers knotting. "They're all gone. Trees take a long time to grow."

"There will be many new trees, Your Grace," Sousten said reassuringly, snapping his fingers again. His assistants rifled rapidly through the parchments to produce the one he desired. "Ornamental trees from all over the Empire. Here, plum and cherry, very beautiful in the spring, with maples for color in autumn…"

She nodded and said nothing more, her hand resting lightly on Remin's arm as they moved through the rest of the grounds. But he could see the busy mind working away behind her great eyes, solemnly absorbing it all, and he wondered irritably why she never just *said* them, all those thousands of thoughts. He had never met anyone who thought so much and said so little.

At the crest of the hill, they came to another stop. Sousten Didion had saved the best for last.

The house.

They had already discussed it endlessly, wrangling over it in person and through messages for over a year. They had shouted. Sousten had quit twice. He had designed a dozen different manors, each more beautiful than the last, and Remin had rejected them all. The last time, Sousten had thrown a tantrum and tore up the design, then disappeared for a week-long bender through the taverns of Segoile.

When he sobered up, he reappeared and began barraging Remin with questions, even consulting Tounot and Juste at various points. Materials, colors, even the shape of the shingles, he had worked for months to extract even the dimmest and foggiest memories.

This was the result.

"It's Tressin," Juste whispered, and Remin nodded. He couldn't speak.

That was his home.

Not a perfect reproduction, of course. Remin was eight years old when the Emperor burned down the ancient seat of his House, and there was so much he couldn't remember. But he recognized the angled towers and deep windows, the rounded rooftop over the main house, the majestic entryway with its wide steps and four tall pillars.

"You…like it?" Sousten asked warily.

"Yes." Remin's throat was tight. He probably ought to have warned Juste; Juste had been born there too, and had seen that ancient and beautiful house burn. His family had been executed alongside Remin's. Tounot had come to foster every summer, and he and Remin had climbed every stair and garret of that old place.

Remin could see in his friend's eyes that it was right.

"Tressin?" The princess echoed, glancing between them, and then her face paled. "That...that was your home, wasn't it? The seat of House ...your family's House."

"It was," Remin said, filled with a grief that was so great, he could say nothing more.

Wisely, Sousten suggested that they postpone further discussion for another day, to give everyone time to absorb the current plans. But Remin found himself returning often to look at the hilltops again, following the game trail that would one day be a riding path, or walking up the wider lane that would become a road. He had fought a war for this place, he could remember every terrifying, horrifying, exhausting moment he had endured to get here, and now he could hardly believe that it would really be his.

And as he rode, he found himself remembering what the princess had said.

Trees take a long time to grow. They did. Remin slid off his warhorse to look at the monster oak near the top of the hill, the widest tree he had ever seen. It had to be centuries old, maybe even millennia. Oaks could live that long, couldn't they? This oak might have been alive when his House was established, eleven hundred years ago. Wouldn't that be something?

A tree like this couldn't be imported, like one of Sousten's ornamental plums. It couldn't be bought for any price. Was that what the princess had meant? All of these trees were old growth forest. Who knew how old? Might there not be other trees as ancient here? Or others equally beautiful in their gnarled and grand old age?

The next morning, he slipped quietly into the cottage in the gray light of dawn to look at the princess, sleeping in her usual place in the center of the bed, curled up small around a pillow. All by themselves, his fingers reached to stroke her soft hair. He liked the thought that trees took a long time to grow. He liked that she would think of such a thing.

That same day, he went to talk to Sousten.

"Leave the trees," he said, ducking through the low door of the architect's cottage. "You can clear out the ones that are in the way of the house, or some other necessary structure, but try to include the rest in the gardens."

"But these are formal gardens, Your Grace," Sousten protested. "A lot of old, wild forest will quite spoil the sightlines. The fashion in the capital—"

"This is Tresingale," Remin said firmly. "It is old, and wild. And you can't buy a thousand year-old oak."

Sousten's mouth shut and his eyes turned thoughtful as the idea struck true, and lingered.

CHAPTER 9 – DANGEROUS CREATURES

The devils had come to Nandre first.

For generations, the tiny mountain village had scraped a meager living from the hillsides of the Berlawe Mountains, sowing the few crops that would consent to grow in the stony soil. Poverty made an unlikely shield, but an effective one; whenever Valleth came, the villagers had only to retreat to the nearby mines until they went away. Nothing in Nandre was worth a siege.

We are made of sterner stuff than stone, they said to each other, a mantra that held true from one generation to the next. Over a century of occupation, as so many other villages and towns were sacrificed to the Lord of Tales, many converted to his worship, hoping to be spared. But Nandre never lost their faith in the stars.

For a hundred years, they watched smoke rise from the valley and listened for the thunder of hooves, the terrifying buzz of the Eagle Knights, swarming like wasps up the hills. They came to rape and plunder and left behind babies with ice-blond hair and blue eyes. But by spring of 822, Nandre knew that another war had begun, and this time, Valleth was losing. Smoke rose from Vallethi fortresses and magicians were often on the road, passing deeper into the mountains. By June of that year, the horses riding up the pass to the village were carrying the black and silver banners of Sir Remin, Knight-General of the Imperial Army.

Valleth must have suffered many defeats, for him to have come so far.

It would be some time before anyone connected those defeats with the arrival of the goat-stealers.

That was one of the problems, in the beginning. Everyone had a different name for the things that had appeared in the night, and often it seemed they were not even describing the same thing. In Meinhem, the great wolves came first, the swiftest of the devils, howling outside their stout log houses, smashing against the walls as if they were mad with foaming sickness. On the high, precarious cliffs of Raida, they called them the slinkers and thought they were some new Vallethi scout, killing the night watchmen in advance of a raid. And in Nandre, where the mountain scrub would not support any animal larger than goats, it was the disappearance of the livestock that first indicated *something* was out there, in the dark.

Was it dogs stealing them? Wolves? They began to hear the noises of both in the night, snarling, rasping growls, and distant howls that froze the blood.

"I'll see to the beasties myself," said Fridolin Creit, who had been one of the richest men in the village until four of his goats went missing. And that was how he became the first human casualty of the devils. For at sunrise, the pen with the goat he had staked out as bait was empty, and so was his perch in a nearby tree.

The people of Nandre began to catch glimpses of…*something*, at dawn and twilight. Furtive shapes in the trees, scrabbling away from the sunlight. Nandre was high enough in the mountains that the trees were fairly sparse, especially near the village itself, where the land had long been denuded to feed the hearth fires. It likely saved some of the village children. In Raida, Selgin, and three times in the old forest of Meinhem, it was children that went missing, rather than livestock.

The first clear sighting of a devil was on August 12, 822, when a sleepy Nelle Vittelich went out early to milk the goats.

Only a few months earlier, Nelle had given birth to one of those ice-blond babies, and that was why she rose early, to spare her husband the chores. Donatin swore he didn't blame her for what had happened by the stream, but Nelle felt herself shamed and disgraced forever. It was her fault she had gone alone, her fault she had not heard the Vallethi warband coming, and her fault that she had not been quick enough to escape. That was why she was star-cursed with a bastard babe, a child she could barely stand to look at.

When she arrived at the stable, there was more misfortune waiting. The door was already ajar, and one of the new baby goats was lying dead just inside.

Nelle clicked her tongue. This would upset her daughter Amalie, who had been hand-raising the kids after an unusual triple birth. It was rare for all three to survive in such case, but it had looked as if the runt might just pull through. Now all of them were dead, lying sightless in the straw.

At the back of the stable, there was a noise. An uncanny chuckling, rasping and breathy, and Nelle's head lifted. For the first time, she found herself looking into the huge, lambent eyes of the creature everyone would soon call *strangler*.

"Monster," she breathed, taking a wobbling step backward. It was skinny, bony, bald, but close enough to human that she hesitated, wondering whether it might not be some feral, motherless *thing*. But then its lipless mouth peeled back from rotten teeth and she stumbled toward the door, tripping over the dead goats. "Monster! *Monster!*"

It was so fast, she only had time for one good scream before it was on her, its breath rasping in her ear. They rolled together into the shadowy yard and those long limbs wound around her, legs clamping tight, bony hands seeking her throat. Its hands were almost like a human's, but long and thin, with an extra joint on each finger. Unable to break free, Nelle threw herself sideways, rolling over, fighting for every inch toward the house.

The fight saved her life. The first rays of sunlight struck the mountain peaks and tipped over them, and the thing gave a grating scream.

"Nelle? *Nelle!*" Donatin burst from the house, cursing and grabbing for a spade. His arms swung up and slammed the hard edge against the devil's head until it let go, and Nelle scrambled free, coughing and gagging.

The thing burst into flames.

It was impossible to say whether the spade killed it, but the sickly green devil's fire certainly finished it off.

All over the valley, others were having similar encounters. On the Talfel Plateau, Sir Huber Adaman lost five horses to a pack of ghouls one night, when they got into the corral and tore the horses' legs off, then couldn't escape the slippery abattoir by sunrise. In Selgin, a blacksmith named Herdegen had a nasty shock one morning when he encountered a wolf demon out by the woodpile, only to be saved by the sunlight as he was fighting it off with a hammer.

It was this common trait that named all of them *devils,* in the end. Crooked, wicked creatures, unquestionably evil, who could not bear the touch of the sun.

But as disturbing as the devils were, the Andelin had been under Vallethi occupation for a hundred years. The horrors of the Lord of Tales were supplemented by the more prosaic dangers of the Andelin wildlife. There were bears. Timber wolves, shaggy and cunning, which made off with sheep and occasionally small children. Foxes. Maned bobcats with tufted ears. On the plateau, there were the coursing cats, leggy felines with pale gold stripes, fast enough to run down a horse at full gallop. Fortunately, they weren't big enough to attempt anything larger than a Talfel antelope.

Thus, after the initial shock of the devils, they became just another hazard, in time. To be sure, it was strange and frightening; it would give anyone a start to suddenly see the huge eyes of a strangler in the dark, and the deafening howl of a wolf demon caused more than a few sleepless nights. But until the spring of 826, everyone just took care to be indoors by nightfall, and barred their doors with iron.

"It's not going to hold."

"It will hold."

In one of Meinhem's sturdy timber cottages, a woodsman named Girnot Briouse moved between his wife and the door with a hatchet in his hand, the largest weapon available. The peasants of the Andelin Valley could rarely spare the iron for something so impractical as a sword.

"Get the children up into the rafters," he said, on sudden inspiration, and boosted up his son himself, the eight-year old boy weeping as he clutched at the rough timbers, only nine feet overhead. His wife Liberie was too big to fit between the close rafters, and their three year-old was too young to hold on. She huddled into her mother, hiccoughing with terror.

Another slam into the door, wood shredding as *things* gnawed and clawed at it.

"Stars, stars, guard us," said Girnot. The hand gripping his axe was shaking. "Stars, witness your children and have mercy, stars, stars…"

The door exploded open.

This was happening in Raida. It was happening in Selgin. It was happening at every fort on the Vallethi border.

That same night, it was happening in the small fishing village of Isigne.

The devils had come in howling, rushing down the Medlenne River like the spring floods. They were not like wolves, which would hunt and eat and then be satisfied. The same wolf demon that would burst through one door would slay and slay and then go straight onto the next, shouldering its way through the tide of slavering, gabbling ghouls. They went for the doors and windows, biting and tearing at them, maddening each other with their blood lust.

"We'll go for the boat," breathed a young man named Siyoun Arpelle, five years a husband and barely that many a man. "The river should be deep enough, if we coast out for a bit. I'll drop anchor in the middle, and we'll be safe until morning. But we'll have to run. Can you?"

"Yes," whispered Oranie Arpelle, binding their fourteen month-old son more tightly to her body in a sling. It was understood that Siyoun would have to carry their daughter.

The fishermen of Isigne lived in rows of cottages fronting the docks of the Medlenne, a tributary of the mighty Brede. Those docks were high and narrow, raised to withstand the spring floods, and it was the thought of those narrow walkways that gave him hope. Narrow and treacherous, yes, but in such a place the devils could not come all at once, and a man might hope to fend them off long enough to make it to the boats.

There was no chance that their door would hold, if this many devils chose to test it.

A few houses down, another door gave way, and at the outburst of screaming, Siyoun shoved outside with an oar in one hand and his daughter in the other, pushing his wife onto the docks.

So many devils. How were there so many devils?

The riverbanks were boiling with them, gray-skinned ghouls and smoking black wolf demons, savaging the figures fleeing for the water. Someone on the hill was waving a torch in frantic arcs, trying to draw the attention of the devils to give someone else a chance to run.

So many devils. Stars, so many devils. Behind him, Siyoun heard a snarling that sent him bolting forward, and he tried not to see the ghouls scrambling onto the far side of the docks, or feel the wood shaking under the weight of the thing behind him. The boards were warped and splintered, gray with weathering, and their repair was one of the many chores the fishermen frequently discussed amongst themselves, and never quite got around to doing.

On such small things, destinies were sometimes decided.

Beside him, Oranie tripped and went sprawling.

"Oranie!" Siyoun whirled to go back for her, his oar swinging out automatically, and so in the light of the moon he saw with perfect, eternal clarity his wife's face frozen in a scream, her brown eyes wide with terror, and the sawtoothed maw of the wolf demon descending.

"Run, Siyoun, *run!*"

All those teeth *crunched.*

His son stopped crying.

Gone. They were gone. Just like that.

Siyoun turned and ran.

There were many young men standing before doors in the Andelin Valley. Many young mothers making desperate last stands for their children. Many elders sacrificing themselves, so that the next generation might live on. There were cowards and traitors, opportunists and scoundrels, and heroes whose deeds would only be known to the watching eyes of the stars.

A hundred miles away, in the town of Ferrede, there was one young man whose worth had yet to be measured.

"Someone mind that window," said eighteen year-old Rollon of Hollisey, a squire who was hoping he would live to see his knighthood. As the last light of day faded from the edges of the shutters, the nighttime chorus was rising, and something struck the door a glancing blow, as if to test it.

Rollon and his small party had been chased into Ferrede that morning with the last of the night's ghouls, after two sleepless weeks on the road. Most of those nights had been spent in treetops, kicking away stranglers and praying their horses would survive the night in makeshift corrals. For one single, blissful hour, Rollon had spotted the smoke rising from the chimneys of Ferrede, saw the stout wooden walls of the cottages, and thought: *we're safe.*

As it turned out, the entire population of the village looked at him and thought the same thing.

But as Sir Huber said, that was what it meant to be a man at arms. Rollon had served as page and then as squire to Sir Huber Adaman throughout the Vallethi war, and though Sir Huber was not a loquacious man, it added weight to the words he spoke. He taught his pages that a sword was a responsibility, and if a man took up a weapon, he had an obligation to use it to defend those who could not defend themselves.

That was the oath a knight swore before his lord. And though Rollon was not yet a knight, he had knelt and sworn it before Remin, the Duke of Andelin: that he would protect the people of Ferrede, and build them a safe place against the devils.

Duke Andelin had only been seventeen when he saved Lomonde, Rollon told himself. And he had been a squire, too.

"Put at least two people on each window," he said, trying to settle everyone else as well as himself. "The windows are high off the ground, and too narrow for anything but stranglers. Even if we lose a shutter, they won't come flying through all at once. Not into a lit room with lots of people watching."

Or so he hoped. All the villagers were crammed into three rooms just like this one, drying sheds raised on stone foundations, with high, narrow windows to let the wheat breathe as it dried. It had stout walls to keep out the vermin, and by daylight, it had seemed like a good idea to get everyone together behind those stout walls, with two armed soldiers on each door.

Now it occurred to him that it just meant every devil for fifty miles would be battering at a single structure.

Ghouls snarled at each other, thudding against the door, and behind him, a child started to cry.

"Sir knight," said one of the women, her voice quavering. This did not seem like the time to remind them he wasn't a knight yet. "There's something scratching over here. It sounds like...*digging.*"

* * *

The glow of torchlight swayed, wobbling from side to side, and then plunged into the dark like a shooting star.

"Get that torch back up!" Remin shouted, moving at once into the new pool of shadow and smashing his shield out, sending three ghouls flying. The devils were streaming into Tresingale like a river, with the larger debris of the wolf demons surging in the flood, and Remin and his men were the riverbank trying to contain them with shields and spears, channeling them into the killing ground of the archers.

Unfortunately, the stranglers were learning to go for the torches.

Tomorrow, they would have to find a way to brace them somehow, Remin thought, moving into position to guard the men working to get the torch tower up and lit again, defending that darkened patch of ground as the devils rushed toward them. They did not fear the light, but they were strongest in the dark, and he went at once for a charging wolf devil, using his own shield as a break wall to smash it up and aside, heaving the beast into an open space in the nearest knot of men. A dozen spears stabbed it at once.

"It's lit, my lord!" called a man behind him, and the line of shields moved at once back into position, bracing for the next wave of devils.

It was not a constant stream of the creatures; not yet. They burst through gaps in the palisade or the wide open stretch in the middle of the east wall, a gap that was shrinking every day, but not quite fast enough. The diggers were working frantically to advance the deep trench, which was nearly as good a barrier as the wall itself would be.

There were the torch towers, discouraging the devils from the hills and slopes. There were shield walls on the ridgelines, shoving the devils onto lower ground, where they were slaughtered in their dozens. Knowing the devils could not be kept out of Tresingale altogether, Remin had arranged the defenses to allow them strategic entry, and placed himself at this critical juncture, a place where the land sloped down between two hills, and the road rose toward the cluster of buildings around the cookhouse, including a certain small cottage.

The devils were not going to go that way.

"Ortaire, push the line forward! Move the wolf toward the archers!" He boomed, half the command lost in the deafening howl of another approaching wolf demon. It was accelerating toward them, shouldering ghouls aside as it charged the lines of armored men.

But for the heavy wolf demons, Remin had invented the *restrati* formation, named for the multilayered fishing nets that Capricians used on the Amati Sea. Instead of blocking the wolf demon, the line of soldiers folded inward to isolate it, shields smashing into its sides to slow it down rather than facing the full force of its charge. Behind them, the second rank of soldiers slowed it still further, enough that the third rank could slash out with their swords, leaving the crippled monster to limp into range of the archers.

Even as Remin watched, the rest of the remaining devils reached the open, well-lit killing ground behind him, and there was a whirring chorus of heavy beechwood arrows, slamming into the survivors. The squires moved among them with their own swords, mopping up.

All the defenses of Tresingale operated on this principle. Slowing the advance of the waves of devils, blunting their momentum, winnowing them down so none of them reached the soft vitals of the town: the masons in their cloth tents, the craftsmen and laborers sleeping in fragile wattle-and-daub cottages, or the princess that would be mother to House Andelin. Remin could not see their house from where he stood, but he felt her presence as keenly as if she were sheltered directly behind his own shield.

"Good, good!" Ortaire called from the line, the voice of a young man who was still not entirely confident in his own command. But he was getting there. "There's a break in the devils ahead, my lord, should we thin them out?"

"Left rank, right rank, forward!" Remin ordered at once, and the two shield walls moved inward, narrowing the gap until the remaining devils were scrambling over top of each other. The spears plunged inward, and the devils died on a hundred points, churning the earth to mud with their blood.

And then, silence. On the distant palisade, torches winked, signaling that all was clear.

Devils tended to come in mobs. And though the night was quiet now, the howling tide of ghouls and wolf demons was only cover for the stranglers, who could eel through the thinnest slices of shadow, as evidenced by the constant threat to the torches. It was hard to credit them with a *plan;* Remin had never heard any evidence of intelligence in the creatures, only malevolence, a hatred of lights and men and men's things, a determination to kill. They came in mobs because they were strongest in numbers, and even wolves had the cunning to hunt in packs.

"Get some weight on the bases of those torches," he ordered, taking advantage of the lull to shore up the defenses. "Ortaire! Have your boys clear those carcasses out of the way."

"Yes, my lord!"

They swapped ranks in the lull between the devils, letting the first rank rest and the second step forward to take the next wave. The rear ranks were not idle. There were archers that needed more arrows, fresh torches to be lit, and the rear ranks swept back through the shadows to make sure nothing was creeping in the dark. They turned up a dozen stranglers that might have otherwise come on them unaware, and Remin almost stepped on one of the creatures himself, crouching in a clump of bushes. His sword lashed out on pure instinct, severing that loathsome head from its neck.

"I'll take it, my lord," said one of the soldiers behind him, dragging the corpse away to be counted with the rest of the devils.

Every night, they counted the dead. The corpses would burn by daylight, all evidence of the creatures blazing away into ashes, and they must *know* if there were more of them, to better prepare for the following night. Every morning, the last thing his soldiers did before they sought their beds was to quarter every inch of the village, combing the fields and forests to make sure they had accounted for every single devil.

It was grueling work, and all too soon, the torches waved in a different pattern from the palisade, signaling that another wave of devils was coming.

Hour after hour. Night after night. Remin stood watch at the east wall, on the palisade, on the hill by the north gate. His men began to fall in twos and threes as the number of devils swelled, cutting away sections of the line and overwhelming them with sheer numbers. Men in armor were hard to kill, but wolf demons could take off a whole limb at the joint, and cackling stranglers dragged the downed men out of the light, yanking at their gorgets with long, thin fingers until they found the bare throat underneath.

"Seven wounded, two seriously," said Jinmin when they convened at Remin's command tent one morning in the gray light before dawn. "Two dead. Stranglers."

"One dead on the east wall, two wounded," said Tounot, ducking under the front flap of the tent and pulling off his helmet. His curly hair was matted to his head with sweat. "And the masons were pitching a fit again as I went by. Could be they're hoping to renegotiate their contracts."

"I don't think that's it this time," said Miche, sighing. He was as bloody and sweaty as the rest of them, his long blond hair caught back in a messy ponytail. "They've been grumbling amongst themselves for a few days, and it's not just the masons. They don't think the camps to the east are getting as much protection as the ones to the west. Maybe a few nights of personal attention from the Duke of Andelin would quiet things down."

"That will cost them you and Tounot," Remin replied, his shoulders jerking with irritation. His commanders were every bit as capable as himself, so this looked to him like an irrational indulgence, but Juste was continually reminding him that the craftsmen did not have three years of experience with devils.

"They ought to count themselves lucky," said Huber, who had been listening quietly. The copper in his eyes flickered. "I wonder how well the rest of the valley is sleeping at night."

That was the real question, and it had been gnawing at all of them. It was one thing if the devils were just appearing a little early; that was inconvenient, but easy enough to overcome. But all those small villages had nothing like the defenses of Tresingale, and no trained, armored men to guard them in the night. Huber had been all over the valley during the war, commanding the mounted scouts that had been Remin's eyes and ears, one of the most effective warfighting tools in his arsenal. Huber had stayed in those villages. He knew better than anyone else what they were facing.

"It might just be us," said Tounot into the silence. "I saw devils pass a small camp if there was a larger one nearby during the war, and more than once. There are more people in Tresingale than in the rest of the valley combined. I expect the devils can sniff us out all the way from the Berlawes."

"Send word to the border forts and have them look in on Raida," said Remin, his black brows lowering in thought. "It's just as well we're supplying them by sea. Where's the map of the Medlenne? We might get a fair distance by river."

"Not for much longer," said Tounot reluctantly. He oversaw most of the supply to the rest of the valley. "The water level will be dropping by now, and there's long, rocky stretches. Here," he said, tracing the section of river on the map as Miche spread it out on the table. "You'd have to drag the boats out of the water off and on for about fifteen miles, and I wouldn't swear that the bottom is deep enough to keep the devils off at night."

"And this is solid marsh for four or five miles," said Huber, tapping another place further downriver. "Fucking nightmare, that was. We lost two wagons and almost lost a horse in that bog. You might get a man or two to Isigne or Selgin, but then they'd be just as trapped as everyone else."

It would be the same in all the other villages. The old roads of the Andelin were overgrown, and most of the bridges had been destroyed in the many wars. The remaining villages had survived *because* they were inaccessible.

"A small party to each village is better than nothing," said Miche.

"A small party to each village is a large party removed from Tresingale," noted Tounot.

All of them understood the problem. Every morning, after he took the numbers of dead and wounded, Remin went out himself to examine the lines of defenses. The blood on the ground, the toppled barriers, the trampled places in the grass where men had stood, fought, and fallen. Every day he examined and improved his own defenses, searching for weaknesses, noting the places where men had died.

Those lines were being pushed back.

"We'll start someplace closer," he said. "Ferrede. There's no cover for the devils in the Iron Hills, and we need to know if Rollon made it."

It was cowardly to wait for someone to volunteer. Remin made the decision.

"Jinmin," he said, turning to the big man. In his armor, Jinmin could withstand a horde of devils, as obdurate as oak. "You will go. Take three others with you."

"Rather go alone, m'lord," said Jinmin, after only a moment's pause. "If there's enough devils to kill me, there's enough to kill anyone with me."

And Jinmin would fight better if he wasn't having to defend his companions. Remin nodded. He had made the offer only as a sop to his own conscience.

Men were not so different from devils. Everyone liked to tell stories about Remin Grimjaw, about Lomonde, about the Charge of the Gresein, but there was no single act of heroism that won the war, and no single act of heroism was going to save his people. Just as the devils threw themselves at the barricades of Tresingale, it was the nature of men to throw themselves at the world, each one spending their lives to move just a little further than the last. Not every man died a hero. Many men died to be planks in a bridge, or stones in a wall.

Only the stars could see where it would end.

The stars were fading in the sky when he finally went home, still arguing with himself. He knew he was doing the right thing, the prudent thing, but he had visited all those villages, too. He knew his people. If they needed help, they needed it now.

Ducking through the low door of the cottage, he quietly shut it and went to wash away the blood. It wasn't his. The devils' blood got everywhere, even drying in stiff flakes in his hair, and it was hard to tell the princess not to be afraid when he came in the door crimson to his elbows.

Setting a kettle over the fire, he dragged his sweat-soaked shirt off and ducked his head into a bucket of cold water, scrubbing.

"...Grace?" said a soft voice behind him, so quiet it was almost lost in the splashing of water. Remin glanced back to find the princess was already awake, sitting up in bed with a pillow clutched in front of her like a shield.

"You can sleep a little longer," he said, resuming scrubbing. It just figured that she would wake up early today.

"I was already awake," she said. "Is...is everything all right? I heard..."

"Everything is fine." It came out sharper than he meant, and he huffed to himself. This situation was in no way her fault. "You are safe, Princess," he said, snapping a towel over his shoulder. "If all the valley sank into the sea, every man here would be carrying you to a boat."

* * *

Under the circumstances, it was incredible to think anyone would be trying to break *into* Tresingale.

The first survivor of the Brede crossing arrived in the beginning of June, and Ophele heard the commotion at the south wall as she was refilling Eugene's water barrels. Now that there were three wells dug in places that did not interfere with Master Ffloce's plans for the artisan quarter, she made three long loops along the length of the wall over the course of the day, rather than multiple trips to and from the same well. The people on the southern end of the wall were doing the finishing work of building tower houses and stairs, since twenty-foot ladders were not something anyone wanted to climb multiple times per day, and certainly not with packs of ghouls running around the base of the wall.

It was incredible to think someone had actually swum across the Brede for the privilege of hearing the devils personally.

"What happened? Is someone hurt?" she asked anxiously as a couple men raced up the hill from the bridge construction site. She was still forbidden to go near it herself, but Sir Miche had taken her to see the massive walls of the caissons stretching all the way to the bottom of a very deep river, so deep in places that men became ill if they ascended too quickly. It was a monumental undertaking, more impressive than a dozen walls.

"No, lady, for a wonder," said one of the engineers. "Lad just dragged himself up on the bank, he swam the width of the river. He's fine, but tired, as you might expect. Says he's come to be a page for the Knights of the Brede."

"I can go get Sir Miche," she said, wide-eyed at the feat. She couldn't swim a stroke herself, and she had seen exactly how deep the river was.

"Would you? That'd be kind of you, lady."

Sir Miche was just as happy to have an excuse to abandon his digging.

"I suppose our first successful swimmer deserves some notice," he said when Ophele hurried to the other end of the wall to tell him. Normally pages were the business of squires, but the shortage of pages made any prospect worth considering. "Of course, it'll be up to Rem as to whether he gets rewarded or punished."

"Why would he get punished?"

"Don't want to encourage this kind of thing," Sir Miche said bluntly. "He's lucky he survived. The river's not just wide. The current is fast and uncertain, you never know when it might yank you under. We tried it ourselves, believe me, before Rem finally decided to charge the Gresein."

Remin Grimjaw, hero of the Gresein Bridge, had become so separate in her mind from the duke her husband that it was always a shock when someone reminded her they were the same person.

"Because other people who try to cross might not be as lucky," she said.

"We've already found some who tried," he said grimly. "It might sound cold-hearted, but we've got our hands full right now. We don't have men to spare cleaning corpses off the riverbank."

She shuddered.

"I want to see His Lordship," a high-pitched voice was saying stubbornly as they approached the river. "I come all the way from Caillmar to be a knight, I ain't leaving 'less Remin Grimjaw tells me no himself."

The boy was bedraggled and dripping in a too-large jerkin, his skinny arms bare and his hair plastered around a rather pretty face. It was a source of consternation to Ophele that a boy whose voice hadn't even broken yet could be so much taller than herself.

"You're leaving if I tell you no." Sir Miche had an uncanny knack for finding the perfect cue to enter a conversation. "What's your name, boy?"

The boy's head tilted back, and his nostrils flared.

"Jacot," he said. "Jacot of Caillmar, as I ain't got no father's name to bless me. I know you, you're Sir Miche of Harnost, the one what they call the maidenslayer."

Sir Miche's hard hand clipped him across the mouth.

"You'll keep a civil tongue," he snapped. And to his credit, the boy glanced at Ophele and blanched.

"Sorry, m'lady." He sounded like he meant it. "Ain't you the princess, eh? Or Her Grace now, sorry. They're still singing songs about you in Celderline, I thought they was all lies."

Songs? About her?

"Pages do not address a noble lady until spoken to," Sir Miche said, as if anyone in the valley had once enforced aristocratic etiquette since Ophele had arrived. But the boy nodded as if he were inscribing the words on his soul.

"I won't forget. Didn't mean no offense. But I still ain't going back 'less His Grace tells me so himself. You can chuck me on the other side of the river and I'll just swim back again."

"I appreciate your enthusiasm, but His Grace is only accepting guests by invitation." Sir Miche crossed his arms and glanced back at Ophele. "This is likely to take a few minutes, if you'd like to get back to Eugene, my lady. Let Guisse know I'll be along, would you?"

Ophele nodded, sparing another curious glance for the boy before she climbed back to the top of the hill where Eugene was napping. The little donkey was an efficient creature; he ate and napped at every possible opportunity.

It wasn't often she saw someone younger than herself. Most boys her age were squires and far too busy working toward their knighthood to spare her more than a bow. The stable boys were a few years younger, usually around fourteen, and while rank was less strictly observed in the Andelin than anywhere else in the Empire, it would still be unthinkable for them to speak to the duke's wife no matter how young she was.

This boy certainly knew how to say what was on his mind, though. Ophele wished she could be so fearless.

Stopping Eugene by the next well, Ophele dropped the bucket and then cranked the windlass to draw it back up again, her slim body swaying with the effort. It took a while to fill all three barrels; she saved herself some walking with the water wagon, but she still had to pull and pour all those buckets, fifteen per barrel. Once they were full, she had to sit down and rest a bit.

"I don't know what I'd do without you," she told Eugene gratefully, stroking the donkey's nose as he lowered his head to investigate her. "Maybe one day I can introduce you to my friend Anzel. You could talk together about donkey things. Like carrots. And whose wagon is heavier. You'd hate Rou's wagon, I bet. He says he doesn't mind the rattling, but I think he's just gone deaf from hearing it for thirty years."

Thirty years. She would still be here in thirty years. The duke had been explicit that even if the river rose up and swallowed every other person in the valley, she would survive, so she could bear his children. On this side of the Brede, she was trapped as effectively as if she were in prison. No one even needed to guard her. There was the river on two sides, Valleth to the north, and the Berlawe Mountains to the east, filled with wolf demons and ghouls and stranglers. The question was, which death did she dislike least. And she was still not unhappy enough to die.

"I wish you could pull me in a wagon," she said, pushing herself back to her feet. She kept a small store of carrot pieces in her pocket and fed Eugene one, stroking his ears as they walked together.

The route along the foot of the wall was a familiar one, and if she hadn't been so tired and sore, she wouldn't have minded this part of her life at all. It was a good thing to bring water to thirsty men, and all of them were so nice to her. They greeted her as they passed, offering gruff compliments, silly jokes, and terrible puns. She was happy to fetch and carry when needed, or even—when Sir Miche wasn't looking—return the odd dropped tool. There were usually a few of those each day, and even as she watched, one of the scaffolders dropped his hammer and cursed.

Ophele had finally learned what word started with *fu-*.

"I'll get it," she said, hurrying forward to retrieve it and scampering easily into the scaffolding. There was an unspoken conspiracy between her and the workers; she pretended she had never climbed anything in her life, and the men thanked the kindly spirit that had come to dwell upon the scaffold and returned trowels, hammers, chisels, and similar small objects.

"Thank you, O Lady of the Wall," the man said loudly to the sky, and Ophele giggled as she slid easily back to the ground. She didn't see why she shouldn't help, if she could, and climbing in the scaffolding reminded her of climbing the old and beautiful trees of Aldeburke.

"My lady," said a stern voice behind her, with an emphasis on *lady.* She turned guiltily.

"Oh, Sir Miche," she said, too cheerfully. "What happened with the boy?"

"I threw him back in the river. You know if Rem ever catches you up there, there may be actual bodies dangling from the scaffolding at the end of the day."

"I was just helping."

"I know." Sir Miche fell into step with her as she led Eugene on to the next set of buckets, the small wagon creaking.

"Why doesn't he want me to do anything?" she asked plaintively. It had been bothering her for weeks.

"In this particular case, he's afraid you'll get hurt. And I agree with him."

"He's not afraid of anything," she said, looking at her feet. No doubt he didn't want his princess to get hurt; he wanted heirs from her. But she objected to the word *afraid*. That implied a level of emotional engagement that did not exist.

"You'd be surprised what scares him," Sir Miche said dryly. "Here, let me do that. I've never seen a spring so hot, no wonder every devil in the Berlawes has decided to come out early."

"It's almost summer," she pointed out, lifting the masses of hair off the back of her neck and fanning herself. Dark clouds had been hovering all day, like a lid on the steaming stewpot of the valley.

"You don't have to tell me," he agreed, winching up a full bucket with such ease that she sighed inside. Thunder rumbled. "Stars, it's going to rain again," he said, frowning up at the sky. "Best get under cover, my lady. I'll start getting the men off the wall."

Sir Miche often said he was useless, as if he wanted to make it clear up front that no one should expect anything from him. But it wasn't true. He had quietly taken over many of the practical complexities of the wall, and he had an eye for detail that spotted disasters before they could occur.

It was oddly…comforting to watch him. Charming, handsome, with that long golden hair, he was like a knight from a storybook. For all the men's jokes about his reputation with women—Ophele could guess what *maidenslayer* meant—Ophele had never seen the least sign of it. He had never been anything but kind and considerate of her.

"What did happen with the boy?" she asked when he returned, handing her an oilskin to keep the rain off and stretching out beside her in his usual lazy sprawl of limbs. She didn't believe Sir Miche had really thrown him back in the river.

"Sent him up to Rem. Not that I want to reward bad behavior," he drawled meaningfully, rolling his hazel eyes toward her, "but we do need pages, and squires. Dozens of them. But no nobleman is going to send his precious spawn to the Andelin right now, even if it is for the Knights of the Brede."

That thought was sobering.

"Is it really so dangerous?"

"Not for you," he assured her. "I'm not just saying it to make you feel better, my lady. Your cottage is near the southernmost bend of the river, any Andelin devil that goes that far has gone through an awful lot of people to get there. Not that you should take it lightly," he added. "There's more this year than we've ever seen before, and it's a worry."

"I just wish there was something I could do," she said, low. "His Grace keeps saying it's safe, but I hear them and I don't know where they are and…"

Her throat closed and she cut off the rest of the sentence. It felt like whining to complain about being afraid when she knew she was better protected than anyone else in the valley, and especially in front of Sir Miche. He always listened with every sign of sympathy, but he was a knight and a hero and he must have seen so many terrible things, her fears could only seem trifling and cowardly.

That was what she told herself, when she was tired and so worn out from working that it seemed like she couldn't walk another step. The duke and his men had surely been more tired than this. More frightened. More lonely.

"Would you have rather stayed in Aldeburke?" Sir Miche asked quietly, and her eyes flew open in surprise. It was a dangerous question. But the downpour was kindly and muffled their conversation. "I'm not blind. I know you're unhappy here."

"I was unhappy there." She wrapped her arms around her knees and propped her chin on them. It didn't matter what she wanted. In her short life she had already learned that there was nothing to be gained from imagining things she couldn't have. So instead, she pondered his question as a hypothetical. It was all very well, after she had been trapped into her marriage, to rationalize it as destiny and a chance to atone for the crimes of her parents. Would she have preferred to stay in Aldeburke with the possibility of one day escaping, instead of marrying the duke, even if it meant that the crimes of her parents against him and his whole extinct House were never paid for?

It was impossible not to think of everything they had done when she could see the scars of it on his body. Every day when he stood at the wash basin, she could see the evidence of his suffering: sharp, straight lines from stabbings, curving slices from glancing blows, divots from arrows, and multiple dark and ugly gouges where whole chunks of flesh had been torn away. Even her fertile imagination couldn't guess what might have made those. But she had seen an assassin come through the window in the dark of night to try to kill him.

Her parents had done that to him.

Didn't she owe him something for it? If she had had a choice, would she have voluntarily delivered herself into bondage, to make it right?

"There must be some parts of it you miss," Sir Miche said gently. "The connection with your mother. Do you remember her much?"

"A little bit," she said, grateful that he hadn't pressed her. Grateful that someone, anyone, cared about her even a little. "I always think of her in the library, and in the woods. We would go walking when it was nice out, and she showed me what things were safe to eat, and how to climb trees."

"Unusual pastimes, for a noblewoman."

"She said that that was what she used to do, back home," Ophele explained. There was a flickering of a memory in the trees, the sensation of being lifted up onto a branch and cuddled in a green bower. "At…Murewood? I think. She said she ran wild there when she was a little girl, and her mother always had to come hunting for her for lessons. But after…everything, the Emperor dissolved their House and took back their lands."

"And so she taught you to run wild at Aldeburke."

"I guess so." She smiled to herself. She had mostly been hiding from the Hurrells, but it was nice to think that something of her mother lived on. "I am sorry for that, though," she added. "Making all of you look for me. I didn't know who you were, and last time…well, I was afraid…I wasn't trying to embarrass His Grace," she finished lamely. "I wanted to tell him that, before. But I could never find the right time."

"I knew that. I found your fire," he replied, making her eyes widen.

"Did you? I thought I'd hidden it."

"You might have, except that terrifying cook told me to look in the trees. Aside from the pines, there wasn't much to the Aldeburke trees at the time."

"Azelma," she said fondly. "I miss Azelma. And her pastries. And her cookies. She cooked for my mother too, you know. I wonder if Sir Edemir could spare some paper so I could write to her. I know it's dear."

"We'll see about it tonight." He stood, offering her a hand up. "Looks like it's clearing. We'd best get back to work. Though I wouldn't like to see another appearance from the Lady of the Wall today."

"I can't help it if the men ask for her help," Ophele said primly. "The good spirits always show up when you call."

* * *

There wasn't much leisure in Tresingale for contemplating the spirits, good or otherwise.

The last day of the week was sacred to the stars, a day of rest and contemplation during which believers gave thanks for the many bounties of the divine. Remin tried dutifully to observe the religious holidays of the Empire, but more than a year after the end of the war, there was still no cleric in Tresingale. The nearest thing they had to a representative of the Temple was the seventeen year-old illegitimate daughter of the Emperor, who looked utterly panicked at the prospect of leading a prayer.

In the Holy City of Jaen, there had been a prolonged struggle over whether to send anyone to Tresingale, or more specifically to the service of Remin Grimjaw. It was a complicated problem. The Emperor was the Beloved of Stars, and Remin was definitely not beloved by the Emperor. Edemir had sent a very polite letter pointing out the increasing number of believers/taxpayers in the valley, as well as the fact that the Duke of Andelin was already incomprehensibly wealthy and would only become more so in years to come. Tresingale *had* planned to build a new temple, the most splendid temple in the Empire, but if no one from the Temple was coming…

A cleric had duly been dispatched.

In the meantime, on the last day of the week, most of the Andelin's faithful contemplated their laundry.

"Princess." Remin ducked his head under the low door of the cottage one Sunday afternoon, squinting to adjust to the comparative dimness. "Come with me. Grab some buckets."

She didn't ask questions. Silent as a ghost, she pulled on her small boots and followed him to the well and back, filling all the buckets and dragging out the cauldron without ever asking why. As he put water over the fire to heat, she hovered behind him, so transparently nervous that Remin's jaw clenched. He didn't know what there was to be nervous about. He had barely spoken to her in weeks. He was tempted just to send her away and get on with her laundry himself, but he had no doubt there were oceans of mystery he had yet to fathom when it came to women's clothing.

237

Mentally shrugging, he turned and waited for the kettle to heat, and then almost tripped over her as he turned to pour it into the cauldron.

"Careful," he said sharply, jerking the kettle back.

She said something inaudible, retreating until she bumped against the wall.

"Speak up," he repeated for the hundredth time. "You can go sit down. It doesn't take two people to heat water."

The way she hastily decamped to the other side of the cottage and hid behind her book made him wonder wearily what was wrong. Why was she so nervous? Had he said something? Mentally, he reviewed the last fifteen minutes and came up empty. Was it because he told her to speak up? How else was he supposed to hear what she was saying?

Scowling ferociously at the teakettle, he waited in silence for it to boil.

"Bring your white clothes over here," he said when the cauldron was half-full of steaming water. It gave him another twinge to watch her rifle through her small trunk. She had put a partition inside it to keep the dirty clothing from touching the clean, and it made him feel both guilty and irritated. He hadn't thought to wonder what she was doing with her clothing, but she hadn't asked for help. How many times had he told her to tell him if she needed something?

"I can do it," she said as she approached, clutching the bundle of chemises and unmentionables. "If you tell me how…"

"Just put them in," he said, waving her over. "What soap have you been using?"

"That," she said, pointing to the washstand, where all her fragrant bath soaps were lined up neatly on a shelf.

"You have to use laundry soap, and lye for white clothing." Automatically, he fell into the brisk, lecturing tone he took when he was teaching squires and pages, and tugged a small pouch from his belt to show her. "Not too much, or it will burn your hands. About this much for that much water, see?"

Her eyes flicked from the small mound of white powder in his palm to the cauldron, and she nodded.

"We'll scrub them first, then put them into soak." Remin crouched beside the cauldron to show her. "Next time, you can do this part yourself, if you want to. Come on, you try."

For a moment, she watched as he methodically crushed the fabric in his hands, scrubbing the lye water into the fibers, then moved to the far side of the cauldron to follow. She was careful not to touch him as their hands worked together in the water.

"You can scrub these, then let them soak," he said, straightening. "I'll be back."

Leaving the clothes to stew for a while, Remin went to scrounge up a large laundry tub, a basket, and a washing bat, determined to do this right if it killed them both.

"We can finish everything by the river," he said, startling her when he appeared in the doorway. "Grab the bedding, too, we might as well wash that while we're at it. You can use this basket for dirty clothes from now on," he added, setting a tall, narrow basket made of woven grass beside her small trunk. It was the only wall space left in the small cottage.

Fishing the laundry out of the lukewarm water of the cauldron, he hid her underthings beneath the rest of the clothing and blankets, then set off for the river with the princess's light, bouncing steps patting on the cobblestones behind him. There was a footpath from the main road to the riverside, winding through tall grass and wildflowers beneath the clear summer sky. On the southeastern bend of the Brede, there was a small inlet and a beach with smooth pebbles and sand, cool underfoot and shaded by tall trees.

Remin sat on a handy rock to take off his boots, basking in a soft breeze. It would have been a nice day for fishing.

"Can you swim?" he asked.

"No," she replied, sitting a short distance away to remove her boots.

"Don't go out further than your knees, then. I'll have to teach you one day." He rolled up the legs of his trousers and tugged off his jerkin, hanging it on a nearby branch. Laundry was messy work. "Usually the river is pretty consistent, but if you're ever down here in spring, you might see sudden floods. See that pole over there?" He nodded toward a sturdy pole a few feet out in the water, marked with black lines at regular intervals. "That marks the river depth. We check it every morning and evening. During the spring thaw, you'll see huge chunks of ice break off the glacier in the Berlawes and fall in the river. If you ever see it start rising fast, run."

"I will," she said, for the first time looking intrigued, rather than nervous.

"We'll do one of the blankets first, they'll need the bat. Tuck your skirts up so they don't drag you down in the water."

Obediently, she tucked them to her knees and then waded after him into the river. There was a small spit of land that jutted out into the Brede, and the water in the inlet was clean, clear, and still enough that he could see minnows darting away as they headed for the rocks.

"First, we soak it, and then scrub it with soap," he explained, producing a rough bar of brown soap from his pocket. "If there are any spots, scrub them harder, but otherwise we just want the whole thing soapy."

She nodded, unfolding the blanket in sections for scrubbing and then taking her own turn with the soap. It took both of them to fold it back up again and set it on the rock, and then Remin retrieved the bat, spinning the handle in one hand. He put a little muscle into it as he smacked the flat end of the bat onto the folded blanket, sending out a wave of soapy water.

"Sorry," he said as the princess brushed suds off her skirts. "We're both likely to get splashed. Turn it over and fold it the other way."

"It's all right." She moved quickly to obey. For a while, they worked in silence, but it was a better silence than the oppressive, anxious tension of the cottage, and the princess was quick and efficient as she plunged the blanket into the river and dragged it back onto the rocks. "Can I try?"

"Sure." Remin handed her the bat and retreated a pace. "You don't need to hit it too hard, you'll wear—"

The paddle cracked onto the blanket and a fountain of water shot up, nailing him directly in the face.

"Oh." The princess dropped the bat and gazed up at him in round-eyed horror, the tips of her fingers rising to cover her mouth. "Oh, I'm so sorry. I didn't mean…"

Remin spat out a mouthful of water.

"—wear yourself out," he finished, the corner of his mouth twitching. Contrary to popular opinion, he did have a sense of humor, and that had been funny. Swiping at his face with his arm, he handed her the bat before it floated off. "It's fine, go on, Princess."

It was hard, tiring work, and in due course he relieved her of the bat and they soaked down the blanket again, dragging it back onto the flat rock. He didn't exactly *plan* anything in particular, but when he brought the bat down it was at an expert angle that sent out an explosion of icy water, and the princess dodged away with a squeal.

"You did that on purpose!" She accused, forgetting her nervousness for a moment as she pushed her wet hair out of her eyes.

"I'm just doing laundry," Remin said blandly. "Come, turn it over, my hands are full."

Warily, she approached to flip the blanket and then rapidly backpedaled, her bright eyes shy and wondering. It made him want to tease her, and it was only belatedly that he realized that it was too late; that was exactly what he was doing. It felt so natural, he hadn't even noticed.

Remin forced himself to focus on the work, using the bat to grind the soap deep into the fibers of the blanket, and then finally waved her back over.

"Hold this end," he said, handing her one end of the blanket. This would be the hardest part for her, and the reason why he hadn't just written her a list of instructions and let her get on with it by herself. Twisting the blanket to wring it out, soapy water cascaded into the river. When it stopped dripping, they plunged it into the river again and repeated the motion, rinsing and wringing until the water ran clear.

"I'm sorry," she said as her hands began to shake with effort. The tighter he wound it, the harder it was for her to hold onto her end. "It's slipping…"

"It's fine. I don't expect you to be able to do this by yourself," he said. He finished wringing it out by himself, his huge hands crushing the water out of the cloth, and then they hung it over a handy tree branch to dry. They repeated the process on the second blanket, and while he wrung it out, he sent her to fill the washtub.

Wading over to her, he tossed all her white things into the tub, along with a few of her dresses, and then bent again with the bar of soap.

"The lye will irritate your skin if we don't wash it out," he explained. "And we do the same thing with your dresses that we did with the blankets, but they're too delicate for the bat. Scrub them down with soap, and then I'll show you what we do next."

It was pleasant, feeling the sun on his bare back and the soft sand gritting between his toes. They traded the soap back and forth, scrubbing, and when everything looked sudsy enough, he rose.

"All right, in you go," he said. "We'll take turns."

"What am I doing?" she wanted to know, lifting her skirts to step into the tub.

"Stomp on them. You have to use your toes and heels to grind in the soapy water. Yes, just like that," he said as she began to stomp first one foot and then the other. White articles bobbed to the surface of the water, the white linen and silk too buoyant to sink down the way her dresses did. Remin poked them. He'd never washed clothes like those before.

"When did you learn how to do this?" she asked timidly, as if she expected him to scold her for asking.

"When I was a squire." Remin sat down next to the tub, stretching out his long legs as she moved in a stomping circle. "I squired for Sir Liyoun Carteret. Ever heard of him?"

She shook her head.

"He was a lancer. That was never my weapon, but he had some skill with it. Most squires have to look after their master's clothing and armor. And it's good exercise," he observed, noting her fatigue with an expert eye. Such work was harder than it looked. "Do you want a break?"

"I'm all right." She paused to twist her long hair into a knot on the back of her slender neck and then soldiered on. She lasted quite a bit longer than he expected, and it was only when he saw her legs begin to wobble that he pushed himself to his feet.

"That's enough, princess, my turn."

"They should almost be done, shouldn't they?" she asked, puffing. "It was almost the same amount of time as when we scrubbed my chem—"

One of those chemises tangled around her ankles and Remin lunged to catch her as she stumbled forward, flinging out her hands with a squeak of surprise. His palm pressed flat against her belly and the shock of touching her tingled through every fingertip, blazing all the way to the back of his neck.

"I'm sorry." Her tawny eyes struck his like flint to steel, and her cheeks flushed pink. "I'm all right, thank you."

"You can go sit down," he said stiffly, removing his hands. "I'll do the rest."

"I was just trying to he—"

"You've done enough," he snapped, and when she scuttled instantly away, even he could tell that she was absolutely crushed.

He hadn't meant to do that.

He almost called her back, even though he had no idea what he could possibly say. He was sorry. He didn't mean to hurt her feelings. He knew she would accept the apology, but then what? He had barely spoken to her for months, and all it took was one afternoon with her to knock him completely off balance.

He didn't know what to do. Stooping, he reached vengefully for the laundry, squeezing and twisting the clothing in his hands. She had done a good job with them. All that was left was to rinse them in the river and wring them out, though that task probably would have finished her off for the day.

Remin kept his back to her as he went to work, spreading her dresses over nearby bushes and hanging them over tree branches to dry in the sun. Repeating the process with chemises, he frowned as he shook one out and found it had ripped in a number of places. When had he done that? Her clothes were so fragile, somehow he damaged them even when he didn't mean to.

Grumbling, he turned to spread it over a nearby rhododendron, and then stopped cold. Behind him, the princess was asleep on the riverbank, curled up in the grass with her slender legs and feet bared by her tucked skirts. A purple butterfly was resting on her cheek, tapping soft kisses onto her skin.

Stars, she was so pretty.

The thought popped into his head before he could stop it. The sight of her filled his eyes and the corners of his mouth tugged upward in a smile so unwilling, it felt as if it should crack the hard lines of his face. He had to look away. He almost stepped backward, a shameful retreat. And even though he knew better, even though a single moment of softness toward her felt like the jaws of a steel trap springing shut, he still spread the torn chemise on the branches above her, shading her fair skin from the sun.

He faced devils every night, but to Remin Grimjaw there was no creature in the world so dangerous as this girl, asleep in the grass with wildflowers dancing above her.

CHAPTER 10 – DEFENSIVE STRUCTURES

To Mistress Azelma Bessin in the kitchen of Aldeburke, in the duchy of Leinbruke, from Ophele in Tresingale:

Dear Azelma, I hope you are keeping well. It feels like so long since I saw you, and it's been so busy here, it hardly seems the same place as when I arrived. Right outside my window, there's a new granary and six new cottages, and a new stretch of road that's almost a mile long.

None of these things were visible, at present. Ophele was writing by the uncertain light of a candle, and the shutters of the cottage had been reinforced so that not a crack of the torchlight outside showed within. His Grace's carpenters had added iron bars to them that morning.

She couldn't decide whether to be reassured by this or not.

But that is nothing, compared to the bridge. They started work on that last month, and let me tell you, what a monument is a bridge! Sir Tounot—that is Lord Tounot of Belleme, but he styles himself as Sir—says that when it is done, it will be wide enough for four wagons to go abreast, and will span the whole width of the river. That is almost a mile long too, but a much grander undertaking, as you might imagine.

At the same time, they are building the footings for the port, and I have gotten to see them at it a little bit. Sir Edemir says it will be even bigger than the ports on the Emme. They are always boasting of the Brede here, and how it is so long, so wide, so wild, more dangerous than any other river in the world, so they must build strong to stand up to it.

245

You will think it is funny, but what I like best is seeing how all the work fits together here, like a puzzle. I told you about how they are digging those huge trenches for the foundation of the wall, but until yesterday I never wondered, what do they do with all that dirt? Well, it turns out they carted a lot of it away to fill in other places around town, like the pond where the temple will be.

Isn't that marvelous? To think that building the wall also means building the temple? Sir Miche says they are to begin laying stones for that next year, and when it is done, our temple will have a spire two hundred feet high, the Point of the Valley Star. The Temple will come and tell us which star looks most kindly upon us, and then the final spire will be aligned to point to it, and catch its light.

Unfortunately, filling in the pond displaced the geese and their babies, but Sir Miche says they are all right; the goslings are old enough to fly, so they have all decamped to the field by the barr—

There was a sudden outburst of howling and Ophele's quill jerked, spattering the page. The noises of the devils were familiar now, but no less terrifying for it as they circled around the cottage, sometimes to the north, sometimes to the east. It made her mouth go dry and her heart thumped painfully in her chest, jerking in spasms of fear. The nightly chorus had begun.

Sometimes she heard familiar voices outside in the road. It might be Sir Miche's voice, drawling and unconcerned, complaining about being bored. Or Sir Edemir, commanding the nearby defenses with the same calm competence he ordered his secretaries. Ophele had learned all their rhythms by now, measuring her nights by the comings and goings of the heroes outside her door.

It amazes me that I may write so familiarly of them, the Knights of the Brede. But they are even better men than we knew, I assure you, always chivalrous and gallant, and very sensitive of propriety, when I am still the only woman in town. Sir Auber says that his brothers and their wives are meant to come later this year, so perhaps I will have a little society then.

Many people have come already, hoping to settle the valley and take oaths to His Grace. Most of them must stay on the other side of the Brede for now, because of the devils, but Sir Tounot says there is much provision for them, and they have negotiated with the local lords to be sure they are all safe and have some work. Sir Tounot is the one that manages them, and I am sure he does it so pleasantly they could hardly mind at all. He is a handsome man with a cleft chin and curly hair, and so well-spoken that one finds oneself agreeing with him no matter what he says, because he says it so well...

She could have filled pages with stories of the duke's men. By day, there would have been a little spiteful pleasure in writing about them, knowing how Lisabe would squirm with jealousy. But at night, she was reminding herself with every rasping snarl outside the windows who it was that stood between her and the devils in the dark.

I have never seen the devils myself, so I cannot know what they look like. But I know all their noises. The ghouls just sound nasty, always growling and snapping, like a rotten dog. Only, there are so very many of them...

She didn't know how many. No one would tell her, not even Sir Miche, which could only mean that there were a great many indeed, so many they thought she would be frightened if she knew. Hundreds, maybe, to make such a racket. Thousands? The noises outside were constant now, an escalating cacophony that built and built until she wanted to scream for it to stop. Rasping, snarling, all of the noises had teeth, tearing at the little town of Tresingale.

I can never decide which is worse, the stranglers or the wolf demons. Remember that one summer when we heard squealing noises in the wood, and it scared everyone to bits until we found out it was just an elk? The stranglers are a little like that, if the elk was laughing in the dark. They call most often at sunrise and sunset, when everything else is quiet. As if they are laughing at their own wickedness.
The wolf demons are more frightening, I think. I can't even tell you what it is like to hear one close by, as if their teeth are iron and they are howling through the metal. I think if I saw one of those, I would just crumple over right there. But I hate stranglers. Sometimes I fall asleep and wake up to hear one cackling, and it sounds so close, like it's right outside the window. I would rather a wolf demon killed me in one bite than to be waiting for a strangler to creep up upon me. I would never wish you to hear them yourself, but oh,

I wish you were here, Azelma. You would laugh at them, I bet, and tell me I am a silly girl. I wish I had thought to ask if you could come with me when we left Aldeburke, for then I would not be so alone. It is hard to be so afraid all by myself.

Sometimes her quill ran away with her.

Ophele scrubbed a hand over her face and hardly noticed when it came away wet. This was not a letter she could send home. Rising, she crumpled it up and thrust it into the fire, reaching for a fresh page.

These letters were not only for Azelma. In the dark of the night, when the fire burned low and it seemed every devil in the world was about to batter down the fragile walls of the cottage, the words poured out of her, the only outlet for her terror. Who else could she trust? In whom could she confide? Certainly not the Knights of the Brede, who went out into the dark with the creatures every night. To them she could only be a foolish girl, at best. They could not know her cowardice. Her worthlessness. For she was the daughter of their enemy, a backhanded insult to their lord.

She started over. She tried to sound hopeful. She tried to sound brave. In the early hours of the morning, she read her letters anxiously again and again, but it was so hard when she had no gauge for what was normal, or what things she should already know.

If His Grace read her letters, he would only despise her more.

Ophele told herself good stories. She wrote about the building of the town, and how beautiful the wheat was, growing green on the hills to the north. She wrote about the wall and how exciting it was to watch it every day, knowing herself a small part of that great enterprise. She wrote about Eugene and Master Didion and the grand manor to be built on the high hill. But she did not write that it was to be made in the likeness of Tressin, the ancient house that her divine father had burned to ashes.

Of her husband, the Duke of Andelin, she wrote nothing at all.

* * *

By the time Remin came home, the fire had burned to coals.

It was not the first time he had found the princess asleep at the table, her head pillowed on her arm and her quill still loose in her fingers. There was a small glass phial at her elbow in a shape he recognized, and he plucked it up, sniffing the dried herbs tied to its neck. Remin had seen enough such beakers to recognize it at once: one of Gen's tonics, and this one for sleep, if he recalled his limited herbology correctly. Gen looked in on the princess regularly, and said she was looking a little worn.

Of all the problems currently before him, the princess's correspondence ranked very low, but Remin eyed the piles of paper as he went to wash the blood from his hands. Her handwriting was too messy to read from a distance, but he wouldn't have done so in any case; it was Juste's task to read her correspondence, to be sure there was nothing dangerous. Even if she was the Emperor's daughter, there were some lines with his wife that Remin would not cross.

That was also why he did her the courtesy of transferring her to the bed, when he would have left anyone else to wake up on their own. Remin held his breath as he slipped his arms under her, but her lashes didn't so much as flicker. She only rolled over and reached for a pillow when he laid her down, curling up small in the center of the bed.

Remin regarded the small bare feet beneath the single ruffle of her chemise, and pulled up a blanket.

Everything about her was a problem.

He just didn't have time to solve everything, as June passed and the devils came relentlessly on. In three years, they had never seen so many. During the war, he had required nightly counts of the carcasses from his men, but even without that comparison, he would have known they were seeing many times that number now.

And summer was just getting started.

It was so hot. The days were long, but the men had to rest in the shade during the hottest hours, or he would have lost dozens to sun sickness. Sweating, he and his knights took their own turns moving stones and hauling heavy filler up to the tops of the walls, a mixture of crushed stone, lime, and other materials that bonded into a sort of concrete. They worked on the palisade, felling a hundred trees a day. They already knew how inadequate that barrier was. The guards on the palisade were being dragged off by stranglers every night, and they were burning through torches faster than they could make them.

Devils were slipping through. A few ghouls got into the cow pen and tore a precious milk cow to pieces. A wolf demon gave the builders at the barracks a terrifying night; they told Remin the next day about the poison-green eyes they saw glowing in the dark, and the shadow pounding against the walls, howling fit to freeze their blood. The barracks stood the test, but two builders did not. They were headed for the Gellege Bridge the next day.

And those were just the attacks Remin *knew* about.

"No sign of Rollon," Jinmin reported, after a week-long attempt to reach Ferrede. Remin and his men were meeting in his tent once a day now, reporting and coordinating their activities and adjusting as information came in. "Only made it fifty miles before I had to turn back. It was bad at night."

During the war, Jinmin had once referred to an ambush by three Vallethi warbands as *a surprise.*

"We'll send men to the other villages," Remin began, feeling a sickening roll in his gut. Isigne. Meinhem. Selgin. Raida. Nandre. He could picture every one of those villages. He had taken their oaths after the war, promising to reward their loyalty with protection. "We can pull them off the border, full cohorts in marching order."

"They'll die if you do," said Jinmin in his flat bull's voice. "Took a day to build defenses myself, just to see if I could stand them off on the ground. I'm only here because the stranglers couldn't get through my armor. Had wolves trying to bash through my barricades all night. You empty the border, that might be enough."

He couldn't do that. And Jinmin was right; it was one thing for entire armies on the march to build a fortified encampment every night, with torches and shell barriers on the tents and all the other defenses Remin and his men had devised over the years. During the war, there had been an entire defensive corps that marched with his army, specifically tasked with keeping the fighters alive at night. He had disbanded them at the end of the war because he hadn't thought he would need them anymore.

"If every man had plate armor…" His brow knotted as he thought aloud. "And builders for a palisade…"

There had to be a way. He couldn't accept this, that he should just *give up* on his people and let the devils have them. For hours, they argued about it, and only the fact that it was *Jinmin* saying this kept him from dismissing it outright. Jinmin was inclined to understate the problem, if anything.

"Take a company from Tresingale, as an experiment," suggested Juste. "Send them a few days out of town and let them try to assemble defenses on the march."

"We'll try it," Remin agreed, after a moment's consideration. "With all the armor we can spare. I won't send anyone to die for no purpose, but we have to try. I will lea—"

But that set off another uproar.

"You absolutely will not," Juste snapped, at the same time that Edemir, Tounot, Jinmin, Huber, and Auber all protested at once.

"Not unless you want to leave Her Grace a widow, m'lord," Jinmin said bluntly.

"We'll draw lots for it," said Miche, with none of his usual lazy drawl. "I didn't take two arrows and a dagger to the back for you just to let you get eaten by a pack of ghouls."

There ought to be a statute of limitations on that sort of thing, Remin thought furiously, but did not say. He was their liege lord, and they would obey his command; they had all sworn sacred oaths to the stars saying so. But it was also true that almost every one of them could have made a similar claim. Miche had only been protecting him longest. Remin was the Duke of Andelin, the last of his blood, and they had fought and won a war at least partially on the premise that his life and his line were more precious than the lives of thousands.

"Jinmin will lead, with one of you to support him," he said, clamping down tight on a wave of helpless fury. He could not go. It was his lot to send others to die instead. "Draw lots for the second position. The question is how many we can send without weakening Tresingale's defenses…"

They labored hours more, answering that question, and in the end, it was Jinmin and Huber that marched out of Tresingale one morning, with fifty men and a dozen horses that Remin really couldn't spare. Huber had gone as if he were daring Remin to protest the decision, the only one of Remin's men who was capable of silencing him with a look.

"We need to manage the town's defenses better in the meantime," noted Tounot. "Localize the alerts when a devil gets through the lines. If we don't let people get some sleep, Rem, they're going to start having accidents."

Everything was like that, a constant balance between *too much* and *not enough.* Remin had a depressing number of similarly impossible quandaries that he could trot out for a little perspective, but he was extremely bitter about the whole thing. And even as he wrestled with these familiar problems of manpower and supply, he was discovering whole new categories of worry.

During the endless week that Jinmin and Huber were outside the walls, Remin was wondering whether it was normal for a lady to keep falling asleep in her bath.

More than once, he had returned to the cottage to find the princess asleep in the water with her head lolling against the rim of the cauldron. He could understand someone falling asleep in a normal bath; those were quite nice. But she was curled up in a little knot of skinny limbs and long wet hair, and he had to shake her to wake her up.

"Oh—what? Did I fall asleep?" She managed to get it together enough to cover her breasts with her hands, blinking owlishly. "I'm sorry, you don't have to—"

It was the third time he had found her like this. Remin fished her out of the water and felt her forehead, his face grim. He kept meaning to look in on her. It felt like he barely saw her these days, and he had a nagging feeling that something was wrong, but no idea what it was.

"Are you sick? I won't be angry if you are." He set her in the chair by the fire and reached for a towel, trying not to embarrass her by looking at her. "I will be angry if you don't tell me."

She shook her head.

"Are you having trouble sleeping?" he asked, in sudden inspiration. Her eyes did look shadowed, and he knelt down before her, draping a towel over her shoulders. "I saw Gen's tonic, and I know it's loud at night—"

"I'm all right." She wouldn't meet his eyes.

"That's not what I asked. If something's wrong—"

"Rem!" Auber shouted from outside. "They're back!"

Remin had to bite his tongue to keep from cursing.

"Get dressed," he said. "I'll be back to take you to supper, but I'm on watch tonight. Don't be scared, Princess. Nothing will hurt you."

He could at least keep *that* promise, Remin thought savagely, hurrying with Auber to the north gate, where Jinmin and Huber were returning with nineteen men, of whom six had lost limbs. There were no horses.

There was nothing to say. There was nothing the Duke of Andelin could do but get out of the way as Genon hurried to do his work among the wounded.

The wide, heavy gates swung shut.

Thirty-one men were dead. Thirty-one. It was nothing compared to the blood Remin had spilled over the previous seven years, but he still had to back off and breathe, containing it behind the hard mask of his face. Should he have anticipated this? Should he have moved men to the villages sooner? He had planned to set up local militias this year, but there hadn't seemed any urgency; the folk of the Andelin knew how to cope with the devils as well as anyone did.

"We can't go," said Huber, coming to stand beside him. His bronzed face was bloody and his eyes socketed with weariness. "We only made it twenty miles before we had to turn back. The stranglers kept going for our torches. Anyone you send is going to die."

"I gave them my word," Remin replied, low and anguished. He couldn't stop picturing a silent Ferrede, with all the shutters and doors torn open, and the acres of wheat blowing in the wind, untended. Elder Brodrim. All those frightened people who had renewed their oath to him.

"I know." Huber glanced at him, an ocean of understanding passing between them. Since they were boys, Huber had been the one to watch the most and say the least. After Victorin's death, he had had little to say at all. But in this case, his silence was simply because there was nothing that could be said. There were no words of comfort he could offer in the face of abandoning hundreds of innocent people to the devils. There should not be any words that would justify such a thing.

"Are you all right?" The princess asked when he returned to take her to supper, looking up at him with solemn eyes.

"Fine."

He was still trying to think of a way to save them later that night, as he stood guard in the lines before the masons' camp. It boasted the same defenses as the lines on the west side of town, with break walls and torch towers and archers. All the defenses the rest of his villages lacked.

Maybe he should try to lead a group of men himself. Didn't he owe it to them to *try?* To risk his own safety, when his common folk had no one to protect them? Perhaps if he took only knights in armor, and they built shelters for the horses…

But what if something happened to Tresingale? What if the town's defenses fell? He had already weakened them with this first experiment. He could not spare the men to guard when he also needed them to build, and it would be a bitter irony if he went out to save his stricken villages, only to find that Tresingale had been devoured behind him.

No one could make this decision for him. And it wasn't the first time he had faced such a terrible choice, but every time was as bad as the first. Where was his duty? Whose lives should he sacrifice? He could not save everyone.

He was too far away to see it when a wolf got through the gap in the north wall.

He heard it, though. Alarms rolled backward in quick succession, and in the quiet air of the summer night he could hear distant shouts. Torches lit in a line, following the trail of the creature. The instructions for defenders were to hold their ground, sound the alarm, but do not pursue. That would only open a gap in the defenses that other devils would slip through. The alarms and cries rampaged southward, down the cobblestones of the only road in Tresingale.

Toward the cottages.

He had taken three steps forward before he even realized it. The wolf demon wouldn't reach them. He knew it wouldn't. And he knew there had been excellent reasons why he was here rather than guarding the cottages by the cookhouse, but at that moment, he couldn't remember what they were.

Who was in charge of the defenses over there? Darri. Cat-eyed Darri, the subtle blade, who had carried out any number of complicated and dangerous assignments. He could trust Darri. He knew that. But the princess was there, with no better defense than mud and sticks, and the sound of a wolf demon howling at close quarters was like standing inside a war horn.

Soft fingers wrapped around his throat, and Remin whipped his head around and slammed it into the grinning face of the strangler.

It was already too late to yell. He had been stupid, walking out of the circle of torchlight. He smacked his sword and shield together as a warning signal and then threw both on the ground; there was no room to swing his sword, the strangler was already wrapping its skinny, squishy limbs around him like the coils of a snake. Yanking his knife out of its sheath, he slammed it into the devil's attenuated body and jerked it upward, snarling into its huge pale eyes.

It gave a rasping scream and Remin grabbed its hands and *tore*. Muscles popped in his wrists and forearms as he ripped that strangling grip loose and smashed the creature onto the ground, crushing its skull under his heavy boot. He was furious with himself. He could hear the other guards behind him signaling warnings to each other, adjusting their positions while he dealt with the creature, and only when he smashed his boot down a second time did it finally die, twitching.

Remin sucked in a huge breath, kicking the body aside. He wanted to cough. His sides were jerking with the need to cough, but it was a matter of pride that he clenched his jaw, buttoned it in, and straightened, picking up his sword and shield.

Even then he couldn't help turning to look as the extra torches by the stables winked out, signaling that the wolf demon was dead. The princess was safe. He had known she would be.

He had never in his life felt so clearly that he was not where he should be.

But it could not be helped tonight. He was on guard *here*. He was responsible for the lives of *these* men. Tomorrow night it would be different, but right now his duty was to the men sleeping behind him.

And just like that, the decision was made. He could not save his villages. All he could do was abandon and endanger the people at his back. There was nothing to be done but endure together. Endure the heat, endure the work, endure the devils and the endless nights. The walls *would* be built, if he had to lay every stone himself. There would be a city, and they would find a way to deal with the devils once and for all.

If anyone survived in his villages, he would see that they never wanted for anything as long as they lived. But he could not save everyone. If he had learned nothing else in all the harsh years of his life, it was that people died, and he could not stop it.

But his gaze lingered on a distant cottage, and in his mind's eye he saw a small woman with a solemn face, who made him feel more uncertain than ever.

* * *

Ophele had just endured another of those long and dusty days.

Sitting on the steps at the foot of the wall, every muscle in her body was voicing the usual complaints, from the blazing burn in her legs to the ache in her feet to the stabbing pains in her arms, as if someone had driven a dagger directly into each bicep. It was a pain she could never have imagined back in Aldeburke, but it was the familiar conclusion of her days now, along with the unsettling feeling that her arms were only loosely attached to her shoulders.

Master Eugene nosed her, and she stroked his velvety muzzle.

A little way up the trench, she could catch occasional glimpses of Sir Miche's blond head, scrambling up and down the huge mounds of earth that lined either side of the pit. The diggers had run into a problem a few hours ago, and almost everyone else had gone home for the day.

She had just crept a little way up the stairs, hoping for a better look, when a voice behind her nearly made her topple off in surprise.

"Good evening, my lady," said Sir Tounot, quickly catching her elbow. "You're still here?"

"Testing the stairs," she said, embarrassed.

"Well, if they are fit for the Lady of Andelin, then they must be an honor for the rest of us," he said gallantly, helping her to her feet. "But if you're waiting for Miche, it will be a bit, I'm afraid. Would you like to go up and have a look?"

"Oh, could I?" she asked, brightening. She had been forbidden the top of the wall, along with almost every other interesting place in the valley. "It wouldn't be any trouble?"

"I was just going up myself to have a word with Ammon," he assured her. "So long as Master Eugene won't take it in his head to wander off."

"No, the cart has a brake now, and he falls asleep whenever he's standing still," she assured him, trotting up the stairs. It was refreshing just to feel the wind at the top of the wall, cool and clean, almost as if the valley's summer humidity was a low-lying phenomenon. And Sir Tounot must have known how much she wanted a look around, because he set her safely in the center and then left her to amuse herself.

Ophele was happily oblivious to the masons sidling nervously along the wall beside her as she explored, as if they feared she might suddenly throw herself over the side. Much of Tresingale was still heavily wooded, and from where she stood, she was looking up at whitebeam trees and wych elms, eighty and ninety feet tall, elderly giants. Closer to eye level were black pines and glossy green holly, and clusters of mossy oak with their distinctive leaves, like finding old friends. There were some wonderful old oaks back in Aldeburke whose branches had cradled and concealed her over the years.

But many of those splendid trees had been cut back to deny concealment to the devils, and she could see more clearing underway on a distant hilltop, where the manor house would soon rise. Nearer at hand were the hills of the barracks and Court of War, and she drifted down the completed portion of the wall for a better look. There were the beginnings of the bridge that would one day butt up against the high wall, a curving fortification that dropped straight down into the river. The masons were very excited about the progress of the bridge footings.

Ophele could have watched this fascinating work all day. Sir Miche had walked with her down the hill to the river a few times, but from there she could only see bits and pieces of the machines involved. Now she could see all of it, creaking away in the fading daylight, and she didn't realize how far she had come until Sir Tounot came trotting up behind her.

"I will walk with you, lady, if it pleases you," he said, offering his elbow. "You can see the treadwheel quite well from up here, can't you?"

"That's what it's called?" Ophele was always pleased to learn the proper names of things.

"A treadwheel crane, yes, my lady. One of the largest in the Empire, according to Master Guisse," he said, puffing comically to make her giggle. "And that's the pile driver beside it. They'll use that to make a coffer dam—that's that diamond shape—and then bail out the water from the middle…"

Well, that was where some of the elms and whitebeams must have gone, Ophele thought, listening with rapt attention as he explained how the dam would become a footing, and the footings would support arches, and the arches would span the river all the way to Firkane.

"I like that," Ophele said, deeply impressed. What she wouldn't give for such a wheel to work the well, and spare her the endless cranking of the windlass. A breeze lifted, combing cool fingers through her hair, and she sighed. "Oh, the wind is so nice."

"It puts me in mind of the wind off the Emme, in the capital," Sir Tounot said reminiscently. "There are great paved walks along that river, and this time of year they are shaded by trees and arbors, with blue morning glories and climbing hydrangeas. But there is no view like this in Segoile."

"Maybe one day we will have walks like that," she said.

"If Master Ffloce has his way, we will exceed anything the capital can boast," Sir Tounot said smugly. "He plans public walks like the ones in Capricia, where even the common folk are welcome to promenade of an evening, and artists and musicians will gather under streetlights to compete for the attention of passersby. In Capricia, they say the Walk of Dreams is sustenance for the soul."

"And we will have artists coming, and musicians?" she asked eagerly, looking down at the river as her imagination painted them over the trees and scrub brush. But then she caught her breath, her hand tightening on Sir Tounot's arm. "What is that? Down in the trees, did you see it?"

"That is a devil, my lady." He halted beside her, his eyes narrowing.

"I thought they didn't come out until night."

"It's dark enough under the trees that they can move a little by day, or they would not be here to trouble us at all," the knight answered somberly. "The hunters have to be wary, when they venture into the forest. But the devils have to stay hidden in whatever holes they have found, for the least sunlight will set them afire."

"I wish it would burn that one," she murmured, looking with dread fascination. She didn't want to see it, but she was also afraid to take her eyes from it. "Do you know what kind it is?"

"Too small for a wolf demon," he said, looking obligingly down at the small shape. "I would say a strangler, my lady. Ghouls are rarely alone, and stranglers like to hide in such pla—"

"My lady!" came a call from behind them, and she turned to find a sodden Sir Miche striding toward them, soaked to the chest in muddy water. He was not smiling. "There you are. Please step back from the edge of the wall."

"There's a devil in the wood down there," she explained as he seized her elbow and drew her back. "Sir Tounot was just—"

"Sir Tounot ought to have more sense," he said sharply, with none of his usual drawling good humor. "All we need is for a bird to startle or that devil to start racketing and give you a fright, and we might as well throw ourselves over the side after you. Please do nothing of the sort again."

"Well, I won't," she said meekly, and he sighed, rumpling up his hair.

"I beg your pardon," he said. "It gave me a turn to find Master Eugene by himself, but I suppose you've earned a look from the top. Just stay back from the edge, I beg, for the sake of my heart. Where's the devil?"

"Over there, you nagging auntie," said Sir Tounot, eyeing him with some amusement. "Though it's ducked back under cover now. Wish I had a bow."

"I expect you'll have another shot at it tonight," Sir Miche said grimly. "With all that water in the ditch, the devils are just going to have to paddle across. I think we've discovered where all the water from the stream at the north wall went. You're going to have a busy night on this side of town if we don't get it emptied."

"Stars and ancestors. You've got them bailing it out?"

"Like bailing out the Brede," Sir Miche said acidly, and Ophele trotted after them to the opposite end of the wall, glancing back at the churning mechanisms on the river behind her. Would something like that work to drain the ditch? Like a water wheel and a sluice down to the river? In her mind, she could see how the pieces would fit together, but she had no notion how hard it would be to build such a thing.

It was on the tip of her tongue to ask, but they were already discussing the matter, their voices clipped and urgent, and Ophele's hands moved anxiously together. She couldn't interrupt them with her nonsense. If it was a good idea, surely they would have thought of it already.

Near the end of the wall, they came to a halt at the sight of the low trench, now a muddy moat where muck-covered men were scrambling about with torches, jamming them into the sides of the dirt piles.

It appeared they had filled one pond only to excavate another.

"Please excuse me, Your Grace," Sir Tounot said, turning to offer a polite bow. "It was a very pleasant promenade. I will hope for another, once we have sufficient safeguards for yonder nursemaid."

His humorous glance at Sir Miche made his intended target clear.

"I would like to watch them building the bridge again," Ophele replied. "If it wouldn't be too much trouble."

"As long as you warn your nursemaid beforehand," Sir Miche said as Sir Tounot departed, drawing her back toward the stairs. "I promised Rem I'd keep an eye out for you, my lady. Not because of anything you might do, but to make sure no misfortune befalls you. There are many varieties available."

"I know. Like that devil."

"That is one virtue of placing you atop a mighty wall," he conceded. "They would have some trouble reaching you here, barring the—careful," he said quickly, grabbing for her as Ophele suddenly swayed, sagging toward the wall and for an instant, supported only by his arm. "Are you all right? Miss a step?"

"Yes. I guess," Ophele said woozily, shaking her head. She felt very peculiar, with a strange buzzing in her ears like a swarm of bees at night. "I'm sorry."

"It's been a long day," he said, but his tawny eyes narrowed as he examined her, and he boosted her directly into the cart when they reached Eugene. "No, stay in the cart. You need a little feeding, my lady."

"Oh, no, I just missed my footing, and Eugene has already worked so hard—"

"If he can pull six barrels of water, he can haul one Duchess of Andelin," Sir Miche replied, light and implacable. "I wonder what Wen's making for supper. Another few minutes and I might settle for a haunch of donkey."

"He said mutton and parsnips," Ophele replied, her nose wrinkling.

"I'll trade my bread for your parsnips, Your Highness." Sir Miche whistled and made her laugh as they set off east, the rickety cart swaying.

* * *

Remin was the first to step upon the completed footing of the bridge.

"Not a wobble," he said, marveling as he watched the dark water of the Brede streaming around the new stone island, an oblong diamond that cut straight and true through that turbulent tide. "You'll be starting the docks next week?"

"Yes, Your Grace," said Master Guisse, examining the sides of the footing with a critical eye. "So long as we have sufficient hands, I do not anticipate any further delay."

"I do not anticipate borrowing any more workers from you," said Remin, who had stolen a dozen laborers to sort out the flooding by the wall. That had been a very long couple of days for everyone.

But even with devils and floods, the work of the valley continued, and he and the master went on to the proposed site of the port, where the first piles had already been driven into the river, outlining its curving form. The machines required to build a bridge were much the same as those that would build the port and its network of docks, and the need for transport across the river was urgent. The long summer days allowed plenty of time to shuttle men and supplies back and forth from the Gellege Bridge, but soon enough the days would begin to shorten, and they could not afford to have wagons racing the devils to the gates. Remin already had another work crew building a fortification halfway between Tresingale and the bridge, just in case.

This port would solve the problems of overland travel. Like everything else, it would grow with time; Master Didion and Master Guisse had put their heads together on the final design, a marvel of engineering where even the cranes would be works of art. The port of Tresingale must be efficient, for all the trade of the Brede would flow through it, up into the valley or onto the bridge, for further transport overland. But it was important to Remin that it should be beautiful. One day, the faces of the stars would look down on visitors from the hillside: Zeraf, the governor of trade, or Nahvet, the star of sailors, a weathered old man with keen eyes, and his lamp ever lifted.

Remin wanted people to *know* when they had arrived in Tresingale.

"We have been considering your competitors, my lord," said one of Edemir's secretaries later that afternoon, a former merchant named Bendir who had charge of the river trade. They were meeting in the new offices above the storehouse, to accommodate their expanding number of experts, and Bendir produced a map of the river, pointing to the duchy furthest east. "Leinbruke charges a passage tariff, a single fee to any merchant that wants to move through the duchy without stopping to trade. It's cheap, but if a merchant sells so much as a hair ribbon, it's considered smuggling. Firkane charges by the mile, but there is no tariff on trade. Norgrede is the worst; they have both a passage tariff and fees at the ports, so they're essentially double-dipping. A merchant who wants to move goods from Leinbruke to the port at Alenre will pay around twenty gold sen. That's why Lein cashmere is so expensive. It costs the earth just to get it out of Leinbruke."

All of this was far outside Remin's experience. But from the excited glances the secretaries were exchanging, he suspected it was good news.

"We can do better?" he guessed.

"A tariff by port, Your Grace," said Bendir, indicating multiple black markers on the map. "You have a monopoly on the river; anyone wishing to use it for trade must use your ships and pay your price. You can charge fees for transport based on portage rather than miles, as that will be the greater constraint. We have done some calculations, to project volume, expenses, and profits…"

He ran through the list of expenses first, being a glass-half-empty sort of fellow, and made sure that Remin understood that there were other factors were likely to crop up that they hadn't anticipated, as well as factors they could anticipate but not quantify: the other duchies were likely to lower their tariffs in response, for example, but who could say when, or by how much.

But when all was said and done, the profit was *staggering*.

"You're quite sure?" Remin's eyes narrowed as he skimmed the figures. He didn't know much about trade, but he knew how much things cost. He knew exactly how much gold it had taken to arm and feed his army. He knew how much it was going to cost to build Tresingale, from the walls to the town to the manor house.

With the profits from the river trade, he could build another Tresingale every three years.

"Quite sure," said Bendir, with the avaricious delight of a born merchant. "The Brede is the only river that feeds into the Sea of Eskai for a hundred miles. And no matter how low the other duchies set their tariffs, they will never match your speed. Travel on the Brede does not require horses or oxen, who must be fed, who might throw shoes, or who might be injured or sicken. The only other obstacle is the port cities. There isn't enough room on the river for you to match a Sideriel or Alenre."

"Then we'll build on the sea," Remin said instantly. His mind was already racing ahead, calculating the position of greatest advantage. He knew the place where the Brede ran out into the sea; on the north side, it was surmounted by the Cliffs of Marren, high and treacherous, stretching all the way from the Brede to the border of the neighboring country of K'ar Yez. There was a reason the Empire had never tried to invade by sea. "We'll dig all the way down to the water and build our own port. Edemir—"

"I know." The knight sighed, resigned, but his eyes gleamed at the prospect. "I'll find out how long it would take and how much it would cost."

"A port on this side of the Brede," Bendir breathed. "Your Grace. I can say with some certainty that you would recoup your investment within a decade, and likely much sooner."

It wasn't even the prospect of money that excited Remin, though if everything went to plan, he would be wealthier than some nations. After a discussion like that, he left the office feeling so exhilarated, he hardly knew what to do with himself. He wanted to see those ships on the river. When the manor house was done, he would be able to watch them sailing by from his bedroom windows. The talk of building a port city of his own made him want to saddle his horse and race to the Cliffs of Marren to tear the earth out of his way with his bare hands.

And what of the world beyond the Brede, and the Sea of Eskai? K'ar Yez was right there, a poor country that was nonetheless rich in resources. They had remained understandably neutral during the last war with Valleth; their country was so rugged and inhospitable that the inhabitants scraped a meager living, and they had been cruelly chastised for supporting the Empire in the past. Every gem in those mountains had to be pried out by the fingernails. Remin was neither an invader nor a pirate, but soon, he would be positioned to make some serious investments. What could he do, if he worked with the clans of K'ar Yez, and gave them passage to his port city to trade the wealth of their lands?

He had barely gotten half a mile down the road, and he instantly turned his horse around and galloped back, bursting into Edemir's office with this latest inspiration.

"We are not a sovereign nation," Edemir reminded him, and not for the first time. "Such trade would have to go through the Court of Merchants, Rem."

That dented his enthusiasm. Just a little.

He could be his own nation, though.

It was dangerous even to think that. It was greedy. And though nothing he had gained could ever replace what had been taken from him, Remin knew when to quit while he was ahead. Or at least pause, and think very, very carefully before he proceeded any further.

He was a young man with his whole life ahead of him, after all. And the Emperor was growing old.

The valley and all its cares sometimes felt so far removed from the rest of the Empire that it was easy to forget they existed. But Remin knew that even if he wasn't thinking about the Emperor, the Emperor was almost definitely thinking about him.

That was the reason for another meeting in Edemir's offices a few days later. Every few days, Remin called his knights together to discuss more sensitive topics.

"They call themselves the Clocksmen," explained Bram, who had forged a lifetime of questionable connections and frequently made use of them on Remin's behalf. Before them on the table was a copy of the tattoo they had found on the assassin in Granholme, the many-spoked clock and slit-pupiled eye. "They say they know the hour of your death."

"Shouldn't they say the minute, if they want to charge for a service?" drawled Miche, unimpressed.

"Go on, Bram," Remin said, though he did appreciate Miche's irreverence. Ever since he was a boy, Miche had been taking the terror out of terrible things.

"They're originally out of Rendeva. Swords for hire who want to pretend they're something more." Bram shrugged one shoulder, contemptuous as always of such conceits. "They have been known to operate in the Empire, so it's not likely they called one just for you, Rem. This fellow in Granholme was likely nearby on another job, and got tapped to do you at the last minute."

"Were there any other deaths in Firkane, or the neighboring duchies?" Juste asked. He would be taking over the matter from Bram, now that they had something to go on.

"There was," Bram confirmed. "Duke Firkane has been having trouble with one of his bannermen. Count Morbray had a hunting accident four days before we reached Granholme. He was forty-three and notoriously cautious, given his relations with his lord."

There was no guarantee it was related. All of it was circumstantial evidence, but it threw the weight of circumstance onto the Duke of Firkane, who loved the Emperor, rather than the Princess Ophele, who had never laid eyes on him.

Something untwisted inside Remin at the thought. But…could she have been in league with him? Could he be *sure* that she had passed no messages, that afternoon in Granholme? Or even just acted to delay him in her bed? His jaw clenched as he looked at the picture of the spoked wheel and its angry red eye. He just couldn't know.

"I'll give this to Juste," he said, as they had all known he would. "I would like proof, Juste. One way or the other."

Juste nodded, his pale blue eyes as placid as ever.

"We'll have to send someone," he said. "Not me. The Knights of the Brede are too well known to be discreet. But we will need people in the Empire more generally, beyond this specific task. Our reach there is too tenuous, at present."

He was volunteering to once again become Remin's spymaster.

"You're entitled to lands in the Andelin," Remin reminded him. "And you have your place as my steward."

He had sworn to himself, at the end of the war, that he would find a peaceful place for every man that had carried a sword beside him.

"I am ever a herdsman," Juste replied gently. "I'll second Darri, if you don't mind. He has an aptitude."

With that, they turned to issues at the other end of the valley. With so many grand designs on the horizon, sometimes Remin became impatient with the small matter of the devils. He did not fear them, himself. He chafed at the restrictions they imposed. But as precarious as the situation was in Tresingale, it was even more so for the folk outside it.

"Our reinforcements have arrived from the border," said Tounot, who had charge of this matter. In his hands was the latest stack of reports, ferried by Remin's fledgling navy since travel overland had become impossible. "They say the men there are holding, especially with supplies from Raida. They've agreed to guard and fortify the village in exchange for foodstuffs."

"Good." Underneath the papers scattered across the table was a map of the valley, and Remin's eye effortlessly picked out the small village on the northeast end, ten miles from the Vallethi border. "Did Raida take many losses?"

"The border detachments sent both men and builders to them," Tounot replied. "All they needed was a stone barracks. At night they shut the doors, post a couple guards, and sleep soundly."

That was more or less what he had intended for Ferrede. Remin was glad to hear it. And he hadn't given up on Rollon and the builders he had sent to the village months ago; there was a better than even chance they would come back as soon as the devils melted away for the winter, none the worse for their adventures.

But he had four more villages, oath-sworn to give him fealty, and he owed them protection. Even after their first disastrous experiment, he still hadn't given up on the idea. The thought of his people out there facing the devils alone made it very hard to sleep some nights.

"There must be a way," he said aloud. "To get to the other villages. I know we're short of men, but I don't want to wait until the walls are up to come up with something. We need a way to get teams of men to the other villages in one piece. Men in armor might survive the trip, but we need to send builders."

"A very small selection of men in armor could survive that journey," Edemir corrected dryly. "Not many of us are up to facing down a charging wolf demon, Rem."

"We can't afford to send all our knights in any case." Remin waved this point aside. He never thought of himself as extraordinary and still didn't really understand why anyone else did. "But I was thinking of the armor in particular. Devils can't bite through metal. Couldn't we have the smiths make something sufficient to protect a small party? They could take turns sleeping during the day."

"I wouldn't like to carry a metal coffin on my back from here to Isigne," said Miche, but he was thoughtful rather than mocking. "But maybe with a supply cart or something, it could work. I'll take that one, Rem. The blacksmiths and carpenters need to make friends. They can knock their heads against this together, or I'll knock their heads off separately myself."

"Trouble?" Remin asked, his black brows lifting.

"Nothing I can't manage," the blond knight said languidly. "People are on edge. They'll get over it when the walls are up."

But it was a warning, all the same; Miche was very good at reading people. It was important to remember that most people in the valley weren't thinking about building ports and arranging trade with K'ar Yez. Most of the valley's inhabitants were enduring long hours of backbreaking work in murderous summer heat, and spent their nights trying not to hear the howling of devils. After a while, that would wear on anyone.

Except for the pages. Remin only sporadically saw the youngest people in his service, but they were all energetic and resilient and didn't have the sense to be afraid. Edemir, Tounot, and Huber maintained connections with other noble Houses and each had a few pages, ranging from eight to thirteen years old. The boys were useful for running errands and frequently did small, mindless chores, though the rest of their teaching had been somewhat disrupted lately.

This fact did not go unnoticed by Jacot of Caillmar, who had swum the Brede.

"Morning, Your Grace," he called one day as Remin approached on his horse. The boy had placed himself in the duke's path more than once, and Remin had several suspicions as to why. "Just finished helping old Wen, need anything?"

"Did you ask Wen if he was done with you, or did you decide you were finished by yourself?" Remin was wise to the ways of pages.

"Well, I saw you coming," the boy said, jogging alongside him at a respectful distance from the warhorse. "And I said to myself, surely in proper order I should ask His Grace first, has he got any job what needs doing. Though it ain't what I expected, being a page. Ain't somebody supposed to teach me to read and play the lute or something?"

"You might not have noticed, but we're a little busy for the fine arts," Remin said dryly. "You can sing by yourself if you feel your musical education is being neglected."

"And so I do," the boy agreed cheerfully. "They said I had a nice voice back home. *In Celderline, he claimed his prize, An exile princess, Imperial heir, And a light like stars was in her eyes, And roses, in her hair...*"

"That's what they're singing now, is it?" So the story of Remin Grimjaw was ending with marrying the princess after all. And she had worn roses in her hair.

"All over Celderline, they never shut up about it. You sure there ain't nothing I can do to change your mind, Your Grace? I'll sing the whole thing, if you like. Or never sing again."

The boy was quick-witted, Remin would give him that.

"Why do you want to be my page?" he asked, mostly out of curiosity. Remin did not take pages. Ever.

"Who wouldn't?" Jacot replied. "Train under the greatest knight in the Empire? It's like walking into a story, innit?"

"This is not a story. You could die here and no one will sing songs about it. You know that?"

"I know it ain't. They wasn't lying about the Brede, for starters." Jacot was completely unabashed. "Was that cold! Thought my balls would never drop back down."

Remin did not laugh. But that was funny.

"If you need something to do, go see Auber at the palisade. He's been saying he needs help moving branches out of the way while they're trimming down the trees." Auber didn't have any pages yet. Maybe it would be good for him to take on the irrepressible Jacot.

"Yes, Your Grace," the boy said, disappointed. He hurdled a ditch and shifted direction toward the north gate. But there were many kinds of danger in the Andelin, and he'd hardly gone a dozen steps more when one of the masons came riding hell for leather toward Remin, shouting.

"Your Grace! Your Grace!" He drew up so sharply he almost went over his horse's head. "My lord, the Duchess fainted by the wall. Sir Miche is down in the river with her, by the bridge, he thinks it's sun sickness."

"Go get Genon," Remin ordered, after a stunned instant, and thumped his heels into his horse.

CHAPTER 11 – TRY

Jacot of Caillmar was right. The Brede was *cold*.

It was nearly evening by the time it was safe to take the princess out of the icy river. Remin thought she was finally cooler; the pink flush had faded from her skin and she had stopped saying that it was too hot, but he was so cold himself, it was hard to tell for sure.

"Better, aye," said Genon, wading knee-deep into the water to check her. His masses of silver-pink scar tissue made him too sensitive to temperature to take a turn in the river himself. "Breathing's finally slowed down, heart's beating regular. I think we can take her home."

"She's going to be all right?" The words had to be squeezed through a throat so tight, Remin wondered that he hadn't strangled.

"I think so." Genon lifted his fingers from the pulse point of her neck. "We won't know for sure until she wakes up."

Remin nodded.

He felt numb. Numb with cold, numb with shock, numb with fear. He knew how to shut himself down when he had to, when he couldn't afford to think or feel, but in this case there was nothing to fight, no action he could take, nothing he could do but endure. He had spent the longest day of his life in the icy river.

"I can't swim," she had kept crying, confused pleas he would never be able to forget. "Let me out, I can't swim, I'm fine, it's just so hot…"

"It's all right." In waist-deep water, Remin held her away from him so he wouldn't warm her, her soaked chemise drifting around her body and her long hair streaming in clouds around her head. "Ophele, it's all right. Didn't I tell you I'd teach you to swim? This is the first lesson. I've got you, all you have to do is float."

She was trying to listen. Her huge, soft eyes tried to focus on his face, on the trees shifting against the sky, seeing everything but understanding nothing, so bewildered that he couldn't stand it.

Remin knew sun sickness. During summer campaigns in the Andelin Valley, sometimes sun sickness felled more men than the battle. Everything her body was doing was working against her, from her racing heart to those panting breaths. In the icy water, she shivered violently, her body's perverse attempt to warm her when she was already burning up inside.

"It's all right," he said again. "Wife, I'm here. Shh, shh. Breathe, a good breath, deep and slow…"

Hadn't he said that, on their wedding night? And then she had trusted him, and they had breathed together. But Remin knew he was no comfort to her now.

A white-faced Miche was waiting when he finally brought her out of the river, and Remin gave her to him for the length of time it took to bring his horse around and mount up. All of the workers on the bridge had kept their distance, mindful of their lady's modesty, but Miche hadn't budged from the riverbank all afternoon.

"She's cooler, thank the stars," he said as Remin nudged Lancer over and reached out for her. His eyes were red. "Rem. She's been working *for you*. She's meant to be the mother of your children. You *have* to take care of her. *Swear it.*"

"I will," Remin promised through numb lips, as Miche carefully surrendered her.

In their cottage, he pulled off her wet chemise and tossed it aside, laying her naked on the bed. Sun sickness was caused by an imbalance of fire. The cooling elements of air and water had to touch as much of her body as possible. Was she warmer? He couldn't tell, his own body was still icy from the river.

Remin soaked a towel in cold water from the well, sponging her with it. Water and air, cool water that would evaporate on her skin. The thought that she might die…

It could not be thought. He wouldn't let it happen. How had he let this happen? What business did she have, laboring day after day in the merciless summer heat? When she woke up, he would never let her lift a finger again. If she woke up. She *would*. Remin bent beside her, his face drawn into stark, forbidding lines, his chest so tight he could barely breathe. What was wrong with him? He was never like this. For some reason he couldn't find the usual icy calm he felt in a crisis, and his thoughts kept scattering.

She was going to be so embarrassed when she woke up. He could already imagine the look on her face. Fainting in front of half the men on the wall, Miche cutting her dress off, and now she was naked in front of Genon. Why did these things keep happening? He never intended to embarrass her, but he failed to prevent it, over and over.

"Going to be dark soon." Genon grunted as he crouched beside the bed, taking the princess's wrist between his fingers. "If I thought there was the slightest danger, I'd stay, but I think she'll live. Miche saved her life, getting her down to the river as fast as he did."

"Will she be all right otherwise?" Remin made himself ask. He had lost many people dear to him over the years, but he had never felt anything like this horrible, hollow helplessness.

"I don't know." Genon never lied about things like this. "It took a long time to cool her down."

"That one soldier, at Creussen. How long did we keep him in the bath?" Remin couldn't remember.

"It's not the same, Rem. He was older, and it was almost two hours before we got him into a cold bath."

That man had been unconscious for two days and awakened an idiot. A drooling simpleton. The Hurrells had tried to convince him she was simple back in Aldeburke, but all it had taken was one good look into her eyes and Remin had known it was a lie. When she opened her eyes, if she opened her eyes, what was he going to see now?

Ruthlessly, he cut that thought off.

"Someone should get Eugene. The donkey." He lifted his head. "Can you check? Make sure someone took him to the stable."

"I will," Genon promised. "I know she's fond of the beast."

"Yes."

Miche said the donkey followed her everywhere, with or without a lead rope.

"I set out some medicine on the table." Genon laid her hand on the bed. "The powder on the left if her head hurts, the elixir in the middle if she's nauseous, and the one on the right she should take regardless, to cool her blood. Mix them with water and have her sip slowly. When someone brings your supper, I'll have Wen send honey to mix with the medicine. She needs sugar and salt. Lots of water, but slowly."

Remin nodded. He was familiar with these measures; he had nursed many sunstruck men when he was a squire.

"I'll let Tounot know not to expect you on watch tonight. We'll manage well enough, just you focus on your wife." Genon heaved himself to his feet and began to pack his bag, rolling up the long, felt case that contained his tools and medicines.

"If you had to guess." Remin couldn't bite the words back. "If you had to make a bet…"

"I don't believe she'll die. We'll know more when she wakes up. I'll be back at first light to check on you." The herbman paused at the door, gripping the handle. "She's too thin, Rem. At least a stone underweight. You didn't notice?"

Remin shook his head.

The door closed and latched. It sounded like a condemnation.

* * *

Color faded with the daylight, and Remin never took his eyes from her.

All this time, he had been trying so hard *not* to see her. Forcing his eyes to go past her, pushing her to the furthest periphery of his life. That had been a mistake. Perhaps it was the reason why he was so wrongfooted every time she appeared. He had never been able to shake her out of his mind. But in this one, crucial area, he had succeeded very well.

Stretched out on the bed, it was impossible not to see it, now. He could see how terribly prominent her ribs were, the jut of her hip bones, even the knobby little protrusions of her wrists. And he knew what she was supposed to look like. Remin remembered every moment of their nights together, how her body had felt in his hands, against his lips, under his tongue. He had kissed those ribs, he had felt those fragile bones jerk as she gasped with pleasure. He had tried so hard to forget, but he never could.

Remin washed one thin arm, noting the bruises dotting her fine white skin, the scratches and scrapes, the stringy, starveling muscle from months of heavy labor. Her hands shocked him. New blisters layered on top of old, ragged fingernails. Those were not the hands of a lady.

This was not what he had intended. If someone had returned a horse to him in this condition, he would have had them whipped. And this was his *wife*.

An Imperial wife, a daughter of the stars, a princess of the House of Agnephus. He had gone through fire and blood to be sure his new House would be built on bedrock, on the divine blood of the Emperor himself, so it could never again be taken away. And for seven years he had imagined the spoiled, pampered princess he would marry, growing up with every kind of luxury, while he starved and worked and fought and froze. And the whole time he had thought: he was going to make the Emperor's daughter work. He was going to show her what deprivation was like. Let her go wailing to her father about the harshness of the world. Let the Emperor gnash his teeth. Let him taste bile. Let him feel helpless.

From the day he met Ophele—no, from the *instant* they met—Remin had been trying to force her to play this part.

And she had never complained. Not once.

Not when he took her from her home without so much as a chance to pack a bag. Not when he forced her to marry him. Not when he hurt her on their wedding night and dragged her straight into the saddle the next morning. Not when, fresh from their lovemaking, he had all but accused her of trying to have him assassinated. Not even after he gave her too much wine and she had been so sick, sobbing into the blankets until Remin wished someone would take him off and hang him.

She had endured it all without a word of protest. Why? Why would anyone do that? Was it just because she was timid? Was she that afraid of him?

Outside, it grew dark, and he rose to light a lamp and set it on the trunk beside the bed, illuminating the sleeping girl. Her delicate face, the eyes that saw and showed so much. He remembered every cruel word he had spoken, every time he had snapped at her, every time he had driven her into flinching, bewildered retreat. All those times she had fallen silent, her words trailing away inaudibly.

More times than he could count.

This was not pointless self-flagellation. Remin was thinking. He had done nothing to earn her loyalty, and a great deal to make her hate him. That had not been his objective, but it didn't matter. The more he thought about it, the more he thought he wouldn't blame her if she *did* try to have him killed.

"Rem," said a voice outside, and he opened the door to find Miche with his supper and a small pot of honey. "Gen said she would live?"

"Looks that way."

Miche closed his eyes. "Thank the stars. The masons brought Master Eugene up to the stable. When she wakes up, she'll likely ask. He's been fed and I brushed him out myself. Is there anything I can do?"

"No." Remin forced himself to meet the other man's eyes. Miche had *warned* him, again and again. "But thank you."

"I'll be here," Miche assured him, gripping his shoulder. "Right outside. All you have to do is call. It's all right. You can make this right."

"I can. I know." Remin took it in like air. Of course, Miche would be there. Miche had always been there, since Remin was ten. No matter what, Miche was always there.

Closing the door, Remin put the food on the table and forgot about it. He heard the shrieking cackle of a strangler in the distance, a sound that made the hair on the back of his neck stand on end. In her sleep, the princess twitched, and he sat down beside the bed, gripping her small hand.

He was doing sums. For example: how many miles had she been walking every day, this girl who had never gone further than the gates of Aldeburke? How many thousands of pounds of water had she hauled from the wells? Just one barrel was two hundred and fifty pounds, almost triple her weight. A *ton of water*. Per day. By herself.

He touched the blisters on her palms, blisters she had hidden under gloves, because he certainly would have seen them otherwise. Wouldn't he?

If he had taken even a moment to think about it, he would never have let her do it. It was hard work, hauling water. At first, it hadn't been too much; the well was nearby and the work crew small. But no one had thought, when they gave her a donkey and a wagon, that it was still one undersized woman filling all those barrels.

He would have hesitated to put one of his squires to the task, and they were training to be knights.

"I don't understand you," he said aloud, to cover the noise of the devils outside. "I don't understand why you did it. You owe me nothing. What has it been? Four months…"

No matter how he turned it around in his mind, it didn't make sense. Why would anyone work so hard, without a single word of complaint, for someone who neglected them so? What possible scheme could involve silently working until she dropped? Even if she wasn't a pawn of the Emperor, it made no sense. Unless her plan was to drop dead beside Eugene and let it be known to the world that Remin Grimjaw could not be trusted with a wife.

Which wasn't a bad idea, in terms of lasting vengeance; Remin would never forgive himself if she died. But that was a rather costly victory from her point of view.

"Prin—Ophele," he whispered. The name felt strange on his tongue. All this time, he had called her *Princess* so he would never forget whose daughter she was. But Wen was right. She wasn't a princess anymore. She was a duchess, his duchess, and had been since the day they were married. He ran the wet cloth over her breasts, tracing the shameful hollow of her belly. "Ophele. Wife. You're nothing like what I expected. I thought you'd be a noble lady like I saw in the capital, but you've never even been there, have you? For some reason, I keep thinking you have."

He could hear the sounds of ghouls outside, and the distant hunting howl of a demon wolf, and kept talking, hoping a human voice would be better than the noises of devils, even if it was his.

"They call them the Roses of Segoile," he murmured. "Because of the thorns. I never had much to do with women. They made me a squire when I was twelve, and sent me off to war with Valleth. Sometimes I went back to Ereguil for a few months, here and there, and I liked the duchess, and the ladies in the castle and the…the girls in the village." His mind shied away from that. "But I didn't really talk to women until the war was over, and I went to Segoile. I don't know what to say. I keep upsetting you, even when I don't mean to. I'm sorry for that. I don't always know what I'm doing wrong, or how to fix it."

His voice went on, circling, wondering, trying to understand how it had gone this badly wrong. He could only hope that she could hear him, that the sound of his voice would make her think, fill her eyes with thoughts. This time, he would ask what they were. He had always wanted to know.

"And those women were terrifying," he said, trying to lighten his tone. "Not like you at all. Miche and Tounot had to teach me how to dodge, or I'd probably still be fighting marriage duels for outraging the honor of some woman I never even met. Duchess Ereguil said that in Dulcia and Capricia, the challenge is getting your daughter married off by the end of the season. But in Segoile it's all a man can do to get out of it alive."

He had to remember to tell her that again, when she woke up. She wouldn't know that, would she? She wouldn't know anything about the capital at all.

"That's what I thought you'd be like. I kept trying to treat you as if you were, but you aren't." Crossing his arms on the mattress, Remin rested his head on them, brushing her hair back from her face with his fingertips. He had tried over and over to paint the Emperor's features onto that small face, but she looked nothing like her father. "I keep looking for thorns," he whispered. "And there just aren't any."

Her skin was cool. He was afraid to touch her beyond that, afraid that even the warm pads of his fingertips might do her some harm. Instead, he ran his fingers through her river of hair, still damp from the Brede.

"When you wake up, we'll start fattening you up. Pudding, if you want it, no matter what Wen says. A dozen puddings a day. Don't ladies like sweet things? My mother's favorite was pudding with custard and strawberries. It'll be different when you wake up, I promise."

But the thought of *different* made his mouth go dry, and Remin fell silent. He had been pushing her away for a reason. She was one of the Emperor's poisoned gifts. The sweetest and most beguiling poison, a poison so seductive that it was almost enough to make him forget all the hard lessons he had learned and just gulp it down. Let it happen, whatever it was. Give up. Give in. Drown. The sweetness would be worth it.

"It'll be different," he repeated, trying to ignore the painful thumping of his heart. "I'll take care of you from now on. No more work, you've done en—"

"But…I want to help…"

The words were so soft, at first he thought his ears were playing tricks on him. Remin looked up to find her eyes were slitted open, the faintest glint of tawny hazel gleaming under her thick lashes. Her face was turned toward him.

"Why?" he whispered back, so relieved that his hand shook as he reached to touch her cool forehead.

"My father..." The words made his blood run cold. She licked her lips. "...my father. Because of what he did. Your House. Your family..."

"You want to help because of what your father did?" he repeated stupidly.

She nodded, tears sliding from the corners of her eyes.

"Sorry. I wanted to tell you...so many times. And Sir Justenin. His family, too...I know. And Tressin. That's why Tresingale, right? I know your family was innocent. My mother told me. I wanted to help. I wanted to give it all back."

Sweet poison. Such sweet poison. It hurt so much to hear it, words that he would have given *anything* to hear over the years. To the rest of the Empire, his parents were traitors, deserving of their public execution. She was the last person he ever would have expected to say unequivocally that she knew they had been innocent. Could he believe her? Could it really be true? For a long moment, they just looked at each other, and it seemed as if everything that had passed between them could be forgotten, for a time, in the forgiving shadows.

"That's why you said you wanted to work," he said quietly. "You never argued. You never complained."

"Yes." Her eyes squinted against the faint light, a crease between her eyebrows that reminded him of his duty.

"You have to take medicine." He sprang up and went to mix the honey and water and bitter powders. It looked as if her head was hurting her. He had to help her sit up, and Remin sat on the bed beside her and propped her against his body. "Sip. Slowly."

It was too much to take in. He was having to apply this new knowledge to everything he knew of her, to every single interaction they'd ever had. Suddenly he was thinking of questions he should have asked long ago, going all the way back to that first day in Aldeburke. Miche, finding the remains of a fire under a pine tree. But why had she been there in the first place? Why did a princess know how to make and conceal a campfire? How had House Hurrell dared to openly conspire against the Emperor's sacred child? What did it say about her father's protection, that they did?

And the wedding. Who let their daughter walk down the aisle by herself? What sort of father couldn't be bothered to send a *representative* to ensure she was treated with honor? A man who valued the loyalty of his child did not abandon her that way. And Ophele had said it herself, the first time Remin had given her wine and loosened her tongue: she'd never had so much as a message from the Emperor. Not even on her birthday.

"I'm sorry," he said as she sipped at her medicine. "Wife, I am so sorry. I have wronged you."

He had not yet begun to calculate the magnitude of the apology he owed her.

"I'm the Emperor's daughter." She turned her face away from the cup. "No more."

"It doesn't matter." Remin was really beginning to believe that. There was just no evidence, none, to prove otherwise. Turning, he laid her on the bed, brushing her hair back to coil on the pillows. Her face was faintly green. "Do you feel sick?"

"A little." Her arms crept up to hide her breasts. "And…clothes?"

Even half-dead from sun sickness, color still rose to her cheeks. Remin squeezed her hand and turned away, fighting to master himself. He had known nothing. He understood nothing. He had *refused* to learn or understand, and he had almost lost her, all her blushes and her soft voice and those extraordinary searching eyes. He had tried to blind himself to her because everything he saw only made him like her more.

"You had sun sickness," he said gruffly as he opened her trunk and pulled out a fresh chemise. "We had to keep you cool. If you start to feel warm again, then we'll have to take it back off. Sometimes it can take a while for the fire in your body to bal—"

She was asleep.

"—lance," he finished. He set the chemise aside and sank down beside the bed, controlling himself only with a colossal effort. It was too much. His breath was squeezed too tight in his chest and he didn't know what to do. Stars, that had happened, hadn't it? She had awakened, and she had spoken.

He would be so careful with her now. Everything she needed, anything she wanted. He wouldn't wake her up to dress. Her skin needed air and water, as much as it could get. Food, and rest, and then…

He didn't know.

He didn't know anything.

* * *

The axe struck the tree with a ringing vibration that shivered all the way up to Remin's shoulders, and it felt good.

This was what he needed. Hard, physical work, the sort that made it impossible to think of anything but the burn of his muscles. Stripped to the waist, splinters and sawdust stuck to his sweating skin as his borrowed axe slammed into the tree, testing himself to see how precisely he could strike, how deep he could make the blade bite. If he moved a distance away from the rest of the work crew, he didn't even need to speak to anyone.

"If you keel over, I'm not dragging you down to the river," drawled a voice behind him, and Remin looked back to find Miche slouching against a tree, watching him work. Miche rarely stood under his own power. "It's murder out here, Rem, are you trying to kill yourself?"

"It's fine." But he did drink from the waterskin Miche offered, then poured more on his head, his shaggy black hair dripping with sweat. "Why aren't you on the wall?"

"Gen says we have to let the men rest this time of day, unless we want to risk losing them to sun sickness," Miche said pointedly. "You know they're taking bets over there on how much forest Remin Grimjaw can clear by himself."

"Are they?" Remin glanced at the swath of downed trees behind him, as if a very localized windstorm had swept past, and shrugged wide shoulders. His skin was browned from years in the sun, and though he felt the heat the same as anyone else, he had worked much harder on much hotter days than this, often in full armor. He picked up his axe. "Guess I better make it exciting for them."

For a while, Miche just watched, arms crossed over his chest. The blond knight was looking unusually scruffy, with several days' stubble on his jaw and his long hair tied back with a rough thong.

"I have to thank you," Remin said abruptly, and turned to lower his head to his friend. His bow was elegant even when he was shirtless and sticky with sap. "Gen said you saved Ophele's life. I'll never be able to repay you."

Miche flicked this away with his fingertips. "I'm not keeping count. How is she?"

"Sleeping." Remin swung his axe, the blade biting with an echoing *thwack*. It had been two days, and she was still only waking up long enough to eat, drink, and perform the necessary ablutions. "Still sleeping. Gen's keeping an eye on her."

Actually, Gen had shoved an axe in Remin's hand and kicked him out of the cottage.

"Must be tired." Miche moved out of the way as Remin set the axe down and shoved the tree over, the muscles flexing in his bare back and shoulders.

"I don't think she's been sleeping." He moved onto the next tree, a sturdy elm. "Before now, I mean. I talked to her guards this morning." *Thwack.* "They said they've seen lamps burning until almost dawn, some nights." *Thwack. Thwack. Thwack.* "Because she was too scared to sleep."

Miche said nothing.

"You warned me. I thought, if she's scared, she just needs to get over it. I didn't think, she's going to sit up every night listening to the devils, frightened out of her wits." The axe swung again, sinking five inches into the elm. "I did wonder why she kept falling asleep. I pulled her out of the bath three—no, five times. That's not normal, right?"

"No," the other man said quietly.

"I thought so." Remin jabbed the axe in Miche's direction. "I thought so. But I told myself that she knows better than I do, surely she'd say something if she was sick or something."

"Most people would."

"Not her. Gen said she wouldn't ask me for a bandage if she was bleeding to death, and I ignored him. She doesn't complain, ever. Stars, I tried to do things to get her to complain, because I was so *sure* she was lying, and eventually she'd break." Remin slammed the axe into the tree, slicing a wedge, and then kicked the wedge loose with a heavy boot. "You remember the women at Iverlach? The ones that wintered with Juste?"

"Through the siege?"

"Gen said she looks like one of them." Another tree went down. Remin went on to the next. "I knew she was skinny. Too skinny. You couldn't tell it, the way she usually covers up, but *I* knew. Did you know that when women starve, or if they're under too much stress, their bleeding will stop? I didn't know that."

"I have heard of it." Miche's face hardened.

"Well, you were the one that taught me about such things." Remin delivered three ringing swings to a sturdy sapling and shoved it over with one huge hand. "Gen said they almost always recover. But it'll be a while before she'll be able to get with child."

There was no one else to whom he would have confided something so personal. Not even Tounot or Juste, who regarded him as their liege first and their friend second. Miche was always just Miche.

"It would be a fitting punishment if she couldn't give me children, wouldn't it? It was the only reason I wanted her, and she knows it. That was the first thing she said to me, after Gen talked to her. She said she was sorry, she would eat and rest and get better. Not for herself. For me, so she can give me heirs."

Remin shoved the last tree over and stood, panting. Sweat streamed down his sides and back, soaking his thick leather belt.

"*She's* sorry," he repeated bitterly. "She said she was sorry for everything her father did, and she wants to make up for it, so she'll have children by a man who wouldn't even comfort her when she was scared. The stars as my witness, Miche, I never meant to do that. How could I do that?"

Sitting down with a thump, he swiped at his sweaty face with a sweaty arm. Wordlessly, Miche handed him the waterskin, and he drank. It tasted salty.

"She said she's sorry for what the Emperor did?" The other man echoed.

"That's what she said when she woke up. She was sorry. She wanted to apologize to all of us for the things the Emperor did. That's why she was working so hard. That's why she never complained. She's trying to give back what he took." It was another bit of supreme irony that the entire time Remin had been punishing her for her father's crimes, she had been quietly trying to pay the debt in her own way. "And she didn't do a *fucking* thing. Was she even alive when my parents were killed? Why would she think she owes me anything?"

"I would," Miche said quietly. "Put yourself in her shoes, Rem. What if it was you? What if it was your family that wiped out hers, had her parents executed, burned down her home, and made her an orphan? You wouldn't feel like you needed to make it right?"

"That's not even the problem." Remin waved this away and leaned back against the tree, gradually catching his breath. "I think I suspected something like that. Not that she was trying to make up for that bastard, but—she's nothing like him. She has nothing to do with him, at all. But all this time, I didn't want to hear it. I couldn't stand to be in the same room with her. Because I knew if I saw her hurt, or scared, or sad, I'd comfort her, and if I comforted her, I'd have to look at her, and the more I look at her..."

"So look. She's a pretty girl."

"I don't want to." Remin's hands clenched into fists. "I think she's innocent. I think she's the most innocent person I've ever met. But what if I look, and I...and then it turns out she's not? I can't *know*. Even now, if I think about it, I can still say *what if it's a trick*. What if she worked until she fainted to make me doubt myself, to make me drop my guard? I think I could still be asking that when she gives me my third child."

"Rem." Miche looked appalled. "That's—"

"I *know*. The problem isn't even her anymore. But even if she hasn't done anything, even if she never means to do anything, the Emperor could still get to her one day. I know it. There's going to be something, some lever, some weakness he finds. He always does, the bastard. He'll tie the strings on if he can't find one to pull."

"Not always." Miche gripped his shoulder, squeezing. "I'm here, aren't I? And Tounot, Juste, Huber, Auber, Edemir, Bram, even that troll Jinmin. You think we all haven't had talks with strangers in taverns, wondering whether we like being Knights of the Brede? I think every third woman I bedded in Segoile wanted to know if I was happy, sworn to Remin Grimjaw. And *happy* is a strong word," he said reflectively. "It's hard, dangerous work, and my lord has no sense of humor."

Remin didn't laugh.

"I was thinking of sending her to Ereguil," he said, resting his elbows over his knees. "The old man warned me. He said the Andelin is no place for a lady. She'd be safe there. Comfortable. She could sleep at night without wondering if a strangler is going to come through the window. Duchess Ereguil would be happy, she's always wanted a daught—"

The waterskin hit him in the face.

"Is that really for her?" Miche demanded. "Or is it just so you don't have to look at her?"

"He was right," Remin shot back. "I think we have proven that I am not fit to take care of her."

"You haven't *tried.*" Miche shoved himself upright. "Nothing in this life would make the Emperor happier than knowing he's got you seeing wolves in every lamb. And you know what, you *do* owe me. I saved her life. That means I get a say in what happens to it. And I say you're going to ask her what *she* wants."

"You know what she's going to say!" Remin snapped. On his feet, he towered over his friend, but Miche glared right back, his hazel eyes shooting gold sparks. "She thinks she has to make up for every rotten thing her father's ever done, she—"

"Then you *respect that,*" Miche said sharply. "Give her a chance. Just *try.* Or you're letting that bastard in Starfall win without even drawing your sword."

* * *

Ophele had never been so tired.

Maybe she just hadn't realized how tired she really was until she was permitted to do nothing but rest and eat and sleep. Everything was wrapped in a haze of exhaustion and often she felt like she was still dreaming even when she was eating, bowls of sweet porridge or savory stew supplied by a kindly giant who bore a striking resemblance to her husband.

"A little more," he kept saying, until she pushed the bowl away and fell asleep again, and the murmur of his deep voice was so pleasant that she wondered wistfully if it all might really be a dream after all, and soon she would wake to an impatient hand on her elbow, and a cold voice telling her to get out of bed.

It might be a dream. The cottage got so hot in the afternoons she pushed her blankets away and tugged restlessly at her chemise, wondering if it was the early signs of that terrible fever. She had never imagined it was possible to feel so hot. She remembered walking with Eugene by the wall, feeling dizzy, and trying to take off her hat. She seemed to remember Sir Miche shouting, then looking up to see the duke above her, telling her to breathe.

And then she woke up in the cottage to find him sitting on the floor next to the bed, his dark head resting on his crossed elbows. For once, he hadn't been cold or brusque. He had even apologized. It was hazy, but she was almost positive that had really happened.

"Are you awake?"

More often than not, when she opened her eyes, he was there. Sleeping on the floor by the door, sitting at the table over stacks of parchment, or there would be the sound of his voice just outside the window. When he wasn't angry or annoyed, it wasn't a bad voice.

"Mmm…" She squinted and burrowed under the covers. "Time izzit?"

"Almost noon." The duke knelt beside the bed and felt her forehead, as he always did. "Feel all right?"

She nodded, sitting up to accept the cup in his hand. For once, it was just water, not a bittersweet concoction of medicine and honey. He was watching her as if he thought she might flop back onto the bed at any moment, and she sipped slowly with her eyes down, uncomfortable with his scrutiny.

Was he really sorry? No one had ever apologized to her before, and Ophele didn't quite know what to make of it. She accepted his kindness as meekly as she accepted his coldness. She had no choice either way.

"Genon said you're to rest for a while," the duke was saying, taking the cup from her and setting it on the trunk beside the bed. "Ready to get up?"

This was a polite way of asking if she wanted to go to the privy, and Ophele was grateful he just made sure she was steady on her feet and then ducked out of the cottage, returning a few minutes later with a bowl of porridge with honey and juneberries, which tasted so good she almost hummed.

"Do you want more?" he asked, eying the empty bowl.

Reflexively, she shook her head, and his black eyebrows drew together.

"I will go get more if you do," he said, looking stern. "Do you remember what Genon said yesterday?"

Every excruciating word. Ophele *wished* the conversation with the surgeon had been a dream, and even more the discussion that followed with the duke. The idea of having children at all was overwhelming, but the thought that she might not be *able* to have children had made her feel as if the cottage was collapsing on her. That was her purpose. That was why the duke had married her. If she failed at that, he would hate her even more.

Maybe that was the reason he was being so gentle now, like he was coddling a particularly high-strung broodmare.

"You're supposed to eat," he was saying firmly. "As much as you can. Are you full?"

Now she just wanted him to stop staring at her.

"I could eat more," she said, looking away.

"That isn't what I asked. Don't placate me, wife. Tell me what you want."

"More. Please." Anything, if it would make him stop asking and go away. The duke eyed her narrowly but decided to accept it, vanishing back out the door.

Ophele leaned back against her pillows and kicked off the covers. Even in her chemise, it was warm, and she could feel the days abed clinging to her skin, making her long for a bath. It was amazing that a place at this latitude could get so hot. Was it because of the humidity? Not for the first time, she wished she had at least some of the books from Aldeburke's library. She was accustomed to being able to look up the answer when she had a question, and in the absence of books, her mind circled, picking at the subject endlessly.

"Here." The duke appeared with another bowl and dragged a chair over to the bed to sit down beside her as she ate. "Do you feel better? Properly awake?"

She nodded, watching him warily.

"I want to have serious conversation with you. And I want you to tell me what you *want*. Not what you think I want to hear. I swear to the stars that I won't be angry, no matter what you say." His black eyes met hers squarely. "Promise? The truth?"

She nodded again.

"I know you haven't been…comfortable here." He had an aristocrat's habit of sitting up very straight, his hands flat, with no gestures to punctuate his words. "I have done nothing to make you comfortable. I am sorry for that." He said it straight out, and looked at her when he said it. "The Duke of Ereguil—do you know who he is?"

She nodded, listening.

"He advised against bringing you here from the first. I ignored him. I thought I had good reasons. And it has been worse than I expected, with the devils," he admitted. "Anyway, if you want, I'll send you to his estate. It's a country estate in the south, probably the safest place in the Empire. He and the Duchess are good people, they would treat you well. Or if you don't like that, I could send you back to Aldeburke—"

"No," she said immediately, and looked down into her bowl. "No. Not there."

"All right." His big fingers touched her hand, making her look up at him. "Wherever you like, as long as it's safe. I said I was sorry, and I meant it. I want to do better by you. So tell me what you want."

The thought of going to another place filled with strangers was almost as daunting as devils. But Ophele thought about it. It was the same question Sir Miche had asked more than a month ago. She would never go back to Aldeburke, though she missed the library, and Azelma, and the familiar sights that still held a touch of her mother's spirit. She never wanted to see the Hurrells again.

She knew nothing about the Duke of Ereguil, except that he had been a close ally of Remin's old House and had protected him after the deaths of his parents. And therefore, he was no friend of the Emperor. Knowing her father, Duke Ereguil and his lady wife had likely suffered their own misfortunes. The thought of a whole new set of people to whom she would have to apologize because her father had tried repeatedly to have them killed made her quail inside. What if they hated her for it, too?

And what of her own resolve, to atone for the crimes of her parents? She still hadn't done *anything* to make up for what the duke had suffered. But maybe she was just making things worse by being here. Maybe she hadn't helped at all. They had already found someone to replace her on the wall. And she was troubling the duke even now, he had barely left the cottage in days and there was so much work to be done…

"Prin—wife?" The duke prodded.

"I don't know," she said, subdued. "I need to think."

"All right. As long as you like." He was silent for a moment, and then said, "You can talk to me. I can see you're thinking. I am not good at talking, but I will try."

"I don't want to trouble you." It was a modest goal, but she hadn't even managed that much.

"Trouble me," he said firmly. "I mean it, Ophele. If I ignore you, pitch a fit. Like Wen does."

"No," she said, her eyes widening at the image, but a small smile escaped her.

"Then hit me. Right here." He took her hand and slapped it lightly against his cheek. "I'll even bend down so you can reach."

"I couldn't," she protested, and she covered her mouth, her eyes widening. Did he really mean it? "I can't hit you."

"No, you wouldn't," he agreed. Her hand was still pressed to his cheek and she wanted to pull it away, but she was afraid he might be angry if she did. Would he really be nice to her now? Or would he turn and snap at her again? Her stomach knotted with anxiety.

"I am sorry," he said again, softly. "No matter what you decide, I will take care of you from now on. But I need you to tell me when something's wrong. I don't know anything about what you need. I wasn't trying to learn, before. I was…there are reasons," he hedged. "But it's no excuse."

"You can't trust me," Ophele replied softly. "I know."

"I didn't think I could."

The words hung there, an admission of possibility. She didn't know what to think. Looking at his strong, tanned hand, all she could see was the contrast with her own, pale and ragged as a wraith's. It was not a capable hand. She didn't know how to do anything useful. What would he say when he found out that she wasn't any kind of princess at all? She had never learned any of the aristocratic arts, how to manage a house and maneuver through society, how to host a banquet or a ball or any of the numerous events that would forge crucial connections for her husband.

She wasn't even strong enough to be useful as unskilled labor. Was this all she had to offer? To be sent away to a safe place until it was time to bear his children?

"Are you done with your food?" he asked, interrupting her thoughts.

Silently, she extended the bowl to him. He didn't smile. She couldn't remember ever seeing him smile. But he looked into the bowl and looked at her, and there was a warmth in his black eyes that made her wonder what it might be like if things really were different.

"That's better than yesterday," he observed, and set it aside.

* * *

Remin Grimjaw was a stubborn man.

This should not have surprised her. It took incredible persistence to endure what he had endured and achieve what he had achieved. But pleasant as it was to hear his apologies—real ones, with all the necessary components—Ophele hadn't *really* thought anything would come of it. He had no choice but to take care of her; for the first few days she got dizzy as soon as she stood up. She had no maid. There was no one else to whom he could delegate the task. But once she was out of danger, she was sure he would go back to ignoring her.

Three endless days later, she realized he had meant every word.

He didn't know how to talk to her.

He had no idea what she needed.

And he was going to sit there and wait until she told him, no matter how long it took.

It was strange just to have him in the cottage. His presence was so enormous, as if the space was too small to contain him, impossible to ignore. Even after he had returned from dealing with the bandits, he was home so rarely that she had gotten used to having the space to herself. Until the devils had come, she hadn't even really minded; she had never had a place of her own before, where she would be left in peace.

But now he was there *all the time.* If she so much as twitched, he glanced over at her, ever vigilant for the least hint that she needed something. Every new task was grounds for a lengthy interrogation about what was needful, what was lacking, and how it should be done properly. Her last bath had been preceded by forty minutes of discussion about how it had been done in Celderline, from the bath oils to the lotions to the nail files, because now nothing would do but for the Duchess of Andelin to be tended as carefully as if every day was her wedding day.

He made a list. The Duke of Andelin sat down with quill and paper and jotted down *scrub brush, nail file, hand lotion, hair oil, towels, hair silk*—she didn't know what the silk they had rubbed on her hair was called, but the duke extracted the information from her as if he were about to tie her down and start pulling fingernails—and a dozen other articles, half of which even *she* didn't know how to use.

"But I don't know what they did with them," she had protested, imagining the luxury toiletries overflowing their small washstand, only for him to scribble an additional note on his list.

...instructions for use.

Was he going to bathe her? Was Remin Grimjaw going to manicure her fingernails? Confined to her bed under doctor's orders, Ophele didn't know whether to laugh or cry.

Other times, he came up with new subjects for interrogation all by himself. In the midst of working through his stack of papers, he would suddenly look up and stare into the middle distance, as if he had just had a divine revelation concerning his wife's shoes. One morning he stood abruptly and went over to her small trunk under the window to rummage rapidly through the dresses there, scowling ferociously.

"These are all wool," he said, glaring at the mystified Ophele. "We didn't buy any other dresses?"

"There are the silk ones in the storehouse..." She had a dreadful suspicion where this was going. It would take *hours* to explain dresses to him.

"No wonder you got sick." He slammed the trunk shut. "The men were going down like tenpins until we started dressing them in cotton during the summer campaigns. We'll send to Mistress Courcy and have her make you something suitable for summer. Will a dozen dresses be enough?" His jaw set grimly as he took his seat at the table, dipped his quill in the ink pot, and issued the horrifying command: "Tell me what to write, wife."

At first, she was happy to be able to sleep as late as she liked and re-read her favorite books. But as the days dragged on, Ophele began to try her strength every time the duke was out of the cottage, frustrated by how quickly she tired. Flopping back onto the bed, she stared up at the thatched roof, trying to figure out how it had been made. She examined the underside of her bookshelves. She peered through the open windows at the blue sky and watched clouds drift by. And, for lack of any other occupation, she stealthily observed her husband.

The duke spent most of his days at the table by the hearth, working through an ever-increasing pile of documents, and Ophele peeked over the top of her book, watching him. He was the most interesting thing in the cottage, even though he was mostly reading, writing, and frowning. Even at rest, he frowned, his heavy black brows drawing together. She had all but forgotten how handsome he was. In the months since they had arrived at Tresingale, her view of him had contracted to include only the signifiers of his displeasure: lowered eyebrows, narrowed eyes, his mouth pressed into a thin line.

But now she was learning his other expressions, particularly his stubborn face, which he wore when he was having opinions about the quality of her bath. His face was a series of interesting angles: the high, arrogant line of his cheeks, the exotic tilt of his eyes, and the square set of his jaw. A thousand years of careful breeding was evident in that rugged, aristocratic face, marred only by the scar on his right cheek.

She was staring. Ophele ordered her attention back to her book, a compilation of poetry from the old masters that she had already read six times. The only sound in the whole world was the sound of the duke's quill against paper.

She fancied that the way he wrote was aggressive, the quill slashing rapidly away. After a little while, the fingers of his left hand began to drum a soft accompaniment against the table. Ophele watched through her eyelashes as he read, paused, drummed, and then wrote, and eventually she found herself craning her neck and counting the beats of his fingers, wondering if there was a pattern.

"Are you well, wife?" he asked, without looking up.

"Yes," she said, retiring at once behind her book. But Ophele had grown up with all of Aldeburke to wander and a vast library of books to read, and in a few minutes she was ready to throw the book off the side of the bed and kick her feet like a five year-old. She wanted up. She wanted *out*. It was hot. She was tired of being in bed. And the scritch-scratch-scritch-scratch of his quill was going to drive her crazy.

"Are you sure?" he asked, reaching for another page.

Setting her book in her lap, she looked at him, wondering if he really wanted to know. Was he just being polite? She hesitated, gathering her courage to lodge her first timid complaint.

"I'm bored."

He glanced at her, one eyebrow lifting. "Bored?"

She nodded nervously. It was a child's complaint and she wouldn't blame him for telling her to go to sleep, or read another book, or anything else that boiled down to *be quiet*. And if he had, it likely would have been the last complaint she ever uttered in his presence. But instead, he glared at her forbiddingly.

"Would you like to see what I'm working on?"

"Could I?"

He dragged the second chair around the table beside him and she padded over barefoot, wondering at the mismatch between his face and his words.

"I've been working with Edemir on supply orders," the duke explained, turning the piece of paper toward her. "We have to keep track of the current population of the valley so we make sure we have enough rations, grains and vegetables especially. You can see here, these are Genon's requirements for nutrition…"

"Oh, you were counting," she said, when she saw the long columns of figures. His eyebrows went up in surprise.

"On my fingers? Well, we can't all of us do sums in our heads." His face was still stern, but after many hours of bored observation, she thought maybe he wasn't offended or being sarcastic. "We have to provision not just the current population, but also all the incoming craftsmen and builders, and Auber's family, when they arrive. So you see, we have to compare how much we need now and add the requirements for the new people to project how much we're going to need then, and get the supply wagons moving. They don't arrive overnight."

"Can I help?" she asked, rapidly skimming the page. There wasn't much to it, just lots of sums.

"Show your work until Edemir is satisfied." The duke picked up a spare feather and pulled out his belt knife to trim a new quill. "He makes all his assistants pass a test before he lets them manage accounts."

"Did you have to take it?" Ophele bent her head over the page. She hadn't had any formal education after her mother died, but there were books on mathematics in the Aldeburke library, and she had occasionally opened them to satisfy her curiosity on some point of geometry or economics. Rou had once explained how he chose his routes through Firkane to visit as many villages as possible in the least number of miles, and she had spent the whole winter with an atlas, fascinated by the problem.

"Yes." The duke sounded amused. He watched her work for a few minutes and then pulled a fresh document from the pile.

This was useful, wasn't it? Ophele wouldn't have called the many pages of arithmetic *fun,* but she was careful with her reckoning and showed her work in long, tidy columns, and there could be no doubt that every page she completed was a page the duke didn't have to do.

"Does it help?" she asked shyly, handing him a sheaf of completed papers.

"Yes," he said, rifling through them. "I hate such work. But it was time Edemir got out of his office, he was getting soft behind his worktable." He bent his head and lowered his voice conspiratorially. "He was counting on me making a hash of the accounts so he wouldn't have to work on the palisade. Won't he be surprised when he sees these?"

She had to cover her mouth to stifle a giggle, shocked by the mischief in his eyes. Never in her wildest dreams would she have imagined that Remin Grimjaw could look like a naughty boy.

"I'll take them to the office now," he said abruptly, pushing out of his seat, and left her staring after him as he ducked out the cottage door.

He often did that; he would make some small joke or tease her and then make an excuse to move away. She didn't understand why he seemed to reach out and withdraw in almost the same moment. And it still seemed like too much to hope that this new friendly feeling between them wouldn't evaporate the next time her father decided to remind the duke of his disfavor.

But the next night, the duke proved again that he was serious about mending things between them.

For the first week after her sun sickness, Ophele slept often and deeply, and it seemed like the moment the light faded behind the cottage shutters, her eyes slammed shut. She had assumed that the duke was going out as he always did after she went to sleep, donning his armor to take his place among the watch. She understood. He was the commander of the army of the Andelin, it was his responsibility to protect everyone.

But it still meant that she felt a growing knot of dread in her belly as she lay in bed that night and tried to will herself to sleep. The curse of an active imagination was that she could summon the sounds of the devils at any moment, whether she wanted to or not, and Ophele's creative mind presented her with dozens of fresh horrors every night.

Surprisingly, though, the duke showed no sign of getting ready to go out. All he did was light the pair of lamps on the table and then return to his papers. At the first cackling shriek of a strangler, she gave up all pretense of sleep and stood on the bed to pull a book from the shelf.

"It will never get anywhere near you," said the duke from behind her.

She nodded, curling up in the corner of the bed behind her book and opening a page at random. She had read her books too many times. Her eyes skimmed over the words without absorbing a single one.

"Wife." The duke came to sit on the edge of the bed and patted the place beside him. "Come speak with me."

"Are you going out tonight?" she asked, moving beside him without hesitation. It was the safest place in the whole valley.

"No."

"Is it because of me?" she asked, subdued.

"Yes," he said bluntly. "But it's not your fault. I haven't done my duty to you. You never even had watch training."

"Watch training?" she echoed doubtfully.

"Yes. Everyone that comes to the valley, even Sousten Didion, is taught about the devils. My soldiers aren't allowed to stand guard until we've told them what to look for," he explained. "You can't expect a man to keep calm when he's sitting alone in the dark and doesn't know what's out there. Anyone would be scared."

"Even you?"

"Of course, even me." He frowned, and she looked down at her lap, her fingers knotting together until his big hand closed over them, quelling the anxious motion. "I was afraid, the first time I saw one. And that was just a ghoul. At the time we weren't sure what they were or if they were even real. Some of us thought they were big wolves, or some new hairless bear, or any damned thing but a conjuring from a Vallethi sorcerer."

"What did it look like?" she asked, torn between interest and prickling awareness of his warm hand on hers. "The first one you saw?"

"It was a ghoul, so sort of human." He frowned again, but he didn't seem angry. "But stringy and starved, like its skin was on too tight. Ghouls run on all fours, but their hands and feet are mostly like ours. That confused us, too, we thought it might be some weird cannibal mercenary Valleth hired. They were desperate in the end. Hired mercenaries from everywhere."

"Why didn't they have to worry about the devils?" she asked, her forehead crinkling as she thought about it. "Valleth."

His eyebrows lifted, surprised. "It's less of a concern in Valleth itself. They have magic there, I'm told the devils are only a problem for the smaller villages. But some of the deserters we talked to during the war said they weren't terribly careful with the common soldiers. They ended up copying us, shell curtains and guards and so on."

"How horrible. I guess that's why—" Outside, there was a long, ululating cackle from somewhere to the east, and Ophele realized she was pressed very nearly into his lap, her heart galloping, and the duke was sitting so stiffly upright he might have been part of the palisade. Forcing herself to detach her hand from his arm, she moved away. It took an effort to keep her voice steady as she asked, "What—what about stranglers?"

"Hate them," he said, his dark head cocked as he listened to the racket outside. "They're tall. Almost my height. Gray skin, bony-looking, but their arms and legs are…hard to describe. They're squishy, when they get hold of you. They wind around you somehow."

"One of them grabbed you before?" she asked, looking up at him with huge eyes.

"Several. And I'm still here," he added, as if this were reassuring. Of course he was, he was Remin Grimjaw.

"How did you get away?"

He opened his mouth to speak, and then paused and reflected.

"Normally when one gets hold of you, that's it. Even for my strongest men. So you know what we do?"

She shook her head.

"Call for help. Make noise. No one fights alone, in an army. If something happened to Dol, he'd bang on his shield so Yvain would know to come and get the strangler off him. They don't kill you right away," he said matter-of-factly. "Takes time to strangle someone, longer than you'd think. And no strangler's going to make it this far into camp. But it's good for you to know. So if one ever did get to your guards, what would you hear?"

"Banging on a shield," she repeated, feeling much better about the whole thing. "What are wolf demons like?"

"Big, black, like they're made of shadows," he began, and as he patiently answered her questions, she forgot to be afraid of the noises outside or nervous about talking to him because it was all so very interesting. The more he told her, the more questions she had. Were the devils magic? If they were, how were they coming into the Empire, which was anathema to magic? If they hired a Vallethi sorcerer, could they get him to send the devils back? Or maybe a Bhumi shaman could do something, had anyone asked? Where did—

"I don't know, and that's enough questions," the duke said, when it was evident that the night would run out before her questions did. But he didn't sound annoyed; he was looking down at her and the corner of his mouth was twitching again. "It's late, and you ought to sleep." He hesitated. "Did this…help?"

She nodded automatically, flushing as she realized that all this time, he had just been trying to calm her down, like soothing a frightened child. But he caught her before she could slide away.

"Tell me if you hear something that worries you," he said, tilting her chin up with a finger to meet her eyes. "Even if you have to wake me. Like one of my men on watch. We have to look out for each other."

"I will," she said softly. She felt both touched and foolish. It was obviously an attempt to make her feel better about disturbing him, but with enough truth in it that it was hard to argue. There was always a chance that she really might hear something dangerous. And he was trying so hard not to overlook a single thing that might frighten or trouble her.

Would it last? The next time one of her father's assassins came, would he blame her again? What would happen when he discovered how useless she really was? Could she learn, somehow? And hide it until then?

But then she would be deceiving him.

These thoughts troubled her more than the noises of the devils. The kinder he was, the more she feared that he would come to hate her again.

Lying in bed, Ophele hugged her pillow close, wondering if this was what Lady Hurrell had meant. Bastards were the seeds of treachery. It was inherent to their natures, and none so much as an Imperial bastard, whose existence was an affront to the Emperor and the stars. She couldn't help deceiving him, she was born of deceit. Of course he wouldn't trust her. But she liked it so much, when he was being this way…

On the other side of the small cottage, Remin paused for a long moment as he laid out his bedroll, looking at the slender back of the girl on the bed, her creamy skin glowing in the hearth light, her long hair streaming over the side of the mattress. He did not smile at the sight. The feel of her body against his lingered, a soft and tormenting warmth, the merest taste of the delights he knew awaited, if only he could reach out to her. If he wanted, he could go wake her right now. She wouldn't refuse him.

But if he did, it wouldn't end in the morning light. Once he had her again, he would never be able to let her go.

And though Remin could not know it, the first of his enemy's agents had already arrived in Tresingale.

CHAPTER 12 – LADY OF THE WALL

"Only for the morning," Remin cautioned as Ophele finished plaiting her long hair and gave herself a final look in the mirror. "And only once along the wall. Slowly."

"I know," she said for the dozenth time, clearly willing to promise him anything if it meant she finally got out of the cottage. "I will. Can we get carrots for Master Eugene? Or maybe apples? I hope they haven't been working him too hard, he needs to rest in the shade during the noon meal or he gets too tired—"

"You need to rest in the shade this morning or I'm not going to let you go," Remin interrupted, collaring her before she could put on her hat. A fortnight of rest and feeding had helped a great deal; her eyes were bright and her cheeks were already rounder, though her gown was still a little large. "Promise me, Ophele. If you feel hot, or dizzy, or at all unwell, you'll stop and tell me."

"I will." She looked up at him, and it was discouraging to see how easy it was to crush her when she was happy, even when he didn't mean to. All the fun was gone from her face. "I promise."

After nearly two weeks abed, Ophele, Genon, and Miche had finally convinced Remin that it was not practical to keep her locked in the cottage forever, though Remin's inclination was to keep her there until cooler clothing arrived or cooler weather did, whichever happened first. He had two fairly devastating counterarguments: first, that people felled once by sun sickness were more likely to be struck down again, and second, Ophele did not have a distinguished record of asking for help when she needed it.

This morning excursion was their compromise.

It was a fitting reward to show her how far the wall had advanced in her absence, though there were practical reasons for visiting, as well. Remin was coping with an increasingly familiar blend of fondness and anxiety as he followed her to the cookhouse, though outwardly his face was as grim as ever. Most of Tresingale's inhabitants were already abroad for the day, but every man that passed paused to offer greetings to their duchess, and they looked so dazzled at her answering smile that Remin was struck with an irrational urge to growl.

"Master Wen?" Ophele paused cautiously at the threshold of the sacred kitchen.

"How many times have I told ye, it's Wen." The vast cook turned with his hands on his hips. "Did the fever affect your memory, Your Grace? You'll find Master Eugene's treats in the usual place. And wash your hands before you touch me cupboards. *Vectors for plague,* the lot of you, that's what Genon says." He relished the words, jabbing a fat finger at the small washbasin to the left of the cabinets.

"The bread smells good," she offered as she went obediently to wash, and while her back was turned, Wen's glare faltered, one beady eye twitching. He had been shockingly willing to provide tempting dishes at all hours of the day for the past two weeks, beginning with thin soups and porridge and graduating to richer, heartier fare, aromatic and subtly spiced.

"It's good ye can offer some compliment today, considering the wrong you've done," he growled. "'Tis a wonder I can hold me head up for shame."

"What?" She turned to face him, eyes wide. "Why?"

"Aye, ye heard me," Wen said loudly, crossing massive arms over his chest and glowering down at her. "Is there something wrong with me cooking, I'd like to know? Is there a reason the Duchess of Andelin should be reeling about and fainting and looking like a chicken someone's plucked?"

That was going a little far, but Remin suspected he knew where this was headed and held his tongue.

"No, there's nothing wrong, it's very good," Ophele said, bewildered. "Thank you for the porridge, I liked the berries—"

"Then *eat!*" The cook bellowed. "If someone were to ask, *who is it that cooks for the wife of Duke Remin of Andelin, hero of the Gresein,* and pointed to a wisp like yourself, I'd be the laughingstock of the whole ruddy Empire! My cooking puts *meat on bones! Meat!* Soldiers march the length of the Empire and chew up armies by teatime because *I* feed them! I will not be defeated by a *picky teenage girl!*"

Snapping a pair of cupboard doors apart, he produced a basket of large, buttery croissants and slapped it down on the end of the counter, all of them studded with berries and dusted temptingly with sugar.

"Croissants?"

"Aye, croissants!" He thundered. "Bleeding croissants! I never thought I'd see the day when I'd be reduced to bloody *pastry!* But by the stars a woman what's fed by Wen of Tallford has fat cheeks and a waist a yard round or I'll know the reason why! And if ye call me Master Tallford just once, then that will be Master Eugene's final carrot! Now take your croissants and get out of me kitchen!"

"I—thank you, I will, I do like your cooking—" Ophele plucked a croissant from the basket and retreated, clearly unsure whether she was supposed to eat or was about to be eaten.

"I said *all the croissants!*" Wen roared, and she grabbed the basket and fled out the door like a rabbit.

"I'll get the carrots," Remin said in a ringing silence, and went to wash his hands. "You couldn't just tell her you hope she feels better?"

"Croissants." Wen was still breathing fire. "To think this day would come. Mincing about the kitchen with an armload of butter like a poxy Caprician pâtissier."

"Thank you, Wen."

"Sod off, Your Grace."

Ophele was waiting outside at the side of the road, hugging the basket of croissants and looking anxious.

"Oh, thank you," she said, when she saw the carrots in Remin's hand. "I only remembered after I got outside, is he really mad about the croissants?"

"It could be viewed as a commentary on his cooking," Remin acknowledged, though from the glance she gave him, he suspected Ophele was wise to Wen's game, even if his bellowing did make her flee in terror.

"I can't eat all this," she said, tearing a croissant in half and offering it to him. "Would he be offended if I gave some away?"

"Eat at least two yourself." Remin bit into the treat with pleasure. After observing his wife for some days, he thought her problem had been overwork rather than starvation. She ate orders of magnitude less than he did, but for her size, he thought she probably did well enough. Just not enough to support the work she had been doing.

It was still early as they walked to the stables together, chewing contentedly on the croissants. The sun was only two fingers above the horizon and Ophele prevailed on him to give his murderous warhorse a carrot as he saddled it, looking longingly at the handsome animal. The horse was velvety black and powerfully muscled, with deep scars over his chest and flanks and fierce dark eyes. Looking at the girl, he put his ears back warningly, as if he suspected her of nefarious designs.

"Come, up you get," Remin said, holding out a hand and feeling a wave of nostalgia as he lifted her into the saddle before him. He was torn between the warring impulses to pull her close and push her away, and his heart beat faster as she settled shyly into place before him, clutching her basket and uncertain whether she should keep her distance.

That made two of them.

"Are they almost to the gatehouse?" she asked, peering east. The walls were three miles away from the main road of Tresingale, at best a vague white line shimmering on the horizon.

"Getting close. We've already got a third crew digging there, it won't hurt to have a pit between us and the devils. The walls should get there in a few more weeks, and we'll be done with the palisade in days." Remin was grimly satisfied with these milestones. "That will leave only defenders on the palisade and behind the barricades at the gatehouse. Soon nothing will get past our perimeter."

"It will be over?"

"For Tresingale." He wasn't ready to broach the subject of the rest of the valley yet; the idea of leaving her when he knew how much the devils scared her was difficult, and he didn't know whether his first duty was to her or to his people.

"It's amazing," she said quietly. "Everyone has worked so hard. They deserve croissants. Is that why we're going to the wall?"

"No, I didn't tell you? Jacot, that boy who swam the Brede, has been trying to fill in for you, but he's lagging, for all that Miche says he works hard. Guisse asked if you'd come show him what you were doing."

"Really?" Ophele twisted her head back to look up at him with doubt in her eyes.

"Yes," he said, puzzled. "They're still trying to figure out how one person kept half the wall watered. Guisse said he'd never seen the like."

"Oh," she said, looking hastily away. "Of course. I'll help. I really helped?"

"You did." Understanding dawned. "You did very well, wife."

It would have taken a stronger man than Remin Grimjaw to keep from tightening his arm around her as she *glowed* at the praise.

If he had learned nothing else in the last few weeks, it was how astonishingly little it took to make her happy. Even as they rode together, she was nibbling another croissant and looking contentedly at anything and everything around her, as if she wanted nothing more from the world that morning. She was so shy, and the least harshness cowed her, but surely it meant he was doing something right if she could look like that.

"Look how far they've come," she marveled as they turned off the road toward the south wall. The wide gap between the two walls was filled with heavy mobile barricades designed to be moved into place at nightfall, sturdy enough to hold back all but the most determined wolf demons. They had hardly gone five minutes before they reached the far end of the diggers, already sweating with their labor, and their shouts rose in a wave as they spied Ophele.

"Hello, good morning," she said, waving and scarlet to her hair. Remin took pity on her and didn't linger, nudging his horse into a trot as they reached the scaffolding. His sharp ears caught some interesting words among the shouting.

"...lady of the wall?" he repeated, and was surprised to see Ophele's eyes shift guiltily away. She was no master of deception.

"I wonder where Master Eugene is?" she said, as if she had gone temporarily deaf, and craned her neck to look south.

"There," Remin said, at the same moment that she gave a cry, and he indulgently galloped over to the wagon where Jacot was leading the elderly gray donkey. She would have leaped off the horse if he hadn't caught her and lowered her, and she only paused to offer a quick greeting to the boy before she rapturously embraced Eugene.

"M'lady? Maybe you oughtn't…" The boy trailed off as the donkey nuzzled eagerly at her pockets, and the fact that Ophele had come prepared with carrots was sufficient to make him step back respectfully, glancing up at Remin.

"The Duchess will be your teacher this morning," Remin explained, leaning over his saddle. "I hope you'll be able to do the job as well as she did."

Jacot's mouth fell open. He glanced over at the small noblewoman, who was cooing over the donkey as if he were a kitten. The boy had given his age as fourteen, but he was eight inches taller than the lady and his long limbs were taut with wiry muscle, strong enough to cross the Brede.

"I will," he said stoutly.

"And treat that beast well," Remin added, with a weight of warning. He hardly needed to say it; it was clear that Ophele had made a pet of the creature, and Jacot was clever enough to see how things stood. "Wife?"

He extended the small basket of croissants, hoping it would be enough to keep her from carrying anything heavier.

"Be careful," he cautioned. "If you feel the least bit tired—"

"I'll sit down in the shade."

"You'd better, or you'll spend another week in the cottage. I'll come find you at the north end of the wall."

She nodded, offering him a shy smile, all the more precious for its rarity. For many reasons, Remin had to fight down an impulse to follow. Jacot of Caillmar posed a challenge. There was no way to ascertain whether he was who he claimed to be; he claimed to be no one, and orphan boys were a dime a dozen. It was entirely possible he was just a brave lad hoping to become more than he was, daring the Brede because he had nothing to lose.

Or he could be one of the Emperor's creatures.

Every precaution had been taken. Only guards on watch and Remin's knights were permitted to carry weapons as a rule, and the clothes the boy had been wearing when he arrived had been confiscated and searched. He had no belongings, and would be allowed none until he was a squire. Unless he ran over to one of the blacksmiths and stole a hammer, he had no weapon but his bare hands.

Seeing wolves in every lamb…

But Remin was trusting him with Ophele. Watching her go, he had the familiar sense that he was drowning, and the harder he floundered, the faster he sank. And he had known it would be that way. He had known that the more he looked, the more impossible it would become to look away.

She hadn't gone twenty paces before she was surrounded by masons and handing out croissants, pleased to have something she could give away.

Remin wheeled his horse around and kicked him into a gallop, feeling shamefully as if he were fleeing.

* * *

"It's mostly counting," Ophele explained as she walked with Jacot of Caillmar, petting Eugene and watching the page from the corner of her eye. The only boy she had known before was Julot, but she was charitable enough to assume he was not the standard for his gender. "The blacksmiths do different things on different days, so some days they'll go through more water than others. If you keep count in the morning, you can usually guess how much they'll need in the afternoon and bring them some extra barrels to get ahead."

"Keep count?" Jacot asked blankly. He had a pretty face for a boy, with rough-cropped brown hair and bright blue eyes.

"Of how many buckets and barrels they go through. It takes an hour to go the length of the wall and back, so if you keep count of how much everyone is using in an hour, then you can figure out the averages…" Ophele had carefully tracked the numbers in her mind over the months, adjusting the averages over time, and after three months she had become fairly skilled at guessing how much water would be needed where. Efficiency was the only way she could have managed the task. She didn't have the strength to muscle through it.

But after a while, she realized Jacot was having very little to say.

"I didn't know there'd be so much reckoning," he said, his brows knotted. "Dunno if I can do that."

303

"Oh." Ophele blinked and flushed. *The Habits of a Lady* said it was a cardinal sin to make someone else feel embarrassed or uncomfortable, but it had never occurred to her that anyone might not know how to calculate averages. "Oh, I beg your pardon, I didn't think…"

"No, I can learn," the boy said stubbornly. "I know my counting. What's a average?"

Compassion made her braver than she would have been otherwise, to make up for her thoughtlessness, and Ophele began with multiplication and division before she introduced averages, though there wasn't nearly enough time to do any of it justice as the north end of the wall approached.

"Sure you're all right, Your Grace?" Jacot asked doubtfully as they turned to head south. "Be my neck, something happens to you."

"No, I'm quite well," she assured him, her mind focused firmly on the problem before her. "The six times is where it gets harder, but if you use your fingers as an abacus, it will help. There are lots of tricks you can use to help you remember, like the trick of nines."

"What trick?" Jacot glanced nervously over his shoulder.

"The sum of any two digits that are the product of nine times any other number equal nine," she said blithely. "Nine two times is eighteen, right?"

She tried not to be discouraged by the fact that the boy's fingers jittered at his side before he nodded his agreement.

"Eighteen is a one and an eight." She held up her own fingers to illustrate. "One plus eight is nine."

"Yes…"

"Now add nine three times." It had been a very exciting day when seven year-old Ophele recognized this pattern. She loved patterns, it was like discovering a secret.

"Twenty-seven."

"And two plus seven is…?"

"Nine." Jacot's eyes widened. He was ignorant, but he was not stupid. "And…thirty-six, forty-five, fifty-four, sixty-three, seventy-two, eighty-one, ninety…"

Ophele clapped her hands, beaming.

"See? It doesn't work with ninety-nine, but then it works again at a hundred and eight, a hundred seventeen…"

"Is there more like that?" Jacot asked eagerly. "I was hoping for some learning when I got here, but all the squires say we got too much work what needs doing to bother."

"Maybe I could lend you a book…" Ophele faltered as soon as she visualized the books on her shelf. There was nothing there suitable for a beginner.

"No, lady, but thankee kindly. I ain't quite up to books yet. And I wouldn't give a f—I wouldn't care what Sir Tounot's lads say about anything else, but I am shamed, being so backward at my age."

"Well, you want to learn, don't you?" she said warmly. "If you don't ask, then you'll never know."

A noise of hooves trampled the end of that sentence, and as Ophele turned to see the duke rapidly overtaking them, she realized with a start that they had come halfway down the wall already. There was a grimness in his face that sent a warning shiver up her spine.

"We agreed you would only go as far as the north end," he said as he drew up beside her. On the other side of Eugene, Jacot gulped.

"It's my fault," Ophele said instantly. "I told him it was fine. I'm all right, I don't feel hot or tired at all."

Unconsciously, her hands moved to cover Eugene's long ears, as if the donkey might be troubled by the tenor of the conversation. The duke looked down at her, his opaque black eyes so dark, it was as if they could devour the world.

"You gave me your word," he said ominously. "Jacot, you may go. Thank the lady for her time."

"I do," the boy said fervently, giving her a bow. "Very grateful, Your Graces. I'll remember the nine times table. And I'll be good to Master Eugene."

He was grateful, but he was still a boy, and departed at speed. Ophele's fingers twisted anxiously before her.

"Come. We're going home." The duke's jaw was tight with displeasure as he nudged the horse nearer. Ophele was frozen. She didn't think he would come to hate her again over something that had seemed so trivial, but his voice had those stiff, frosty tones she remembered all too well, and all the friendliness was gone from his face. It felt like a weight of ice had settled solidly in her middle.

"I'm sorry." She had to force the words out, her tongue feeling clumsy, a moment from rooting itself to the roof of her mouth. "I didn't mean anything, I wasn't thinking…"

"You're speaking too quietly." The duke held out a hand, his brows knotting together. "Come here. I can't hear what you're saying."

"I said, I'm sorry." She made herself take his hand and let him lift her into the saddle. "I didn't mean to go so far."

"I don't like it when people break their promises." That handsome, arrogant face could look so forbidding. She didn't know what to say. It had seemed like a small thing to tell Jacot, *no, we'll go on,* meaning no harm and thinking they would only go a short distance further. She hadn't considered it in the light of a promise broken, and certainly not something that could fracture the fragile peace between the duke and herself. The bare thought made her struggle against rising panic.

But wasn't breaking a promise the same as telling a lie? He already couldn't trust her; she shouldn't dare to stir a step without making her intentions clear. What should she do? The silence prickled between them and she could feel the scant, stiff inch between her back and his chest like wind howling through a chasm. They rode in silence down the length of the wall, and turned onto the east road.

"Why did you do it?" he asked abruptly.

"Jacot doesn't know how to do averages." She answered quickly and had to remind herself to speak up. "That was how I kept track of how much water everyone was using. The buckets and barrels. He was just giving everyone the same amount. But I had to teach him multiplication and division first, and I wasn't done when we got to the north end, and I didn't realize how far we'd gone until you came. I'm sorry."

He waited, eying her to be sure she was finished.

"I understand. But you promised me. It might seem like a small thing, but this is a dangerous place." He nudged her to make her look up at him. "Wife. I want to be able to trust you."

"You do?" Ophele was nearly holding her breath. She had not expected it to go this way, at all.

"I do." He shifted in the saddle, and she realized that he was uncomfortable, and the shocking thought struck her that maybe this was as difficult for him as it was for her. "Promises are important to me."

"I'm sorry," she said again, laying a hand on his arm. "I didn't think of it that way. I won't do it again."

"Then that's the end of it."

And that really was it. His arm tightened around her and Ophele settled back into the comfortable crook of his shoulder and chest, feeling so light she could have laughed, or burst into song. Was it really so simple as that? Could it really be this way between them?

"He said he can't read," she told him impulsively. "Jacot. The other boys are making fun of him."

"There will be time for such things when the wall is done," the duke replied. "He will have to learn to cope with insults on his own, wife. Believe me, he will not thank you for intervening."

"But it would help him on the wall if he knew more arithmetic, at least. Perhaps I could teach him again tomorrow, in the morning?"

"Will you keep your word to go no further than the north end?" There was a pleasant rumbling in his voice, even though his face was stern.

"I will."

"Then yes."

It was so nice. She didn't want the ride to end. She wanted to see anything, everything, and it was so comfortable to ride with him this way. And surely he was as tired of the cottage as she was.

"Is there somewhere else you have to go?" she asked, thinking of the many projects underway throughout the valley. "To see Master Didion or Master Ffloce? The planting? Or the palisade? Or that new building by the river?"

He still wouldn't tell her what that was going to be.

"The planting is done," he said, slanting a look at her that said he wasn't fooled. "But they're laying the foundation of the manor house today."

"It's still early," she said, glancing east, where the sun was now a handspan above the horizon. It would be a hot day, but not yet. "I don't mind, if you want to go look…"

"That's very gracious of you." The corner of his mouth twitched.

The duke wasn't wearing his armor today. Ophele could feel his heart pounding against her back as he turned the horse south, down lanes lined with sticks and string, like the shadowy outlines of a dream.

* * *

In the dark hours before dawn, Remin jerked awake.

The cottage was still dim and sketched silhouettes of familiar shapes: the chair he was always knocking his knees against, the washstand at his feet, the bed a scant foot past his head. His eyes flashed underneath it, checking the frame automatically for the shape of concealed weapons before he sat up, careful of the many breakable objects nearby. Even if he had survived another night without anyone trying to murder him, living in such a small space meant he lived in constant, hunched terror of knocking things over.

It was early, but there would be no more sleep. Yawning, he scrubbed his eyes with his palms, trying to drive out the dream still rattling in the back of his mind like an unquiet ghost. His skin was slippery with sweat.

His dreams were starting to wear on him.

Rising, he went to scrub his face, then built a fire and put on a kettle of water to heat. Soon, there would be an actual bathhouse with water piped from the river and constantly heated by furnaces. Nore Ffloce's eclectic background served them well; it would be a bathhouse in the luxurious Benkki Desa style, clean and practical, easily expanded when the time was right. Already there were two teams of bathhouse workers on the way from Abharana, with a Madam Imari Sanai to manage the women's half.

He was saving that as a surprise for Ophele.

There were a number of other gifts creaking their way to the valley in various wagons, some of which she knew about and others she did not, but it was sheer coincidence that they would arrive around her eighteenth birthday. Remin deserved no credit for remembering it. It was Miche who had wondered aloud if the Duchess had attained her majority yet, and that had been a nasty moment, when Remin realized it might have already passed. He suspected that was another thing he would have heard about for the next fifty years, if he had forgotten her birthday.

Ophele didn't so much as twitch as the teakettle whistled. Remin washed, shaved, and dressed, foregoing his shirt and making do with a simple cotton jerkin that left his arms bare. It was too hot for layers. He couldn't imagine how Ophele endured all the drapery that fashion decreed was required, and every day he sent an impatient inquiry to the Gellege Bridge, asking if there was news of the order of clothing from Mistress Courcy.

What did women wear elsewhere in the world? Imperial noblewomen mostly stayed indoors, so maybe it wasn't such an inconvenience elsewhere in the Empire, but now that he had seen how impractical his wife's clothes were, his opinion had turned resolutely against them. Remin felt no obligation to abide by the foolish conventions of the Empire. This was his valley. They would wear what they liked.

Maybe he could find a tailor and some seamstresses who would appreciate a little creative freedom.

"Ophele." Kneeling next to the bed, he peeled the covers off and shook her. "Wake up, wife, it's morning."

"Iss mornin…?" Her eyes were still closed as she sat up.

"Would you rather stay and sleep?" he asked, unable to resist teasing her when she was still mostly unconscious. She was so pretty with her face all soft from sleep. "I wanted you to go with me today, but if you're too tired…"

"No, I want to go." Her eyes snapped open, and he repressed a smile.

"Here," he said, putting her hand around a cup of water, and as soon as she managed a sip, he stepped outside to let her wash and dress. By the time he went to the cookhouse for breakfast and the stable for his horse, she should be ready to go. And sure enough, she was waiting outside the cottage when he rode up, looking creditably awake.

"Where are we going?" she asked eagerly, taking his hand to be lifted into the saddle. She was dressed in a pale green gown with slashed sleeves and a curving neck that revealed the upper swells of her breasts. The sweet scent of her soap wafted as Remin set her before him.

"We'll have a look at the palisade first," he said gruffly, trying to ignore these temptations. "Something's been gnawing at the end near the ridgeline. Then Auber wants to take a look at the land west of the wheat fields. It's all hilly forest, might be good for an orchard."

"Apples?"

"And cherries, and whatever else we can get to grow."

"Apples are my favorite." Ophele settled against him as they swung north, chewing on a breakfast biscuit. "What about you?"

"Peaches. There was an orchard at Rospalme, in Ereguil." It was peculiar how even this simple answer made him feel as if he were giving another tiny piece of himself into her keeping. Remin twitched his shoulders and tried to ignore his unease.

Before her sun sickness, he had been accustomed to making a circuit of the valley in the morning, looking in on the various projects to see their progress with his own eyes. He had been ashamed to realize that she had never seen any of them before. Until her illness, she had never gone anywhere but the cookhouse and the wall.

Today she would go with him. It was cool enough in the morning that he thought it was safe to go out, and he found himself wondering what she would say. She had been getting braver about speaking, and every time she dared to offer an opinion or started a conversation, it felt like a victory.

"We're on the same latitude as Abharana, in Benkki Desa," she said thoughtfully. "They grow peaches there. And black plums and white cherries."

"Did you memorize that book?" he asked, amused. Ophele had already trotted out tidbits from *A Survey of the Nations of the Sea of Eskai* several times, which included information on the major exports in the region.

"I liked how that sounded together, black plums and white cherries. I tried to get Azelma to buy some, but she said they would never make it to Segoile, let alone Leinbruke."

"Benkki Desa's a long way away, isn't it?" Remin said thoughtfully.

"Eighteen hundred and forty miles by boat," she replied. Remin looked down at her in surprise.

"How many miles over land?"

"3,472 to the border of Argence." Ophele looked up at him with her best solemn-owl face, as if everyone memorized mileage charts. "Why?"

"Black plums and white cherries might be considered luxuries, if they can't be had outside Segoile," he said. Her eyes lit up.

"We could grow them here and sell them?"

"I don't see why not. But I also know nothing of orchards."

"Different trees need different soil, and they do something called grafting to put the branches of one tree on another, though I don't know why." The words tumbled over each other in her excitement. "At least they do with apples. Didn't Master Didion say we would have a small orchard by the house?"

"On the east slope, yes. You want apples handy?"

"And peaches," she said, giving him a full, beautiful smile that made Remin feel as if the air had suddenly filled with wine.

"We'll mention it to him," he managed, setting his heels to his horse and making her grab for his arm as the black beast sprang forward. She was just full of surprises.

It looked like ghouls had been chewing on the west end of the palisade, judging by the shape of the bite marks, and after confirming that a six-foot stretch of wall would have to be replaced, Tounot rode with them to look at the prospective orchard site with Auber. It felt a little ridiculous, once they got there. Three knights sitting on their horses, looking at a hilly bit of forest, agreeing that sure, it looked as if fruit trees might grow there. What did any of them know? Orchards were to farming what siegeworks were to swordsmanship: adjacent, not overlapping.

"We'll have to send for someone to manage it," Auber said, nudging his bay forward into the trees. "Though at some point you're going to have to look at some short-term investments, Rem. Everything we're building isn't going to turn a profit for a long time. I don't know much about orchard trees, but I know you won't see a harvest for a while. Trees take a long time to grow."

"I have heard that," Tounot agreed gravely, as Ophele flushed pink. An arborist they had consulted about the huge oak at the manor site had all but promised his firstborn child if they would preserve it until he could come see it personally. Apparently, any oak thirty-five feet wide was likely to be very old indeed. Ophele's words had been making a circuit of the town ever since, to be trotted out whenever it was even vaguely appropriate.

"Maybe if you started with older trees?" she offered hesitantly, as if she wasn't sure whether they were making fun or not. "Since Master Didion is bringing in older cherry trees and maples anyway…"

"Valleth's paying," Remin said with a shrug and a great deal of internal satisfaction. Valleth's invasion had destroyed the valley, it seemed only fair that they should pay to restore it. "I wonder if there's anything left of the old orchards. Do we have any old maps of the valley?"

"We'd have to send for copies," Tounot replied. "Edemir wouldn't have much use for maps a hundred years out of date."

"There were old orchards?" Ophele asked, looking intrigued.

"The valley was settled, before," Remin explained. They had found the remains of many towns and burned-out cities over the course of the war, charnel offerings to Valleth's Lord of Tales. Even worse, Valleth hadn't even done anything *useful* with all that dreadful magic. Squandered, all of it, on the infighting between warlords.

"Someone said something about finding orchards…three years ago?" Tounot remembered. "When we were pushing into the mountain passes, going for the forts."

"Victorin," Auber said. "Victorin and his men found them. Apples of the gods, he said, but then they were hungry at the time."

"I'd like to find those," Remin said slowly. Victorin's apples. That would be a good thing to have to remember him by. "Remind me, when we get back. We'll send out some inquiries."

That was the first step to any new project in the valley, and they wandered among the low hills for a little while, speculating how long it would take to clear the forest, and how long it might take for fruit trees to be transported to the valley, particularly if they were coming from Benkki Desa. Maybe he should see about acquiring some Benkki Desans to tend them.

"The caravan's ready for your inspection, Rem," Tounot said as they were turning back toward Tresingale. "If you want to take a look, it's on the way."

If Tounot had a fault, it was that he had a knack for saying the exact thing that Remin least wanted to be said.

"I'll look later," he said shortly, trying to communicate with his eyes that this was not a subject he wanted to discuss in front of his wife.

"The blacksmiths have been arguing about it with the carpenters," Tounot went on, blissfully oblivious to these signals. "They're trying to get the weight down, but if it's going to last all the way to Ferrede and keep the devils out, then it can't be too—"

"Devils?" Ophele echoed, looking up at Remin with a flicker of disquiet. One night's conversation had not allayed all her fears.

"It's nothing you need to worry about," he said stiffly. He still hadn't decided whether to tell her about the expedition to Ferrede; he might not be going at all, and he was almost positive that even if he was, such purely military matters were no business of a noblewoman. In any case, he knew she was still scared of the devils and he didn't want to bring up the possibility that he might have to leave unless it was actually going to happen.

Remin was pretty sure that ship had just sailed. No, Tounot had *launched* it and then fired flaming arrows into it.

"I'll meet you there," he told Tounot and Auber, spurring his horse toward the gate and giving Tounot a glare that promised later reprisal.

Of course, Remin hadn't the least idea what he was going to say, and he knew by now that if he didn't say something, Ophele never would. He used to think she was sulking when she did this, wielding her silence like a weapon to make him feel guilty. He had never been able to abide such tricks. But now he understood that Ophele didn't sulk. She just…retreated, he thought, frowning down at the top of her head. Instantly and completely. He didn't understand why, or what to do about it.

"I mean that I don't want you worrying," he finally said as their cottage appeared ahead. "Nothing's been decided."

She nodded without the least indication as to whether she would actually continue worrying, and Remin's jaw tightened.

"We'll talk about it later," he said, frustrated. "Stop worrying about it, wife. Don't leave the cottage while it's hot."

He wanted her to say something, anything, but she only nodded again as he set her down beside the road in front of their cottage, and he left with the feeling of a job poorly done. If only she would *talk*. He couldn't imagine what she was thinking, and he didn't know what to say to make it right.

* * *

It wasn't difficult to put it together.

In the cottage, Ophele sat down with a stack of papers the duke had set aside for her, figures that needed adding, letters that required responses. There was so much work underway in the valley, no doubt including countless items she didn't know about, but she understood perfectly well what Sir Tounot had been talking about. The duke and his men must be trying to find a way to help the other villages in the valley. What else would they need with a caravan, especially one built to withstand devils? And he hadn't brought it up because he thought she would be scared if he left her alone at night again.

And she would be.

Ever since her sun sickness, he had been scrupulous about explaining things to her. If he stood watch, it was always on the main road; he explained all the defenses from the gate onward, so she would understand how many men stood between her and danger. He had even showed her exactly where he would be standing, and he was never gone all night anymore.

"There's nothing to be afraid of," he had told her, the first night that he went to stand watch. And seeing him fully armored and massive, so tall he had to duck his head to keep his black hair from hitting the rafters, it did seem impossible that anything could stand against him. "I've killed stranglers with my hands, wife. None of the devils can bite through good steel. Nothing can kill me."

This was obviously not true; he was as mortal as anyone else. But her father certainly hadn't had much luck. Neither had Valleth and all their mercenaries, or the three preceding years of devils. And she had felt so foolish that he was going to such trouble to reassure her.

"I know," she had said.

"Nothing will hurt you," he said firmly, and then knelt down in front of her and gave her a shake. "Look at me. Nothing can kill me, and I won't let anything anywhere near you."

He had said those words before, but never like that. And looking into his black eyes, she had believed him.

Ophele knew what she should say. She had read the words in countless books. She should bid him to go and do his duty, and be careful, and tell him she would take care of his home while he was away. That was what a proper noblewoman did.

Dipping her quill in an ink pot, Ophele bent over the first page, adding the first column with her eyes. Sir Edemir had come to the cottage a few days ago to give her a few math problems and let her do them in her head, and had looked so surprised that she wondered uncomfortably whether she had done something strange. Her reward was more accounts to manage, but at least she didn't have to show her work anymore.

If she could do that, maybe she could do this.

She heard him coming even before he knocked on the door, some time before supper.

"Wife?"

"Yes," she said, sitting up very straight.

He kicked the dust off his boots before he ducked through the low door, his face set in its customary frowning lines.

"You've been working?" he asked, sitting down at the table beside her.

Ophele nodded, suddenly anxious.

"What have you been working on? No, tell me," he said, when she moved to hand him the stack of papers. "I want to hear you talk."

"Orders for the kitchen," she said, looking up at him and wondering what this was about. "And medicines, for Genon? And I answered some of the letters we talked about yesterday. From the weavers and dyers. And the man who wanted to know about mining. And a few others."

"Is that it?"

"Yes? There were a lot of orders for the kitchen," she said, apologetic.

"No, I'm sure you did plenty of work," he said dryly, looking at the stack by her elbow. "But I want you to tell me about all of it. I want you to get used to talking to me."

He was wearing his stubborn face again.

"Oh." Her eyes flicked up to his, surprised. "Oh. Well, I also answered a few more letters, people asking if they could come live here, and I told them what you said about not letting anyone else come until next year…"

The duke listened patiently as she explained the other letters she had written, and then they looked through the food orders for the kitchen, speculating about what earthly use Master Wen might have for a bushel of dried persimmons. Though she felt embarrassed that he was going to such trouble, she knew better than to resist; he would sit at the table all night if that was what it took to make her talk. He was so stubborn.

And thinking that, for some reason she had to look down to hide a smile.

"So let me tell you about the caravan," he said when she was done, and described what she had already deduced about trying to get a team of men and horses to Ferrede. "The hard part is the horses," he explained. "We can hardly put them in the wagon, so we have to come up with something to protect them overnight that they can haul. The carpenters are calling it a mobile palisade. But if it's too heavy, we need more horses to pull it, which means the palisade needs to be bigger to protect them, which means more horses…"

He spread his hands and Ophele nodded. It was an interesting problem.

"But we have to go help Ferrede, and the other villages," he went on. "I guess you've figured that out. I didn't tell you because I still don't know who will actually go, or when. I didn't want you worrying about it in the meantime."

"I'll be all right," she made herself say. But this time his frown was a real frown.

"Stop saying you're fine when you aren't," he said sternly. "It makes it hard for me to tell what to do. Tell me what you're thinking, not what you think I want to hear."

"I'm thinking that they're your people. My people," she said, which was still an incredibly bizarre thought, but was nonetheless true. "Because I'm the Duchess of Andelin. Ferrede, Meinhem, Raida, Isigne, and Selgin. Is that all of them?"

"Nandre. And Raida is fine, they're by the border wall."

"Nandre," she repeated, giving him her own version of a stubborn face. "I didn't think about what might be happening to them, all this time. But they don't have knights, do they? Or soldiers."

"No, they don't," he agreed.

"And they swore to obey you as their lord. They swore to the stars."

"Yes."

"Then you have to go."

"I don't know if that's true," he replied slowly. "I was thinking about it. It bothered me, even before. I swore to protect the people of Tresingale, and I thought I was doing my duty, standing guard for them. But I only swore the protection of my body to *you*. Not the protection of someone else's body. I thought it was the same thing as long as you were safe, but Juste would disagree, I expect."

"But you said I'm safe," she said, refusing to be diverted even with such tempting intellectual fodder.

"You don't sleep when the devils are about," he said bluntly. "You're always awake when I come back."

She flushed.

"It's not as bad as being out there with no guards at all," she said, her ears pink. The people of the valley shouldn't have to suffer because she was a coward.

"Why do they scare you so much?" he wanted to know. "If you explain it to me, maybe there's something we can do about it. Is it just the noises?"

It was the noises, but Ophele thought that wasn't all. And he was asking so directly, and had been so patient, she thought she owed it to him to at least try.

"Where do they come from?" she began, her fingers twisting together. "The devils."

"Vallethi sorcerers."

"I know that, but from *where*," she said, voicing one of the many questions she had asked herself so many times. It felt good to say it out loud. "Are they from the underworld? Or somewhere else in this world? Or somewhere in Valleth?"

"We don't know," he admitted.

"Why do they go away in the winter?"

His lips twisted. He was an intelligent man, he likely already knew where she was going. "We don't know."

"Why are there more this year than there were last year?"

"No idea." He looked at her expectantly.

"Then how do you know there won't be more tonight than there were last night?" she asked softly. "A lot more, maybe. Too many."

"I can't know. But we've planned for it," he said, to her surprise.

"You have?"

"Of course. The Vallethi army showed up in places we didn't expect, and often with more people than we expected. Though I can't send out scouts against the devils," he said, in a tone that let her know he was treating her question seriously. "Huber brought it up. He's always the one with the questions that keep me up at night. But after that last expedition outside the walls, we made plans, just in case we were ever overrun."

Ophele's expression very clearly said, *do go on*.

"We've drilled organized retreats from three main areas. Here, let me have your quill, I'll show you," he said, reaching for a blank piece of paper.

"Here's the palisade. It only admits stranglers, but that's still a vulnerability. Then here, northeast, is the gap between the palisade and the wall, and the gap between the north and south sections of the wall." The quill slashed briskly between his large brown fingers. "There are barricades here, mostly for the wolves…"

In a few minutes he had sketched out the defenses for the town, then showed her how it folded inward, and how the masons would be evacuated to the unfinished barracks while the people in town would be moved to the cookhouse and storehouse. As Yvain and Dol had said, she herself would go to the storehouse, but in Ophele's mind it had been a chaos of screaming men and devils running in all directions, not this well-ordered retreat.

"It wouldn't be fun," he said, looking down at the finished diagram, with its many arrows and dotted lines. "And we could likely tighten this up, there's a hill here that would slow down the retreat, another barricade would buy them more time…anyway," he said, returning his attention to her. "We can't prepare for everything, but we have prepared for this. You're not likely to wake up one night with a mob of devils surrounding the cottage."

"I was more worried about the storehouse," she confessed. "I thought—it sounds silly, but I thought of Yvain and Dol taking me there and locking me inside, and then in the morning I would come out and find I was the only person left."

Her voice faded as she spoke her worst fear, and the duke's stern face softened.

"I guess that would scare anyone," he said, and hesitated only a second before he covered both her hands with his. "But I'd say that's very, very unlikely, wife."

It wasn't magic. Her heart didn't pound any less frantically later that night, when he went out to guard the road and she heard a strangler cackling in the distance. But when she went to sit by the fire, thinking she would read, she found that he had left the plans for retreat in the center of the table, with all the buildings in town neatly labeled and the path from the cottage to the storehouse marked. And in the storehouse, he had added two figures, labeled in his slashing, jagged script: *Ophele. Remin.*

She didn't hear him come in that night. She was already asleep.

A few days later, she plucked up her courage to ask him whether or not a decision had been made about the caravan.

"Well, *I* won't be going," he said. His face was as austere as ever, but she was learning to see the humor in his eyes. "Remember how I told you they were trying to figure out how to keep the size of the caravan down, to compensate for the palisade?"

She nodded.

"They succeeded." The corner of his mouth twitched. "I won't be going, and neither will Jinmin. Can you guess why?"

She thought about it, and it actually startled a laugh out of her.

"Nooo…" she said, looking up at him with wide eyes. "You can't fit?"

"They'd have to grease me up to get me in there," he said, and gave her something very close to a smile as she burst into giggles.

* * *

With the caravan finished, and the gaps between the city walls being whittled down daily, Remin judged that it was time to take another chance.

Or rather, to send someone *else* to take a chance.

It was the lot of a lord to send other men to die, but even after years of experience, Remin still could not reconcile himself to it. Tomorrow, Huber would be leaving for Ferrede to see if anyone had survived this cruel summer, along with a small group of soldiers and young Sir Ortaire, who had been willing to fight every other man in Tresingale for the dubious honor.

There had been no slackening in the devils. Every night they came in waves against the small town, and Remin was counting every man in the defenses. The loss of two knights and six soldiers was no small matter. Nor could he easily spare the four horses needed to pull the metal caravan. But that was why it must be Huber. If anyone could persuade horses to go into the teeth of the devils, it was Huber, and Huber had always been something of a dark horse himself: a wild card, appearing unlooked-for at the moment he was most desperately needed. And as the former master of Remin's scouts, he knew the valley better than any man alive.

No doubt Huber would also have preferred to go *quietly*. But nerves were stretched thin from hard work and relentless heat, and Miche and Juste thought a leavetaking was an excellent time for a feast. Which was how Remin found himself in the same position he had been on the first night in the valley: down on one knee beside Ophele, squinting at something called eyelets as he helped her dress.

At least this time he hadn't made her cry first.

"Why does it have so many ribbons?" he grumbled, rummaging through the ridiculously tiny box.

"Maybe so we don't have to sew it together," Ophele said, examining the pieces of the gown with an absorbed expression. She was dressed only in a chemise and still rosy from her bath, having spent hours happily wallowing in her new basin. The scent of her filled his senses like a drug, so sweet and heady that he wanted nothing more than to bury his face in her.

"Oh, I see, it laces up the sides," she said, holding out a slender arm to demonstrate where the bodice laced together, with trailing golden ribbons meant to dangle in streamers alongside the red silk skirt of the gown. Remin tied first one side and the other, tightening them together so silk and velvet hugged her slim waist and cupped her breasts. The colors suited her. The deep red made her skin glow and her eyes looked more golden than ever, as if the metallic leaf-and-flower embroidery had flecked color onto her irises.

Gently, he set the matching circlet on her head, brushing her hair back from her shoulders. Ophele, Duchess of Andelin.

"It fits you well," he said, admiring the ribbons and beads glinting in the rich umber of her hair.

"I heard in the capital, we would be dressed to match for something like this," she said, turning pink and busying herself with the mysterious jars now overflowing their washstand.

"It would be hard for anyone to match you." The words escaped before Remin could stop them, and when Ophele glanced up at him in surprise, he reddened like a fool.

"It makes me feel conspicuous," she said. "I'll be the only one all dressed up."

"They will be pleased to see you so," he promised. "It is a great honor to keep company with a lady."

"Is it?"

"Most of my men don't often get the opportunity," he said, lifting her easily at the door. The new road stretched for more than a mile, but there was still plenty of mud in Tresingale. "They will see you and think of their sweethearts, their wives, their sisters, and their daughters. All the women they left back home. When the wall is done, maybe they'll feel safe to send for them. Especially if they see you, looking so…"

In the middle of the lane, he trailed off, lost in her golden eyes and searching for any words but the ones that had so nearly slipped out.

So beautiful.

"…like such a fine lady," he finished lamely. "Try to have words with them, if you can. Especially with the men that will be leaving tomorrow. You will give them courage."

"I will," she said, her small face solemn, though she gripped his shirt front tighter as he approached the doors of the cookhouse and set her down. He could see her draw a deep breath as she moved into her place at his side.

The doors opened, and the cookhouse fell instantly and completely silent.

"Your Grace," said one of the men at the nearest table, springing to his feet as everyone else hastily rose. "My lady, we're glad to see you well."

"Cordiot," she said, surprised. "Thank you. And you are, too? Your ankle, I mean?"

"Sturdy as a plank, my lady," he assured her, and Remin was astonished at the number of similar conversations as they moved toward the high table. He hadn't thought of it, but this was the first night they had come to supper since her sun sickness. His men weren't just pleased by the sight of *a* lady, however lovely and charming. They were glad to see *their* lady.

His lady.

They teased her. They laughed with her. The color was high in her cheeks as she bobbed her head like a little bird, and he drifted behind her like a man in a dream. They were talking to him too, and he was sure he answered, but his eyes were so filled with the small figure in scarlet, nothing else seemed real.

It was Tresingale's first real feast, and Wen and his boys had outdone themselves. The good smell of roasting boar had been filling the town all day, and the huge slabs of meat were so tender, they melted on the tongue. There were heaps of roasted potatoes and thick slices of bread with butter and cheese. The pageboys had been dispatched to go berrying and returned with a bounty of blackberries, fat and juicy. Remin remembered chewing, but he tasted nothing.

He had to shake himself as the platters were taken away to offer the customary speeches and toasts, both for the men leaving tomorrow and to thank the stars for the renewed health of their daughter. All his men were putting their best foot forward, and after the wine was poured down the table, Remin rose to offer a toast of his own.

"All of you have worked hard to secure this place against the devils," he said, lifting his cup to the whole cookhouse, and indeed, all of Tresingale. "Sir Huber Adaman and Sir Ortaire of Berange have volunteered to dare the road to Ferrede, and go to the aid of our people. It is your work that has made it possible for us to spare them. We hope to find Squire Rollon and his builders waiting in Ferrede, fat and lazy after this summer. May the stars bless the journey, and the men who undertake it."

Both Huber and Ortaire had come to kneel before him, and Remin glanced at Ophele. Her sacred hands were the ones to offer that blessing.

"Please be careful," she said, as both men laid their brows against her palms. "You are very brave to go. Come back safe, as soon as you can."

"Thank you, Your Grace," Huber promised, and every cup in the cookhouse lifted to salute them.

There was not much time left before sunset, but Remin called for a little music, nonetheless. Part of every knight's education included learning to play the pipe, the lute, or the mandolin. Darri of Ghis had a surprisingly sweet voice, and the rest of Remin's men all took their turns leading the singing, everything from *My Sweet Lady Awaits* to the comical *Where is Squire Ness?* This was what he had dreamed of, when he imagined his own banquet hall, though he waved away demands for a song of his own. He was not quite ready to serenade his wife.

Then someone a few tables down the hall stood up and began to sing.

Oh you can search the Empire wide
And never find a better guide
To the precious things you unfortunately let fall

For to the scaffold you are bound
No matter what goes tumbling down
There's only one gentle-hearted spirit you can call

There went me hammer off the side
And me trowel's in a glide
Oh come and save me, nimble lady of the wall!

"Oh, *no!*" Ophele gasped, as Miche threw his head back and roared with laughter. Remin glanced between them. He had heard of the lady of the wall before, but he had decided not to inquire closely; a good lord let his men have their fun.

Her reaction was likely everything they had dreamed. Scarlet to her ears, she was covering her face with her hands and peeking through her fingers at Remin as if her whole castle of lies was collapsing at once. Every verse was more absurd than the last and before long the entire cookhouse was singing the ridiculous song, including the Knights of the Brede, who thoroughly enjoyed such jokes. And though Remin would have a word with her later about whether it was really advisable for a noblewoman to climb about in scaffolding, at that moment she was laughing so hard she was breathless, and he was just so *proud* of her.

"My lady?" Miche stood and offered an extravagant bow. "Will you honor me with a dance?"

"I'm…not very good," Ophele said apprehensively, as she gave him her hand.

"You won't need to be," he promised, and the men cleared a space before the high table so they could dance the Lady of the Wall off her feet. She looked a little pale to be under so many eyes, but Miche whispered something that made her laugh and spun her into the music, then handed her off to Juste for the next song and Huber after that, who knelt to ask for her hand with deadpan gravity. Ophele's eyes widened and she dipped a curtsy, smiling.

If she had needed to dance, they would have thoroughly exhausted her, but her feet scarcely touched the floor. By the time Bram set her into a neat figure at the end of the next song, her eyes went immediately to Remin, happy and laughing and wanting to share it with him, and suddenly it felt as if everything else in the world dissolved away, leaving only her. The loveliest thing he had ever seen.

Ah.

He loved her.

He knew it. He knew it as surely as he knew his own name. It was like flying and it was like drowning, beautiful and dreadful, and somehow inescapably inevitable. How long had he suspected that he would love her? When had he actually begun? The Lady of the Wall. Who else would have become the Lady of the Wall for him?

His hands felt like ice as he rose to go to her, and his heart was hammering fear and love, love and fear. But he still went, though his legs wanted to carry him past her and out the cookhouse doors.

"My lady," he said, offering her a big hand, and Bram relinquished her with a bow.

"Your Grace." Ophele's fingers vanished into his and he wrapped an arm around her waist, swinging her easily into the next song. Boots stomped the rhythm around them. Hands clapped. Remin knew how to dance, even if his long-ago dancing master had once witheringly described it as what one might expect to see if a fireplace poker decided to promenade through a ballroom.

But it wasn't like that with her. In his arms she felt like warm, living silk, a wisp of a girl with long skirts and hair whirling in the turns. It was so easy to move with her. Maybe it was because he already knew her body so well. He had held her, carried her, picked her up and pinned her down, helped her dress and tended her. He remembered all of it as he danced with her, the times he had seen her drunk and weeping, sick and heartsick, the times when she was laughing, delighted, and crying out with pleasure.

Faster. The song was swifter on the chorus and Remin heard the roaring of the singing, matching his quick feet to the music. Ophele's face was flushed with exertion as she tried to keep up with him, her small red slippers beating a tattoo. Looking into her golden eyes was like falling into the stars. He wanted to kiss those red lips. He wanted to love her and make love to her and keep her by his side always.

And if he was wrong about her, she would cut out his heart.

Faster. Faster. The song had a tongue-twister of a chorus, light and quick, and at the end of it they landed together so perfectly, it was as if the whole world took a breath. Her body was pressed against him, her breath panting with his, and her face was turned up to his, glowing. Her eyes. Ah, those eyes. He could see nothing else.

Now was the moment, if he wanted to seize it. Now was when he could bid them all goodnight and take her home to their bed. Maybe it didn't have to be this way between them. Maybe it wasn't too late to make her love him. Maybe…

Remin bent his head and pressed his lips to the back of her hand, a gesture filled with the courtly elegance of the nobleman he had been born.

"Thank you for the dance," he said quietly, relinquishing her to Tounot. There was a flash of confusion in her face; he must have betrayed himself, somehow. But though he tried to look reassuring, he had reached the limits of his endurance. As the men burst into another song, he faded back through the crowd and slipped out the doors into the twilight.

At the high table with his brother knights, Miche of Harnost watched through narrowed eyes, reading the tale before him with deepening disquiet.

CHAPTER 13 – GREATER THAN FEAR

In a curious contradiction, the building of the walls opened the town.

To be sure, the soldiers' barracks had been under construction for some time, and all the arriving merchants and tradesmen had already been on their way to the valley long before. But almost overnight, it seemed Tresingale transformed from a settlement under siege to a frontier town. At last, the defenses began to move away from the vulnerable camps and sleeping places, tightening around the gaps in the walls, and now men could sit around their campfires at night, talking and drinking and dicing, then seek their beds without fear.

Those beds had moved at last from the cookhouse to the barracks, which left room for other society, the first real society Ophele had ever known. After supper in the evening, whenever Remin and his knights were not on guard themselves, they lingered by the fire, spreading their maps over all the tables and endlessly planning. For hours she listened with fascination as Sir Bram spoke of planting vineyards on the hills east of town. Sir Justenin wanted to build an observatory overlooking them, for the peaceful study of the stars. Sir Tounot dreamed of a town of his own, beside a shining blue lake on the plateau.

He had looked oddly sorry when he said it, but Remin had only nodded and marked the site on the map, making Sir Tounot the first Marquis of the Andelin, master of lands yet unnamed.

"The rest of you had better hurry up and make your claims," he said, looking at the enormous expanse of territory, a fifth the size of the entire Empire.

Ophele had little to say in such matters; it was all foreign to her experience. Not merely the building of a new duchy, but even this rough society. She had never known anything as simple as sitting beside the fire in company, listening to the unwinding of a conversation. It had always been just her and her mother at Aldeburke, and once Lady Pavot died, the best she could hope was to be ignored by the Hurrells.

It was wonderful. Whether they were planning the planting for the next five years or recounting war stories when they were in their cups, Ophele was content to sit at Remin's side for hours, soaking up all this knowledge.

"No, it has to be the trebuchets outside Jardingard," Sir Auber contested, when they were discussing some of their more lunatic exploits. "That was *pure* luck, it never should have worked."

There was some dispute among the Knights of the Brede as to what their all-time stupidest plan had been. In her opinion, Sir Jinmin's one-man assault on a supply gate at a fortress called Bittern *sounded* the most insane, but apparently there was some stiff competition.

"Jardingard is one of the border fortresses in Valleth," Sir Tounot explained kindly to Ophele. "Rem was making it clear that he was going to invade if they didn't surrender. Though we would have preferred not to."

"We'd likely still be laying siege to Mindelind if we had," said Remin, grimacing. Mindelind was the capital of Valleth, and its walls were famously twenty feet thick.

"If you'd been a second later on those trebuchets, they might have flung you halfway there," Sir Auber said acidly.

"If I'd had three or four more Jinmins, I wouldn't have gone," Remin retorted. "Too many of you short bast—none of you could reach to cut the lines."

"If you'd waited a day, Juste would've shown up with reinforcements. But what do you think he did instead?" Sir Auber addressed this to Ophele. "He and Jinmin stole some Vallethi uniforms and infiltrated the lines, figuring that Valleth would never guess our general would be stupid enough to go wandering around the battlefield by himself—"

"And they didn't," Remin pointed out.

"—and while he and Jinmin were ripping the machines apart, the rest of us mounted a charge to reach them before Valleth could move archers in to turn them into pincushions." Sir Auber shook his head.

"When I got there, Rem was dangling off the arm of the last trebuchet and if just one of those Vallethi sods had the sense of a goat, they would've cut the block weight loose and pasted our general against the walls of the fortress he was defending."

"No," Ophele breathed, her eyes round at this picturesque image.

"I think the most amazing part of the story is that Rem and Jinmin found Vallethi uniforms that fit," Sir Miche observed dryly, to a burst of laughter.

There were dozens of stories like that, most often recounted later in the evening, after they had consumed a fair amount of wine. Ophele loved the stories about Remin best; he would never tell her such things about himself, and it was so good of his knights to do it for him, boasting of their young lord over his own protests. When they walked home together afterward, she couldn't help looking at him, marveling. Not because he was the great military genius and hero, Remin Grimjaw, but because now she understood how he had done it. And most often, it was with creativity, courage, and brute stubbornness rather than superhuman strength.

Oddly, the more human he became to her, the more she admired him.

But it wasn't just the stories. The workings of his mind were a constant source of fascination to her, being both opaque and relentlessly rational. Once he made a decision, it was almost as if he set up mental tripwires for the required conditions of the next step, and never mentioned it again until they had been met. Ophele herself had forgotten that she wanted to teach Jacot arithmetic until the day Remin gathered up a selection of books, took her to the cookhouse, and thrust her in front of the boy with the announcement that the time had come.

"Now?" she asked, as Jacot hastily swallowed his lunch and scrambled to his feet.

"Didn't you say you wanted to teach him? We've space for it now, and it's cooler here than the cottage with the doors open." Remin looked surprised that she had not been preparing all along for this day.

And that was how the Andelin Valley acquired its first school, with a single student and a wildly inexperienced teacher. Every afternoon, Jacot left Eugene on some shady grazing by the wall and bolted back to the cookhouse, determined to learn as much as he could.

"Master Eugene is well," he always assured her as he took his seat. "And Sir Justenin says he's going to get another donkey to haul water for the west side of the wall, did you know? Digging wells and all just like they did on our wall."

Jacot was as smugly superior with this arrangement as if he had devised it himself; the men who had worked with Ophele were very proud of their water management scheme. And as gratifying as this news was, Ophele seized on a much more interesting possibility: *baby donkeys.*

"Oh, I hope he gets a female," She said rapturously, wondering if there was any way she could drop a hint.

"Dunno if Master Eugene is up to being put to stud, lady," Jacot replied, bolting down bread and cheese as if he thought someone might take it from him. By now he knew where the lady's priorities lay. "He's slowing down a mite."

"Nonsense," Ophele said firmly. Master Eugene was the finest and noblest of donkeys, he would breed splendid babies. But Jacot did only have an hour, so she turned her book where he could see it, pointing to the poem they would be reading. Her book of poetry was the best primer available; the necessity of rhyming kept the vocabulary fairly simple, though Jacot did not appreciate the flowery language. "I have a good one today," she promised.

"Is it?" The boy said doubtfully.

"*The Hero of Vindelein,*" she read, encouraging. "Penniless, fatherless, a son of the stews…"

"With a smelly old jacket and holes in his shoes," Jacot said through a mouthful of bread, chortling.

"Stop that." She would not laugh. Ophele felt less shy with people younger than herself, and though she had never had a teacher of her own, she had the idea that they should be very serious. "Here, go ahead and read the next line."

Jacot was an ideal student. Eager and quick-witted, he gave Ophele the confidence to expand her efforts to the rest of the pages, who soon began to assemble for lessons during the hottest part of the day. Ophele never dreamed that the pages' real first lesson had been on the horrors that awaited them if they *once* upset their gentle teacher, delivered by everyone from their squires to the knights to Remin himself, who promised he could throw them quite a good distance into the Brede.

Even a month ago, she couldn't have imagined a life like this. It was as if the whole world had burst open, so far beyond the narrow boundaries of Aldeburke that she was scrambling to keep up. The wall. The building of a town. So many new people, a home of her own, work that she could do well, and devils and knights, like something out of a story book. It was so much and so far beyond her pitiful experience that sometimes she felt dizzy, thinking of it all.

But from the moment she opened her eyes every morning, Remin was there. Gentle and unsmiling, the unshakable bedrock beneath every step she took.

How wonderful it would be, if he would always be there.

* * *

Yet somehow, as the weeks went on, she began to wonder if something was wrong.

It was a ridiculous thought on its face. There was no concrete evidence she could point to; outwardly he was the same as ever, or at least unchanged in this new, kinder iteration of himself. He wasn't perfect. He was stiff and cold by nature, and often abrupt, though she thought he might not mean to be. There were so many things he didn't know that he was trying to learn for her sake, and even his clumsiest efforts were touching.

But even as the town grew safer, her worry for him grew.

There were the guards, for one thing. Folk still went cautiously in the dark, and no one ever went anywhere alone after nightfall, just in case. But for the most part the standing guard in town was gone, except around the cottage. Every night, Yvain and Dol came to stand at their posts on the front and back of the house, and Ophele had finally realized they weren't there just for her benefit. The Duke of Andelin slept there. And it wasn't safe for him to sleep without guards.

And then there was an incident at the cookhouse one afternoon, when she had arrived a little late for the noon meal and caught Master Wen flaying a newly arrived builder alive. To that point, Ophele had privately thought that Master Wen yelled just because he *liked* to yell, and maybe he didn't really mean it. But that day there was no doubt that he was deadly serious.

"…something wrong with your ears, ye lackwit? I told ye to stay on that side of the line. That line, on the floor, it's white and it's there for a fucking purpose. Cross it again and I'll gut ye."

His victim made some reply, which Ophele couldn't hear from ten feet outside the door.

"No, this is *my* kitchen and His Grace's fucking food, and if ye move one inch nearer to it, I'll shove a spit up your ass and roast ye for supper. What ye see in that cupboard is what ye get, and ye let me watch your blooming hands while ye take it. Slow. Now ye've got your biscuit, get the fuck out and never do that again or ye can go hunt devils for your dinner."

It was the angriest she had ever heard him, and for a while, she didn't understand why. She had written off the periodic explosions from the kitchen as Master Wen's unique way of expressing himself. But he had said, *His Grace's food.* The duke was fed from that kitchen. Master Wen rigidly controlled all access to the food he ate, and was ferocious as a mastiff to anyone that tried to get near it.

And then she remembered that even in Aldeburke, they had heard about Remin getting poisoned. More than once. The Emperor had been outraged, *outraged* that someone would attack a noble-born boy, but nothing ever came of the investigations.

That thought would have shamed her before, but now it made her *furious.* How *dared* someone do that? All this time, she had been trying to repay her blood debt on principle, but suddenly she felt a fierce urge to protect him. It was a ridiculous idea, considering he was three times her size and the greatest knight in the known world. He had never been unhorsed. He had never been defeated in combat. The only way anyone could get to him was with sneaky, despicable things like poison.

Again, she remembered that morning months ago, when he had so nearly struck her. She had been frightened at the time, but she had learned to read his face better now, and it was not because he had been angry. Those widened eyes, the careful way he had stepped backward, hands up…

If it had been anyone else, she would have said he was *afraid.*

Remin. Every day she was learning something new about him, unraveling some mystery, discovering virtues he hardly seemed aware of himself. He wasn't modest so much as adorably oblivious, as if he really didn't know he was one of the most handsome men in the Empire. Sometimes just looking at him made her feel flustered.

And other times, it made her worry. His black eyes were as opaque and unreadable as ever, but sometimes when she looked into them, she had to fight the inexplicable impulse to lay a hand on his forehead, to see if he was well. He did look tired. He never looked tired. Was that it? Was that why she had the strange sense that something was wrong?

"What's this?" he asked when he came home one evening, to find a steaming cup of tea waiting for him at the table.

"Tea." The town's first merchant had arrived, and claimed that this blend was good for calming and promoted sleep. "Mr. Guian had a dozen tins of it and I asked him to save one for me. There's even a little honey or sugar, if you like it sweet."

"Where did you get the money?" he looked at the tea with an unreadable expression as he stirred half a spoon of sugar into it.

"I had something put by." Ophele's eyes slid away from his. She had sold one of her books. "I can get milk next time, if you take your tea that way. Master Wen says if I want milk, I have to get it from the cow myself."

"This is fine." The corner of his mouth twitched, the nearest Remin Grimjaw ever came to a smile. "Is something else different?"

"Maybe." Ophele watched him, nervous and excited. She had never surprised anyone with presents before. There had never been anyone to surprise. She had cleaned up the cottage as best she could, lit the lamps on either end of the mantle, and put out fresh bouquets of flowers, but there wasn't much to work with. She watched as his eyes drifted over the neatened shelves and tidy washstand, then landed on the mantle.

"Where did you find that?" His dark eyes fastened on the small glass bear, set prominently in the middle.

"I was looking for teacups in the storehouse and saw it," she explained, hoping he wouldn't be angry. It wasn't pretty exactly, but there was something touching and a little melancholy about the bear, seated on its haunches with one paw outstretched. "Do you like it?"

"It looks good," he said, with a nod that encompassed the whole of the cottage. "I always wondered why you asked for a bear."

"I like bears." Ophele felt her cheeks heat and looked down at her own teacup. "I took these cups from a set, I hope it's all right."

"It's from the Duchess Ereguil. She sent a full tea service as soon as we settled here. I don't think she understood what Tresingale was like last year."

"Will they ever come to visit? The Duke and Duchess?" The prospect made her nervous because of course they would, one day. The whole point of having a vast manor was to host guests, sometimes dozens of them at a time. Ereguil was one of the great duchies of Argence, an ancient and noble family whose House was as old as the House of Agnephus, the House of the Emperor. And the Duke and Duchess of Ereguil were the nearest thing to parents that he had.

"Next year, most likely. I'm hoping to have a respectable place for them to stay, and they both say they want to see the valley. Maybe that was why she sent the tea service," he added reflectively. "She's the greatest lady I know. If you decided to go and stay with them, they would bring you back when they visit."

The words were as sudden and shocking as a slap, and Ophele hastily lowered her eyes to hide her hurt. He hadn't mentioned the possibility of sending her away since her sun sickness, and she thought he had forgotten. With the wall nearing completion, it didn't seem there was any reason for her to leave.

Unless he didn't want her here.

All this time, he had kept his word to take care of her. But maybe he still didn't like her. Maybe he was just doing what he had to do to make sure she was healthy enough to bear his children. Maybe he would rather she was out of the way until she was strong enough to do so.

Strong enough for him to bed her, without love.

Her mind shied away from that thought as unbearable. Before, she thought she could do it. As long as he didn't actually strike her, he was an improvement over the Hurrells. And she had given an oath to do it; the most important thing she could do was to secure his succession. But if he didn't love her…

"Is that what you want?" he asked quietly.

It was the hardest thing she had ever had to say. To screw up her courage to tell him the truth, especially when she didn't know what would happen after she did. But she didn't want to go. She wanted to help him. She wanted to be here for the building of his dream, which she had thought was becoming *their* dream.

Be brave, and don't tell lies.

"No," she whispered. "I want to help. Do…do *you* want me to go?"

"You have helped," He replied softly, and his big fingers brushed hers, to make her look at him. "I hadn't realized how much. But I want you to be safe. I don't want you to be afraid anymore. I know this place is hard for you."

"I don't mind."

"You *should* mind," he said, and when his black eyes met hers, she felt the jolt to her heart. "You're a lady. You're a *princess*. And you deserve so much *better,* you should have everything, and I can't—I thought, when you first came here, that you *expected* it, but Ophele, you're just so…"

She was looking at his lips. Suddenly, he was so near that she would only have to turn her head a little, and he would kiss her. She could see herself reflected in his eyes, and his voice was so deep and aching that she could hardly breathe. She wanted him to say it, whatever it was. She wanted it so badly, it was as if the fate of the world hung in the balance.

"What?" she whispered finally, and her hand reached for his all by itself.

"Nothing. Nothing," he said, rising so abruptly his knees banged the table. "Never mind. It's just my foolishness. I should go and help on the wall, I meant to go earlier. I'll be back to fetch you for supper. Don't go outside until it's cooler, Juste thinks it will be another scorcher this afternoon…"

He was pulling on his boots as he spoke, and Ophele watched, hurt and bewildered and for some reason unspeakably disappointed.

"I won't," she said, as if she had a habit of roving the countryside in the heat of the day. It didn't make any sense. If he didn't like her, why did he look at her that way? So many times, he would forget himself and laugh, or his eyes would get so warm, and then when he touched her…

But it wasn't only his touch. As she watched him gather his things, Ophele considered and rejected the possibility that this was a purely physical phenomenon, or, contrariwise, a matter of simple obligation. By now, their nights together seemed almost a romantic dream, a chance encounter with a mysterious stranger that would never happen again. But she had never forgotten that kindling between them, and she had come to know Remin better, since then. The man that listened and explained, patient and persistent, a brave man that tried even when he didn't know how to do things.

She liked this man. She liked him very much.

And he had already told her that he didn't know how to do this.

"I'll be back soon," he said as he ducked out the door, and Ophele nodded, her eyes watchful.

"Be careful."

Take care of His Grace. That was what Sir Huber had told her, when they were dancing together the night of the banquet. And of course, she had agreed; that was what a wife was supposed to do, even if the husband was Remin Grimjaw and the wife was manifestly unqualified to take care of anything.

But Remin's men all seemed to think he needed care, and Ophele quietly picked over the evidence. She knew little of the world and nothing of men, but when she put forth the proposition that he didn't care for her, the weight of evidence did not seem to support it. His observed behavior flatly contradicted it. If he had wanted only to be rid of her, he would have seized this chance with both hands.

Which meant there was something *else* troubling him, and as Ophele's eyes drifted toward the door he had closed so gently behind him, she understood that this was a puzzle, of a kind she had never attempted before.

* * *

I need to speak to you privately, please.

The note was scrawled on a small scrap of paper, rolled up in a tight scroll and hidden under the edge of his dinner plate.

It was hardly the first time that Sir Miche of Harnost had received such an invitation.

Automatically, he transferred the note to his lap, noting the messy, childish handwriting. Really, that was sufficient all by itself to identify the guilty party, but his eyes went to the small woman some distance down the supper table, who was doing her best to pretend he didn't exist.

Ophele's ears were *scarlet*.

You can find me in the stable before supper, read the rest of the message, and Miche flicked it into his sleeve, amused. Of course, he was ever the obedient slave of a lady, but it wasn't going to be easy to have a private word with the Duchess of Andelin. Not even for Miche of Harnost, who modestly considered himself the cleverest man in the valley.

In the first place, everyone was busy from sunup to sundown. Having discovered that his destiny lay in ditch digging, Miche was loathe to stop, especially since that troll Jinmin had suddenly decided *he* wanted to be Master Earthmover. Miche would be damned if some upstart would best him, even if he was eight feet tall and built like a drawbridge. Miche had charge of the east side diggers, Jinmin was on the west, and by the stars, they'd see who made it to the gatehouse first.

The lady was hardly less occupied, for all that she no longer worked at the wall. Ophele had become a fixture in front of Remin on his big black horse, poking her small nose into all the business of the valley and offering her hands to anyone who had a use for them. It did Miche's heart good to see her so happy. She had been a silent, solemn little shadow for so long, and he bitterly reproached himself that he had not intervened sooner. This clumsy invitation meant she had grown brave enough to set her hands to the levers of the world.

How could he refuse her?

"…give us a hand at the gatehouse tomorrow?" Bram was saying beside him, and Miche made some rapid mental calculations.

"Yes," he said, with such a dazzling smile that the other man bristled in instinctive alarm.

It was a perfect opportunity.

Miche spent the next day arranging matters to his satisfaction and wondering what she wanted. The problem seemed obvious to *him,* but he wouldn't have blamed Ophele for being confused; it would be a thorny challenge for any young woman, let alone the Exile Princess, and Remin was just *lost.*

He had kept his word. He was trying. Stars, he was *succeeding,* there were few endeavors in the world more warmly received by their beneficiary. It had upset Miche terribly to realize it, but Ophele did not expect to be treated kindly. Every gesture, no matter how small, was received with touching surprise, and she paid them back with smiles and thanks and little gifts of her own. She and Remin were both being so *careful* around each other, tiptoeing forward with each new offering as if they were asking, *is this all right? Are we all right? Is this what you want?*

It was a vicious cycle that threatened to make them deliriously happy, and in the process was making Rem so wretched that Miche couldn't believe no one else saw it. But then, he knew Remin very well. When Tounot had been barred from even writing to his former liege lord and boyhood friend, Miche had been the one to tell Remin the news. While Juste was tending sheep in his monastery in the mountains, Miche had been tasting Remin's food for poison. And when old Duke Ereguil decreed it was time for his foster son to learn how to stand a watch, Miche was the one who stayed up all night to teach him how.

Rem was very good at hiding his feelings. But sometimes, when he looked at Ophele, there was something so trapped and desperate in his eyes that it made Miche's blood run cold. He knew that look. It was not a good thing when Remin Grimjaw felt trapped.

Miche went to the stables that evening to find Ophele grooming Master Eugene, a task she would not allow anyone else to perform. Normally, Rem would already have been there with her, but through a series of minor manipulations, His Grace had been needed out at the wall. Jinmin and his boys had run into a little trouble.

"...and your ears," she was saying as Miche entered the stable, a contented little burble of chatter that made him suspect she was used to talking to herself. "I wonder if long ears are a sign of beauty among donkeys. In Daitia, they go half naked except for these amazing hats—"

"How scandalous," Miche drawled, making her turn with a start. He grinned. "Evening, my lady. Please tell me more about these hats."

"You creep about like a cat," she said frankly, but she was smiling. "They have a language of hats, in Daitia. If you saw someone with a gray hat and gold trim, it might mean, *I am sad and rich.*"

That made him laugh, and he sat down on a convenient hay bale, laying his sword over his knee. He was filthy and sweaty from the day's digging and made a face as hay dust whiffed upward to stick to his bare arms.

"I wonder if we could adopt the custom," he said, entertained by the idea. "Rem seems to be cannibalizing architecture and customs from half the nations in the known world."

"No, you wouldn't want to wear some of these hats." Mischief lurked in her eyes, a shy humor that she was just beginning to share. "They have punishment hats. People have to wear them for thievery or bribery or shirking work."

"I will have you know that the east side crew has already surpassed yesterday's digging." The subtle jibe made him smirk. "We'll have the north wall done before winter, you'll see."

"I know His Grace will be relieved." Her hands worked smoothly, brushing the donkey's fuzzy gray flank. "Sir Miche, I have been wondering, is there anything…troubling him?"

"What makes you ask that?"

"He seems so to me," she said, frowning. "I wondered if it might be something to do with my…my father. He wouldn't tell me if there was, I guess, but everyone is being so careful to guard him, I thought maybe—"

"Everyone is always careful, my lady," Miche said somberly. "There are many measures in place. Rem's never alone, even if it looks like he is."

"I never thought about how complicated it must be," she admitted, exchanging her brush for a curry comb. Miche had never seen a donkey so well-groomed as Master Eugene. "But when I wanted to buy tea from Mr. Guian, I thought, how can I tell if the tea is safe? Sir Tounot said Mr. Guian could be trusted, so I bought it, and then I thought, how can I *keep* it safe? No one's in the cottage most of the day. If I left the tea there, how could I be sure someone didn't sneak in and do something? I had to ask Master Wen to keep it for me. If we want tea, I go get it from him, one pinch at a time."

Miche was actually impressed that she had thought it through so far. And surprised that Wen had consented to be the Keeper of Tea.

"And Rem drinks it?" he asked curiously.

She glanced at him, her forehead crinkling.

"Yes…" She said slowly. "I saw him sip. He wouldn't pretend to drink, would he?"

"He would." Even though he had come here to have precisely this conversation with her, Miche was still sorry to see her face fall. "He's good at it. He likely spills a little while your back is turned. Does he empty the cup?"

"No," she said quietly. "I thought he would like it. I was so careful to make sure no one could get to it. Or is it because…"

She cut the words off, but Miche could read what she was thinking well enough. *Is it because I gave it to him?*

"It's not just you." Miche was sorry he'd ruined it for her now; if Rem had gone to the trouble of pretending to drink, he'd been trying not to hurt her feelings. "Rem wouldn't eat a haunch of mutton unless he'd been personally introduced to the sheep, I'm afraid. You know he grew up on Duke Ereguil's estate? Since he was eight."

"Yes."

"He was nine the first time someone poisoned him. I wasn't there, but Duchess Ereguil told me about it. Windweed seeds, from Noreven. It's a nasty poison. I hear it's like lockjaw, the joints swell up and stiffen, and the muscle spasms are so bad, they'll break bones. And nothing stops the pain. He screamed for days. It was weeks before they could talk him into eating again."

It still made Miche *furious* every time he thought about it. Even in Segoile last year, Remin had frequently gone hungry rather than eat food from someone he couldn't trust. Ophele stared at him, aghast.

"But I suspect it's a nearer trouble," Miche went on, sighing. "There was a girl he liked when he was fourteen, in Rospalme. Mind, he wasn't old enough to be courting, even if the girl's father would allow it, which of course, no sane man would. She was older than he was, sixteen or so. Merrienne, that was her name. It seemed every bit as harmless as you'd expect. Rem used to give her flowers. Just shoved them at her because every time she talked to him, he'd turn red and clam up. Couldn't say a word."

"Really?" Though it was obvious that something terrible was coming, she couldn't help smiling. It was sweet to imagine Remin as a blushing boy.

"That was another reason I didn't have much hope for the match," Miche said dryly. "He was going to have to learn to say whole words out loud first. But she seemed to like him. Took the flowers, anyway. They kept meeting accidentally in town, and finally she got him to agree to slip out one night to see her."

"Alone?"

"Yes. I probably would've let him go, if I'd known." Miche was candid in acknowledging his own faults. "I just would've followed him. But he didn't breathe a word of it, and when I looked in on him that night, he was gone. I imagine he was sick of being guarded all the time, and didn't like to have anyone listening while he was trying to woo his first sweetheart."

"And she betrayed him?" Ophele asked, her eyes round.

"Worse. She tried to kill him."

"Oh. No." Ophele looked at him in horror, her hands lifting to cover her mouth. "No, no, no, a sixteen year-old girl?"

"She *said* she was sixteen. She'd arrived in Rospalme a year before, with people that said they were her parents. They vanished that same night. Anyway, by the time I found him, Rem had already killed her. She kissed him, then tried to stab him. You might've seen the scar on his back." Miche slapped at his left shoulder. "And he hit her. He was always big for his age, and he was scared. I don't think he meant to kill her, but...it was very hard for him, after."

"That is so awful. That is so *awful,*" she whispered, tears welling and overflowing. "How could anyone *do* that, that poor boy! How could anyone—"

Wordlessly, Miche extended a handkerchief as she wept. It was hard. He was sorry to tell her how hard the world could be, but Remin would never tell her this story. After all these years, maybe he didn't even know how. Maybe the weight of all those hurts had been so vast, so relentless, he didn't have the words to speak of them. But Miche would do it for him. Miche had never forgotten that fourteen year-old boy, clutching his bleeding shoulder and asking was Merrienne really dead, it had been an accident, there must be some mistake, why had she done that to him?

"I don't believe you'd do that," Miche said, squeezing Ophele's shoulder. "Down to my bones, my lady, I know you never would. And Rem thinks so too, that's why he's been letting you close. But there's part of him that just can't ever *know.* You see why?"

She nodded, scrubbing at her face with her sleeve.

"I know. I know. I *hate* him. The Emperor," she said thickly. "I know I shouldn't say it, he's the Beloved of Stars, but I *hate* him, I don't believe he can be the Divinity when he does something so awful. Remin never did anything, and neither did his parents, it's all a li—"

"We don't say that even here." Miche looked at her sharply. He would have thought she was too young when her mother died to know such dangerous things. What was common knowledge among Remin's knights was treason everywhere else in the Empire. "You should talk to Juste, if you have questions. What he says goes over my head, but you're bright enough to keep up. No, keep it," he added, waving a hand as she offered his handkerchief.

"I miss talking to Sir Justenin," she said, dabbing her cheeks with it. "I liked talking to him on the way here, he always made me think."

"There will likely be more leisure, in a little while." Miche had his own ideas about why the quiet, gentle Juste might have been keeping his distance. "And you probably know better than to ask Rem about any of it, but he won't appreciate it if you bring it up."

She nodded, red-eyed.

"Why did you tell me?"

"Because you need to know. Especially if you've guessed enough to go poking yourself," he added approvingly. "It's not your fault, but it will be hard for you. Hard for him. You see why?"

"I do."

"And now that you know, you can help him," Miche said, encouraging. "You wouldn't think it to look at him, but he takes a sight of looking after."

"That's what Sir Huber said." She gave a wobbly smile. "Before he left."

"Huber was always sensible. Don't look so serious," he added lightly, and she was quick-witted enough to understand the warning. "Tell me more about these Daitian hats."

"Daitian hats?" Rem asked, appearing at the end of the stable, and Miche was happy to explain the fundamentals while Ophele curried the donkey within an inch of his life.

* * *

Remin had a few memories of what life had been like, before.

The memory of Tressin was as vague and lovely as a dream. It was an old land, a beautiful land, peaceful and sedate. His father had been very proud of their well-ordered duchy, and from the windows of his nursery, Remin could see the forest to the east and the acres and acres of wheat fields to the west. That was his best memory of the land: the golden wheat waving under the summer sun, and a deep blue sky.

The sheaf and the sword were the sigil of his House. Remin's father always said that one could not exist without the other.

His father was Duke Benetot, lord of a House whose name it was treason to speak. He married Sidonie of House Roye when she was eighteen and he was twenty-one. It was probably a political marriage, but

Remin remembered them being happy. In the evenings they always went for a walk in the garden after supper, and his parents spoke easily together, and laughed often.

His father was a very important man. Everyone bowed when he passed and said *Your Grace,* and though he looked like a stern and terrifying giant, he made a happy fool of himself playing with his son, chasing him up and down the stairs, flipping him upside down, throwing him up in the air and onto various soft objects.

"Benetot," Remin's mother admonished, covering her eyes with her hands as if nothing bad could happen so long as she didn't look. "Be careful, what if he falls?"

"He'll get up again," his father had replied. Benetot was convinced that rough play made strong boys, and Remin was going to be a knight, just like his father.

His mother was always worried because Remin didn't have any brothers and sisters. Over and over she said she was going to have a baby, but then she would get sick and the baby would go away, and another small stone would be added to the family memorial in the woods.

"I'm here, Mama," Remin had tried to reassure her, when she was sad after she had been sick again.

"So you are," she had said, pulling him into the bed beside her. He still remembered how her voice had tickled his ear as she hugged him. "My heart's greatest treasure."

As a daughter of House Roye, his mother knew better than most that treasures could be stolen or lost. Multiple children were a hedge against cruel chance.

And he remembered the night when Duke Ereguil had come for him, only minutes ahead of the Imperial Guard. His mother's parting kiss on his forehead, the feel of her tears on his cheek. There had been no farewell from his father. Benetot had gone to Starfall and never came back again. There had been no final words to remember, no parting benediction. Only his mother's choking sob as she whispered, *good-bye, my treasure.*

"You're sure about this, Rem?"

In the closet of an office above the storehouse, Edemir eyed him as he set his own seal and signature to several packets of documents, all thick, heavy parchment with Remin's instructions painstakingly detailed. These were not mere lists. These were the formal orders of the Duke of Andelin, written in triplicate, witnessed and signed, with all the formal ribbons, toggles, and wax seals required to prove their authenticity.

"You've been nagging me to do it for a year, do you want me to tear it up now?" Remin asked absently, scrawling his sharp, slashing signature in all the appropriate places. Edemir was not required to know the contents of these documents. Indeed, in this case, Remin was requiring him and Tounot to sign without having read a single word, attesting that Remin himself had provided these documents and signed and sealed them in their presence.

Remin was entirely within his rights to do so. Especially if the documents might concern Edemir and Tounot themselves, which these did.

And given the tide of people surging to the valley, it only made sense that Remin would get his affairs in order. Soon enough, the first ships would go skating across the Brede, carrying goods and passengers, and Remin was already looking long at the new arrivals, wondering. He had been careful and lucky for a long time, but if one of the Emperor's assassins made it through the gauntlet of precautions, it was best to be prepared.

He was not wrong to worry. It would be many months before he learned that there were now two traitors in Tresingale.

"I never thought I'd see the day when I came to bless the Andelin devils," said Tounot, affixing his own seal and signature as second witness. "It's a lot easier to watch the riverbank when we only have to do it from inside the walls. If anyone manages to survive the devils outside, I'm inclined to shake their hands and give them my blessing."

"You can make that the policy in Tounot Town."

"Not everything has to be alliterative, Rem."

"Makes it easier to remember." Remin signed the last page and set down his quill, his fingers cramping. He felt better, having it done. The sheer complexity of his instructions was a kind of testament to what he had built, and with the east wall finally complete, he could rest knowing that he had done his best to defend his people.

They had been finished only yesterday, with a little ceremony as Master Guisse and Master Misler had laid the final stones at either end of the wall. Remin had gone so far as to don one of his better jerkins for the event, playing Lord of Tresingale to mark this significant milestone.

"Five miles of wall in six months," he had called, when the watchers demanded a speech. "It would be an achievement to boast anywhere in the world. You dug to bedrock, cut and shaped the stone, and laid every block with care. I can only hope that the rest of my city will be built so well. And when the devils come tonight, the night watch is going to stand on this side of the pit and salute the filthy buggers."

That brought a burst of cheers, savage and triumphant. The east gatehouse was yet only a hole in the ground, but so deep and wide that it was nearly as an effective barrier as the wall itself. And there among all the shouting, laughing men, there was Ophele, a solitary spot of color in her new pink gown. She had endured as much as any of them to see that this day would come, but there was no sign of hardship in her face. Her smile was swift and bright as sunrise when he looked at her, as if there had never been a hard word between them at all.

Before, he would have suspected it for a lie. But now he knew that was just her, so swift to bloom with only a little encouragement. Ophele did not hold grudges.

That was why he was about to make one last, massive gamble upon her.

Tying off the last of the ribbons, Remin bound up all three copies and locked them away. One day, he might be able to tear them up and write something better. But if this was the culmination of his life, he would not be ashamed.

He left Edemir's office with a lighter step. Ophele was waiting for him at home, and the prospect of seeing her made his heart beat faster. She always seemed to have some small gift or surprise for him these days, from a new belt to a sachet for his pillow or even just a pretty stone she had found down by the river. Sometimes it was food, and if she had scones today, he was going to eat one for real.

"Yes," she said when he knocked on the door, careful as always to warn her.

Ophele was already dressed for dinner when he stepped inside, so beautiful even in her simple blue gown that his chest tightened. She turned to smile at him, and the fronds of her long hair hung around her in damp tendrils, like an enchantress from an old story. Maybe she was one of those dangerous, beautiful women, luring him so subtly and so sweetly that even Remin Grimjaw couldn't resist her.

"Here," he said, taking a seat by the fire and holding out a hand for her brush. He was inclined to indulge himself today, and he liked brushing her hair. He liked the feel of it in his fingers, liked feeling it change into silk as it dried in the heat by the fire. He liked turning his hands to a gentle task. "Are you well, wife?"

"Yes. Are you?"

"Fine. You keep asking me that," he remarked, drawing the brush through her hair. "Actually, I was thinking of something my mother told me, when I was a boy."

"Oh?"

"Have you ever heard of the Diamond Cygnet?"

She shook her head, watching him with large, solemn eyes.

"It's an heirloom of my mother's House. Sidonie Ileane of Roye, that was my mother's name. She told me it was a golden egg as big as both her fists, decorated with jewels to show a forest surrounding a lake. There was a little key that unlocked it on top, and when it opened, there was a swan made of diamonds inside, with a ruby this big for its heart."

He indicated his own large thumbnail.

"It sounds beautiful."

"It was a gift from my many-times great-grandfather to his wife, Neda the Swan. She was a great beauty of the time. It was a masterpiece, one of the chief treasures of the family. But House Roye was on the border with Dulcia, before it was absorbed into the Empire, and four hundred years ago the family estate was attacked and looted, and the King of Dulcia took the Cygnet."

He could remember his mother's voice as she told him the story, holding his small body in her arms. Of course, she had used simpler words then; seven year-old Remin was *just* old enough to understand treasures and war and loss.

"My mother's family never forgot it. The story of the swan passed from father to son, mother to daughter, because even if it was in the Dulcian King's court, it still belonged to House Roye. And sooner or later, the chance would come to get it back."

"The Annexation?" she asked, quick as always to make connections.

"Just so. Two hundred years ago, Earl Sigedore Aolo of Roye led the Emperor's forces into the capital of Dulcia. He fought his way through the Dulcian King's guard and captured the entire royal household. And he only asked the Emperor for one thing as a reward."

"The Cygnet." She smiled with appreciation.

"Mmm-hmm. It wasn't just a matter of pride," he said thoughtfully. "It wasn't that the Cygnet belonged to House Roye and they wanted it back. They remembered, over generations. They waited. And when the opportunity came, they took it. My mother said that was the sort of thing that makes a noble house a great House."

"I always thought that was just a thing for romances," Ophele said thoughtfully. "Fathers telling their daughters they have to marry so-and-so for the good of their House, when the daughter wants to run off with a stableboy. But I guess if you want to have a great House, sometimes you can't run off with the stableboy."

Conversation with her was confusing because he enjoyed it so much. There was always more to say, and he could see all those thoughts crowding behind her eyes.

He just didn't know, he couldn't know, if anything she said was real.

Quietly, he brushed. The locks of her hair dried, gleaming in his hands, maple twined with umber, so beautiful against her skin. Before he realized what he was doing, he had touched her, his fingers gently tracing the smooth skin of her forearm, bared by the shorter sleeves of her soft blue gown. All this time he had been careful never to touch her more than necessary, denying his desire for her.

"Your Grace?" she asked softly, and he withdrew.

"Fine," he said, setting the brush down on the table. "Come, we'll be late for supper."

Supper was a raucous affair these days, and with so many new people coming into the valley, the high table was a necessity. Remin sat surrounded by his knights, eating only from the dishes Wen personally provided, and even then, only after Tounot and Miche had tasted them.

"Thank you," Ophele said as he cut her meat for her, a courtly grace. Soon there would be silver, it was already on its way, but he liked watching her eat, her slim fingers picking at the morsels, her tidy manners. Her hands were so pretty.

"Sousten says you'll be needed at the house tomorrow, Rem," said Juste from a few spaces down the table. Juste had taken charge of the day-to-day building of the manor house. If something happened to Remin, then the house would belong to him.

"When?"

"Midmorning. They're framing the first floor and need some muscle."

Remin nodded. It was a pleasant thought that one day his son and Juste's boy might play together in halls very like those at Tressin. But the vision in his mind had altered somewhat, and now the son he imagined had Ophele's golden eyes, watchful and intelligent. Daughters that were their mother in miniature. He had planned a dozen children as a hedge against fate; he understood his mother's fear all too well.

But now he looked at Ophele and he could imagine his life with her so clearly, it was as if Sousten Didion had painted it for him. The vast concept of *a* future, and everything he had endured to ensure that there was one, had narrowed to a singular vision consisting of her. He could see nothing else.

Walking home in the gentle light of dusk, his heart was pounding in his throat. It wasn't just the future that lay before him, the home and the children and the garden he wanted to build. A thousand years of ancestors stood behind him. He had been born to carry that burden, but sometimes it was so heavy. He had fought for so long for them, so everything they had struggled and sacrificed to create would not have been in vain.

He lived a lifetime in the short distance from the cookhouse to his cottage. Every step felt as if it were the culmination of all the steps he had taken in his life. The long years of painful, arduous training to become a knight. The determination with every new attempt on his life that he *would not die,* he wouldn't give the Emperor the satisfaction. The endless years of war. Remin was twenty-four years old and he had spent half his life at war.

All the while he had known that if he failed, if he died, then his blood would be gone from the world forever. His parents' blood would be gone, as if they had never been. All of it depended on him.

And he was about to risk it all.

Yvain and Dol were already waiting, trying not to look curious. He'd had a word with them that morning, asking them to move back some from the cottage, as he was wanting private conversation with his wife. They were his men; they would obey. Even if they heard him murdering her, they wouldn't approach.

Inside the cottage, there were a few minutes of homely chores, building the fire and lighting the lamps. Ophele put on the teakettle, setting out the tiny parcel of tea she took from Wen every night, careful to let Remin see that it remained sealed until he himself opened it. She was so smart. It was a habit now to have tea while they worked through the endless stack of correspondence together, one that Remin liked very much. But tonight, he had a different set of papers in mind.

"I want to talk to you, wife," he said, steering her to a chair and producing his copy of the document Tounot and Edemir had witnessed, still sealed and wrapped in black and silver ribbons. The colors of the House of Andelin.

"What is this?" she asked, sitting obediently. There wasn't a flicker of suspicion in her large, tawny eyes.

"My will. I want to give you something." He sat down, taking the knife from his belt and pushing it across the table to her, hilt first. "This."

CHAPTER 14 – ENDURING HAPPINESS

"I'm sure your father would reward you richly," Remin went on, as she sat stupefied before him. "But I have made provision for you, all the same. Tounot and Edemir witnessed my will today. You can see it is sealed, with a stamp that means it is sworn in the light of the stars. It is my will that if you kill me, no harm will come to you. No one will lay a hand on you. In the morning, you will be given safe transport anywhere you want to go. Segoile, if you like. Anywhere in the world. There's a draft waiting for you against my accounts for a thousand gold sovereigns, with a further thousand to be paid annually. Once the valley starts producing—"

Ophele's head shook slowly as she listened, disbelieving. None of this made any sense, she didn't understand, why—

"Please, just listen." The strong brown column of his throat worked as he swallowed. "Once the valley starts producing, you'll receive a percentage of its profits, including the river trade and the port. You will never want for anything, the rest of your life. You will be safe. We can even call in the guards to watch you do it, if you like. To prove I let you." He smiled very gently. "You couldn't get me unless I let you, Princess."

"What—what—w-why?" she stammered, bewildered. "Why, I don't understand, why would you—"

"Because I love you." He said it straight out, with such sadness in his eyes that she felt tears burn in her own. "I love you, and I would rather…you lived. But I'm tired of waiting for the axe to fall. If this is another trick—"

He had to stop. His jaw tightened.

"Then you win," he whispered. "I concede. Just do it now, please."

"No." Her lips trembled. "No. No, I don't want to, Remin—"

"I know you might not want to. Maybe the Emperor is forcing you somehow. I don't blame you if he is, wife. It's happened before." His big hands covered hers. Warm hands. "It's all right. I understand."

His hands squeezed, and she felt the hilt of the knife under her palm. He had put the blade into her hand himself.

"You won't be hurt, I swear it to you," he repeated softly. "You won't ever get a better chance than this. I just don't want you to…surprise me. I might strike back without thinking and if I hurt—I would *rather* die, do you understand? Please. This way, you'll be safe—"

"No. No, no, *no.*" That broke her paralysis. Ophele stumbled out of her chair, clutching the knife in her hand like a live serpent. "No, I won't, I don't want to, I won't!"

She didn't know what to do, and she realized she was still holding the knife and flung it into the corner with a cry, scrubbing her sweating palms on her skirt. Oh, she did understand. It took her only a moment to put it together. This was what Sir Miche had been warning her about. This was why he had told her that terrible story, and the reason Remin had tried so hard to push her away. This was what had been tormenting him from the very beginning.

Remin couldn't be sure of anyone. Ever.

He loved her? He was afraid to love her. Ophele, the daughter of the Emperor. How could he ever believe she was not her father's tool, placed at his side and waiting only a single moment of weakness? How could he *know* that she would not be like Merrienne, who had beguiled him and won his trust and then not only tried to lure him to his death, but forced him to kill her with his own hands?

What could she possibly say? Her tongue was rooted to her mouth, blocking all questions and objections, and she had never been good at finding the right words when it mattered most. He was right to be afraid. There was her father, implacable and vengeful, who might very well decide one day he had a use for his bastard. There was the nameless crime of her mother, and all the many poisons Lady Hurrell was carefully hoarding. But it was just as her mother had said: Ophele could not control what the Emperor would do, or what Lady Hurrell would do, or what her mother had done. All she could control was her own hands.

"Wife—" Remin began, rising from his seat. "If you would just read—"

Her eyes fell on the parchment on the table beside him. His will, wrapped in ribbons, witnessed and sealed, his intent in writing that she could take his life and go unpunished. And just like that, she knew *why*.

He was giving her this chance to kill him. He was giving her every possible reassurance that she could do so without repercussion. He had done it because he desperately hoped *she would not*.

Ophele lunged past him and thrust the parchment into the fire.

"No," she said, whirling to face him, throwing out her arms to keep him from retrieving it. "No, I won't. I won't, *ever*. I—I swear…" Frantically, she searched for words, any words, magic words that would once and for all remove all the doubt and fear from his heart. "I can't promise for my father, or Lady Hurrell, or anyone else, but Remin…I swear, I swear if I ever lay my hands on you with violence, may all the stars in heaven strike me dead. I never will. I swear. I *swear.*"

Those were his words. That was the oath he had made to her the first night they came to the valley, a spell of protection. Tears streaked hotly down her cheeks as she gazed up at him, but even with her eyes blurring, she saw the change in his face.

"You'll—you'll be safe if you do it," he began, wavering. One hand gripped the back of a chair as if he needed the support. "There's another copy, Edemir has it—"

"I don't care. I'll burn that, too." Her voice cracked as she swiped at her eyes. "This is my chance to kill you, right? Without any punishment. I could be rich. I could go anywhere, and—and I won't, I won't, I don't want to! Remin, I won't, *ever*—"

He took a stumbling step toward her and she wasn't sure if he pulled her down or if she fell with him, but he dragged her against him, his hands gripping so tight they hurt. He wanted to believe her. Oh, how he wanted to believe, she could feel it in his desperate grasp, the way his fingers trembled as he held her. This was the greatest test of his life. Not whether he had the courage to offer his throat to her, the daughter of his enemy, and risk everything he had to ask her this question.

The test was whether he had the strength to believe her answer.

"I won't," she repeated. She didn't even realize she was sobbing. "I won't. I really won't, I'd sooner go in the Brede—"

"Don't say something so terrible. I can't—you won't. You really won't?" He sounded strangely breathless, his voice more wavering and uncertain than she had ever heard it. "You're not…tricking me?"

"No. Never." Her hands reached to cup his face, to look straight into his black eyes and let him see her own, transparent as glass and filled with certainty enough to sustain them both. She could promise him this. She could promise him this with all her heart. "Remin. *Never.*"

His eyes flickered as if he had been struck. He twisted his head out of her hands and his throat worked, his chest giving a traitorous quiver before he managed to suck everything in and shove it down hard, hiding it all behind the cold, stern mask of his face.

"All right," he whispered after a moment, catching her to roughly wipe away her tears. "All right, I'm sorry. Don't cry. Please don't cry, I'm sorry, I had to…I had to be sure. I'm sorry, wife. I…believe you."

"You do?" she asked, looking up at him with fresh tears welling. "If my father does something terrible, you won't hate me again?"

"No," he said huskily. "No, he has nothing to do with you. Nothing at all."

His arms went around her and he all but crushed her against the wall of his chest, a place so solid and safe that it was inconceivable that it could ever cease to be. His heart pounded frantically under her ear, but that was all right as long as it was still strong and beating, and the warm, masculine scent of his body was so comforting. And gradually his heart slowed, and her tears ended, and his deep voice rumbled through his chest under her ear.

"I'm sorry," he said again, stroking her hair. "I couldn't think of any other way. It was driving me mad, wondering, and I never really thought you would, but I…I couldn't stop imagining…but that's not your fault. I will make it right, I swear. Every grief I've given you, I will repay. Ophele, I love you." He pushed her back gently to look into her face. "I love you so much. I hope one day to make you love me."

His gaze was as stern and direct as ever, as if he meant to win her love with the same awkward, stubborn, touching persistence with which he had dedicated himself to taking care of her after her sun sickness. Locking them both in the cottage, Ophele a captive in her bed while he interrogated her about her shoes. It made her laugh and cry at the same time.

How could she tell him anything but the truth, when he had just bared his heart to her?

"You remind me of a bear," she whispered, her fingers stroking his high, arrogant cheeks. She loved every part of his face, from his tip-tilted eyes to his thick black brows, so quick to frown. "From the first day we met. Remember, when you pulled me out of the tree? You looked just like a bear, your hair, and your eyes. And you grumble like a bear. And I was scared, at first, but you were so nice that day in Granholme, and so I thought…"

Her eyes went to the glass bear on the mantle above them, small and melancholy, with one large paw outstretched.

"I like bears," she whispered, feeling heat rise to her cheeks.

"Oh." Remin blinked, looking from her to the bear and back again, his dark eyes wide. "Ophele. Ophele…"

She hadn't dared to hope that he would kiss her again. That slow, considering kiss that she had never forgotten, his lips brushing hers so steadily, it was as if he was mapping their terrain, learning every contour. And she wanted him to learn it. No land had ever yielded itself so completely to Remin Grimjaw, her soft mouth moving to match his, following his lead, sensitive to his growing urgency.

It was like falling. It was like drowning. She could feel the waves, warm and dark, a churning heat that matched the rhythm of his stroking tongue, a tangling wet roil. The grip of his hands matched the motions of his mouth, holding her so tight against him she could feel his ribs expanding when he breathed, deep and ragged. They breathed together. They fell together. They drowned together.

"Wife," he whispered against her lips. "May I share your bed tonight?"

Her eyes fluttered open. Everything was hazy and her lips were tingling, almost bruised from the intensity of his kiss. She wanted more. Her head nodded and she felt his hands at her back, tugging at the laces of her dress. His mouth kissing her neck, her shoulders, deep, hungry kisses that almost hurt, devouring kisses of teeth and searing hot breath. Her gown pooled on the floor and Remin slid his hands under her chemise, sliding it up her body and over her head.

Her arms automatically lifted to cover her breasts, but in this golden dream, suddenly it didn't seem like something she should be ashamed of. Looking up at him, she thought she wanted to be naked for him. The look in his black eyes made her shiver inside. And she wanted him to be naked for her.

Her fingers were nervous and fumbling as she tugged the laces free on his jerkin, and he bent silently to help her push it off his shoulders. Remin. Her heart ached to see all those scars on his body, to feel the gauges and gashes and stippled indentations. And he was so beautifully made; broad-shouldered and deep-chested, tapering to a narrow waist that was so sculpted, she wanted to run her fingers over it and feel the ridges.

Every one of those ugly scars was someone's attempt to take his life. He had come to her tonight prepared to die.

It was unthinkable that he should die. Never, she wouldn't let it happen, no matter what. No one would touch him. He loved her, and she loved him, and every inch of his skin was precious to her.

"Ophele…" he rumbled above her, and she looked up at him as she unbuckled his belt and slid his breeches down his long thighs, baring all of him. She did blush when she saw him, already erect, his male part twitching and flushing red as he hardened. It must be strange, to have such a part. She had so many questions. Curiously, she reached to touch him, her fingers closing around him.

Oh, he liked that. Remin groaned, his face flushing as he watched her stroke him, slow and unsure. He felt different than she had expected, almost velvety, warm and living as he throbbed in her hand, and seeing the pleasure in his face made her own breath come faster. This was him, and he was hers, and this was their secret.

"Slowly," he breathed, muscle rippling in his jaw as he bit back another moan. His hand covered hers, gently guiding. "Like that— *ahhh*…yes. Your hand is so soft…"

He was getting harder, and hotter. She could feel him throbbing, and for some reason it sent an answering pulse between her thighs. Her fingers slid over him, her thumb brushing the thick head, and he jerked in her palm.

"Enough," he rasped. Shivers ran through his body as she stroked him, his breath coming harder. "Enough, or you'll finish me right here. When did my wife become so brave?"

His mouth covered hers as he dragged her up with him, her bare toes skimming over the rushes on the floor. The blankets of the bed struck her back and the lumpy woolen mattress shifted as he knelt above her, his shaggy black hair falling forward around his face.

"We'll have to be quiet," he whispered. His hands slid up her body from her waist, cupping her breasts, and he bent to stroke his tongue over a nipple. "Can you?"

She nodded, and he almost immediately made a liar of her when he drew her nipple between his lips and suckled so that she had to clap her hand over her mouth. His fingers moved between her legs to find her already wet, deftly playing with her breasts and nipples and the flushing, heated opening between her thighs. Her body rose as she gasped, hearing the soft, almost chirping noises of his lips suckling, licking, making her writhe. Everything felt as if it had slowed, as if her body and her thoughts had been coated in warm honey.

"So beautiful," he breathed, his lips moving slowly from breast to breast as one long finger sank inside her. "Are you ready for me?"

"Yes…" Her voice came out so high and breathless and strange, it hardly sounded like her. Inside, his finger tickled, and her hips arched and her thighs tightened automatically, her body seeking to pull him deeper. "Hngh, yes, yes…"

Oh, she was ready. She was wanting. She was aching. She could see his member as he moved above her, lowering to push against her opening.

"Remin…" she breathed, looking up at him, and felt him press inward, so big. His hands gripped her thighs and there was a burning stretch as he penetrated her, painful and exciting.

"You're so…small inside," he gritted, his huge shoulders knotted as he forced himself to go slow. "Tell me…ahhhh, ah…tell me if it hurts…"

"I will…" Her voice was reedy and breathless. He drew back and her body jerked, feeling the friction as he withdrew, and then a surge of pressure as he pushed in again, deeper. Ophele's back arched, her inner channel contracting strongly against that hard length, so tight she could feel him throbbing inside her. She dug her nails into his shoulders, barely stifling a high, gasping moan.

"Ahhh…if you do that…" His deeper moan vibrated in the depths of his chest as his hands wrapped her thighs around him, and he sank all the way inside her in one long, smooth stroke.

355

So full. So much. She couldn't cry out, she couldn't even breathe, she had forgotten how intense it was to take all of him, her small body straining to contain him. Remin thrust, driving still deeper when she thought it was impossible, his hard hands sliding to her waist to hold her in place. Ahhhhhh. He drew back, a melting, liquid rush as his manhood tugged out of her, and then rolled in again with pleasure so powerful she sucked in a breath and barely remembered to stifle her cry.

"Remin!"

"I know, I know," he panted. She could see the pleasure in his face as he thrust again, his black brows knotted together, lips parted, his eyes squeezing shut as his hips drew back and surged forward. "But we have to be…quiet…"

"I can feel you…*hhhhn, nnngh*…oh, good…"

His mouth covered hers, muffling both their moans in a tangle of tongues and breathless panting. Every thrust felt so good, she felt it all over, inside, outside, everywhere, his skin shivering against hers. Another stroke, so deep, and his hips caught against her and ground forward and made her whole body surge upward. White flashed behind her eyes.

"Shhh, shhh, ohhhh, Ophele…" His stubbled jaw rasped against her neck as he strangled with the effort to keep quiet.

"It's so good, it's so good," she gasped, her arms trembling as she held onto him, feeling his body levering against hers unstoppably. If anything, he went harder. She thought she was going to suffocate or explode or die underneath him, and she felt him stiffening inside her, pulsing so hard she felt it bounce against the top of her skull. His breath was huffing out of him in a deep *huhn, huhn, huhn,* faster and faster.

"Remin…" Her voice quavered upward. She could feel herself tightening inside, working him as she trembled on the edge. Her eyes were open, but she saw nothing, the feeling of him inside her blotted out everything else in the world. "Remin, nngh, nngh, *ohhhhhh!*"

His lips covered hers to devour her cries and he shoved hard, deep, making her inner thighs scream a protest. Oh, *there!* It was like he was hammering the fracture points of her body, finding the fault lines, the pounding of his powerful body would break her into pieces. Every stroke reverberated to her fingertips and she felt herself shivering inside, clenching tighter, as if her body desperately wanted this thing that would blow it apart.

Ophele clutched his shoulders and *shattered.*

Remin's body jerked against her, slamming into her, grinding down into her as he filled her in huge, hot jets, spending himself inside her. The surges of his body felt so good she could have screamed with pleasure, her heels skidding over the blankets as she tried to push herself up to meet him, feeling the mechanisms of her body finish him, wringing him dry. All of him. Everything.

She felt like she was floating. As if they had become dust, light and ephemeral and mingling together in the air, and when she put herself back together, Ophele was sure he would be there, built into her bones. Part of her forever.

Remin panted, his head between her breasts as shudders rippled through his body like aftershocks. Even though her own body felt so distant and disconnected from her that they seemed like someone else's hands, she lifted them, caressing the back of his neck, running her fingers through his black hair.

Against her skin, she felt his lips curve into a smile.

"I love you," he murmured, and moved over her to kiss her. "Wife. Ophele. I love you."

"I love you," she whispered back, tracing his cheek with a fingertip, and felt that her heart would burst with happiness as he nuzzled his face into her palm.

* * *

There would be no sleep that night.

It was impossible. It wasn't just his desire for her, though Remin barely managed to restrain himself long enough to let her catch her breath before he wanted her again. He was *alive.* He was alive, when he had expected to die. He was alive, and she loved him, and she had consented to lie with him, and all those things he had dreamed about a home and their children and making a garden of this valley might really come to pass...

It was too much. He had never really believed that those things would actually happen. It was too painful to contemplate such happiness.

He knew how to suffer. He knew that endurance was a question of scale. He had been able to survive years of war. Months of scorching summer heat. Weeks of hunger in the winter, when the supply trains were stretched thin, and blizzards delayed them in deep snow. Days of pain from healing wounds. Hours of torment as Genon stitched him back together. And minutes and seconds of agony when he had been shot or stabbed or poisoned, sometimes thinking only of the next breath when it hurt too much to contemplate anything further. He knew how to hurt.

Now, he was having to apply this harsh lesson to a joy so great, he couldn't even grasp the outlines of it yet.

Instead, he thought of Ophele, real and tangible, his joy made flesh. Wrapped in sheets and blankets that smelled sweetly of her, naked together in the dark, there were no walls between them. There was barely the barrier of skin. He had never known it was possible to talk to someone else like he was talking to his own soul.

"I think it started in Granholme," he said, brushing her hair back from her face. He had already made love to her twice and thought he might have taken the worst of the edge off. Now he felt only a dreamy lassitude, wrapped in the warmth and dark as if they could drift together in this small space forever. "I liked you that day. I think that was the first day I ever heard you really *talk*. And that night, I didn't want to leave your bed. I don't sleep anywhere without guards, you know. Miche or Tounot usually take turns guarding when we're traveling. But then when that assassin came…"

Her fingers grasped his as she listened.

"I felt stupid," he admitted. "I know now you didn't have anything to do with it. But you'd talked to so many people that day, and the lock on the shutter was broken. That's not proof. But if it had been you…I couldn't stand that thought. It happened before. Someday I'll tell you about it."

Not tonight. He didn't want to ruin this night with such a tale.

"You mean Merrienne," she said unexpectedly, making him stiffen at the name. "It's all right, Sir Miche told me. You don't have to say it. Unless you want to."

Remin's lips tightened and his brows drew together, but he supposed he could forgive it, this once. She knew, and he didn't have to talk about it.

"Well, that was why," he said, shrugging as if that would push that long-dead girl out of his mind once and for all. "I tried not to love you.

I think I knew almost from the beginning that I would. You even knew my House's words, the day we married."

"I read them in a book," she said, which no longer surprised him. Her fingers played in his dark hair. "But…you love me now?"

"More than anything." How strange it was that saying it could make him feel so light. The words had sat in his chest like a stone for so long, a secret he had hidden, probably even from himself.

"Even if the Emperor does do something again, though, you won't…" she said hesitantly, and suddenly he remembered how she had looked, that night in Granholme, and her red and swollen eyes the next morning.

He could really be appallingly stupid.

"No. No, I won't," he said firmly, pulling her against his body, his hands rough with apology. "I believe you. I'm sorry. I will believe you always. But if anything happens, if anyone tries to threaten you or blackmail you, tell me. No matter what, I won't be angry. I gave you my heart," he added, lifting her chin to look her in the eyes. "That means my life is yours to take, if ever you have to. Never forget that I chose your life tonight."

Her lips trembled and she buried her face in his chest, filling him with regret. There had been so many misunderstandings. And so many refusals to understand on his part, so many times when she had offered a hand and he had chased her away. Gently, he stroked her hair and waited. He had made his apologies. He would not keep saying words. He would show her.

"Well, that's too bad." She said, muffled. Sniffling, she lifted her head and wiped her eyes with the back of her hand. "Because I chose your life. And I threw my pardon in the fire."

The corner of his mouth twitched.

"Then we'll have to talk to each other about it, if it happens," he said, resting his forehead against hers. Stars, how he loved her. He loved her eyes. He loved her lips. He loved her little snub nose and he kissed that too, and her feathery eyebrows, soft arches. He loved her breasts very much indeed, and lavished them with such attention that her breath turned shallow and panting and she arched against him, clearly as hungry for him as he was for her.

There was so much to learn. He was discovering what made her writhe. He played at giving pleasure and then withholding it, teasing his shy wife, and was delighted every time she surprised him.

"What do you want?" he asked, his voice rumbling the question as he licked and tormented her nipples until she was squirming underneath him. But he was utterly defeated when she looked at him through her thick eyelashes and touched the rigid length of his manhood, her fingers stroking the swollen, throbbing head.

"That," she whispered, meeting his gaze with a mixture of shyness and shamelessness that made his desire claw its way to a mountaintop and *howl*.

That was a clear victory to Ophele.

Unfortunately, the walls were thin and there were two guards and a dozen cottages nearby, so howling had to be kept to a minimum. They were both rather vocal with their pleasures and Ophele finally grabbed for a pillow to muffle her cries while Remin died a dozen deaths, swallowing his own groans. Privacy was a luxury he would never enjoy while the Emperor lived, but he still didn't care to broadcast their activities to half the town.

The bed was another problem. It had not been made to withstand this sort of activity and every time he really got going, it started smacking against the wall. Rhythmically.

"Shhh, oh, Remin, they'll hear," Ophele whispered, breathless and horrified at the same time, and Remin stuffed a pillow between the frame and the wall so they could finish together in a strangling, simultaneous orgasm.

They dozed, lying limply together in a tangle of limbs. They made love again. He lost count of how many times he had been inside her; it all blended together in an endless, blissful dream, sleeping and rousing and coming together again. Telling secrets. Telling truths.

"Why were you in the woods that day?" he asked. She was sprawled partway on his chest, and the curve of her slender back fit perfectly under his fingers as he stroked her. "When we came to Aldeburke."

He was trying to tread lightly; Remin was aware that he was not always the most delicate of men. But there were a number of things that gave him pause.

"I didn't know who you were," she said instantly, as if she had been dying to tell him this. "I was sorry as soon as I found out, I didn't mean to embarrass you."

"But why were you there, little owl?" he asked it as gently as he could, his finger trailing along the large outer orbit of her eyes. His little owl, so solemn. "Hiding in a tree, of all places."

"I was afraid there would be trouble," she said, her lashes lowering to conceal her splendid eyes. "I thought, so many knights…"

"The lord never told you I was coming?"

"No."

"So I scared you," he said regretfully. "I thought it was an insult. The Emperor enjoys such tricks. But…Ophele, if it wasn't an insult, why were you dressed—"

"Well, I didn't need anything nice around the house…"

Could that be right? She had been a prisoner. But it felt like there was something she wasn't telling him, and even worse was the way she was avoiding his eyes. And she still hadn't explained why she would see strangers and *hide,* he realized. She had answered so neatly it had almost gone right by him.

He frowned. She was a formidable opponent.

"I see," he said quietly, and let his fingers play over her lower lip. He wasn't sure what to do. Now that he thought about it, she had always had little to say of herself, and was so good at turning questions aside. "Considering that I began our acquaintance by shouting at you, I wonder that you ever came to love me, wife. Explain yourself."

Under his fingers, he felt that soft lip curve.

"Well, I didn't at first," she said, relaxing against him. "But I was listening on the way here, when all of you talked about Tresingale. I liked that. I'd never thought about what it takes to build something. And then when we came here, I realized that you didn't come out of a book. Remin Grimjaw. I heard about you from when I was a little girl…"

He could have listened to her soft, drowsy voice forever as she went on, telling her story. It was odd to hear about the Remin Grimjaw she had heard about, a man that was nearly as strange to him as he was to her. He hadn't really known what was said about him, when he was growing up. He had been too busy trying to live long enough to grow up.

"But none of those things happened by themselves," she said. "You had to figure out how to do all of it. All of this. And I was always sorry about what my father had done, everything—everything," she said, touching the scar on his cheek. "I knew he wanted to kill you, but then I started thinking how terrible it would be if you died. And, in Granholme, before…I thought it would be nice, if you loved me like that. And then I realized I couldn't bear it, if you didn't."

Her voice grew softer as her shyness got the better of her, and Remin held his breath, not wanting to miss a single word.

"But I think it started with Tresingale," she finished, resting her head on his chest. "It's your dream. And I liked your dream. I love your dream."

"Come here," he murmured, tugging her toward him and covering her lips in a slow, caressing kiss that singed the edges of every nerve. Lifting a hand, he traced his thumb along the delicate ridge of her jaw, feeling it move with the soft slide of her lips over his own.

"Remin," she whispered, a musical little purr as his other hand slid down her back to her lovely round backside. Remin had not had much opportunity to contemplate his favorite parts of female anatomy, but it was so satisfying to squeeze her. "Again?"

"I think so," he said thoughtfully, and rolled on top of her as she giggled, sliding her legs apart. She had gained back much of the weight she had lost in the weeks since her illness, and her thighs felt so pleasingly round and smooth in his hands, he had to kiss them before he insinuated his big body between them.

She was still wet. He had filled her so many times, this was not surprising, and though he thought there was small chance his seed would catch, it gave him pleasure to sow her thoroughly. Even if he did get her with child tonight, the main house would be done before she delivered. He entered her in a long, deep stroke, the plump pink petals between her legs wrapping tight around him, with just enough friction to make him lightheaded.

"Oh, you're so deep…" she moaned, her hands sliding over his back. His hard member rasped her as Remin pushed still further, sheathed to the hilt and feeling her tight channel grip him.

"Too…deep?" he managed, grinding himself there because it felt so good he could hardly stand it.

"Nooo…" she breathed, pulling him down to her, and her small, silky body lifted to push against him eagerly, a rolling motion that made him push up, in, and made them moan together as he rubbed in her. "Come deeper…"

When they first met, he thought she would have died of embarrassment before he saw her chemise. He had never expected his shy wife to be so honest in bed. She never lied to him, he thought, dizzy with pleasure. Not even here. Her legs wrapped around him and her voice rose in breathless whispers to urge him to go faster, harder, her nails scoring his back until he thought he was losing his mind.

"You get too loud when I do that," he panted, almost ready to say to hell with the entire listening world.

"But there, there—ahh, Remin, there's something…" she gasped, her eyes squeezed shut, her face screwed up with pleasure.

"What, what?"

"When you—oh, *nnnngh!* Oh there, there, what you just did!"

He did it again. He had no idea what he was doing, all of this was as new to him as it was to her. But he found something inside her, maybe that rough spot Miche had told him to find with his fingers, and angled his body to rub the hard length of himself over and over and over it, rolling his hips upward to strike it as precisely as he would jab a spear. The effect was extraordinary. Her body bucked underneath him and she gave a gasp and her body gripped him and yanked him inside her, so hard that he barely had time to get a hand over her mouth before she came.

"Oh, there, there, there," she sobbed breathlessly as he pounded her, pushing her through a climax that probably made Yvain and Dol think he was murdering her. And it hardly felt any less good to him; Remin managed only a scant few seconds before he was coming so hard, it felt as if he were turning inside out, every muscle in his body straining with the force of his climax. And as he filled her again, this time it was Ophele that had to clap her small hands over his mouth.

"You're…poking your fingers…in a bear's mouth?" he asked as he fell panting beside her on the bed, and she jerked them back as he bit her fingertips.

"They're going to hear you roaring otherwise," she said, her eyes widening with surprise and delight that he was playing with her.

"It'll be better when the house is done," he promised, maneuvering her into the comfortable shelter of his body. He hadn't slept in a bed in six months. It felt almost decadent to lie on a mattress with her soft, silky self against him. "And a better bed. This one sounds like it's going to come apart."

"Do you think anyone heard us?" she whispered, a little anxiously.

"It's so late, everyone should long be asleep," he evaded, though he was already planning to make sure Yvain and Dol had cleared out before she left the cottage that morning. There was no point in trying to keep secrets from guards and servants; they saw and heard everything, and the good ones took pride in their silence. But he thought it was probably better to introduce this idea gradually.

"I want to go see the house tomorrow with you," she said, turning her chin up to look at him.

"Today," he corrected. Already he could see her face better than he had a few minutes before, large eyes and red lips, swollen with his kisses. "It's almost dawn. And only if you're not too tired. You have to tell me if you are."

"I will," she whispered, and soon she was asleep beside him, her lashes curving dark over her cheeks.

To Remin, sleep seemed both very far away and entirely unnecessary. And maybe some part of him feared that if he fell asleep, the spell would end, and he would wake to find that all of this had been a dream. Beside him, Ophele turned on her side and reached for a pillow, hugging it to her breasts. The familiar sight made the corner of his mouth curve upward.

Carefully, he rolled onto his side to shape himself around her. He had never shared a bed with anyone before. It had always been too dangerous. It was strange, but pleasant. He just meant to enjoy the warm and lovely weight of her beside him, but the sound of her soft breathing lulled him, and he closed his eyes. Just for a few minutes.

But he could learn this. He could learn to endure happiness.

* * *

The stern discipline of a lifetime allowed Remin to wake on his own a few hours later, a slow and blissful rousing that was like coming into a dream rather than out of one. It was a bit disorienting, with the sun too high in the sky and the cottage already a little too warm, but Ophele was in his arms and there was plenty of evidence that the previous night's passion had been very real. Closing his eyes, he buried his face in her hair and breathed.

For all that he'd hardly slept, he felt better rested than he had in weeks.

Normally he would have risen straightaway, but for once, he indulged himself. Part of him wanted to claim illness and wave away the day altogether, to stay in bed with her. An increasingly large—and hard—part of him wondered if he would hurt her if they went just one more time. She was already naked. He was right there.

Reluctantly, he rejected the idea. There was a certain rawness to more delicate parts of his own anatomy, making him worry that he might have already been too rough with her, and besides, he was the Duke of Andelin. He had to set an example. Bending, he kissed the top of her head and tried to slip out of bed without waking her. He was big and the bed was small. It was tricky, trying not to jostle her.

Perversely, her eyes opened anyway.

"Mmm?" she asked sleepily, squinting. "Time izzit?"

"Midmorning." Remin crouched beside the bed to put his face level with hers, brushing her hair back. She was barely conscious, but he found he needed to see if the magic was still there. "Wife."

"Hmm."

"Do you still love me in the morning?" he asked, and her lips curved.

"Yes," she said, her eyes slitting open. "Do you still love me?"

"Yes." He rumbled with contentment as he kissed her. "More than anything."

She burrowed back into the covers, but he could see her smiling. He had never felt like this before. Not just in love, but *safe*. So many times, Ophele's face had replaced Merrienne's in his dreams. But now he had seen her flinging the knife away with his own eyes.

Washing, shaving, dressing, he couldn't stop turning to look at her, in the same place she had been for the last five months, if only he had been able to reach for her sooner. In due course he would find a hundred ways to make up for everything that happened between them. But for now, he could only be humbly grateful that somehow, his life had led him to this place.

Tugging on a fresh jerkin, Remin shrugged at a stinging itch in his back and belted it around his waist, then went to wake her properly.

"Ophele," he said, kneeling beside her and peeling back the covers. "Do you want to stay and sleep?"

"Nnngh."

That sounded no-ish.

"You'll have to get up, then." Sitting her up, he put a cup of water in her hand. Normally, he would have left her then, but she looked so tempting. Naked in bed with her clouds of hair tumbling around her shoulders and the marks of his mouth all over her shoulders and neck, her nipples red and swollen. It made him want to push her back down and leave more marks.

Unfortunately, the forequarter of Ophele's mind finally creaked into motion, and one arm moved to conceal her breasts.

"Could you get me my chemise?" she asked, her ears turning pink, and Remin propped his chin on his hand and gazed up at her adoringly.

"In a minute."

"You're already dressed, it's not fair," she said, but though she was blushing, she was laughing, too. That was good. He didn't want to embarrass her, but he had always liked to tease her.

"I'll get it. And some water for washing up." But he couldn't be settled in his mind about leaving until he had kissed her twice more and then retreated stiffly, a little unsettled. Not only was he acting a fool, he couldn't stop.

It was already hot outside, the sun bouncing off the cobblestone street, and he looked with satisfaction at the building underway. There were several more merchants clamoring to set up stores in a valley where an awful lot of men currently had nowhere to spend their wages, and in the distance, he could see the baths nearing completion. The women's bathhouse would only have one customer for the present, but Auber's clan would arrive any day now. Hopefully more would follow.

In the kitchen, he ignored Wen's curses over the late request for breakfast with the equanimity of a man in love and went to the stable for his horse. Ophele was waiting at the door of the cottage when he rode up, looking like a pretty Celestial sister in a modest violet gown.

366

"What's this?" he asked, flicking at the heavy wool with a frown as he settled her before him. Her long hair was loose too, hanging around her shoulders, and she tugged it down when he tried to brush it back.

"I had to cover up," she said, her eyes fleeting up and down the lane as if she suspected listeners were waiting to spring out from beneath the daisies. For a split second, she pushed one side back to show him the marks on her neck, as if she were revealing the brand of a criminal. "You made so *many,*" she whispered, scandalized.

"I was hungry," he said, presenting her with an apple. But he would restrain himself, in future; it was one thing to tease her when it was just the two of them, and something else altogether to *advertise.* Especially if it meant she had to wear one of the hated wool dresses.

"But what if someone sees?" One hand tugged down her long locks to keep them from flying as Remin nudged his warhorse onto the road.

"We'll be careful," he promised, pulling her comfortably against him, one arm wrapped around her waist. "Are you hurt at all, wife?"

"I'm all right. Really," she added before he could ask, and there was no telltale line between her eyebrows.

"Tell me if you are. Or tired. Or anything."

"I will," she said, and when she lifted her eyes to his, for a dazzled moment he completely forgot where they were going and what they were doing and even that he had a horse he was supposed to be directing. The smile that spread across his face almost felt like the shattering of a mask, he used it so rarely. But it was also completely out of his control when she was smiling back at him, wide and foolish and beautiful, and he hadn't known it was possible to be so happy.

Sousten and his men were already busy on the hilltop, and Juste was consulting with the man himself as they rode up. There was a gratifying number of workers present, darting over and around a foundation made of solid Andelin granite that stretched deep into the hill. Sousten's plans called for an absolute warren underneath the house, storerooms and vaults, kitchens and servants' quarters, with a delivery entrance on the back of the hill.

Dismounting, Remin lifted Ophele down and fed her apple core to his horse. She was still trying to woo the fierce animal, but so far he was having none of it.

"I was beginning to wonder if you'd come," said Juste, offering a bow to Ophele. "My lady. I'm glad to see you looking so well. I'll let Sousten explain what's what, he's like to burst otherwise."

"It's a pile of stone," the architect said bluntly, waving both hands at the large square foundation behind him. He was wearing his version of work clothes, compensating for rugged leather boots with a great deal of lace at his wrists. "Today it will become a box. Here you see the bones of the grand entry: the deep portico, the wide stairs, and there are the bases for the pillars, Your Grace, as well as the pedestals for the guardian dogs." He gestured to the two square plinths at the base of the stone steps. "The stars must bless our work this day that you have appeared so fortuitously. It needs the hands of a fair lady to make this box a thing of beauty, and there are no fairer hands than the lady duchess, the flower of the Andelin."

He bowed to Ophele, who looked rather startled by the compliment. "It does?"

"Indeed. It is the duty of the mistress of the house to make it a home. This will be the first house in the valley and the grandest. A daunting task lies before us. His Grace has flung open the doors to the world to seek inspiration. Will we have sun palaces as they do in Daitia, or Bhumi water gardens? Would you like your bath in the Benkki Desa style, or the sunken pools of Argence? We will wed these functions to the form of the Andelin Valley, with which we will build a harmonious whole."

He clasped his hands together, looking at the house as if he could already see it.

"And of course, we must incorporate the characters of our chief players, the Andelin's first duke and duchess," he added, flinging out his arms to encompass them both. "It is your home, but it must also be a stage, a place to display the fairest flower in the valley, to showcase the lady's delicacy and charm." He bowed again. "And also a fit setting for His Grace. Austere," he explained, waving a hand in Remin's direction. "Aloof. Difficult to please."

"You earn your gold, Sousten," said Remin, unperturbed.

"It is a historical undertaking!" The architect declared passionately. "We are not building a peasant's hovel, no tepid merchant's town house! There is no other place in the world like this! In centuries to come this will be the beating heart of the valley, where all of its nobility will come to marvel at the splendor of the House of Andelin! They will dance upon floors that *you* have selected, my lady! They will eat in your grand banquet hall! The guardian dogs that we set upon the doors of your House will stand watch over your children's children's children!"

He ended this ardent speech on one knee before Ophele, clutching her fingertips in his, as if he were already honoring her for this achievement. Remin felt an inexplicable urge to applaud, but Ophele looked daunted at the prospect.

"Are—are there books I could read?" she finally offered hesitantly, looking at Sousten with worried eyes. He blinked, as if his leading lady hadn't quite nailed her lines, but soldiered on.

"Yes, my lady," said Sousten Didion, clasping her hands reverently. "There are books."

"We will need walls first," Juste observed, recalling the architect to mundane reality.

Life was hard, for a man with a vision.

"Stay in the shade," Remin said as he walked with Ophele beneath the ancient oak. Its roots were so high, they made a convenient bench. "Don't worry, we'll get all the books you like. We'll build another storehouse for them, if we need to."

"I can do it," she said, her lips firming in her own version of a stubborn face. His hand reached to give her a caress all by itself, as if it were possessed.

"I know," he said, and went to go lift up the first wall of their house.

It was closer to noon than morning and the very air smelled hot, the sweltering, wavering depths of an Andelin summer. The structure of the house would be a blend of stone, plaster, and timber frames, using the ancient trees that had been sacrificed to clear the home site. Remin didn't mind being called on for heavy labor. He was proud of every stone he had lifted in the valley, and every tree he had hewn.

"Right, lads!" shouted the foreman. There were multiple crews of men standing by ready to lift the massive frame, some of them on ropes, with a few like Remin waiting to push from the other side as the frames were pulled upward. "And…three…two…one…*lift!*"

The men heaved. The massive frame rose, and Remin got his hands under the post and shoved, muscle bunching in his shoulders and back as he took the weight and bore up beneath it. Braces thunked into place at the ends of the frame, and carpenters hurried forward to hammer pins and toe holds into place. The heavy frame would support itself, once all four sides were up; they would lean on each other and last for centuries.

For now, they were just building the main house. Remin could already see where the hallways to the wide wings would be, and as they lifted the frame, where tall windows would look out on the valley and the river. He couldn't help glancing at Ophele, watching with fascination from her place under the tree, her large eyes taking everything in. Her gaze caught his and she glowed in his sight, and Remin turned back to his work, suppressing another smile.

As the day heated up and he began to sweat, his back stung like fury, and halfway around the house he slid his shirt off and hung it over a handy shrub, shrugging his broad shoulders. Between his size and his scars, he was used to being stared at, so he thought nothing of it when the men nearby kept giving him sidelong glances. Particularly at his back.

"My lord." Juste leaned over to murmur while Remin was holding the latest section of the frame in position. "Did you run into a cat yesterday? It appears one might have been at you. Perhaps you should put your shirt back on."

"No," Remin replied, mystified.

"Perhaps you were tangling with a cat last night," Juste said meaningfully. Remin blinked. His eyes automatically sought out the cat in question. Or rather, the owl.

The owl would never stand up under questioning. Ophele was staring at them in mortified horror, peering through her fingers and scarlet to the ears, shaking her head slowly. The guilt couldn't have been more clear if she'd been wearing a Daitian punishment hat.

"Thank you," Remin told Juste with great dignity, and went to retrieve his shirt.

So much for being discreet.

The rest of the framing was done by midafternoon, and Remin accepted a dipper of water and a small loaf of bread and cheese from Wen's wagon and then went to go see how Ophele was faring. It had been some time since he replaced his jerkin, but she moved to sit with him out of sight of the builders without meeting his eyes. Silently, he broke his loaf of bread in half and extended it to her. Tearing off a bite of his own, he waited.

"Everyone saw it," she finally whispered, clutching her bread. "Remin, your whole back, it looks like you lost a fight with a bobcat."

"It itches," he agreed, twitching his shoulders as if the scratches bothered him. Honestly, he hadn't known there was anything there. He had to fight to keep another foolish smile from escaping. "You scratched the devil out of me, wife. I don't know how I can bear the shame."

"I didn't do it on purpose, why didn't you—" she began, and then she finally looked up at him and stopped short. A giggle escaped, and she covered her mouth and looked away. "You're horrible."

"We're married," he told her, and since they were safely out of sight, he lifted her onto his knee and kissed her soundly to prove it. "Everyone already knows. Miche is always quoting that one philosopher, what's his name. The hedonist."

"Thiolas Laval."

"The greatest blessing under heaven is a lusty wife. That one," Remin agreed, and she burst out laughing.

"That is *not* what he said," she said reprovingly, but settled against him comfortably to eat, her toes dangling above the grass. Sheltered by the ancient oak, they watched the house coming together like a vast wooden puzzle. The builders bawled orders, hammering and pegging, finishing the toe holds and driving huge wooden dowels into place to pin the massive timber frames together. The wood would be protected by a façade of stone when it was done, and those timbers might stand forever, if the builders did their work well.

"That's really going to be our house," she said, watching with fascination. "It's so big. I don't know what we'll put in it."

"Books?" he offered, to see her smile, and laid a big hand on her flat belly. "And babes, in time."

"I will," she said firmly, placing her hand on his with the same air of resolve she had given the house. "I asked Mr. Hengest and he said I shouldn't have any trouble, as long as I eat well and—"

"No," he interrupted. "Not the noble children of House Andelin, scions of Ospret Agnephus. Our children. Yours and mine. I want children with *you*."

"I—what—why?" she stammered, searching his face, and then looked quickly away, as if she had realized how much she had revealed with that question. Remin looked at her steadily. He was not a stupid man. After almost seven months of marriage, he had at least learned not to attempt a frontal assault on this shy, wary opponent. It would only make her retreat.

"It seems I have grown greedy," he said instead, toying with her slender fingers and allowing her to avoid his eyes. "The more I have, the more I want. I defeated Valleth, and won the war. I am made duke again, which was my birthright. I have the Andelin Valley for my duchy, which they call the jewel of the Empire. And I have married the daughter of the Emperor, so that my heirs will be protected by his sacred blood for all time. I thought that would be enough. It's the foundation for a dynasty."

She was listening, watching his fingers caress her.

"But it wasn't." He pressed his lips to the back of her hand. "I needed my wife to love me. I want children with her, and no other. And I will love them better, because they are like their mother."

As so often happened, words failed her. Ophele's lips trembled and then firmed, her eyelashes veiling her splendid eyes, hiding all those thoughts. How much did she think that she never said? But he thought he understood her a little better now, and his hand drifted over her back, a caress to make the silence comfortable.

Really, they had only begun to know each other.

"I will be a good lady to you," she said finally. "And to your people. I will learn."

"We will both learn," Remin agreed, and sealed it with a kiss.

There was time. This was only the beginning. Before him spread the wide valley, the distant villages whose fate he still did not know, and the devils that lurked in the shadows, waiting for nightfall. His own house was little more than a foundation and timber frame, but in time, it would shelter them all from wind and rain. In time, he would make it a home, and a garden for all his people. In time, it would hold the new family he would make with Ophele of Aldeburke, the woman that he loved.

In time, it would be a beauty and wonder.

Thank you for reading! If you enjoyed this book, please consider leaving a review on Amazon. Reviews make a world of difference in how often Amazon displays and recommends a book and are one of the best ways you can support an author.

Read on to find an excerpt from book two of the
Empire of the Stars, *Stardust Child.*

Prologue

Year 794 of the Divine the House of Agnephus

"Do you think it's too late to run?"

"The lady's carriage has departed the estate," said Laud Ereguil, shutting the door on a messenger. "If you're going to go, Divinity, you're going to have to do it out the window."

"I would make a capable mercenary," said twenty year-old Bastin Agnephus, two years the Emperor of Argence, and soon to be married.

Imminently, in fact.

Thirty-one years before Remin Grimjaw lifted the first beams of his House in Tresingale, Emperor Bastin Agnephus was getting married.

He stood with a young Duke Ereguil in an upper room of the Temple of Imele Mer, a soaring structure of crystal and stone upon whose tower rested the light of the stars. The Emperor was splendid enough to rival them in his wedding attire, a blue-black doublet the color of the night sky, studded with the purest white diamonds. He had the thick brown hair and blue eyes of the House of Agnephus, and he was a well-made man, elegant and spare, his body trained with rigor and discipline in the use of sword and bow.

It was not the body of a weak man. He could not abide weakness.

"You think so?" The recently raised Duke of Ereguil laughed. "I hear they're hiring in Rendeva."

"I would never go to Rendeva. Backhill peasants." Bastin leaned against the deep stone window ledge and looked out into the streets below, where flower petals were falling so thickly, he could barely see the crowd. Was that a carriage, at the end of the road?

"I don't think you'd get along with the other mercenaries, Divinity."

He would never have a chance to try. There was no escaping his destiny. Bastin Agnephus, Beloved of Stars. He had been born in their sight and would die in it.

Ordinarily, he would have been attended by a half-dozen of the highest-ranking nobles in the land, but Bastin had kicked them all out an hour ago, leaving only Laud to stand this final vigil. Both men were young for their responsibilities, but theirs was a generation of orphans. So many of their fathers had been lost on the battlefield of the Andelin Valley, in yet another failed bid to take it back from Valleth. The former Duke of Ereguil had perished along with a full third of the peerage of the Court of War. It had been all they could do to hold Valleth back at the Brede.

But Bastin's father had not died honorably on the battlefield. The previous Emperor had died in his bed of a wasting illness, weak to the very end. And before he died, he had bowed one last time to his nobles and betrothed his son to Esmene of Melun, the eldest daughter of that powerful House.

Bastin had been fighting to get out of the betrothal for two years. And Laud Ereguil had supported him all that time, the nearest thing he had to a real friend. It was very hard to tell sometimes. Everyone always wanted something, and the divinity of the Emperor intimidated many of them. Maybe other Emperors had believed in their own celestial origin, but Bastin had always been all too aware of his own mortal frailty.

"You are the blessing on the land, my son," his father had told him, over and over again. "Our lives are the covenant between the stars and the Empire."

That was the bargain, as Bastin had always understood it. He was born into wealth and splendor, raised and guarded as the most precious treasure of the Empire so that the blessing would endure. In all the world, the Empire of Argence was the only land without magic. There were no Stone Teeth left in the hills, none of the chaotic bursts of wild magic that twisted men into beasts and beasts into men or melded the two together. In Benkki Desa, a man might walk into the forest and find twenty years had passed when he walked out again. In Bhumi, he might carve a wooden totem for his door and wake up the next morning to find it had come to life and was gnawing on his toes. In the Empire, a statue was always a statue. A song was just a song.

But if the lives of the House of Agnephus were the binding covenant for this blessing, it was a very flimsy one. His father had been ill for several years before Duke Melun had won his way into his chambers, where he kept the Emperor closeted for three days, then emerged with a signed betrothal in his hand. The Emperor had died soon after. It had been humiliating, but Bastin had gone before the Court of Nobility to argue that his father had been weak and sick, and it ill-served Argence to bind its Emperor against his will.

It had been the first great challenge of his reign, and he had lost.

"That's her," he said, clenching his teeth. That was definitely a carriage, moving slowly down the road toward the temple, giving the commonfolk a show. "She will never be an Agnephus."

"It might be more productive to try to make her one," Laud replied, pragmatic as always.

"There have been three Melun Empresses." Bastin knew his history. "Their ashes rest in the Melun crypt at Ereseide."

He did not doubt Esmene Melun would follow suit. He had met her three times since their betrothal: once when the engagement was first announced, again at the summer Turning of the Stars, when he had been browbeaten into making an appearance with her, and the last time after he lost his bid to break the engagement and had been forced to go before the Five Courts to formally present his future Empress.

There had been no mistaking the triumph in her eyes.

He saw it again when he stood at the temple altar and watched her approach, resplendent in a silver gown that suited her cold beauty. In her heeled slippers, she was of a height her soon-to-be husband, and three years older as well, though she wore her silver-blonde hair loose in the style of a maiden. She was already wearing a delicate silver crown.

Before she had even been crowned Empress.

"Blessings upon this night," said Duke Dardot Melun, bowing deeply to Bastin and then turning to kiss the back of his daughter's hand. Bastin had been so distracted, he had barely noticed the true author of his misfortune. He was not required to acknowledge the duke, so he didn't; his eyes passed right over him, as if he did not exist.

"Greetings to the Divinity Bastin Agnephus, Beloved of Stars, Emperor of Argence, Dulcia, Capricia, and the Four Isles," said Esmene, sinking into a deep and graceful curtsy.

"Greetings to the Lady Esmene of Melun," Bastin replied, with only the merest nod, as befit a man of divine origin. He was an experienced courtier and could assume a mask of serenity even when he was being shackled to a harpy. The House of Agnephus had suffered many humiliations like this over its long history. There were some that called it the House of Marionettes for the number of weak Emperors it had produced, figureheads protected only by their sacred blood. Divine puppets.

Esmene's slender, well-formed lips curved with satisfaction as they turned to face the Seer together, and in his heart, even as he spoke his marriage oath, Bastin swore another: he would find a way to be free of her.

Thirty-one years later, he was still trying.

From the wide windows of his office in the Imperial Palace, the vista in the garden below might be regarded as evidence of this failure. In those gardens walked the Empress and his half-Melun daughter, Selenne, who was the same pale platinum beauty as her mother. The birth of Selenne was a victory for the Empress that he could never undo, but for all that he had tried to hate the child for the crimes of her mother, he had failed there, too. Though Esmene had done her best to keep his child from him, Selenne still came to walk in the gardens he had forbidden to anyone else, and he endured the hated presence of the Empress.

Among the begonias a short distance from the two women, a small white animal appeared and vanished again, swift and silent as a ghost.

"Divinity," prompted one of his secretaries. "The petition?"

"I am minded to grant it," the Emperor said, turning away from the window. Picking up the letter on his desk, he skimmed it again, feminine writing that used many more words than necessary to obscure its vulgar quid pro quo. "Draft the necessary documents and I'll sign them."

"Yes, Divinity."

The years had not been without victories. Bastin was not the weak man his father had been. Over the decades, he had reminded the Empire that he was sacred in ways they would never forget. He had built his power and influence, augmented by the enormous increase in Imperial resources that came in the aftermath of the Conspiracy. He had tripled his lands and wealth from that incident alone.

And Bastin had learned that even in defeat, there were still ways to snatch a species of victory.

"Send for Master Geheim," he ordered, prompting an exodus of scribes from the room. Master Lariot Geheim's visits with the Emperor were not recorded for posterity. That was a victory in itself. It had taken twenty years of patient work for Bastin to bend the Tower of Scholars to his will, but now the record of his reign was under his control.

Turning back to the window, he watched as the Empress waved farewell to her daughter, sweeping off into the roses with her ladies behind her, fluttering like so many aged, dignified butterflies. Empress Esmene was fifty-five now, and her slender elegance was beginning to show signs of brittleness. It was an aging court. But as long as she died before him, Bastin would count that a victory, and every day of life without her would be sweeter for her absence.

Crown Princess Selenne was another matter. Bastin had been preparing the battleground for her betrothal almost since the day she was born. She would not be bound, as he had been. She was his last chance to set things right. His last opportunity to triumph over the House of Melun, and make the House of Agnephus a power in its own right. It would be ironic but satisfying if his enemies aided him in this final victory.

"Divinity?" Master Geheim stepped inside and bowed, a lean man who might have been any age from forty to sixty. His black hair and gray eyes conveyed all the warmth of a puddle. Nominally, he was in charge of the Emperor's Land Office, with its vast network of couriers and messengers, who often carried more unofficial orders. Over the years he had handled a great deal of the Emperor's clandestine work.

"Master Geheim." Bastin waved him to a chair and sat down on the other side of his desk. "We have some messengers to dispatch."

Scan here to order Stardust Child, *coming April 2025!*

GLOSSARY

The Nobility of the Empire and Consecrated Knights, in Order of Precedence

1. House Agnephus

    a. **Bastin Agnephus:** *(bah-STINN ahn-YEH-fuss)* The Divine Emperor, Beloved of Stars. The ruler of the Empire.

    b. **Selenne Agnephus:** *(sel-LENN ahn-YEH-fuss)* Crown Princess of the Empire and Ophele's younger half-sister.

    c. **Esmene of Melun:** *(ESS-men-nay MEH-luhn)* The Empress of Argence and eldest daughter of the powerful House Melun.

2. House Andelin

    i.   **Duchess Ophele of Andelin:** *(oh-FELL ANN-deh-linn)* Her Grace, the Duchess of Andelin, and Princess of Argence. Daughter of the Divine Emperor and colloquially known as the Exile Princess.

    ii. **Duke Remin of Andelin:** *(REH-minn of ANN-deh-linn)* His Grace, the Duke of Andelin. The son of traitors and despised enemy of the Divine Emperor, he is sometimes called Remin Grimjaw.

3. **Laud Ereguil:** *(LAWD err-GEEL)* Duke of Ereguil and foster father to Remin after the execution of his parents.

4. House Hurrell *(in exile)*

    i.   **Lord Meverot Hurrell:** *(MEH-veh-roh HUR-rell)* Former lord of Hurrell lands in the eastern Empire, lost and exiled after the Conspiracy.

    ii. **Lady Bette Hurrell:** *(BET HUR-rell)* Former lady of Hurrell and foster mother to Ophele.

iii. **Julot Hurrell:** *(ZHUE-loh HUR-rell)* Son of the lord and lady and notionally foster brother to Ophele.

iv. **Lisabe Hurrell:** *(LISS-uh-beh HUR-rell)* Daughter of the lord and lady and foster sister to Ophele.

5. **Lord Tounot of Belleme:** *(TOO-noh of bell-EMME)* First son of the Earl of Irenvale, estranged after his father's repudiation of Remin. Commands the Tresingale garrison as well as the unauthorized visitors camped on the south side of the Brede.

6. **Lord Edemir of Trecht:** *(EDD-eh-meer of TREKT)* Second son of the Count of Trecht, a Leinbruke lord with lands close to the Brede. Master of Treasury, Exchequer, and Supply.

7. **Sir Huber Adaman:** *(HUE-bur ADD-uh-man)* A knight from a long line of knights in Ereguil and childhood friend of Remin. Master of Remin's scouts.

8. **Sir Justenin of Tresingale:** *(JUST-enn-inn of TRESS-in-gale)* The son of one of Remin's father's retainers, unnamed for his own safety. Master of Beasts and counselor for Remin and his men.

9. **Sir Auber Conbour:** *(AW-bur CONN-boor)* A farmer's son that joined Remin's army at its mustering by the Gresein. Volunteered for the charge over the bridge and was subsequently knighted. Has charge of Remin's farmlands.

10. **Sir Bram of Lisle:** *(BRAHM of LILE)* Former mercenary who served Duke Ereguil for various activities before the war, and volunteered for the Charge of the Gresein. Assists Edemir with the Tresingale garrison, as well as other sensitive activities.

11. **Sir Miche of Harnost:** *(MEESH of HAR-nohst)* Remin's long-time bodyguard and friend, who was assigned to him exclusively when Remin was ten. Master of Digging and manager of Remin.

12. **Sir Jinmin of Oskerre:** *(JIN-minn of OH-scare)* Originally from Norgrede, he switched loyalties to Remin during the war. The only knight capable of posing a physical challenge to Remin.

13. **Sir Darrigault of Ghis:** *(DARE-reh-goht of GHEES)* The Subtle Blade. One of Remin's knights who is frequently trusted with tricky or clandestine work.

14. **Squire Rollon of Hollisey:** *(ROH-lone of HALL-iss-see)* Son of an Ereguil lord and squire to Sir Huber Adaman.

Recognized Masters, in Order by Name

1. **Ammon Misler:** *(AM-monn MISE-ler)* Master mason, has charge of all stonework along the wall.

2. **Cam Sharrenot:** *(KAM SHARE-ran-noh)* Master carpenter, specializing in ironheart oak.

3. **Nore Ffloce:** *(NORR FLOCE)* Master architect, chief planner of the city of Tresingale.

4. **Odan Guisse:** *(oh-DAN GISSE)* Master engineer, chief engineer of the walls, harbor, Temple tower, and similarly massive projects.

5. **Sousten Didion:** *(SOH-stenn DIH-dee-ohn)* Master architect, chief designer of Tresingale Manor, as well as the future Court of War, Academy, Temple Tower, harbor, and similar projects.

Commonfolk, in Order by Name

1. **Azelma Bessin:** *(uh-ZEL-mah BESS-sin)* Cook at Aldeburke and friend to Ophele.

2. **Dol:** *(DOHL)* Trusted soldier who serves as Ophele's guard at night.

3. **Genon Hengest:** *(GEH-non HEN-ghest)* Herbman and surgeon for Remin and his army.

4. **Istaire Guian:** *(ISS-stare GEE-ahn)* First merchant to arrival in Tresingale; provider of tea.

5. **Jacot of Caillmar:** *(JACK-uht of KALE-marr)* Page boy who won his position by swimming the Brede.

6. **Wen of Tallford:** Camp cook and guardian of Remin's food.

7. **Yvain:** *(ihv-VANE)* Trusted soldier who serves as Ophele's guard at night.

ABOUT THE AUTHOR

Melissa Cave is a project manager and a veteran who has spent most of her life traveling, first as a military brat and then on behalf of the military herself. She has always been fascinated by new places, cultures, languages, and history, and there is no better place to indulge it than in fantasy writing. She currently lives in Virginia, where she is failing to grow strawberries for the third year running.

Follow Melissa on X @melissajcave, on her website at melissajcave.com, on Amazon, and don't forget to subscribe to her newsletter for information about advance reader copies, pre-orders, and bonus materials!

Subscribe here!

Printed in Great Britain
by Amazon

56294387R00218